RANDOM REVENGE

DETECTIVE ROBERT WINTER SERIES #1

William Michaels

Varzara House
Orlean, VA

Published by Varzara House
Copyright © 2018 William Pursche and Michael Gabriele.

Library of Congress Control Number: 2018934314

ISBN: 978-0-9998161-0-3

10 9 8 7 6 5 4 3 2

P6c

ACKNOWLEDGEMENTS

Special thanks to the law enforcement officers and members of the military who have graciously provided their insights and expertise, especially Captain Luke Durden of the Fairfax County (VA) Police Department and retired Detective Steven Gabriele of the Coventry (RI) Police Department. Also many thanks to Dallas Hudgens, Guy Williamson, Kim Pursche, and Deborah Atella.

Police procedures and policies differ across jurisdictions, and any errors and omissions are the sole responsibility of the author.

RANDOM REVENGE

CHAPTER 1

Lenny G was the hippest guy around, and he should know. Sure, he wasn't quite as with it as the dudes back in LA—those guys *defined* hip. But here in Marburg, he wasn't even in a gang, yet he was more down than the local gang leaders. Not that he had met any; they might not even have gangs in this backwater city. An hour away from a million plus metropolis, and it was like being in the sticks. Shit, an hour outside of LA and you were still *in* LA.

Lenny sauntered down Main Street. *Main* Street. Any city so pathetic it had to name a street Main was obviously desperate for respect. Lenny was here—on Main Street—because it was, unfortunately, one of the few places where he might score a shot. Not like LA, where there had been a hundred, a thousand, places where he could make a few bucks with his camera. LA teemed with actors, singers and junkies, often all wrapped up in the same body. Even a halfway decent pic could get him a cool couple of hundred from a celeb website, even more from a print rag.

Celebrity photographers like Lenny Gruse—he hated the term *paparazzi*—came in two flavors. One kind did their best to make the subject look good, whether it was a red carpet shot or when catching some hot actress out shopping in her flats and little makeup. Actresses who were a little too long out of the limelight, craving a little freshen up exposure, would tip off one of these puff photographers to where they would be, picking up the kids from day care, having lunch with a new beau. Remoras sucking exposure from a shark. Lenny G—that was his official handle—could always spot these fake candids; the actress would be looking at the camera, casually doing a non-pose pose, not running out the door with a quick brush hair, but polished after having it styled hair. Definitely eye makeup. All bullshit, screaming out to Lenny, the fans clueless. Real celebs who wanted to stay incognito wore ponytails under Dodgers caps, yoga pants, and sunglasses. If the celeb actually wanted to be *noticed* in their disguise, they wore ridiculously large sunglasses.

The other celebrity photographer, like Lenny G, snared the surprise shot. The hot new actress caught kissing her married co-star. The supposedly righteous talk show host snared leaving a not so secret rehab facility. The kind of shots that went viral. The kind of shots that could put not only the celebrity on the news, but could make the career of the photographer.

Lenny stopped in front of a Korean hair and nail salon to check his reflection, the garish pink neon sign announcing *Manicures* making his eyes look like a horror movie demon. Lenny kind of liked it. Hanging in the window were photos of models sporting a menu of hair styles. Lots of spikes and mullets. Marburg couldn't even keep up with hair styles, spikes and mullets were so last year. He'd probably have to go all the way into Boston to get his hair done.

His reflection wavered, shifting, forcing him to refocus. A short Asian lady was staring out at him, her already narrow eyes squinting so hard it was a wonder she could see. Maybe a Korean pissed off look. Or maybe she was studying Lenny's much more up to date hair style. The crone gave him a little shooing motion with her hand, and Lenny ignored her for a bit, just to make it clear she couldn't order him around, and then gave her the finger and took his time walking off.

*Man*icures. What a bullshit name, what kind of man got his nails done? Metrosexuals, wimpy actors. He couldn't imagine letting someone touch his nails. The Korean lady—would she have understood it when he gave her the finger? He'd heard that in other countries it might be the first finger . . .

Lenny continued his stroll, his eyes constantly searching for anything of value to shoot, his hand in his pocket, poised on his quick shot camera. The larger bodied camera with the long lens he held tucked along his side, mostly out of sight. If he needed something fast he would make do with the pocket unit, but if he could sneak up unawares he could draw the telephoto and get off a few shots. It was always a real time decision, like being in a war maybe, which weapon to use. Picking the wrong one could mean a poor image or being spotted, the subject employing the dreaded hand over the face defense, ugly but effective.

Two women were heading toward him now, wearing too tight tops and flip flops, cheesy. No woman in LA would be caught dressed like that on Rodeo Drive. Not that Main Street was Rodeo Drive, but it was the closest Marburg had to something like it. Two hundred thousand people lived here, yet there wasn't even an upscale store where he might spot a celebrity doing some shopping. A Maxfield would be too much to hope for, but even a Lanvin would work. Marburg didn't even rate its own Niemen Marcus.

Lenny ignored the women, not meriting even the no cost digital memory. Another woman caught his eye, coming out of a restaurant called The Café. Younger, with a little swagger, she knew how to walk, maybe a model or an actress. Lenny fingered his camera unconsciously, but a rear end shot was useless unless the ass could be connected to a name, someone famous.

The possibilities of running into someone famous in Marburg were pretty low right now. Lenny was looking forward to June, when the East Coast Theater festival would get its annual migration of actors looking to pad their resumes with a little stage, the ticket to break out of a typecast, like too many zombie movies. Lenny had missed the spring film festival; he'd been making the cross country drive with the U-haul, listening to his mother gushing about opportunities out here. She talked about jobs for Lenny. *Her* big opportunity was with a guy named Tom; she had finally convinced him to let her move in, saving all that cross country travel for his nookie. Now she'd work on him until he was husband number three. Tom hadn't realized that Lenny was part of the deal until his mother had already taken over most of the closets.

The restaurant the hot chick had left could have potential. Lenny hadn't been in there yet, and had been meaning to check it out. The up and coming actresses, who hadn't yet made the leap to the West Coast, would be working for the theater festival and all the businesses that lived off it: the equipment rental shops, the staging companies, even the restaurants. Actresses were like sparkling peppermint gum to restaurants, pop in a new piece, get a nice hit in the form of new eye candy for the diners, and spit them out when they asked for a few days off for a screen test.

A very few of these actresses, the lucky ones, the few with just the right amount of that special something, would make it big.

And Lenny G could help make that happen.

LENNY LINGERED IN THE DOORWAY of The Café, getting its vibe. Faux leather lined the walls, not a good sign. To the left, a long bar, all wood, not bad, but above it, a sign announcing karaoke night, that in itself two strikes against the place.

Midday, the place was not crowded. Three men at the bar, ogling the young female bartender in a black button down shirt uniform that showed nothing. Booths along the walls, lit with industrial looking pendants, a failed attempt at retro chic. A few servers moved about, all in the same drab uniform. All women, all young, mostly blonde, a menu within a menu, something for the male customers to salivate over.

A sign invited him to seat himself. Lenny took a minute to scope out the talent, figuring out who had what station. Two possibilities: the tall, very young looking Scandinavian blonde, and the not quite petite one with the tight body. Lenny watched as she talked to a male customer, her fingers touching her hair as he spoke, giving the customer just the hint of a smile. Lenny G nodded appreciatively, she was good, flirting without being suggestive, enough to up the tip without having to even suggest anything inappropriate, the kind of woman who made a guy feel good about himself without anything actually being said. Subtle and powerful.

She had potential and would be one to watch; he'd do some research on her. Her station was the fullest, which also meant she had some regulars, guys who knew her tables. Lenny expected she'd be busy even when there was a hostess; she'd be kicking something back to always get the most and best customers.

Too busy even on this slow day for Lenny to work her. The other girl, the model wannabe, would be easier. Lenny headed for one of her tables.

He sat in a booth, facing out into the restaurant. Thought about it, then placed his expensive looking camera on the table. The tall blonde glided over, practicing her runway walk.

One glance at her up close and Lenny realized she wouldn't be his ticket, nor would she make it big. Not that she wasn't good looking, she was actually very pretty. Perfectly pretty. Symmetrically pretty. That sounded good, but perfectly pretty hadn't been in vogue for twenty years or more. There were thousands of symmetrically pretty women. Even her boobs were probably exactly the same size. None of these women stood out in any way, they were like widgets, nothing to catch the eye of a photographer, a model agency, an agent, a customer. Marburg would be the end of the line for her.

But all was not lost. Just because she wouldn't put bucks in his pocket didn't mean she wouldn't be of use. She was probably a bit older than she looked, she had to be twenty one since they served booze. Old enough to be legal, not old enough to be especially wary, probably grew up on some hick farm . . .

"I'm Leah," she said, as cheery as a time share agent. "I'll be serving you today."

You might be at that, thought Lenny. *Leah.* Shit, I hope she's not Amish or something. "Leah. Nice name. I'm Lenny G."

"Nice to meet you," said Leah, actually sounding sincere. "Lenny Gee? Like Gee whiz?"

Maybe she was younger than he thought. "No, just the letter G. It's my professional name." Lenny casually gestured toward his camera. "I'm a well known photographer. You may have heard of me."

"I don't think so, sorry."

"That's okay. You're very pretty, and tall, and you have great eyes. I saw you walk, I thought you were a model, and I've shot models, a lot of them know me."

Leah's cheeks reddened, blushing, her eyes opening wide, interested. "I *am* a model. Becoming one, anyway. I've already done some sessions. I've been in some circulars."

Lenny shuddered. *Circulars.* Local department store glossy ads in the Sunday paper, the kiss of death for a model, doing tee shirt and underwear shots. He had nailed it. Still. . . she *was* cute. Underneath that stupid uniform she probably had nice legs. "That's good, that's good. Get you some *local* exposure. But these days, it's hard to break out, to get noticed where it counts, out in LA. That's where I'm from, by the way."

"Really? You shot models in LA?"

"Mostly actresses there, actually." Lenny leaned toward her. "I've made a few of them famous. Sometimes just the right photo is all it takes."

Leah glanced over her shoulder. "I need to go check on my other customers, but I'd love to hear more about it. Can I get you something to drink?"

"Sure." Lenny was about to order a Coke, but that didn't sound very West Coast. He did a quick calculation in his head, remembering exactly how much, or how little, he had in his wallet. "Chivvas, on the rocks."

"Okay. Um, can I see some ID?"

Lenny hated being asked for ID, he was way past twenty one, although he realized he looked a little young for his age, a genetic problem of light skin and the inability to grow good facial hair. "Gotta card everyone who looks under forty, huh?" he said, as he pulled out his wallet.

"Wow, you still have your California license. Hollywood. That's exciting."

She's obviously never been there, since most of Hollywood was a dump, all that his mother could afford, even with Lenny being forced to chip in. Leah was still examining his license, her mouth moving silently. *Can she even read?*

"You're older than you look," said Leah, handing back the license.

Now Lenny was sure she'd never make it, picturing her trying to butter up a producer or an agent with a line like that, not even realizing the implied insult. She better be able to do something else with those lips besides sound out words . . .

Leah catwalked off to get his drink, Lenny reassessing his chances with her, wondering if he should change his approach. Fuck it, go with what's worked, how he could make her famous.

And it was the truth, at least one time.

Back in LA, he'd had a tip about an after-hours place about to get raided for drugs. Not designer drugs, but heavy shit. Normally, no one in LA would care about a drug bust; half the city was dealing, the other half using. But who would be in the bar—that could catch interest.

Lenny wasn't the only one who got the tip, he got it from a guy who got it from a guy who worked the door in an escort agency where one of the girls was doing the afternoon delight with an aide in the prosecutor's office. By the time the news filtered to Lenny, even at two a.m. the front of the bar looked like the waiting line for the new Apple phone. Photographers with cameras, long lenses, tripods. Anybody famous would smell the cameras from inside and find another way out, cops or no cops.

Every shooter out front would get the same shot, making it basically worthless money wise. Lenny had been to the club before, trying to sneak some indoor shots, only to be shown the back door. So this time he angled that way, down an alley ripe with dumpsters. Amazingly, only two other shooters had the same idea. The three of them had bullshitted and smoked some weed while waiting.

The thump of music behind the door stopped at a little after three. Lenny and the others locked their camera focus on the door. No one barged out; the cops must have uncharacteristically corralled the crowd. The other shooters started to walk away, so Lenny was the only one whose camera was still pointed at the door as it popped open. Lenny automatically started shooting with both hands, stills and video. A woman emerged, looking back over her shoulder. When she turned Lenny caught her full with the flash just as she was pouring enough designer coke down her bra to supply a barrio for a month. She was so wasted she didn't even register what was happening, giving Lenny enough time to get a few more shots, her sultry eyes wired, a full line of white powder on her upper lip. Even without her trademark nose ring she would have been recognizable anywhere, Francis Martine, an on-the-cusp actress who had been jilted on a reality matchmaker show by a rich bachelor.

Lenny sold the shot to the first celebrity rag he contacted, and they ran it under the headline "Got Coke?" which Lenny had actually suggested. The flash had given the picture a mug shot look, adding to its allure.

The exposure Martine was about to get from this photo would put her *over* the cusp, and a career as an adult industry actress, known everywhere else but LA as a porn star, would be born. And Lenny Gruce would become Lenny G.

LENNY PEERED OVER THE TOP of his menu, checking out Leah and the other possibilities. The other waitress, the one with *the look*, was far more interesting, but he could tell just by the way she interacted with her customers that she'd be a harder nut to crack. Too confident, too experienced. Manipulative. He upped his estimate of her average tip to thirty percent.

She wore her hair in a half updo, designed to look styled and casual at the same time. Her pants were definitely tighter than Leah's, not because she was overweight, far from it. It looked like she had the waist taken in to accentuate her butt, which was pretty amazing, and Lenny had seen a lot of LA booty. She also had just one top button of her shirt undone, probably the restaurant's dress code, but for some reason more skin showed. Lenny smiled, realizing what she had done. She had removed one button, moving it down, and then added a new button hole. It was an old trick, making it look like you only had one button undone, but giving a little peek show, no one noticed the extra button hole. So she *was* talent, or looking to be.

He put his camera on the bench out of sight and went to the bathroom as an excuse to get a better look at her, timing it so they'd have to pass through a narrow aisle between the tables. She was focused on the tray she was carrying, so Lenny was able to check her out as she approached. She was even hotter up close, even in that ugly uniform. Nice cheekbones, her eyes just a little too big, a small sexy overbite, pert breasts straining against her top—she probably had tightened that as well. Probably five seven, too short to model, but just right for an actress; she'd be able to work with the shorter actors who the film people always had a problem shooting next to taller women. But it wasn't one thing about her, it was the package, *she had it*, and she knew it, and she used it.

What the fuck was she doing in Marburg?

Maybe she just needed her big break. Maybe she just needed Lenny G.

In the tight space between the tables they had to turn to face each other, Lenny taking it all in, her faint hint of perfume, the in vogue no excuse eyebrows, her boobs pointing at him, drawing his eyes down.

"Excuse me," she said, with just an edge to it, the way you'd say it if it was the other person who was in the way.

"Sorry," muttered Lenny, her aura overwhelming him. It was those damn tits, she used them like a weapon, aimed at him.

Their eyes locked for a second. She had amazing eyes, glittering, maybe with a little annoyance at her job, but alive, eyes that would convey emotion without speech, eyes that would reach out from a photo, promising anything, any man looking at those eyes would read into them whatever he wanted.

She seemed to look right through him, and then she was gone, and Lenny stumbled, hoping she hadn't noticed. He ogled her as she walked away, a walk that said *follow me.*

Lenny didn't need his camera, every pore of her face was locked in his mind, every strand of hair. And those eyes . . .

He'd also seen her nametag. *Melanie.*

Lenny forgot all about the bathroom and went back to his table, trying not to stare at Melanie, but failing miserably. He had to find out her story, she could be *the one.*

Leah returned with his drink, Lenny reluctantly redirecting his eyes to her. Leah was actually prettier than Melanie, in a technical sense, but Leah paled in comparison, even though she was taller, had better skin, nicer hair, big blue eyes. Living proof that it took more than beauty to have what it takes.

Leah set his drink down. "I have a few minutes to talk, you're my only other table."

"Sure," said Lenny, magnanimously. "Are you new here, too? I noticed you didn't have a name tag."

"I just started. They are making one for me."

It was one of Lenny's favorite approaches, find something in common with a woman, build some rapport, but then subtly make it clear he was more powerful than they were. Truth be told, words by themselves hadn't worked that much in LA. Although he had got his first piece of ass this way, later in life than he deserved, but it was hard to get in a girl's pants when you lived at home all the way through community college . . .

"You working between shoots?" asked Lenny.

"I haven't actually had any since I moved here. I couldn't afford a place in Boston, but this is close enough, plus there's the film festival. I'm hoping to get a job in the office there, meet some people."

"That's a good idea, for a start. But a lot of other girls will be doing the same thing."

"You think?" Leah looked crushed. "I thought you said you just moved here?"

Lenny nodded sagely. "It's the same all over, even in LA. Actors, singers, models, anyone trying to make it, they need to get noticed, you know? So they try to get jobs in the agencies, the offices. Just a portfolio isn't enough, I should know."

Leah twisted her hair, an indication of confusion, not guile. "What works?"

"You got to stand out from the crowd. You have to be willing to do anything to make it." Lenny put just the slightest stress on the *anything*, not overplaying it, just to get her mind going that way.

"I am," said Leah. "I know it's not easy, I'd be willing to volunteer in an agency office, do some free modeling. Whatever it takes."

Lenny tried not to roll his eyes. A hundred other girls would be trying the same thing, and much more, doing some partying, offering up their bodies. He actually hadn't seen it, but he knew it must happen, how else would those slimy agents and producers get the women they all had hanging on their arms?

Lenny leaned over to her, sharing a secret. "I don't tell many people this, but I like seeing someone like you make it, up against all those women who don't play fair. Usually it's not so much being lucky as managing the process. Making your dreams a reality. Taking control."

Leah stepped closer to the table, her voice low. "What do you mean?"

"Well, the right photo, it gets around, goes viral, just like that," Lenny snapped his fingers, "and all the right people see you, people who aren't likely to be picking up a circular you happened to be in."

"What kind of photo? You don't mean something nude, do you?" Leah backed away a step.

"No, no," assured Lenny. "Nothing like that. There's plenty of that for free on the internet, you don't want to be in that camp. Besides, you are too pretty." He glanced around, caught Melanie looking at him, her eyes shining across the room, making him lose his chain of thought. Was she checking him out?

Shivers ran up both his legs. Melanie had reached across to him, touching him with her eyes. He sensed a connection to her, even more than when they had brushed past one another. Something was fated to happen, he knew it.

"Lenny?"

Leah shifted position, blocking his view of Melanie, forcing him back to the present, picking up his spiel. "Yeah, like I was saying, not a nude. You just need to be in the right photo, with the right people, you know, someone famous, maybe an actor here for the summer theater. A picture like that will end up in the Hollywood Reporter, the *Los Angeles Times* even."

"I've *seen* those pictures," said Leah. "But I don't know any of those people."

"I can help you out there," said Lenny. Not that he knew any of those people either, but it was amazing what creative cropping and a little photo manipulation could do. Position Leah just right and it would appear she was walking arm and arm with the next Matt Damon. No reputable magazine would publish it, but Leah wouldn't know that. Not that he would bother. Leah wasn't worth the effort, Melanie sure, but Leah . . . he'd just string her along, get her to give it up for him a few times, then move on, maybe use her to get a little info on Melanie.

Leah was staring like she just met Santa. "Would you do that for me?"

"We can talk about it. What time do you get off?"

"Ten."

"How about a drink? There's a place just up the street, Stripes."

"I've seen it, but I've never been there."

"It's good," said Lenny, having scoped it out. "Not a dive or anything. I can meet you there, tell you more about how things work."

"Okay. Hey, do you want to order something to eat?"

Lenny had blown his daily meal money on the scotch. And he'd need cash for tonight, although maybe he could get Leah to think paying for their drinks would be her way of saying thanks for his mentoring. "I ate a late lunch. How about just some fries and a salad?" Immediately regretted it, she'd think he was gay, ordering a salad.

"I'll be right back."

Leah almost trotted off, a new spring in her step, seeing her chance at a big break. Lenny would normally have been wired, he had a live one on the line, and she was actually better looking than any woman he had been with, not counting the handjob he got from that redhead Cinder, who he later learned started to charge for them.

As soon as Leah was away from the table he sought out Melanie, and damn if she wasn't still staring at him even as she was getting a drink order filled at the bar. As Leah put in the order Melanie drifted over to her, the two women's heads together, Leah animated, nodding toward Lenny's table, sharing her good fortune.

Melanie looked over at him, and again Lenny felt the connection. Melanie would cut Leah out so she could get in on the action. *His* action. He started thinking of a different set of lines, he instinctively knew he'd need a better rap for Melanie. Melanie would be the kind of girl who would know what she would have to do, he wouldn't have to work up to it so much, not after seeing how she worked her customers, using her sexuality. He could just lay it out, the price she'd have to pay for fame.

He wouldn't even have to slip her a roofie to get her in bed.

MELANIE UPTON HALF LISTENED TO Leah's breathless chatter, a story she'd heard before, some slimeball making the moves, pretending he could help a girl out, blah blah blah, all bullshit. She could have finished Leah's sentences, even while not paying attention, her eyes now locked on the guy who called himself Lenny G. She'd been dealing with guys like him since high school, ever since her drama teacher had suggested that if she just came to his house for some private tutoring he'd show her how to connect with the audience just by pursing her lips, a silent way to communicate emotion. Even at fifteen, Melanie had known what part of his body he wanted her lips to be emoting.

When Leah got to the part about Lenny taking staged pictures, Melanie had heard enough. It was one thing to hit on a girl, shit, she made half her tips letting guys think they were getting somewhere with her, but that was all play, even the guys knew what she was doing, it was a game. But taking advantage of Leah was something else. Melanie had steeled herself for the big time, and could handle herself, just as she had handled her drama teacher and the football coach and the boys in drama college. But Leah was so naïve she'd get taken in even by a would-be photographer.

"Let me help you with the order," said Melanie, picking up the salad, not giving Leah a chance to protest. She led Leah to the table, the poor girl so innocent that if Lenny had been for real, Melanie could have stolen him away and Leah wouldn't have seen it coming. Melanie kept her eyes on Lenny the whole time, watching him lock on her, clueless he was over his head. His clothing was as artfully planned as hers was, but she could pull it off. He just looked like he was in a costume, and no one had told him that there was no masquerade party. He didn't look hot, just out of place. He was wasting his time, no one in Marburg knew hot, not the way she did. She'd studied it, she knew, she felt it, she didn't have to put it on. She'd get to the big time, blow by the Leahs like they were standing still, leapfrog over the Lenny G's.

At the table she gave Lenny a little look, getting his attention, and then she dropped the salad platter on the table with a bang, making him jump. "Whoa, there, big boy, no need to get excited over some iceberg."

The guy looked at her, already on the defensive, his hand over his camera, protective. Melanie pushed on. "Leah tells me you've worked in LA."

Leah, setting down the fries, chiming in, like she'd known Lenny for more than a few minutes, "He's got a lot of experience, for his age."

Melanie gave Lenny a good once over, making him squirm. His

hand came up to his face, subconsciously hiding his ridiculous attempt at a scruffy look, his streaky brown hair in some kind of tangled mess, a homemade styled mop. A small scab glared from his left ear, probably a self inflicted piercing attempt. "Looks pretty young to me, what are you, twenty five?"

"Older. And I'm from LA, I didn't just work there."

"Yeah? If you're such a hotshot, why are you here? Run out of money, have to come home to live with your mama?"

"I told you, I'm *from* LA."

Melanie gave him the hands on hip look, the I don't believe a word you're saying stance. "What's the camera for? Looking to score some upskirts? All the waitresses wear pants, you're out of luck."

"What's an upskirt?" asked Leah. She paused. "Yuk, is that for real?"

"She's just playing with us," said Lenny, a smile frozen on his lips. He turned to Melanie. "I don't do that kind of photography. I shoot big names."

"Like who?"

Lenny reeled off a list of actresses, Melanie knowing right away any dimwit could print photos off the internet, pass them off as their own shots.

"I do my thing, I can even help someone along, you know, the pic goes viral."

Melanie didn't fall for it, the unspoken promise; she used that ammo herself on her customers. What was different was that she could deliver the goods if she wanted, unlike Lenny. It wasn't that she was oblivious to the reality; a good photo could put her in the limelight. It would be a shortcut to her current plan, hanging out with the up and coming actors from LA who were out for the summer theater. It's why she had this job. They'd end up here sooner or later, even if they partied in Boston.

Melanie took her hand off her hip, pretending to be taken in a little, opening herself up, sending out the vibe that she was listening, that Lenny's rap was working on her. "You could do that? Get a photo to go viral? For Leah?"

"Sure. For anyone," said Lenny, perking up. "If they have what it takes."

Both of them knowing they were only talking about Melanie now, Leah was out of it, if Melanie wanted her to be. Leah was nice, but Melanie wouldn't hesitate for a second to run Leah over if it would in fact get her to LA, to a big time gig, but Lenny wasn't going to be the one to get her there, no matter what he was peddling. Melanie grazed her lip with her tongue, telling her mouth to hint at a smile—her drama teacher had been right about that, at least—and leaned a little over the table, watching Lenny's eyes pulled like magnets toward her chest. She waited until he was pumped up; the higher they felt the harder they fell.

"It must be so *hard*," she cooed, "deciding where to point your— *camera*. Deciding who to help get over the top."

Lenny smiled stiffly, a half frown, probably not sure if he was being made fun of, but being a guy, still responding to her implications.

"I can handle it," he said.

"I'm sure you can," said Melanie, turning and walking away, pulling Leah along with her, not bothering to hide her laughter. Melanie was going to make sure that the only one who would be handling Lenny would be himself.

Once clear of the other customers, Melanie turned to Leah. "Maybe your mother already told you about the birds and the bees. Time for me to tell you about the snakes and the foxes."

LENNY WATCHED THE TWO women walk away, feeling good, that had gone well. He hadn't been imagining that connection with Melanie, it had been real. She felt it too, it was like Leah wasn't there. Melanie had pretended to be tough with him, showing off for Leah, signaling Lenny that she had an edge. It was all an act, Melanie was just trying to get noticed. Noticed by him. Even that crack about living with his mother. Although he hadn't admitted it was the truth, only a woman with some kind of psychic connection to him would have made that crazy thought pop into her head, she couldn't really believe someone as cool as Lenny lived at home with his mother.

Melanie had understood his secret communication to her, she got it, she knew what he could do for her. It would take more than one night at a bar and a few drinks, but she knew the game, and once Lenny proved to her how he could help, she'd be so grateful she'd do *anything*. Melanie was going to make it big, he was sure of it. Even if the monetary payoff didn't come now for him, it would later. He'd have photos of her before her success, the rags loved those, the before and after pictures, before the plastic surgery, before the celebrity wedding. Before Melanie met Lenny G.

And he'd get laid. Get to see her ass out of those man pants . . .

Lenny grabbed his camera and managed to get two shots of Melanie as she walked away, breaking his rule about booty shots, because someday, *that* ass was going to be famous.

CHAPTER 2

HOT AND A LITTLE SWEATY, Melanie stuffed her waitress uniform in a laundry bag and shoved it in her locker. Her shift had been longer than necessary because her bitch manager, Lyn, set the day schedule from 11-7—who the fuck did that, anyway? Leaving at seven meant missing your tips from the early dinner crowd, so everyone on the shift stayed late, which was probably just what Lyn and the owner wanted so they could avoid hiring a few more servers. Just another example of the bullshit she had to deal with.

Any other night she would have plenty of time to go home, shower, and change, but tonight she wanted to get to the Marquee early. A location shoot was planned for tomorrow morning, with makeup call at six a.m., so if Jason was going to hit the club he would do it early. This might be her one shot to catch him.

Melanie hung a short, black knit dress—her emergency outfit—on the employee bathroom door. Something silky would have been better, but it would wrinkle like hell in the locker, and someone would probably steal it anyway. Melanie suspected Lyn rummaged through the employee stuff.

She splashed water on her face, pulled down her hair, and put on fresh makeup. A little more than usual, it was dark in the Marquee. The bathroom's fluorescent lights weren't flattering, if she could make herself look half decent here she'd be okay. On the wrong side of twenty five, if Melanie didn't get a break soon she never would, so every one of these potential hookups was a big deal.

She slithered into the dress, adjusting it to show as much cleavage as she had, wondering again if she should get a boob job, it was basically a toll these days, tits and tucks and veneers. Who would have thought that a woman in the prime of her life would need so much work? For movies and even television, women had to be perfect, look just so . . . which of course made them all look pretty much the same.

Her hair looked like shit, but with any luck the focus would be on all the leg she was showing. She stepped back into her ugly work shoes, she'd change into her Jimmy Choo pumps in the car—no way she was going to leave those for Lyn to find—and then hit the only club in Marburg where anyone who was anyone would ever show up.

THE VESTIGES OF A VELVET rope drooped in front of the Marquee, put there by the original owner who had grandiose dreams of long lines. A heftily built bouncer with a buzz cut sat on a stool, spinning a keychain around his finger. He was more useful than the velvet rope; the Marquee sat on the other side of the literal railroad tracks, fights and stabbings were common enough they didn't make the news. Melanie gave the bouncer's biceps a squeeze as she walked past him, no fucking way she was going to pay a cover, even if the club was stupid enough to charge a single woman to get in. The bouncer had long since stopped flexing his muscles in expectation of her touch. He knew she wasn't going to put out, but he held the door for her anyway. Melanie practiced a new smile on him, the one that said elegant, challenging herself, because after nine hours of slipping in deep fryer fat she felt anything but.

The room was running as if a capacity crowd was present. The sheer size of the place a pipe dream of the founder, who after two club bankruptcies was reportedly making good money delivering essentials like bottled water in BPA free containers, kale salads, and high quality weed to in town actors. Some kind of techno pop fusion blared from an overburdened sound system, rattling Melanie's teeth.

The place was actually pretty busy for midweek, no doubt the word getting around about the location shoot for the new television series. Wannabee actors and actresses would be at the club angling to get spotted by some casting director for a role as an extra in a walk by or crowd scene, or, hope against hope, a U-5, a union category of up to five lines of dialogue that could in some cases actually get you a screen credit.

Melanie was here for basically the same reason, but she had much loftier goals, wanting to slip past all the paying your dues bullshit, at least as far as it came to small roles. Although even she had no illusions that some dues of the more personal kind would have to be paid.

The club was brighter than usual. The new owner, an actor has-been himself, had turned on every bulb in the place, maybe discovering for the first time how few of them worked. Melanie was sure the irony of the club name and the dead bulbs was probably lost on him. The place looked more like an old movie theater in need of a face lift, gaudy, Marburg's attempt to imitate the look and feel of some imaginary New York City club by someone whose only view into New York was watching *Saturday Night Fever.*

Melanie bypassed the main bar, only gawkers hung out there, and skillfully wove through the crowd toward the back room, not really a separate space, but an L-shaped extension of the club. Along the way she spotted half a dozen actors who actually had a few credits. One girl, who definitely had not been carded on the way in, but should have been, had already cut an album that was getting good airplay. Others were the countless men and women who were in some way associated with television and movies: actors, writers, stage hands, gaffers, dancers, costume designers, caterers—the cast of the cast of the industry. Some were no doubt at the club because they were part of tomorrow's shoot, others were here because it's where people from the industry hung out in Marburg.

A few of them nodded to Melanie as she passed, two even worked at the same restaurant as she did. No real smiles, especially from the women, seeing Melanie just as she saw them, as competition. She spotted a guy who dressed like an FBI agent but who was actually the local source for ecstasy, molly, and the drug of need for actors, amphetamines. He'd get you plain old coke, but that was a little passé these days, even here in the relative boondocks. In the corner of the back room, a guy who looked like a doctor, because he was a doctor, sat at a table, nothing but a small pad in front of him, a line beginning to form for this modern day version of a house call, where after a five minute consult he'd write a fully legal prescription for Ritalin, speed you could carry around with impunity because the bottle had your name on it.

The savvier part of the crowd gravitated to the back, most of them aware of another private room beyond this one. Melanie had only been in there once, and hadn't stayed long when it was pretty clear that the young director who had invited her was only interested in getting some head, ammo that Melanie saved for producers, or at least directors who had a better track record.

Melanie didn't spot Jason, so she headed for the smaller bar in the back. There were two empty stools, one next to three good looking but amateur college boys, and the other in the midst of a bunch of what looked like accountants. Melanie slipped between them, catching a few glances, and then she twisted on the stool, crossing her legs, letting her dress ride up a little, making subtle adjustments to her posture until she was sure that every man who could see her had checked her out. It was another challenge, like the smile; she was disappointed whenever she couldn't get the entire room to at least look.

Tonight was easy, she didn't even have to do the heel dangle. When she had hit her goal she turned to the barmaid. "Hey, Fiona."

"Bosses suck," said Fiona, putting a Southern Comfort down in front of Melanie without being asked.

"I feel for you," said Melanie.

"The douchebag wants me to close every night this week. Which means I'm working three doubles in a row. Just so he can be with that slut."

Melanie took a sip of her drink and nodded understandingly.

"I have a three year old kid," Fiona continued. "Does he care what a pain in the ass it is to find somebody to watch her every night?"

One of the college boys called out, and Fiona rolled her eyes. "Speaking of a pain in the ass . . ." She headed off down the bar, in no particular rush.

Melanie listened in on the accountants. " . . . if we can combine the Marburg production incentives with the state tax credits and the lodging tax rebate, we can save almost twenty percent on location shooting costs."

"Still need to factor in the higher union scale for the crew."

"Sure, but that's a wash with the kickback, excuse me, the cash rebate."

"The talent isn't going to like it."

"Fuck em. Only one big name to worry about, and he's going to have his mind on other stuff."

There was a general round of laughter, and the conversation drifted to more accounting talk. Melanie had actually followed quite a bit of what they had said. Just because she wanted to act—wanted to be what the accountant had called *the talent*—didn't mean she was stupid. She'd taken a few classes on entertainment accounting at one of the larger universities in Boston—well, she hadn't taken them, she'd snuck in, no one checked or seemed to care—and had learned quite a bit about how production companies made money, hid money, and, if they were fronts for not so legitimate businesses, lost money on purpose to create tax havens or launder cash.

Already the night had one good outcome. The accountant was likely talking about *Shock and Awe*, the series they were doing location shoots for, about a young rat pack group of hackers. It sounded like the show might be in town for a while, which meant more opportunities for her to hook up with Jason, who had been cast as one of the leads, his first big role after a few years of off Broadway, regional theatre, commercials, and the usual run of supporting cast roles.

Shock and Awe was being produced by the wildly successful movie producer Scott James, and Jason was also being seriously considered for the lead role in one of his new movies. That would be the leap to the big time that every actor salivated over, since even a flop Scott James movie could make your career from just the visibility and the contacts you'd make.

Not many people knew this, since Scott James kept his casting under wraps until the last possible moment. Melanie knew it for a fact, because she had been giving Jason some pretty good oral, or so she thought, but obviously not good enough since he had taken a call from Scott James in the middle of one of her ministrations. Jason waited until Melanie had finished him off, and then he had matter of factly told her he wouldn't have time to reciprocate, or probably ever set foot in her dump of an apartment again, because he'd be moving to LA.

*   *   *

AND YET, HERE SHE WAS, hoping he'd walk in, Jason being even more a possible ticket for her now than when he had been cast in the television show. Any halfway decent looking girl could hook up with a new series lead, but a Scott James star, that was something else entirely. Jason moved to LA only to find out that the shooting for the series was going to take place on the East Coast, and in Marburg of all places, where he had spent years doing exactly what Melanie was doing, trying to connect with industry people in town for the film festival or summer theater.

Fiona drifted back, expertly replenishing the accountants' drinks. Melanie was impressed by how she turned on a good smile for them, sucking up her anger over her boss, knowing the smile, some banter, and maybe a brief touch on the hand would get her a bigger tip. Melanie automatically filed Fiona's smile away, it was a good one for her own repertoire, a big flash of teeth, the mouth a little open, inviting, followed quickly by a comment, so it looked natural. Now if Fiona could just sparkle the eyes . . .

After Fiona finished with the accountants, she turned to Melanie, flicking her head toward the other end of the bar. "The college boys offered to buy you another drink, and take care of your first one too. I took the liberty of telling them I thought you were waiting on someone. I figured you didn't want to have to deal with pawing barely legals. I can go back and tell them otherwise if you want."

Melanie hadn't paid for a drink in years, but she was picky about who she drank off of. "Thanks, you did right. The blond one is cute though."

Fiona flipped back her hair. "Letting a cute guy at a bar buy me a drink is what got me pregnant the second time." She poured Melanie another Southern Comfort. "I'll run a tab until you decide who is going to pick it up."

"The night is young," said Melanie.

"Tell me about it. I'm dead on my feet already." Fiona glanced over Melanie's shoulder. "Hey, isn't that Michael Stevens?"

Melanie casually swiveled back to the crowd, it wouldn't do to appear too excited, even over a big name star like Stevens. He was sitting in one of the corner tables, with another middle aged man in a suit and a younger guy. Stevens looked as good in person as he did on the screen, a little shorter maybe, but virile, a little gray giving him some gravitas. "Yes, that's him."

"I heard he's a sleaze, I'm not sure where, TMZ maybe."

Melanie sipped her drink. "He is."

"You know him?"

Melanie shrugged. "Guys like him."

"I read he sleeps with women and promises he's going to help their careers but never does anything, just strings them along, then dumps them when he's tired of them. I can't believe women fall for that."

Melanie turned back to Fiona. "They do it because it works."

"Really?"

"How do you think a lot of the actresses in Hollywood got their first role? Or their bigger role? They sleep with someone. Have you been to LA? Half the women look like they could be in the next Maxim, and the other half have *been* in Maxim. The women have to find a way to stand out from the crowd."

"Still," said Fiona. "He sounds like an asshole."

Melanie nodded her head toward the accountants. "Are you planning on sleeping with one of them?"

"What? Of course not."

"But you gave them a big smile, flirted a little with them. Don't get me wrong, I do the same thing at the restaurant. It's a game. You're promising something you aren't going to deliver. Everyone understands, no one gets pissed off or hurt. But I'm sure you've slept with customers before. You gave them something. Even if the odds are low, guys will keep trying. So will women."

"I guess you're right. But I'm not powerful, I don't have much to offer."

Melanie's smile was genuine. "Don't sell yourself short. Never underestimate what you're worth."

Fiona was looking back at the men at the table. "Who's the younger guy with him? He's hot."

"His name is Jason Ayers. He and Stevens are shooting a new series. Jason is basically a younger version of Stevens, he's got just as much asshole potential."

"You know him too?"

"Biblically."

"Hmm," said Fiona. "You think he'll pick up your tab?"

Melanie downed the rest of her drink and stood up. "That's a good question. Let's find out."

" You're not gonna cause a scene, are you?"

"Are you kidding? There aren't enough people in here to make causing a scene worthwhile."

STEVENS WAS FACING OUT toward the room, so he noticed Melanie first. She didn't strut or wiggle or act suggestive, that always looked too forced. She didn't know Stevens's favorite type and really didn't care. Fiona was right, he was a sleaze. If none of the other women he'd slept with could parlay him into a role, neither could she. Being a realist had saved her a lot of wasted sex.

Stevens did check her out, maybe because she was approaching with purpose, not some wide eyed star. Jason had noticed her too, a frown flashing across his face, Melanie getting a sudden urge to make a fuss, just to see his reaction, see how he'd handle it in front of the big shots.

Quickly dismissed the idea; it would be fun but she'd waste the chance with Jason, who could still be her ticket, especially if the series and the movie peaked at the same time.

The men stopped talking when Melanie reached the table, not especially annoyed, she was attractive enough to get her few seconds of opportunity. "Mr. Stevens, sorry to interrupt. I just wanted to say hello to my old friend Jason. Jason, it's been a while." She gave them all the business smile, the one that said: I'm being polite, now show me it's worth my time to stay here and talk to you.

Jason glanced over at Stevens, who was unabashedly staring at Melanie. He was a star, he could afford to ogle. Melanie thought Jason looked good, the same killer blue green eyes, the square face that was not quite perfect, making him more approachable, more alive, no chiseled model. He even had the dense, dark eyebrows, not really Melanie's thing, but very much in vogue. His haircut was better, and so were his shoes, he must already be on payroll.

Jason, perhaps taking his cue from Stevens, not shooing her off, finally acknowledged her. "Melanie."

"You know this beautiful young lady?" asked Stevens.

Melanie marveled at the pitch of the question, just the right tone to get Jason to give up exactly how he knew Melanie, or more specifically, whether he had slept with her. Stevens might be a sleaze, but he sure could command his voice, something else Melanie was working on. Unless Jason had matured a lot in the last year, he'd have no chance in this contest against Stevens, so Melanie jumped in. "Jason and I go way back, Mr. Stevens."

Stevens' eyes narrowed just a bit. Anyone else might have missed it, but Melanie studied actors, she had surprised him with her own perfectly pitched volley, pregnant with implications, and by taking a bit of control of the conversation.

"Call me Michael. And it can't be that far back. You're too young."

Just the way you like them, thought Melanie. Now she batted her eyelashes dramatically, play acting for them. "Oh, Michael, you say the sweetest things."

Melanie had ignored the third man, as had Jason and Stevens once the verbal sparring had started, the age old competition of preening. The third man didn't count in all this, he was just a suit.

Jason was still frowning, marring his striking features, he'd caught on to Melanie's game. "We're kind of busy here, Melanie."

"Nonsense," said Stevens. "Would you care to join us?"

A lot of women would have jumped at that, but Melanie wasn't going to appear easy to get, and the last thing she wanted was to let Jason think she'd been claimed by Stevens, it would spoil her plan. "That's so kind of you, but I'm sure you all have some business to discuss." Hoping that Jason realized what was happening, she was turning Stevens down, surely even Jason would understand the implications. Not wanting to leave it to chance, she added, "I hope to see you around soon." She directed the comment to the table, but she was looking directly at Jason, and now she was talking with her eyes, the magic sparkle, the same look of unspoken promise she had used the first time she had snared him.

But Jason had turned to the suit, he'd missed it. "You were saying something about finding some seedy places for location shoots? I might have a few ideas." He turned to Melanie. "Or better yet, Melanie might. Still living in that same dump, Mel?"

Melanie thought she did pretty good holding it together, Jason trying to put her down, making it clear there was nothing she could do for him, he didn't need her. And at the same time signaling to Stevens and maybe even the suit that she wasn't worth their time.

So Jason would be a tough nut to crack. Not that she hadn't expected that; he had something she wanted, and they both knew it. She actually relished the challenge. "You always were more comfortable in dangerous situations than I was," she said, building him up in front of the other men. "I moved out of there." Melanie thought fast, what would be a place that Jason would think of as nicer but also believable? Of course she hadn't moved at all, still in the same hellhole.

Jason took the bait, or maybe he was testing her. "Oh? Where to?"

Melanie needed something upwardly mobile, neat, stylish. Like someplace her sister Gigi would live, a neighborhood with successful professionals, art studios, chic boutiques, trendy restaurants . . .

"Lakeview," she said, which was perfect, because it was in fact where Gigi lived. "I've got a nice garden apartment. Quiet, a corner unit, away from the pool."

And everything suddenly fell into place, the whole plan, she could use her sister's place, Gigi always traveling for her job. Melanie wouldn't have to figure out how to get past security at the shoot, wouldn't have to keep finding ways to run into Jason, wouldn't have to worry about Stevens seeing her in whatever hotel the talent was staying at.

All she'd have to do was figure out how to get Jason to Gigi's apartment.

CHAPTER 3

T HE SUN FIRED SHARPLY through a bare window in the makeshift attic bedroom, hitting Lenny squarely in the eyes, a sniper sent by Mother Nature. The heat made Lenny's eyelids twitch but he refused to surrender, groaning and burying his head in the pillow. Far too early to get up.

He'd have to get a curtain for that damn window.

Sharp voices reverberated from below, loud enough to be heard right through the thin mattress. Lenny pulled the pillow over his head, trying to drown out the noise and the light. After a fruitless few minutes he tossed the pillow on the floor. The alarm clock told him it was almost noon, not early morning at all.

Downstairs, the voices, obviously an argument. His mother, Patty, and her boyfriend, Tom. They had only been living here three months and it was already clear that Patty and Tom could argue about anything at all. This morning it was about replacing the refrigerator. The argument would morph into broader themes, usually involving money, or the lack of it, and then would end up, as it always did, about the move from Los Angeles.

Lenny wasn't a big fan of Tom, but he could at least sympathize with what the guy was going through. Tom had a cushy job outside of Boston—*had* being the operative term—before his life had changed rather quickly. Tom's wife, now ex wife, had found out about Tom's dalliances on his West Coast business trips, and had given him, but not his house, the heave ho.

Patty had been one of Tom's dalliances, and she had taken the opportunity to explain to Tom how much better off he was, and didn't this just give them the chance to spend more time together? Offering housekeeping skills she hadn't practiced in years—Lenny knew this first hand, since he was still living with her in LA—Patty convinced Tom it would be a great idea if she moved east to be with him.

Tom was happy with the promise of uninterrupted sex, less so when he found out that Lenny was part of the package. He stashed Lenny in the attic, out of sight. Their uneasy peace came crashing down when Tom's ex found out Tom was shacking up with Patty. The entire divorce suddenly became public and ugly.

Tom's publicity shy bosses at his company didn't like that at all, and had added injury by doing their own heave ho. Tom was suddenly homeless, jobless, and with an alimony payment based on income he no longer earned.

Lenny tuned them out. He'd heard it enough times to know what each of them would say next. Patty pushing Tom to get back on his feet, sounding supportive, but Lenny knew she was already calculating how to find another meal ticket, since this one was looking like a bust. She'd screwed up making the move before the divorce was final, gambling, worried that some other woman would take her spot. Lenny didn't care; his mother would end up on her feet either way, as she always had since his father had left them when he was six. But right now Lenny was trapped. He didn't make enough money to live on his own, so his mother's dilemma was his.

His own meager income from his photography career had taken a sudden dive. He wasn't exactly pulling down the big bucks in LA, but he got by and was always on the cusp of making it into the big time. The move east had squashed all that; he'd had to virtually start over learning how and where to get tips of celebrity sightings.

Luckily they had ended up in Marburg, which had the film festival, and was only an hour from Boston, not exactly the mecca of filmdom, but a large enough city to attract some movie shoots and the occasional TV show.

The location gave Lenny a chance—however slim—that he would appear in the right place at the right time and the next photo would give him enough money to move out.

Lenny pushed himself up and automatically reached over to the nightstand for his cell phone.

Which was not there.

He'd left it downstairs to charge, because the attic didn't have any plugs. It was also hot and stuffy, since the window didn't open either. Still groggy, Lenny padded barefoot across the small room, ducking his head to get through the miniature door. Halfway across the adjoining spare room—why couldn't Tom clean all the shit out so Lenny could use this for a bedroom?—Lenny remembered he was dressed only in his boxers; his mother had given him shit about walking around Tom's house in just his underwear. Wasn't this their house now? It's what he had always done in the morning. He went back to pull on a pair of shorts. He struggled with the button, he'd put on a few pounds, all that beer drinking, hanging around bars, waiting for someone important to show up so he could get a picture.

Downstairs, his mother was smoking a cigarette at the kitchen table. Tom sat morosely drinking his coffee, staring blankly into space, a scattered newspaper in his lap.

"Anybody seen my phone? Ma?"

Patty took a deep drag and blew the smoke out toward the ceiling, a sure sign to Lenny of an imminent lecture. He glanced over at Tom, who picked up the newspaper with a sudden interest, but not before flashing Lenny a glance, as if to say, 'I wouldn't if I were you,' something deep in Tom's testosterone sharing a warning with the other male.

Lenny picked up on it too late, still focused on trying to skip out before his mother launched into whatever was on her mind, which was obviously not the refrigerator. "Ma, my phone! You seen it?"

Patty stubbed out her cigarette. "You spend way too much time on that phone."

"Ma, it's for work. It's the way I get information about where to shoot. And I need to be available, in case I get a call from a tipster."

"Tipster? What are you, some kind of public prosecutor? Oh, no, wait, that would mean you actually had a job."

Lenny wasn't going to get ensnared by this argument again, he'd been having it with his mother for years. And he knew the comment wasn't directed at him anyway; it was really meant for Tom. Lenny caught his mother glance over at Tom—she was a good manipulator, but she'd be terrible at poker—but Tom was safely cocooned behind the *Marburg Times*. Probably, Lenny thought, looking through the help wanteds, if for nothing more than to get Patty off his back.

Patty gave Lenny a little smile, an invitation to join her team, to help her work on Tom. Lenny had learned his skills of manipulation from her, and they both knew it. As well as the fact that they needed Tom, or someone like him.

Unlike most children, Lenny was able to look at his mother with the dispassionate eye of a photographer who knew what people found attractive in a woman. And Patty, though in her late forties, had a lot that men wanted. Raven red hair, oversized, still vibrant eyes, and a pleasant fullness in all the right places—her lips, her breasts, her hips. Guys like Tom, who might still lust after twenty year olds, but who were realistic, loved having a woman like Patty on their arm and in their bed.

Any other child talking about his mother this way would lead to psychologist talk about Oedipal complexes, but to Lenny it was just the hard facts of the superficial laws of attraction. Personally he liked the twenty year olds, and was at the age when he still had the chance to land a few now and then. Which reminded him of Leah, at the restaurant, and even more, of Melanie, although she was more Lenny's age. And to have any chance with Melanie, he needed his phone.

Lenny shook his head, turning down his mother's offer to gang up on Tom, and walked out of the kitchen.

Patty, without missing a beat, was already back to working on Tom, her voice following Lenny like a dark shadow. "You have such great skills, hon. You just need to get out of this funk, go on some interviews. You'll have a real job in no time, we can get a nicer place to live. Come here, let me make you feel better."

Lenny needed to tune this out more than the argument, so he closed the door to the kitchen before searching the living room for his phone.

He finally found it on the coffee table in the den, sitting under the newspaper, opened to the help wanted section, which obviously Tom hadn't been reading after all. This was just the sort of twisted way his mother liked to torment him.

There was a sticky note on the phone, a grocery list stuck to two twenties, things Patty wanted him to pick up, too busy herself doing whatever she did all day. She had worked a little in LA, a hostess for a catering company doing fancy parties, but she hadn't worked at all since the move east.

Lenny shoved the forty bucks in his pocket, crumbled up the list, tossed it in the air, and swung at it with his fist, but missed.

He could still hear his mother cajoling Tom. Fearing that the discussion would move to cringe inducing topics, he went out on the back porch and sat on a creaky lawn chair. It was already humid, sticky even in the relative shade, the webbing of the chair damp on his legs. Lenny was famished but the urge to get connected kept his hunger at bay for a bit.

Only one text, from one of the tipsters he was cultivating, a harder job than he had expected, the whole sub rosa celebrity sighting information business not well established here in Marburg. The tip was cryptic, *a possible scenario going down at the Marquee at 7 p.m.*

Lenny had scouted out the place, the only halfway decent club in Marburg. Not that he'd had much luck there, mostly wannabees and a few hasbeens, now and then some suits, maybe scouting out the suburbs of Boston for shooting locations or in town trying to negotiate tax incentives. Still, it was the most likely place to see a celebrity.

He went online, squinting at the phone—he really needed a bigger screen, something else he couldn't afford—and pulled up the website for the Marquee. The usual fluff, images of celebrities who had been there, most of the pictures all looking like they had been taken at the same events, probably around the time of the film festival or the awards shows.

The club had a *Meet the Staff* tab, which surprised Lenny, who gave a shit about the staff at a club? It brought up a list of photos, the largest ones showing the owner, an overly dressed little putz, smiling widely in various shots with mid level actors and actresses, all of them sporting that fake smile that Lenny recognized, the celebrity cringingly putting up with the guy who was letting them drink for free. The second largest picture on the site was of a blonde in one of those ridiculous over the shoulder poses, obviously taken by a rube local photographer. Lenny clicked on the image and the woman's resume popped up, an actress with a few local commercials. Lenny immediately deciphered the code—the owner had convinced the staff they'd get noticed at the club, which got him low cost help. He had sweetened the offer by putting up their resumes and photos on the site—which no one in the trade would ever look at, but the help wouldn't know that—the owner also probably promising he had connections who could help them. Lenny nodded, it wasn't a bad idea. The woman with the biggest photo was likely the one the owner was currently banging.

Lenny figured if the Marquee did that, the other business owners in Marburg where actors hung out might have glommed onto the scam, so Lenny pulled up the website of The Café, where he had spotted the two best looking women he had seen in Marburg, Leah and Melanie.

Sure enough, another web page with staff photos. No bios, but last names.

Melanie's sparkling eyes leapt off the screen, grabbing at him, Lenny feeling a tingle in his crotch, she was that good, probably able to turn her sexy gleam on and off at will. He didn't even scan the rest of the page for Leah.

Melanie Upton.

Lenny tried the IMDB database, the Linkedin for the acting world. Immediately got a hit, with several entries, including *Her Long Comment*, an off-Broadway thing that got some decent press, as well as a few non speaking roles and a list of her commercials.

With enough to narrow down an internet search, Lenny found a few images on second tier websites, three or four photos that popped up repeatedly, good shots of Melanie, eyes big and shiny and mischievous, making Lenny suspect she had planted the pictures, maybe giving a little something of herself, or the promise of it, to get the photos online.

One link led to a video that Melanie probably hadn't wanted circulated, a dark, jerky image, probably from a cell phone. Melanie, maybe a little drunk, in between two guys, good looking in that superficial actor way, fancy haircuts, all black, slightly too tight outfits. One of them appeared to be enjoying being with Melanie, who was showing a lot of very nice leg in a little black dress and strappy heels.

Whoever took the video kept zooming in on Melanie's breasts and legs, Melanie laughing along, preening, showing off a tribal tattoo high on her inner thigh. The other guy, the better looking of the two, seemed a little less sure, keeping just a bit of separation from Melanie. Some kind of asexual, thought Lenny. He wondered what Melanie was doing with him, he didn't seem her type. But he was the one Melanie kept looking at.

Even a little tipsy—an act?—Melanie looked hot, that same sex appeal Lenny had experienced in the restaurant coming through even in the video. He kept replaying it, advancing frame by frame, freezing on the best parts. Melanie's sultry smile. Her hand on one of the guys. The sexy tattoo. Lenny wondered if she had more ink even higher up. Lenny shifted in the chair, wincing as the cheap straps dug into his leg. Damn, just a picture of Melanie cut off his circulation. He *had* to have her.

Lenny studied every image and link very carefully, telling himself it was all for research. In order to be a good photographer you had to get in the head of the celebrity. Figure out what they might do, so you'd be there when it happened. Uncover their weakness. Drugs, sex, whatever. Melanie Upton had a weakness—everyone did. He'd find it and exploit it to get to her.

The Café restaurant website boasted that big name producers, agents and talent often frequented the place for lunch or early dinner. Of course Melanie would be sharp enough to get a job at a restaurant that attracted what little Hollywood royalty would be in Marburg. Lenny knew her game.

Gotcha.

Melanie would hang out at the Marquee, he was sure of it. In fact, he was surprised she didn't work there. Maybe sleeping with the little creepy owner was the cost of the job, and she didn't want to waste it on him. Either way, Melanie would be part of the nightlife, looking for her break.

Back in the house, Lenny was about to hit the kitchen to find something to eat, but his mother was still at it, and now Tom was talking back, not a good sign. Lenny checked his wallet, barely enough money for lunch, gas, and his tipster.

He ran back up the stairs to shower and change. When he was

done, he crept back down the stairs, hoping to sneak out without being heard.

With that annoying maternal psychic sense, his mother called from the kitchen, "Don't forget the groceries!"

Lenny picked up the wadded list, letting the back door slam behind him.

CHAPTER 4

LENNY STOPPED AT THE 7 ELEVEN, grabbing a slice of pizza, a Monster, and a two packages of Twinkies. The rows of cigarettes behind the counter reminded him of the grocery list, and he asked the clerk for a pack of his mother's smokes, adding in a few flavored cigarillos, which he found helpful in breaking the ice with women. When it came time to pay Lenny pulled out his wallet, quickly calculating in his head about his share versus his mother's, decided her tally was higher than his, and so paid for everything with one of her twenties.

He ate at one of the small tables in front of the convenience store, his eyes on his phone, scanning the celebrity sites for any hint of upcoming Boston-based shoots, a tedious process of endlessly following links.

Nothing sounded promising, so he looked at the state's office of business development website, where bureaucrats bragged about how much tax money they gave away to production companies that weren't even located in the state, but supposedly benefited the local economy. Sure enough, a page of films and shows supposedly lured by the political geniuses. A few more searches and Lenny had a list of possible shooting locales.

It took the better part of the afternoon for Lenny to scout them out. Some were so vague as to be useless, no hint of a schedule, or even if the deal was in the bag. Others mentioned Marburg but were too general, the entire shoot probably nothing more than creating a few background clips that would be used over and over to introduce scenes that were actually shot on a studio set out in LA.

Although Lenny didn't find a single shoot in progress, the time wasn't totally wasted. He was out of the house, doing something, working his gig. Although the chance of coming across a valuable shot was pretty low, it could never be discounted, so he had his camera gear on the seat close at hand. He was getting a feel for the area, and if he got a tip on a location he'd know how to get there quickly.

He ate dinner a strip mall Wendy's, staring out at the parking lot to a chain grocery store, reminding him of the grocery list. He reluctantly stopped at the market to gather the rest of what his mother wanted. He'd have to hurry if he was going to be at the Marquee in time to meet his tipster.

LENNY SPED UP CANTERBURY STREET, glad for once of the big motor in the squishy Cadillac, a car that always seemed to look even more outdated than its age, this one a gift from an ex boyfriend of his mother's, a veritable pimp mobile. Lenny hated tips that demanded you be somewhere at a specific time because it forced him into a schedule, and he hated schedules, they took away his freedom. Right now he didn't have a choice, he was desperate for a tip.

In town he passed by The Café; he'd check later to see if Melanie was working. He parked on the street while still several blocks from the Marquee. It was a pain in the ass to walk but he didn't want anyone to mark his car as paparazzi wheels.

Lenny moved like he was on a military mission, his camera held loosely like a weapon ready to fire, his eyes darting everywhere, always looking for a shot. But the streets were uncommonly quiet, that in between time after work and before the nightlife began. From behind a parked Kia he studied the area in front of the Marquee, looking for any sign of an impending newsworthy event. It was unlikely he'd missed anything. He would wait because he knew about unpredictability, and it wasn't like he had much else to do. He lit one of his cigarillos to pass the time and so he wouldn't appear to be loitering. Just a guy outside for a smoke.

After forty five minutes of squinting at every passerby, trying to identify who might be someone important, Lenny ground out his last smoke, swung his camera around to his back so it would be less noticeable, and crossed the street to the Marquee.

He felt a little out of place, not dressed for a club, but it didn't matter, the place was dead. A few men sat at the bar getting an early buzz, the mid shift staff clustered in the back listlessly chatting, barely giving him a glance. The throb of music was ridiculously loud in the near empty room. It took only a few seconds to see that there were no brass or celebrities.

Back outside, Lenny's tipster JT was hopping from foot to foot, his forehead hidden in a hoodie, a walking cliché of an informant. Either that or high on crack.

"Where you been?" JT asked in a loud whisper, the squeaky voice more from his nose than his mouth.

"I waited forty six minutes for something to happen. Then I went inside to have a look around."

The hoodie turned toward the street, a bobblehead in the wind. "Yeah? Well, while you were looking around, you missed it."

"Missed what?"

"Darren Kent and Violet Calmly of *Sideways* drove by in private cars."

"So?"

"*Separate* private cars. Word on the street is they ain't having a good time on their reality show."

"You dragged me here to watch two people, who aren't married, drive by in separate cars? Are you fuckin' kidding me?"

"Dude, why ain't you getting this? They're on the *same* show. They're supposed to be having a thing going, hot and heavy. If they were that into each other they'd be riding in the same car. But they hate each other. So they're in separate cars. It means their reality show is a fake. If you got a picture you could reveal the whole secret."

"Nobody in the world would pay me a fucking cent for a picture of two cars."

"Well, you'll never know, now, will you? Because you went inside to have a look around."

Lenny resisted the urge to slap some sense into JT, a temptation he'd had many times in life about many people but had never actually acted on. This would be a good time as any, JT nothing more than a stick on legs. But JT had been the only local contact he'd managed to cultivate. Maybe he just needed a little seasoning, some of Lenny's expertise.

"How did you know it was them in the cars? Did you see them get in?"

"I didn't, someone else did."

"Who?"

JT's eyes narrowed. "Hey man, you aren't trying to get me to give up my source, are you?"

Lenny hadn't been, but it was a good thought. "No, I just want to know how good your info is."

JT bopped left to right and back. "I know one of the limo drivers," he mumbled.

Lenny stashed that piece of information away for the future. "Okay, watch." He swung his camera around and deftly shot six quick photos of passing cars, panning, letting the autofocus do its thing. He pulled up the first image on the screen and held it out. "What do you see, JT?"

JT peered out from his hoodie. "A car."

"No shit. What else?" Lenny flicked to the next image.

"Someone driving."

"Who?"

"Shit man, I don't know. I think it's a woman."

"Exactly," said Lenny. "You can barely make out who it is." He clicked through all six images. "See? Car shots are useless, you can never tell who's driving unless the windows are down."

"Yeah, but if you say it's them in the photo, who's to know?"

Lenny shook his head. He hated dealing with amateurs. "It's just no good, JT. Keep that in mind down the road."

"I guess this means I won't get my ten bucks?"

"Bring me something good next time." Lenny snapped his camera around his back, holstering his gun. "And JT? No more of this clandestine shit. If you have something, just text it to me."

JT called out after him. "Hey, Lenny, you at least got a smoke?"

*   *   *

THE QUESTION DID REMIND Lenny of his mother's cigarettes, and the groceries, which he hadn't remembered to take home before his trek around town. The milk was no doubt spoiled, another few hours wouldn't matter now.

Instead of heading back to the Caddy he went the other way down Main, angry now; he'd have to get more milk or risk his mother's wrath. The incident with JT hadn't helped. He just couldn't get a single fucking break, *one* break was all he needed, was that too much to ask?

Lenny spotted two women on the sidewalk ahead, walking toward him, in high spirits, laughing. A blonde and a brunette, dressed elegantly, one in a designer skirt outfit, the other in a great dress, both in heels. Even from a distance Lenny recognized the expensive handbags. The blonde put her hand on her friend's arm, and Lenny forgot all about the milk and JT, thinking, wow, that's hot, wondering if they were lesbians or maybe bi.

He was openly staring as they neared, taking in everything, both wore wedding rings, huge diamond studs, all the trappings of well kept women, married to rich guys. Exactly the kind of woman Lenny expected he'd get once he made it big, graciously giving his wife a platinum credit card to buy sexy clothing, bringing her to clubs in his Corvette. No, a Masarati. Or maybe a chauffeured limo. His wife so thrilled to be with Lenny she'd put out for him anytime, maybe even in the back of the limo. Maybe even with one of her girlfriends.

Lenny was so taken by his fantasy he didn't even think to get a photo of them, one of the few times he'd missed a chance to add to his personal real life porn stash. As they passed him he purposely brushed against the blonde, just a graze, but enough to make his legs weak.

Neither one of them even glanced at him.

Lenny turned, watching them walk away, their asses seductive, his mind chasing after them, catching them, transporting himself with them to another place, a bedroom . . .

Some old guy skirted around him, and Lenny reached out to push the geezer away, the asshole was blocking his view.

The old guy spun around, an aged hippy with long hair. "What's your problem?"

Lenny took in the deranged eyes, the faded ink on the guy's arm. "Nothing," he muttered. He glanced down the street, the two women were gone.

Lenny left the crazy hippy behind and stalked off, continuing up Main. The guy yelled after him, but Lenny's mind was already on Melanie. Hooking up with a woman like Melanie could be his ticket out of poverty. If he could just spend some time with her, make her see what kind of talent he had. He'd make her famous, and not only be along for the ride, he'd get to ride her. A twofer.

Across the street from the restaurant Lenny leaned against the wall of a Starbucks. He reached for a cigarillo but he was out, hopefully he wouldn't look too suspicious. Outside The Café the tables were filled with diners, Lenny praying that Melanie was working and had the outdoor station. An older waitress came out, definitely not Melanie. He considered going in to the restaurant to check, decided it would look too obvious. He didn't want Melanie to think he was stalking her, or desperate.

A halfway decent Latina was sitting alone at one of the Starbucks outdoor tables, immersed in her laptop. An empty seat against the window would give him a nice view of her legs, so Lenny went inside, ordered a basic coffee, and hurried back out. Two old ladies had taken the table he had scoped out. Lenny gave them a dirty look and sat at another table where he could keep an eye on the restaurant, but unfortunately not on the Latina.

A slow hour went by, Lenny's coffee long gone even though he had nursed it. But the cup on the table made him look like a customer, and no one bothered him. The Latina was gone, but fortunately so were the two old ladies, so Lenny was able to grab the table against the window, where he had a clear view of both the women coming in and out of the coffee shop as well as the restaurant. Still no sign of Melanie. Lenny was trying to figure out when the shifts would change, maybe she'd be coming on or off duty. He toyed with his phone to kill time. Maybe call the restaurant, ask for Melanie? He could always hang up, at least he'd know if she was working. Too risky, she might pick up, see his caller ID.

If this were LA, just sitting here would be a joy, so many good looking women walking around, as good as surfing porn. Well, not quite as good, but there was something about seeing hot women in the flesh, no photo or even video could duplicate that. Lenny had spent many hours just like this, sitting with an empty cup, checking out the ladies, all shapes and sizes, Asians, Latinos, black, white, a rainbow of possibilities. It was amazing how many beautiful women were in LA, not just in Hollywood, not just near the studios, but everywhere, women from all over the world descending on the city to try their luck. The locals fought to keep up, knowing the men would always be on the lookout for some plaything.

But here it was different. Really attractive women were the exception, not the rule. Lenny thought about what power that must give them, how they probably got their pick of the men. That one over there, the blue eyed blonde, for example. In LA, she'd have to jump up on the table and flash her boobs to get noticed, but every eye at the Starbucks was on her, men walking by checking her out, even though her clothes were just a little off, like she had read about chic instead of understanding it. Not that Lenny would kick her out of bed. Maybe he'd try his line on her, offer to take some pictures, even though she was too short.

He fondled his camera, about to make his move, working out the dialogue in his mind. Maybe lay his usual rap on her, about helping her build a portfolio for commercials, try to get her away from the crowd at the Starbucks, wondering where he could take her for some privacy. He fingered the last of the roofies in his pocket. He'd never tried putting them in coffee, he could offer to buy her a cup, get her in his car . . .

Two guys were at the table in front of him, doing exactly what he was, checking out the female scenery. One of them said, "Shit, look at her," Lenny thinking they were talking about the blonde. He was so immersed in his plan for her that it took him a moment to realize the men were looking across the street, where Melanie had just stepped out of the restaurant.

She was wearing a short tight dress, not likely what she had gone to work in, meaning she'd changed in the restaurant. A date? Lenny slunk down but Melanie wasn't even looking his way.

Lenny let her get a few steps before he stood up, just as one of the voyeurs in front of him said, "Just think, some guy gets to hit on that," which is just about what Lenny was thinking, only instead of sitting around mentally masturbating like these two losers he was going to make sure he'd be the guy they were talking about, the one Melanie would be with.

He walked down the street, keeping watch on Melanie. Surprisingly, she still had on her clunky work shoes, not what he expected of her, a fuck me dress with bulky flats. Melanie turned into the restaurant parking lot, heading toward the back, maybe where her car was parked. Lenny was blocks from the Caddy, he'd never get there in time. He stood helplessly on the corner, undecided.

For once the gods were with him. In two minutes Melanie returned from the parking lot, walking right toward him, a forward gait, now in tall heels, Lenny so entranced by her legs that he waited too long to turn away, she'd notice him for sure. When he looked back up, though, Melanie had turned onto Main.

Lenny paralleled her from across the street, now and then pretending to look in a window in case Melanie glanced his way, but she seemed to be in a hurry, not looking around at all. Lenny dodged through the early evening strollers, ignoring even the good looking women. He matched Melanie's cadence, in his head hearing the click of her heels on the sidewalk, even over the rush of cars. Maybe he could cross over to her side, get a better look at her ass. Too risky, she might turn around . . .

And right then she did, Lenny so surprised he tripped, and almost expected her to as well, feeling the connection. They were *linked*, that had to be it. Had she been unconsciously looking for him, wanting Lenny to be there? She had swung her head back around again, never breaking stride. Lenny mentally willed her to look his way. It would be worth the risk, it would prove that something was going to happen between them, like when you were speeding down the street and you made the light change to green just with your mind.

But Melanie didn't look, she was on some kind of mission, fully decked out in her sultry weapons, those perky breasts, those legs. At the next corner the light was against them, Melanie impatient, jostling to the front of the pedestrians, Lenny doing the same on his side of the street. At the next corner Melanie didn't cross the side street, she was going to come across Main, toward him. Lenny missed the move, he was already in the crosswalk, too late to stop, he'd stick out like a sore thumb.

He kept walking, slower now, glancing back every few steps, praying for the light to change. He turned to look in a shop window, the display not registering, listening for the traffic behind him to stop, a signal that the light had turned red. Only then did he risk a quick peek over his shoulder, seeing Melanie coming his way. Frantic, Lenny stepped into the shop, an image flashing in his mind of Melanie heading into that very store, was this how they were fated to begin their relationship?

"Can I help you?"

Lenny spun to see a gray haired woman with too much makeup looking at him expectantly, the shop completely empty, no place to hide.

"Uh, no, just looking around." Lenny pretended to do just that, his mind still wrapped up in the connection to Melanie, expecting her to come in behind him. The clerk was staring at him, a smile frozen on her lips, Lenny thinking he was making her day, this good looking guy showing up in her shop. Over her shoulder stood row upon row of female mannequins, wearing only underwear, not sexy underwear, but girdles, thickly padded bras, something that looked like a fucking diaper. A sign read, 'Living your life with incontinence.'

Stunned, Lenny swung around, the entire store a sick orgy of adult pads, walkers, bedpans. The clerk said, "Don't be embarrassed, it can happen at any age."

Lenny felt himself shrivel, he couldn't let Melanie see him here, he had to get out, out, and was reaching for the door just as she walked past. The glass was all that separated them as she crossed by, so close he could have touched her if the door hadn't been closed. He leaned forward involuntarily, her pull was that strong. Then she was gone, in his mind hearing the swish of her thighs, forced together by the tight dress.

He waited as long as he dared, then stuck his head out the door, almost getting it knocked off by a kid on a skateboard, then he was out, free, the woman calling from the shop, "Come back soon!"

Lenny shivered, shaking off the feel of the shop, keeping a few people between him and Melanie, Lenny getting hotter with each step. Two blocks later she turned, and Lenny laughed, a partial release of pent up excitement. Melanie had gone into the Marquee.

A BOUNCER WHO HADN'T been there before stopped Lenny. "Ten bucks."

"A cover? You gotta be shitting me," said Lenny.

"Ten bucks," repeated the bouncer, his tone suggesting he didn't care whether Lenny went in or not.

"I just saw someone walk in without paying."

The bouncer looked Lenny up and down, taking in his black khakis and midnight silk shirt. "She's dressed better than you are. Better legs too."

Lenny bit off a retort about his legs being pretty good, not wanting to appear to come on to the guy in case he was gay. "Covers are just stupid."

"Ten bucks."

Lenny dug in his pants, came up with his mother's second twenty. The bouncer took his time giving him change, ten ones. Lenny stepped into the club, muttering, "Jerkoff," only half hoping the bouncer would hear.

Inside, the club was already surprisingly crowded, Lenny wondering where all these people had come from in just a few hours. If this had been LA it would have been empty, no one hit a club before eleven, and usually much later for the good ones, which the Marquee would never be.

Lenny drifted toward the main bar, and not finding Melanie there, he bumped his way through the throng to the back room. He was a little underdressed, good thing even his casual clothes were stylish. He spied Melanie on a stool at the bar in conversation with a good looking waitress.

He chose a table at the rear of the main room where he wouldn't be so noticeable but could still see Melanie. The whole vibe of the club had changed since he had been there earlier, people must have come in after work. Keeping half an eye on Melanie, Lenny checked out the action.

Every nightspot had its own feel; Lenny had been in enough of them to know. This was the hopeful crowd, hoping to have some fun, get a buzz, maybe a hookup. He spotted the budding actors right away, trying not to look obvious as they scanned the room for agents and producers; the too thin models, trying to look bored; and the suits, the production company execs, ignoring everyone except who they were with. Lenny wasn't quite in the club, but he certainly knew what its members looked like.

A gap in the crowd gave Lenny an unobstructed view of Melanie, looking good even in profile, her dress hiked up to her thighs. The waitress was giving Melanie another drink. Their heads were pretty close, friendly, Lenny thinking maybe the waitress was Melanie's date. Nah, she couldn't be gay, it would be such a fucking waste. Besides, he would have picked up on that.

Melanie turned away from the bar, Lenny's eyes drawn like a magnet to her legs, simply amazing. She was looking deeper into the back room, as was the waitress, so Lenny followed their eyes. He immediately spotted Michael Stevens, in the corner with two other men. Lenny had shot Stevens a few times, mostly with almost under-age women, the first time thinking he had a real scoop, then finding out that shots of Stevens with women less than half his age were a dime a dozen. Most of the photographers only shot Stevens to get pics of the girls to keep for themselves. Stevens had good taste in women.

Surprisingly, Melanie turned away from Stevens, back in conversation with the bartender. Melanie didn't seem too impressed, not like everyone else in the club, who were all surreptitiously eyeing Stevens, probably trying to figure out how to approach him. Which would be disastrous; famous actors hated being bothered in public, especially by wannabees. Now and then condescending for an autograph for a fan, sure, if in the right frame of mind. But being hit on by some talent, no way. A guy like Stevens picked who he wanted, it didn't work the other way around.

So Lenny was stunned when Melanie got up and headed right for

Stevens. No, no, she was doing it *all wrong*, she'd blow her chance for sure. Lenny jumped up, he needed to stop her, tell her the error of her ways, she'd be so grateful for his help. He'd get her alone and explain how things worked. Stevens would be useless, he wouldn't help her career.

Two steps later Lenny realized he was too late. Stevens had already noticed Melanie, a slow motion train wreck unfolding. Lenny was already planning ahead, he'd give Melanie a shoulder to cry on, tell her how to do it next time . . .

Lenny slumped against the wall, resigned to the inevitable. Even with the booming music the room seemed to hush, conversations drying up, all eyes on the table, where Melanie now stood talking to the men, half the crowd jealous of the attention Melanie was getting, the other half amazed at her balls. Lenny was pretty amazed himself; it was obvious that Stevens was captured by Melanie. Maybe not so surprising, come to think of it, she was that hot.

Mixed feelings now: rooting for her, wanting her to be the one who could be different, who could approach a powerful man like Stevens in a roomful of people and get away with it, yet miffed, Melanie was *his*, or would be soon, Lenny was going to be her ticket, Stevens could spoil *everything*.

Melanie turned, slowly walking away, the music louder, a hundred held breaths let out.

She had failed.

Lenny's heart went out to her, she'd be so depressed, getting blown off in public. She'd need him now.

LENNY STEPPED IN FRONT of Melanie as she left the back room. He wanted to reach out and hold her, she was so beautiful, her eyes dancing in the lights, not the look of depression that Lenny had expected. She moved to dodge him, so he took the chance and reached for her arm, the touch electric, his hand clammy, the skin on the back of his neck prickling. He wanted her so bad . . .

Melanie turned her eyes on him, ablaze with annoyance, actually looking down on him. Must be the shoes giving her height, he wasn't *that* short. Then the recognition, pleasing Lenny. She remembered him.

"Take your fucking hand off me."

Not quite the reaction Lenny wanted, but he figured she was pretty upset about the whole Stevens fiasco. He jerked his hand away. "Hey, I just want to help."

"What are you doing here? You stalking me?"

Lenny's legs grew weak. "What? No, really. I hang here. Kinda, I told you I'm new." He rushed, he didn't want to miss this chance. "I saw what happened with Stevens, I can help with that."

"You know Stevens?" Disbelieving, but she didn't walk off.

"Not exactly. But I know what he's all about. I've shot him." Lenny lifted his camera. "I'm a photographer, remember? Listen, I know what you are trying to do, you're trying to get discovered. I get it. I'm doing it too. We have that in common."

"I very much doubt we have anything in common." She moved past him.

"Look, I know you're upset, getting blown off by Stevens in front of all these people."

Melanie spun on him. "What the fuck are you talking about? I didn't get blown off."

"Don't be embarrassed. You had guts to try it. You need a break, you thought he'd be the one to help, you took your shot. Half the room wished they were brave enough to do what you did."

"You moron. They asked me to sit down."

"Yeah, right, Michael Stevens wanted you to join him and you walked away?"

Melanie took a step closer to him, in his space now, Lenny delirious with her presence, her scent. "What I'm doing is none of your fucking business. Or anyone else's around here." Her eyes slid past Lenny.

Lenny caught the look, seeing it for what it was, Melanie was worried about what the crowd had witnessed, it was his chance. "Give me five minutes and I'll tell you a surefire way to get what you want, and you won't have to suck up to Stevens or anyone like him ever again."

"How would you know?"

Lenny smiled, he *had* her. "Because I've helped an actress do it before. Come on, what will it hurt to listen?"

Melanie's eyes flicked back to the crowd, Lenny waiting, trying to relax. It was impossible, so close to her, he could feel her heat. Someone brushed by, a silicone blonde in a tight dress, Lenny feeling her eyes on Melanie, the chick shaking her head, a look that said *loser*, not to Lenny, but to Melanie. Melanie turned, her lip curling, it would have been ugly on anyone but her, Melanie's hand coming up, maybe to slap the bimbo.

Lenny grabbed Melanie's wrist, surprised by her strength, barely managing to check her swing. "Not the scene you want to make," he said urgently. He jerked his head to the back room. "You want the suits to see?"

Melanie shook off his hand. "Fuck that bitch," she said to the retreating woman.

Lenny guided Melanie toward the bar. "I'll give you a way to get what you want without having to fuck anyone," he said. *Except me.*

Lenny was confident now, because he knew what he was going to suggest to her would work. That, and the fact that the bimbo woman had actually helped him out. Melanie had an ego—everyone had to have one, in this business—but Melanie was acutely aware of public perception, she wanted the publicity, the adoration. It would rankle her that people thought she had struck out with Stevens. It fit perfectly into Lenny's plan.

Lenny was feeling the eyes on *him*, the crowd probably thinking he was Melanie's main man, what a rush that was. He kept pace with her, not wanting it to look like he was following, she was with him, following him, that was the way it was supposed to be. He did a little skip to get ahead, beating her to the bar.

No stools were empty, he was stymied trying to make some room. Melanie didn't give him a chance, she just stood in front of two guys who were eying her, and they immediately jumped up to offer her a seat. Lenny was amazed, she didn't even have to smile, such was her allure. Melanie took one of the stools, giving the guy a quick nod, but immediately turned away from them. Lenny took the other stool, ignoring the frown from the guys.

"Five minutes," said Melanie. "And only if it's good. Otherwise

I'm out of here. And I want a Black Russian."

"Sure, sure." Lenny signaled for the waitress, the same one who he saw Melanie talking to earlier. "A Black Russian here," he said.

The waitress, whose name tag said *Fiona*, waited for Lenny's order. He shook his head, he needed to keep his focus. The waitress glanced at Melanie, some kind of look passing between them, then she was gone.

"Make it quick," said Melanie.

Lenny launched into his spiel. "Look around this place. Everyone here is trying to get noticed. Must be a few hundred people looking for a break. There are clubs and restaurants and modeling agencies and casting companies all over the country, filled with people like this, every one of them doing the exact same thing. You could win here, and still not make it, because there's an ocean of people just like you. The odds just aren't in your favor."

"So far you're telling me what I already know. And I'm not just one of them, I'm better."

"Hey, I know that. I can see you got it. I lived in LA, remember? I know the scene. But even the suits here might not be good enough to recognize what you got, and even if they do, might not have enough pull to launch your career. You have to get into the big time, connected with the right people."

"You're still telling me things I already know."

Lenny pushed on, feeling the pressure. "You got to get to a place where people think you are in the A-list, where they associate you with the heavy hitters. It's like a club, a private club. Once you're in, you're in, and people don't care how you *got* in, they forget. But here in Marburg, you don't have much of a chance to make the leap. You're working at the right restaurant, you're in the right hangout, you took your shot with Stevens, even with all that, the odds are a million to one, even for a woman as beautiful as you."

"And you can improve my odds?"

Fiona returned with the drink, giving Melanie a little smile. Lenny waited for her to leave before he went on. "I can. I've done it." He told Melanie about his success in LA, the photograph, blurring over some of the details, and not mentioning it was a one time thing. "So just hooking up with Stevens, a lot of girls try that, you know a single actress who got anywhere from it?" He went on before Melanie had a chance to reply. "That's because no one did. He uses them and spits them out. You've got to turn the tables on him."

"Spit him out?" Melanie took a sip of her drink, her voice even.

Lenny didn't know if she was teasing him, he marveled at how she could turn his mind to sex. "Something like that. Here's a question for you. What good is it if you sleep with Stevens? Nobody will know, and if they do, nobody will care. On the other hand, if there was someone else we could get you next to, not quite in a compromising position, but in a photo that would go viral, you'd be noticed. Instantly. No more trying to hope the stars align to bring the right actor or suit in your orbit so you can make your pitch. No long road to getting just a shot. It will happen like *that.*" Lenny snapped his fingers. He couldn't hear the snap over the music, but he thought he had made his point.

Melanie turned, her face registering some kind of emotion, Lenny could feel the connection, they were on the same side. She was thinking about it, he was getting somewhere.

"Of course," Lenny added, trying to sound matter of fact, "we'd have to find a way to get you in the right place at the right time." Already talking like they were a team.

Melanie's eyes went to the table where Stevens and the other men were still sitting, Lenny holding his breath. He'd taken his shot, he didn't want to blow it now by pushing too hard. After an eternity Melanie turned back to him, meeting his eyes full for the first time, then downed her drink. "I'll think about it."

Melanie nodded toward the bartender and flicked her head toward Lenny. Fiona smiled, coming over. Melanie gracefully slipped off the stool and walked away, Lenny staring at her ass, that amazing body, not believing his luck, he was almost there, so much faster than he had expected. She was just trying not to appear desperate, she'd come around.

Fiona tapped him on the shoulder. "Thirty six dollars."

Lenny forced his mind off of Melanie's ass. "For a Black Russian?"

"She had a tab."

Lenny stuck his hand in his pocket and pulled out what remained of his mother's cash. He might just be able to cover it, but there'd be nothing left for the groceries, his mother would be pissed. "Fuck me."

"In your dreams," said Fiona.

CHAPTER 5

MELANIE KICKED OFF HER HEELS as she unlocked the street side door that led up to her apartment, ignoring the pebbles that bore into her bare feet. It had been a long day, she had a major league buzz going, and there was no way she was going to walk up a steep flight of stairs in four inch heels, Jimmy Choo or not.

The overpowering scent of curry filled the stairway, courtesy of the Indian restaurant on the first floor, her crappy apartment even worse because the food there sucked. A dim yellowing bulb on the landing was the only light, but Melanie knew these stairs even in the dark—it was the only time she was here. If she hadn't been so focused on Jason she would have lined up a guy to sleep with tonight, someone with a fucking elevator.

The loose lock rattled as she turned the key. Melanie wondered why she bothered with it, her shoes were the only things worth stealing, and she had those with her all the time. Inside, the room was surprisingly bright, the thin curtains no match for the streetlight which glared into her window.

Melanie dropped the shoes on the floor, and her purse and the copy of the local *Herald*, which she had lifted from the entrance to the Indian restaurant, on the kitchen counter. *Kitchen* being a bit of a misnomer, the appliances stacked against one half wall in an ell. Though she had a separate bedroom, the apartment was really just a studio; she'd sweet talked a guy into illegally walling off the bedroom area. Even in Marburg a studio was all she could afford, every dime she made burned up going back and forth to New York for screen tests, what little was left spent on clothes. If the restaurant didn't let her eat for free she'd probably have starved to death by now.

Standing in front of the open fridge, Melanie pulled the top of her dress away from her skin, trying to cool down, the refrigerator her only source of air conditioning. Two cans of beer, a wrapped half sandwich and an opened pint of yogurt. Melanie grabbed a beer and the newspaper and padded back to the couch, not even bothering to turn on a light. She would've turned the tv on, out of habit, but the cable had been shut off two days ago. Melanie peered at an ashtray on the coffee table but there was nothing in it worth trying to smoke.

She flipped idly through the paper as she took a hit on the beer. One headline caught her attention: *Mayor To Announce Filming In Marburg,* that being what passed for big local news. She skimmed the article, the only useful tidbit being the mention of a press conference the next day.

Melanie put the beer on top of the paper and laid her head back on the couch, the night replaying in her mind like a TMZ clip. The only thing missing was a microphone stuck in her face. Jason, always a bit full of himself, now a full fledged pompous shit after getting cast in the new series *Shock and Awe.* Still looking good though, maybe even better. Her time with Jason in the sack had its fun side, although even there he was more into himself than into her. She giggled at her own stupid joke, realizing she was a little drunk. She'd worked her restaurant shift through dinner and so had done all her drinking on an empty stomach.

Meeting Stevens was somewhat unexpected. Melanie knew he and Jason would be on the same show, but usually the big star didn't want to be seen in public with the newbie, unless it was arranged by the publicity department. But running into Stevens could be a real turning point for Melanie, although she'd have to achieve what all his other women had not. Her whole plan had been to leverage Jason, but maybe Stevens could fit into the picture. It wouldn't be the first time she'd slept with a guy old enough to be her father, if she thought he could do something for her.

Lenny. Disgusting troll. Oblivious to how common he was, a guy who hung around the actresses, trying to score. But even a troll could have a good idea. A timely photograph with the right person, in the right situation, one that might be viewed as scandalous, or at least newsworthy, could get Melanie some good publicity. Maybe even on TMZ.

Jason or Stevens, which one to use?

She picked up her beer, the cold can leaving a ring right around the word *Shock* in the newspaper article, and all at once, as if it was destined, she had her answer.

THE PRESS CONFERENCE. Lots of people, celebrities, press. The perfect place to get attention. It would take some planning, but Melanie was confident she could pull it off. Who should she be photographed with, Jason or Stevens?

And who would take the picture? It was unlikely Lenny Gruse was the right photographer for the job. Melanie would want a proven commodity. Someone who had the skills, the connections, but also was enough of a sleaze to do it for the right reason.

Someone like Tim Tazik.

Taz had done some publicity photos for Melanie, always at a significant discount, usually free. What he really wanted was to get in Melanie's pants.

"You are quite a work of art," Taz had said during the first photo shoot.

Melanie knew it was the usual photographer bullshit, trying to get the subject to feel good, but she played along. "And you're the artist who's going to make me famous?"

"Hey, I've shot plenty of women. They don't come close to you."

"Better switch to boots," said Melanie. "It's getting thick in here."

"Just telling it like it is. We can go far together, you'll see."

Taz had pushed a little harder in each shoot, Melanie managing to keep things professional. Taz was married, and for the most part, Melanie had drawn the line there, the last thing she needed was some deranged wife coming after her. But Taz would be perfect for this.

Melanie rummaged through her purse for her cell phone and checked to make sure she still had Tazik's private number, the one he said his wife didn't know about. He'd given it to Melanie in the hopes she might change her mind about hooking up. Too late to call him now. Tomorrow. Using the private line would give Taz the idea that she'd finally succumbed to his charms, which was just what she wanted anyway. At least until after he did what she needed.

MELANIE AWOKE STIFF, a crick in her neck from falling asleep on the couch. She pulled at her twisted dress, unzipping it, letting it drop to the floor now that it was hopelessly wrinkled. She ate the rest of the yogurt as she heated up some instant coffee and opened her one working window, greeted by curry tingled humid air. Not even mid morning and it was already hot.

As she sipped the coffee she was flicking to Taz's number on her phone. Just as she would for a screen test, she took a few moments to get in character. She was playing the part of a coy vixen, negotiating with a potential lover, using her feminine wiles to get him to break his bonds of matrimony . . .

"Taz? It's Mel."

"I was hoping I'd get a call from you on this line someday."

Okay, so it wasn't going to take a lot of skill to get Taz over the moral quandary of infidelity. "It's that day. I was hoping I could borrow you for a while this afternoon."

"Borrow me? Is that shorthand for use me? Some new kink of yours?"

Melanie rolled her eyes. "Probably not in the way you're thinking, Taz."

A disappointed hesitation. "Okay, I'll bite."

"You'll be at the press conference today?"

"Of course. I don't know anyone who won't be."

"I need you to take some pics for me."

"Pics for you or of you?"

"Of me. An attention getter."

"Hmm . . . You're not going to make a scene, are you?"

"Why does everyone ask me that? No. I just want a shot with . . ." Melanie flipped a mental coin. "Jason Ayers."

"What for?" asked Taz, suspicious.

"He's an old friend. I just want a picture of us together, so I can remember being there when he made the big time."

There was a pause. "Mel, if he knows you, you can do a selfie."

"I don't want a selfie, Taz, I want something professional."

"So you can use it for your own publicity."

"Come on, Taz, this is what you do for a living."

"How much were you planning on spending? It being my livelihood and all."

Now it was Melanie's turn to be quiet. If she had to come right out and say it, the game was lost.

"Maybe we could work something out," said Taz.

Melanie smiled. She had him. "I'm sure we can, Taz." Only it wasn't going to be exactly what Taz had in mind.

"The press conference is at one. Where do you want to meet?"

"We won't have to, not before, anyway. Just have your gear, and be clicking away when you see me."

"Video too?"

"Why not?"

"Okay. This better be worth it, Mel."

"Believe me, Taz, it will be."

For her, anyway. Melanie hung up. She had a lot to do before one o'clock.

THE PUBLIC BATHROOM at the community park was nicer than Melanie's. She balanced her phone on the vanity, taking another look at the cast on the *Shock and Awe* webpage. The face of Lisa Vista—where had she come up with that stage name?—stared out at Melanie, a hard stare, as if she knew what Melanie had in mind.

Melanie gave Lisa's picture the finger. She'd met Lisa a few times on shoots. They were about the same age and same height, although Lisa had more experience on the screen, having started earlier in life, playing the good little girl parts. Melanie had been stunned when Lisa got the role in *Shock and Awe*, the bitch just didn't have the right attitude for the role, no rough edges, no spontaneity, no spunk. She was a ballet dancer trying to do freerunning, she had the look but not the moves or the toughness. Melanie could have nailed it, but she hadn't even been invited to a casting call. Maybe Lisa had slept with Stevens to get the role. Melanie had even read a few articles online suggesting that Lisa's casting had been a mistake. Damn right.

Melanie deftly spun the brush through her hair, working in the gel, doing what she could to tame her waves to match Lisa's perfectly straight hair. Melanie was good with hair. Her mother had been a stylist, and Melanie had sat many days after school in the salon, toying with the tools of the trade, the ladies giving her some lessons when things were slow. It was at the salon where Melanie had read all the gossip mags, and it was there that she decided to be an actress. One day little girls would be looking at Melanie's picture in one of those magazines, women all over the country would be copying *her* latest hairstyle . . .

Right now, she just needed to look a little like Lisa. The clothes had been no problem; the entire cast of *Shock and Awe* had been wardrobed by some goth flameout, black on black, stuff Melanie had in the closet but had stopped wearing years ago. The best thing was the black beret, the signature of Lisa's cast role, the part of the outfit that would make the viewers think it was Lisa even when a double was doing her stunts. Melanie had found one just like it at a second hand shop on the way to the park. And a red one as well.

Earlier that morning Melanie had called the hotel where Jason and the rest of the cast would be staying, that being no secret, as there were only two halfway decent hotels in the city. Melanie had a friend there who confirmed that Lisa was not a guest. In fact, besides Stevens and Jason, the only others in town were the lesser supporting cast. That would make things much easier, although Melanie had a backup plan in the event that Lisa had made the trip.

The mayor's voice reverberated through the bathroom, the sound system actually piped in, so no one would miss a word. How the show was going to bring jobs to Marburg. Marburg welcoming back its own, Jason Ayers, a smattering of applause, blah, blah, blah.

Jason's name gave Melanie's heart a little flutter, not from any kind of love, but it was like a cue for showtime, the five minute warning. Though she'd scouted out the location, her act would require a

little bit of improv. She'd watched the beginning of the press conference from the edge of the park, and had memorized where the cast
was going to be, it was just like blocking out a scene. But she wasn't
the director, she couldn't tell Jason where to stand, she couldn't freeze
everyone else in place while she made her play. She'd have to rely on
her quick thinking.

It could backfire. But she didn't have much to lose. And burning a
bridge with Jason wouldn't be the end of the world. Shit, it might get
Stevens even more interested in her.

Satisfied with her hair, Melanie set the black beret on her head,
tilting it to match the photo of Lisa. Once she got the feel, able to put
it on without a mirror, she stashed it in the pocket of the leather
jacket, on the opposite side from where she had the red beret. Now
there was nothing to do but wait.

When Melanie heard the press start to ask questions, she slipped
out the bathroom and headed for the back of the stage.

THE STAGE WAS NOTHING MORE than a large bandstand used for
summer concerts in the park. Behind it, a large wooded park flowed
with hiking trails. Facing the trees behind the bandstand was a concession booth, now closed and locked, and the lattice structure holding up the stage. No one was there, the crowd around front, focused
on the press conference.

Melanie kept out of sight, not furtive, just lounging against the
side of the concession stand. She couldn't see who was on the stage,
but she could see half the audience. No Taz. She walked to the other
side of the booth, and there he was, right in front with the other photographers.

Melanie had been to a few press conferences like these; after the
mayor's announcement, there would be a Q&A with each cast member. Then the cast shoots, supposedly candid but carefully orches-
trated. Stevens was there only because no one would have showed up
if he hadn't put in an appearance. Jason was the newsworthy local.
The audience wouldn't be expecting Lisa if they hadn't already seen
her on the stage.

Melanie did her little thing, getting in the role, *feeling* it. Not pretending she was Lisa, but stepping into the role Lisa would have on the show, but in the way it *should* be played. A hot, sexy woman, independent, with a withering look that could make even a strong man turn away first. A woman who could take care of herself, who wouldn't accept any bullshit, a woman who would do whatever was necessary to get what she needed.

A woman like Melanie.

To that she added her own history with Jason, the first time she had snared him, how she had turned him on. She wouldn't have to fake it, just pull it up out of her memory file; with Jason it hadn't all been acting.

The last of the questions died down, the photographers scurrying into new positions. They knew the drill. Another announcement of the shoot, more to give the makeup people a last chance for touchups. A group cast photo first, then Stevens. While he was being shot, all the rest of the cast, including Jason, would wait at the edge of the stage, or even off of it, so that all eyes and cameras would be on Stevens, the biggest name and the biggest ego.

A bustle from the mass of photographers, Stevens was up. Melanie slipped around the back of the booth, hoping no one would be using this opportunity to sneak a smoke. Someone did come around, Melanie turning away, but it was just some guy looking for the bathroom.

Melanie peeked around the corner. The cast clustered at the bottom of the steps, waiting to be called up for their shots. Jason was there, puffing himself up. At the side of the stage he would be in direct view of the photographers.

Melanie heard someone yell, "Mr. Stevens, just one more!"

Showtime.

In one motion Melanie set the black beret on her head, cocking it just right, striding through the group, in the role, changing her walk, her posture, changing everything. Two people now between her and Jason, the makeup gal and a little guy with a too tight leather jacket. Jason hadn't seen her yet . . .

Melanie walked right through the makeup woman and the guy in leather, the woman taking a step back, Melanie shoving the guy away, hard, he fell on his ass, the commotion causing Jason to look and the photographers to redirect their attention.

Jason's eyes widening in confusion, something was wrong, the black beret making him pause, and that gave Melanie all the time she needed. She threw her right arm around Jason and pulled him in, and with her left hand, the one closest to the photographers, she grabbed Jason's wrist. Her lips were on Jason's before he could react, her tongue in his mouth, Jason's body reacting before his mind did, maybe some remembered chemistry of his time with Melanie.

Melanie got in a pretty good kiss before Jason came to his senses, his eyes shooting open, recognizing her, trying to pull away, but Melanie, her adrenaline flowing, held on to his wrist. Taz better be catching this part.

Melanie lifted her leg along Jason's, like she was in bliss, her hidden hand slipping to Jason's crotch, giving him a playful squeeze. Melanie pulled away before Jason had a chance to. Like everything else, it was *her* decision, it was what the beret girl from the show would have done. Melanie looked right at the photographers, who were all busily snapping away. She didn't smile, that wasn't in the role.

Melanie pulled the black beret from her head and dismissively tossed it aside. She put her hand on Jason's chest and pushed him away, the femme fatale rejecting her suitor, and pulled on the red beret, tilting it just right.

A half pose, just a few beats, just enough so everyone would think it was a surprise part of the press conference.

Then she disappeared around the back of the stage, heading for the wooded area, hearing the shouts of the photographers, and more important, the clicking of their cameras.

CHAPTER 6

LENNY GOT TO THE PHOTO SHOOT in the park early, scouting the place out. A crew was setting the stage with a podium, basic folding chairs, and a banner proclaiming Marburg as the 'Hollywood of the East.' A few old ladies in the audience, this likely the highlight of their week.

Lenny checked the angles. The best shots would be getting the arrivals, although there would be competition. Sure enough, another photographer arrived, a weasely little guy Lenny had seen around who always dressed in brown—brown pants, brown shirts, brown jacket. Where the hell did you even buy a brown shirt, a UPS store? The guy gave Lenny a nod. Lenny nodded back, brown-dressed weasel or not, the guy was kin in some way.

Lenny drifted over to the front of the stage, where a crew member, a nerd who was trying to grow a chinstrap beard and failing miserably, was roping off the photographer stall in front of the audience. Lenny flashed the guy his credentials, a $49 annual purchase from the Independent Guild of Photographers. It usually worked, but the skinny beard must have been honing up, looking for a way to use what little power he had, and he just shook his head. Lenny didn't even try to talk his way past, he wasn't sure he wanted to sit there anyway. The photographers in the stall would have the same angle for every shot.

"How about a schedule then?" said Lenny, and the guy paused, maybe trying to figure out why he should say no, but he had about a thousand of them, and reluctantly handed one to Lenny. Lenny sat in one of the uncomfortable audience chairs in the back row and read it over, lighting a cigarillo.

Pretty standard, the mayor, the full cast shoot, Stevens, then the Ayers guy Lenny had seen Melanie with at the club. Melanie . . . had to keep that fire lit, get with her tonight.

Stevens would duck out after his shoot, Lenny was sure of it. No way the star would wait around for the lesser cast to be photographed. That's when Lenny would make his move, he'd find a spot where Stevens would be picked up, be ready.

It was a nice day, sunny, a perfectly clear sky, all a rarity in Marburg. Another thing Lenny missed from California, good weather. It was always so frigging humid here, barely lunch time and he was already sweating. People were wandering into the park, a few cops lazily lounging along the walkways. A couple of vendors selling cold drinks, some kids playing frisbee. The stage where the proceedings would take place was a tiny bandstand, a make-shift structure of metal and wood that Lenny thought looked rather amateurish. There was no sign of any celebrities yet, not even lower tier wannabes.

Two large box trucks sat to the right of the stage, blocking Lenny's view of the road along the park. Lenny immediately recognized it as the perfect spot where celebrities could enter and leave the area somewhat inconspicuously. That's where he would position himself, just before Stevens finished on stage.

Now that he had a plan, Lenny focused on the people in the park. Two young ladies who didn't look like the usual actress-wannabes had walked in from the street, babbling in animated conversation. *Two ladies, two chances.* Probably just a couple of college students. Lenny got off a few quick shots of them, then swung the camera around to his side, his photographer shtick was not likely to work on them.

Neither one looked his way, so Lenny called out, "Are you here for the big announcement?"

This had the desired effect, the girls glancing briefly at Lenny and then to the stage. Lenny thought they were both pretty good looking, probably early twenties. The one with the better face had blue eyes, her hair in a braid, draped along her shoulder from under a Red Sox cap. She was a little dumpy though, her loose sweatshirt probably masking the fact that she was flat. The other one had a much better body, and she was showing it off in a tight shirt and jeans. But her face was just the wrong side of average, her dark brown eyes shrunken. Always my luck, thought Lenny, half of what I want.

"What announcement?" asked the blonde.

Lenny tried to act nonchalant, but his heart was thumping. Getting them talking was always the hardest. Which one should he go for? He gestured toward the staging. "Some scenes from a new TV show are going to be shot here in town. I know for a fact they are going to announce it today."

The girls shrugged in unison. The blonde said, "I didn't hear about it."

"Me either," said the hollow eyed one, not sounding very impressed with Lenny's implied inside information.

"You should hang, I could fill you in on some dirt. You might see yourself on the news if they pan the audience."

"Who watches the news?" brown hair asked.

The blonde was nodding. "I don't. Too negative."

"Right," Lenny said, pushing on. "Well, this is a good thing for the local economy. Marburg gets publicity. People get noticed. You get noticed, good things can happen. Fame and fortune." He was motor mouthing nonsense, it happened every time he got next to a halfway decent looking woman.

"Are you a reporter or something?"

Lenny grinned. "Kind of." Trying to sound mysterious.

The brunette took him in, dismissively, turning to go. "Whatever."

"Let me buy you girls a drink."

"I don't think so!" said the brunette, her voice a mocking singsong.

"C'mon, I don't bite. My name is Lenny."

The girls were already down the path, laughing to each other, the brunette wiggling her ass. Lenny bit his lip. They were laughing at him, he was certain of it.

He tried to be nice, and this is what he got from women.

Fucking bitches.

*   *   *

LENNY TOOK A FEW HALF HEARTED shots from the back row. The press conference had been a bore, Lenny's mind drifting toward the audience, trying to catch a glimpse of some good looking women. It was slim pickings.

Still pissed about the two college girls. Maybe the east coast women needed a more direct approach, they might have had their fill of wimpy guys. He had to try something new, come on hard, the alpha male.

A buzz snapped his attention back to the press conference, where some kind of commotion was taking place. A small crowd had gathered, blocking Lenny's view. He wasn't that interested, someone probably fell off the stage. A few cries, people in the front row now standing to get a better angle.

On the stage, the mayor and most of the others had turned to look, except for one guy who was rushing away from the commotion, down the stairs on the other side. Stevens. Lenny grinned, the whole thing was probably some kind of diversion so Stevens could make his getaway. Camera at the ready, Lenny ran after him.

Or tried to. Everyone was standing now, the folding chairs so close together that the rows were blocked like rush hour on 495. Lenny swore and pushed his way through, knocking over chairs and drawing a few shoves. Finally clear, Lenny rushed down the aisle, heading for the stage, only to be blocked by the same jerk in brown. The guy was already shaking his head at Lenny.

"Hey, someone over there is having a stroke!" yelled Lenny, pointing.

The crewman was having none of it, he just crossed his arms, barring the way. Lenny took a sharp right, crashing into a big guy with meaty biceps. Lenny bounced off him like he'd run into a NFL lineman, toppling over the front row of chairs, gamely holding on to his camera, taking the brunt of the fall on his elbow. He screeched in pain, untangled himself, and was up and running around the stage.

The two trucks were still there, and Lenny wove between them and a dumpster. He cleared the corner just as a limo sped off.

Lenny slumped against the dumpster, breathing hard, twisting his arm to examine the broken skin on his elbow. Fuck it all, always one step away from a break. He didn't even bother taking a shot of the departing limo. Car photos were, as he had explained to JT, completely useless.

LENNY TOOK THE LONG WAY HOME, needing time to clear his head. He had to turn his luck around, and fast. He only had a couple of bills to pay but he was making so little money that he was always behind. He'd been drooling over a new long lens that could be used in low light. Lenses like that cost a fortune.

There had to be a way to get on track.

His cell phone chirped, a Google alarm he had set to go off any time there was news about Marburg. He flipped his eyes back and forth between the road and the screen, keying it to start a video clip from the local news channel. The headline read: *Shock and Awe at Shock And Awe Press Conference, Cast Change In The Works?* Of course it was about the conference. He'd left before it was over and missed out. Again.

Lenny listened to a breathless reporter standing in front of the now empty bandstand:

"Hollywood is invading Marburg. At a photo shoot today in Marburg Park, the mayor announced that Marburg would be the background shooting locale for the new drama, Shock And Awe. Cast members Michael Stevens, Sean Gentry, and Marburg's own Jason Ayers were on hand. But the big buzz took place off the podium, completely upstaging the event, when Jason Ayers was caught in a lip lock with a woman in a black beret. The woman, who Channel 12 has identified as Melanie Doyle Upton, then replaced her black beret with a red one before disappearing. Upton also currently lives in Marburg and has worked with Ayers before. This has led to speculation that the changing of the berets was a tease that Upton might be replacing Lisa Vista, a no-show today. Rumor has it that Vista's contract is still not finalized and she's asking for more than the studio is willing to pay."

A blaring horn forced Lenny's eyes back to the road. He'd just run a red light. He pulled into a gas station parking lot, dazed, staring at the frozen image of Melanie, the red beret cocked on her head, smiling at the camera, at Lenny, mocking him.

Melanie.

The fucking bitch had stolen his idea!

Lenny pounded on the steering wheel and let out an anguished cry.

No way she was going to get away with this. He continued to slam his hand into the steering wheel, not feeling the pain, his eyes locked on Melanie.

THE CADDY WOVE AIMLESSLY, Lenny still raging, slow, then fast, tail-gating, swearing at the cars, at his bad luck, at Melanie. Not only did she steal his idea, she'd done it all wrong, she'd *ruined* it. She wasn't going to get anything out of Jason, he wasn't a big enough name, a few seconds of local publicity with him wasn't going to do her any good at all. The big stations and websites wouldn't bother to carry a kiss of two small time actors, even one with Melanie's good looks.

Jason looked like such a wuss, what the fuck was Melanie doing with him?

It had *all* been Lenny's idea. She'd stolen it, but she'd fucked it up big time. It was like putting your name on someone else's photo, pure plagiarism.

Photos. Lenny had seen a video, had Melanie found another pho-tographer to take some stills?

Lenny jerked the big car to the side of the road, spinning through his phone web browser before he'd completely stopped. Nothing would be on Google yet, so he surfed to the largest local celebrity site, and there it was. Three shots of Melanie in the bright red beret, her hand on her hip, capturing the essence of both Laura Croft of *Tomb Raider* and Uma Thurman in *Kill Bill*, or maybe Jessica Alba from *Dark Angel*, tougher actually, like she'd wipe up the floor with all of them.

Posing. Not like Melanie had been caught unawares, but playing for the cameras, and probably one in particular. The images were credited to a Tim Tazik, whoever the fuck that was.

So the photo had been planned all along, just as Lenny had sug-gested. But instead of having Lenny take the shots, Melanie had set it up with some other photographer. Probably some guy she'd end up sleeping with. Exactly what Lenny had planned to do with Melanie in exchange for the photos.

Fuck fuck fuck.

Lenny dropped his head on the steering wheel. He just couldn't get a break. No, that wasn't it, people kept fucking him over, making fun of him, taking advantage of him. His mother, making him run her errands when he had better things to do. Melanie, stealing his idea, probably laughing at him right now.

He banged his head against the steering wheel, waiting for the pain, wanting the pain. But it didn't come. Just as when he had slammed his hand against it, he didn't hurt, all the hurt was in his head, his mind so beaten up by all the bad luck and assholes that his body was somehow inured.

To prove it, Lenny slammed his fist against the door. Nothing.

He bet that Tim fucking Tazik would feel it if Lenny hit him that hard. Or Melanie.

The thought brightened him, and, proud of his calm, Lenny put the car in gear and headed off to find someone to hit.

LENNY WANTED TO SEE Melanie's reaction when he told her he was going to beat the shit out of Tazik. That would show her she couldn't fuck with him.

He parked the Caddy two feet from the curb in The Café's valet zone, no one there, the street mid afternoon empty. Lenny pushed through the restaurant door, a few eyes turning his way. No Melanie.

He caught Leah, the waitress from his first visit, rolling her eyes before picking up a menu and approaching him.

"Table for one?" she asked, her voice suggesting Lenny would never have a lunch partner, especially a woman.

Lenny didn't have time for her. "I'm looking for my friend Melanie."

"I didn't know she was your friend."

"I'm sure she doesn't tell you everything. Is she here or not?"

Leah pursed her lip, Lenny fighting the urge to slap the look off her face with his newly discovered pain free hand.

"She called in sick."

"Was that so fucking hard?" Lenny didn't wait for a reply and stalked out. Of course Melanie wouldn't come to work, she'd be playing hard to get, a little mystery to let her story build. The headlines running through Lenny's mind: *Who is Melanie Upton? Was her appearance a publicity stunt by the studio?* Except the only places the stories would run would be in some local rag, because Melanie had blown it.

Maybe he could still salvage this, at least get Melanie to put out; he'd given her the idea after all. She probably did it all the time, a little personal thanks would be no big deal for her.

He hadn't found out where Melanie lived, he'd have to work on that. In the meantime, where would she go if she was trying to feed the story about her joining the cast of *Shock and Awe?* Obviously that whole idea was bullshit, Melanie wouldn't be working at the restaurant if she had a series lined up.

The hotels. She'd go to where the cast was staying, just to be seen there.

Maybe Tim fucking Tazik would be there too. Lenny would get two for one.

LENNY GOT HIS FIRST PIECE OF LUCK in ages in the parking lot of the Hilton. A small blue Toyota was parked forlornly between two limos, Lenny remembering the car from the parking lot of The Café. It had to be Melanie's.

Inside the hotel, sure enough, there was Melanie, sitting at the almost empty bar, chatting up the bartender, strategically positioned so that anyone walking through the atrium would notice her. She was all in black, leather jacket, tight leggings, calf hugging boots.

Lenny crossed the atrium, the sound of an indoor waterfall meshing with the pounding in his ears. Lenny feeling it, a surge of strength, only the dreary low key muzak threatening to spoil the mood, in his head a powerful scream of heavy metal.

With each step he grew in power. He couldn't even feel his feet hit the floor, his strength building, this was what he was meant to be,

Melanie would recognize it immediately. He'd never felt so confident in his life.

Until Melanie turned to him. Lenny tripped on nothing, the power of Melanie's sexiness smashing into him, her tight physique, her perfect legs. Lenny had to forcibly lift his gaze away from her amazing body into her eyes. Instead of awe, or joy, or even cowering in fright, she scowled. A thunderbolt swatting at a fly in just her look.

Lenny's knees shook and he had to grasp for a bar stool to keep from falling.

Melanie's eyes narrowed, her lips barely moving. "What the fuck do you want?"

"You, you—stole my idea!" Lenny sputtered.

Melanie turned away from him, in that one motion dismissing him utterly. She casually picked up her drink. "Tough shit."

"That's not fair. It was my idea. *Mine*. You *owe* me." Lenny hearing his own voice, more a whine than the cool toughness he was trying to project.

The bartender, a red-haired kid who barely looked old enough to drink, turned on Lenny. "Melanie, this guy giving you trouble?"

Melanie's eyes glinted. "If I said yes, would you throw him out?"

The redhead puffed up his narrow shoulders. "Sure."

"Try it, fuck head," said Lenny.

Melanie looked back and forth the between the two men, a slight smile playing on her lips. After a beat she said, "Don't bother, he's harmless."

Lenny's hands wrapped around a dish of peanuts on the bar. "I'll show you harmless."

"Hey, calm down, man," said the bartender.

"You owe me," Lenny repeated.

"Tell you what," said Melanie, lazily. "I'll let you pick up my tab. Again. That's probably all you're good for, anyway. Glen, give me another one of these. Make it top shelf this time."

The bartender laughed, the sound setting off a latent fuse in Lenny. He smashed his hand down on the bar, forgetting he was still holding the glass dish, the peanuts flying everywhere, the dish breaking into pieces, toothpicks scattering like pickup sticks.

Melanie turned her eyes on him, blazing now, fury personified.

Lenny wilted under her scornful gaze, not even having the ability to open his mouth, much less speak. What could one possibly say to a storm about to smother him?

With no other option, he ran from the room, humiliated, feeling the eyes on him, the hotel guests, the doorman, the asshole bartender, and most of all, Melanie.

His hand hurt like hell.

CHAPTER 7

MELANIE, lying on the floor in her celebratory hot pink underwear, legs up on the couch, her tablet balanced on her bent knees, pulled up the article on the TMZ site again to see if they had made any updates. None yet, but she still felt good about the coverage of the press conference. Her plan had worked perfectly, hence the special occasion underwear. The media world, or at least the part of it that covered cable channel produced TV series, was abuzz with the reputed casting change for *Shock and Awe*. TMZ had failed to get a quote from Scott James, the series producer, but TMZ made it sound like a no comment, implying that something *was* in fact going on, that he was dodging the press.

It would be wild if the show *did* make the casting change. Stranger things had happened. Melanie glanced at her phone on the coffee table, willing it to ring.

It did, and she jumped, pouncing on the phone. No way the show would be calling, not yet, but maybe the press. Melanie was ready for this, she'd been practicing, it was just another role. Play coy, drop a few hints, she didn't need to lie about anything, just be vague, they'd fill in the holes, making it juicy. *Scott James and Melanie Upton refuse to comment on Shock and Awe cast change.* Just getting mentioned in a headline with Scott James would be a win for her.

An LA phone exchange, could it be?

She composed herself before answering. "Melanie Upton." Like she was expecting a business call.

"What the fuck were you thinking?"

The screaming voice, familiar, but hard to place, a raucous buzz rattling Melanie's eardrums. "Who is this?"

"You sure as shit know who it is." Still shrill and not much quieter.

"Jason." Melanie was expecting this call too, but not so soon. "What's this number?" She propped her legs back up on the sofa, she could handle Jason.

"Never mind. I'm the one asking the questions. What was that stunt you pulled at the press conference?"

"I'm reading the coverage now, it went well, don't you think?"

"What the hell are you talking about?"

Melanie sighed theatrically. "Jason, Jason. You got the role, but you still haven't learned the business. It's all about publicity."

"Publicity? Is that what this was about? Wait, did someone put you up to this?"

Melanie hadn't thought Jason was that dumb, but she went with it. "Maybe."

A long silence, Jason probably thinking it over. "You're full of shit."

"You got to admit, I'd be a better choice than Lisa what's her name."

"Lisa Vista. Shit, Mel, have you thought about what this will do to her? People are talking about her getting replaced. She's already called, asking me what's going on."

"Why did she call *you*? Are you sleeping with her already?"

"She's probably calling everybody. And I'm not sleeping with her, not that it's any of your business."

Mel's voice hardened. "I don't give a shit about Lisa Vista and neither do you. When did you start to care about other people? Did you even put in a word with Scott James to get me a reading for that role? It was okay to fuck me and dump me, but now you're worried about how *Lisa* feels?"

"Mel, this isn't right."

"Bullshit Jason, you'd do the same thing." *If you'd been smart enough to think it up.*

"No, I wouldn't. So no one put you up to this, right? That means they aren't considering a cast change and giving Lisa's role to you or anyone else. You did it just for your own publicity."

Melanie rolled her eyes, not believing she thought this guy could be her ticket. Maybe she should have hitched herself to the Michael Stevens bandwagon, as crowded as that probably was right now. "Jason, honey, I did it for you too."

"What?"

"Think of all the publicity this brings the show. Last week it was just one in a long list of new series. Now everyone will be talking about *Shock and Awe*. You just watch, the producers will milk this, pump up the drama for the first show, people tuning in to see who is in the cast. They'll probably call me after all."

"Mel, I won't be part of it. You can't pull me into this."

"That was *you* kissing me on the stage. The photo is all over the place, there's even video. You are *already* in this."

"No I'm not."

"You think anyone is going to believe that? With our history?"

"Mel, you think TMZ is following your love life, or even mine? No one outside of Marburg knows about that."

"They will if I tell them. Or," Melanie toyed with her hair, just as she'd be doing if Jason were there, breaking his focus, she'd have him for sure with this next line, so natural it wasn't even like playing a role, "I could post a few selfies we took."

"I've got selfies with a lot of women."

Melanie smiled, a little catch in Jason's voice, defensive. She buried the hook. "With you naked? In my bed?" She didn't have any such evidence, but Jason would never know, he always fell asleep right after sex.

A pause. "You don't have pictures like that."

Melanie didn't argue, Jason knew she might. And damn, she should have thought of it, not only with Jason, it would be in her arsenal with every guy from now on. Whenever she needed some extra punch, maybe feed them to that weirdo Lenny. Wouldn't that be a kick, tell him to run with it.

She let Jason worry a bit longer, then shifted her tone. "Maybe we should talk about this in person." Running her fingers up and down her legs, letting her near nakedness drift into her voice, hinting at more than talk. If she could get Jason alone she'd be able to knock some sense into him, even if she had to put out. All she needed was for Jason to tell the press he didn't know anything, which was the truth. If she worked him right she might even get him to be non committal, like he wasn't admitting what he knew.

"How about now?"

Melanie smiled, she had him. "Sure. Where are you? I'll just throw something on. Unless you want to see me the way I'm dressed now. Or not dressed now."

"I'm right outside your apartment."

"What?" Melanie scrambled up, peering out through the blinds. A few cars driving by, a bum across the street near the recycling dumpster, the usual. "At my apartment?" Buying time.

"The new place you told me about, Lakeview. Although I don't see a lake. Which unit was it again?"

Christ, he was at Gigi's apartment complex. Good thing Gigi was on a business trip. Did Gigi have her name on the mailbox? Melanie leaned against the wall, thinking fast. "I'm not at the apartment right now."

"So what was all that about me seeing what you're wearing?"

Melanie recognized that gloating tone, Jason thought he had her cornered. "I was just teasing. I'm at a friend's place, I'm trying to avoid the press."

"I thought you said you wanted the publicity?"

"I do, but I have to play this right. Listen, Jason, we can work this so we both get a win out of it."

"There's nothing to work out."

"Then why did you call? Why are you at my apartment?"

"To try to talk some sense into you."

"Or you wanted a booty call for old time's sake? Or maybe you want to start up again, since we might be working together."

"I don't need anything from you. I can get all the ass I want, I always could, and now with the show women will be begging me. Shit, I can do better than you just by taking the ones Stevens doesn't want."

Melanie tucked the phone under her chin and went into the kitchen to get a beer. If Jason thought his bluster would get her down, he really didn't know her. But she played the part. "No need to be mean. We did have some good times. We can keep doing that. I know what you like."

"I won't say this again. Leave me alone, and stay the hell away from the show. If you don't drop this right now, I'm going to talk to Scott."

Like he was on a first name basis with Scott James already. "And tell him what, exactly?"

"The truth. That you're a lying, conniving bitch, and he shouldn't touch you with a ten foot pole."

That was harsh, what the hell had she ever done to Jason? Show a guy a good time and this was the thanks she got? Like he didn't get anything out of their relationship, like he wouldn't have tried to glom onto her coattails if she had landed a big role? "I'm helping you out here. I could just as easily have gone up and kissed Michael Stevens at that press conference, he would have rolled with it."

"Stevens spits out women like you every day. You think you can con him, con Scott James? You're nothing but a small town hustler."

Melanie, hardening. "And so were you, just a few months ago. I'm just doing what I need to do, what everyone does."

"It's all about you, Melanie, I've always known that. You think I bailed on you just because of the show? I knew you'd try to use me, and I was right. Using your body to get a screen test? I get that, okay. But you—you'd run over your own grandmother for a casting call. You're not only selfish, you've got a mean streak."

God, he was cliché. "Jason, just let it go. Anything you say to anyone, Scott James, the press, will just dig you in deeper. Just play dumb, you're good at that. You won't have to act at all."

"Fuck you, Melanie. And I'm warning you, stay away. I'm going to talk to Scott when I get back to LA and tell him all about you. He'll make sure you never get a decent role anywhere."

The line went dead. Melanie stared at the phone. She knew Jason would have to be managed, but she hadn't expected this. That was the most emotion she'd ever seen out of him, even when acting. She needed to get a handle on Jason, or he could screw things up big time.

Jason had spoiled her good vibe. She pulled on a pair of tights, no longer in the mood for pink, wanting to cover up, a little defense in order.

She finished the beer, toyed with the bottle, and was about to throw it in the trash. Remembered the recycle bin on the sidewalk when she had peeked outside. She rinsed the bottle out and set it on the counter. She'd recycle it, just as she would Jason.

Who the fuck was Jason Ayers to call her selfish? There was nothing selfish about recycling.

CHAPTER 8

LENNY POKED AT THE KEYBOARD with his left index finger, his right hand useless, wrapped in gauze and covered with a frozen bag of peas. Sweat beaded on his forehead, courtesy of the lack of air conditioning in his attic apartment. But he didn't want to sit downstairs and deal with the questions his mother would no doubt have about his injured hand.

Lenny playing detective, trying to discover Melanie's home address, which was turning out to be harder than he expected. Around Hollywood, you could buy celebrity address lists for fifty bucks. He'd yet to find such a list on the east coast, and Melanie was no celebrity, shit, she'd *want* to be found by agents, producers, anybody. She should be wearing a neon sign with her contact information. But so far, nothing.

All afternoon Lenny's mind replayed the scene from the Hilton. Each time he rewrote the memory, changing his style, his attitude, his approach, what he said to Melanie, what she said. In some of his edits he jumps over the bar, pounding the snarky bartender, impressing Melanie. In others she just agrees that she owed him, taking him by the hand, telling him she'd get them a room.

If he could only get her in bed. Melanie wouldn't have to do her posturing in front of an audience, she could drop her act, just be herself. Underneath all that bluster Lenny was certain she wanted to be tamed.

Sure, she'd be feisty, that was the whole vibe she gave off. She probably liked it a little rough, he could go for that.

And she owed him big time. He'd find a way to collect, either on the photo or from her. Preferably both.

He pulled up Melanie's entry on the IMDB database again. Nothing about a role on *Shock and Awe*, although even if it were true, which Lenny doubted, it wouldn't be listed yet. No direct contact information, but a number for an agent. Lenny smiled when he read the listing, a Hollywood telephone exchange, a number he recognized as a front for a service that struggling actresses used to look professional. He clumsily thumbed in the number.

"Hello. You have reached Starlight Representatives." A recorded greeting. "All of our representatives are helping other clients at this time . . ." A list of options, except the one any caller would want, the chance to talk to a real person. A click, followed by music that must have been lifted from a porn movie, or maybe *was* a porn soundtrack, a private Starlight Representatives joke on any caller who didn't have a direct number to a human being.

Lenny pictured some aspiring actress at the switchboard, leaning back in her chair, doing her nails, chatting with her BFF on another line. "Answer the phone, bitch," he mumbled.

After an eternity of fifteen minutes a ringing cut into the music. "Thank you for calling Starlight Representatives. This is Max, how can I help you?"

A guy. Just his luck, Lenny hated talking to guys, he couldn't use his smooth spiel on them. He pushed on, he'd bowl Max over. "This is Lenny Gruse"—saying it like the guy should obviously recognize his name—"and I have a photo shoot with Melanie Upton I need to reschedule. My assistant took my cell to get a new battery. I need Melanie's number."

"I'm very sorry, sir, but it's against company policy to give out our clients' phone numbers."

"Dude, I know it's against company policy, I've dealt with companies like yours for years. I'm doing a favor for your client even taking this shoot."

"Sir, there is nothing I can do for you." Like he was reading a script.

"Look, she knows me. Her number is on my cell phone. It wouldn't be there if I wasn't in the business, right? I need to reach her." Lenny tried to keep a firm grip on the tone and volume of his voice.

There was a long moment of silence, Lenny thought the guy hung up on him.

"Hello," Lenny said.

"Mr. Grouse—."

"It's Gruse!"

"Well, Mr. Gruse, I've explained, there is nothing I can do for you. I cannot give out any personal information on any client, for any reason. If I do, I get canned. You'll have to find another way to solve your problem."

This time, the guy hung up.

"Fuck!" Lenny shouted. He fumbled for the redial button, getting the recording again.

Why did everything have to be so fucking hard for him?

LENNY DIDN'T START THE CAR until Melanie was well down the street. He'd been waiting for an hour, his hand throbbing. In his rush to get here he'd forgotten to bring anything to eat or drink, and he had to piss.

Earlier he'd walked by the restaurant three times trying to spot Melanie through the window, finally catching a glimpse of her from behind. But he'd know that backside anywhere.

He rolled along slowly, feeling a little better now that he had Melanie in his sights. Lenny had a lot of experience stalking, it's how he got most of his celebrity photos. He could even shoot one handed out the window, a skill he was particularly proud of. He snapped a few shots of Melanie as she walked.

Melanie popped into a Starbucks, Lenny letting the Caddy idle at the curb. The Starbucks made him think of coffee and cakes and a bathroom. Melanie was out sooner than he expected, sipping a grande, heading back toward the restaurant. If she was going back to work he'd have time to take a leak.

Melanie turned into the parking lot, looking fine, her ass swaying seductively. Maybe she knew he was watching? Women like

Melanie could turn that walk on and off like a switch.

Her blue Toyota pulled out into the street. Lenny let two cars go by before pulling out to follow.

LENNY WAS AT IT AGAIN the very next night, this time across the street from the Lakeview Apartments. This was the second night in a row he'd been here after following Melanie from the restaurant. Hers was a garden apartment with yellow daisies in a box under the front windows, filled with cheery suncatchers. Not what Lenny had thought would be Melanie's style, but women never ceased to amaze him.

The neighborhood was unfamiliar to Lenny, so during the day he had driven around, getting his bearings. The apartment building looked new, a lot of young professionals, a bustle of activity in the morning, the place particularly deserted during the day, no kids around anywhere. The building, odd shaped, a curved U ending in a hard L, like a question mark, an architect who wasn't sure about his own horseshoe fetish. The curve opened into a pool, not much privacy, but the rear of the L side faced a quiet alley lined with bushes and trees. After Melanie had left for work Lenny had taken a stroll, like he lived there, out for a walk. The garden apartments had back doors that opened onto the alley. Each unit with a small fenced in garden, the fence a joke, more for show. Melanie's was the corner unit, easy to find even from the back.

He'd planned better today, plenty of snacks, a few Monsters, even a piss bottle. But at midnight he was getting antsy, Melanie not coming home right after her shift, maybe at the club. The street was quiet; not a late neighborhood, lights off in most of the front windows, everyone in bed. Melanie in bed, now there was a thought to keep him occupied.

At half past, Lenny couldn't take it any longer, he got out of the car and headed toward the back alley. From his earlier scouting he knew the bedrooms faced this way. A few lights in the windows, squares of life behind the shades. Farther down the building, about five units away, one window was open, a casement that swung outward, drapes hanging over the sill.

*   *   *

MELANIE'S APARTMENT WAS TOTALLY DARK. Lenny hadn't seen her come home, she was probably off working on her publicity idea. *His* publicity idea. The one she'd stolen from him.

Lenny glanced around, saw no one, and slipped through the gate. Manicured boxwoods lined the back wall. He stood quietly in the small garden, breathing, making himself part of the apartment, his nostrils flaring to catch a hint of Melanie's essence.

Too floral, the garden full of flowers, a girly scent. Lenny having trouble getting a feel for Melanie, this was so unlike what he expected. Need to get a little closer . . .

Once amidst the boxwoods he was virtually invisible from the other apartments to the right or from the street to the left that led into the complex. Someone walking along the back alley might see him, but Lenny was sure he'd hear anyone approaching, it was that quiet.

A double window to the left of the door, no drapes, a small glow of what was probably a nightlight, more suncatchers. The kitchen, the raised windows over the sink. Beyond that, the living room. Two windows on the right side of the door, dark.

He stepped onto a stone path that led into the garden, reaching out. He stood there silently, his palm against the wall, feeling for vibrations, of movement, of Melanie. Warm. Lenny smiled in the dark, that was more like it.

He moved on to the bedroom window, took one more look at the street, and peered in through a small crack in the drapes.

The bedroom door was partially open, a dim light in the hall, maybe another nightlight. A bureau, overwhelmed by a huge flat screen television sitting on top, Lenny thinking that's where Melanie watched porn with her boyfriends. Across the room, the bed, with what looked to be a wrought iron headboard. Hard to see anything else.

Lenny couldn't take his eyes off the bed, especially the headboard. Melanie, hard as nails on the outside, probably all an act, he bet she had another side, he'd heard that tough women had a hidden desire to be dominated. Maybe she'd bought that headboard so she could be tied down, made to do a strong man's bidding.

He'd been fantasizing about what he'd do if he got her alone, what he'd say, how he could convince her he was the man she needed to be with. Take a more direct approach, just like he used when following her to find out where she lived. He was done talking. When he did get to her, he'd just push her against the wall and kiss her, take the initiative, like she had done with Jason Ayers at the press conference. She'd see the appeal in that, feel his power.

The headboard pulled at him, tantalizing, spurring his fantasy. If he got her in the bedroom, he could even skip the kissing, just throw her on the bed. Do it in the dark, or wear a mask, let her get worked up, she'd love it. Then he would reveal himself, and she'd be shocked, it would turn her around, she'd look at him in an entirely new light. A man of power, a man she needed, not only for her career, but for her heart.

He ran back to the car, not caring who might be watching. Time to make a plan. Time to act.

TWO DAYS LATER, Lenny was ready.

As he drove he fingered the shopping bag on the seat. He'd discovered that the local discount store was a goldmine for hiding his identity; a ski mask—on the shelves in the middle of summer!—dark glasses, a flashlight with a red lens, a small pocketknife. In the camping section he'd found a camera that took photos at night. He hoped he could find a way to set it up outside Melanie's bedroom window, or even get it inside.

Best of all was the flat plastic package, women's pantyhose. He'd been a little self conscious picking them out at the store, at the register mentioning to the bored cashier they were for his girlfriend. His fingers fondled into the package, the slick material sensuous. He'd seen guys in movies robbing banks with stockings over their heads. He was looking forward to trying that out, hoping he'd be able to see well enough to watch Melanie's reaction.

One cruise past the restaurant, that was all he'd risk. Lenny slipped on the new sunglasses and his baseball cap. The street was busy with late day traffic, so he had to concentrate on his driving and couldn't get a good look in the window of The Café.

Too soon to go back to Melanie's apartment even if she wasn't working. Lenny headed the other way, across the literal and proverbial railroad tracks, looking for a place to hang. The neighborhood changed character quickly, the streets narrower, shabby, mostly industrial buildings. A few more blocks, shifting again, old style houses, different colors and angles but all the same feel, kids in the streets, teenagers on stoops, laundry hanging over window ledges.

Bars, lots of bars, men on the corners, smoking, throwing dice. Mostly white, some Hispanics, separated by just a few steps of sidewalk but enough to demark a different world. Curses, yelling, even some singing.

Some eyes on the Caddy, dull interest, the car old enough it wasn't tempting.

A bar would be a good place to wait, but not these bars. Lenny didn't fit in here. He didn't fit in on Main Street either, but even less so here.

Back he drove, leaving town in the other direction, fewer but nicer bars, mostly Irish themed. He picked one out at random and pulled into the small lot.

Lenny's fingers slid over the stockings one last time, a caress of Melanie's legs, before hiding the bag under the seat.

On the way in he counted his money, thirty two bucks, twenty of which he had bummed from his mother for gas. The rest was what was left of his monthly hundred dollar allotment he got from his mother's disability check, a flow that would dry up if she couldn't find a local doctor who would continue to support her contention that she had carpel tunnel from a prior job as an Entertainment Promotion Specialist, a gloried title for pushing time share scams by phone. Lenny didn't want to think of how she had convinced the doctor she was still injured four years after she had quit the job.

A sign said "Tables for dinner patrons only," and though Lenny was hungry he couldn't splurge on a sit down meal, even in a place like this. The place was surprisingly busy, the after work crowd. He forced himself into a spot at the far end of the bar, drawing curious looks from the regulars.

A freckled barmaid, more girl than woman, finally ambled over, chatting with some guy she passed, barely looking at Lenny as he ordered a Bud on tap. She wasn't his type, too skinny, pasty skin, but she could have at least smiled. If she didn't do better on the next round he'd stiff her on the tip.

Lots of laugher around the room, people without a care. The tables filled with couples, married, on dates. Lenny a wistful voyeur; why couldn't he be that lucky, eating a nice meal with a girlfriend like Melanie, or even his wife Melanie. He'd recount his day to her, a big photo scoop, she'd listen attentively, nodding knowingly, still so thankful that Lenny had given her her first break.

Instead, here he sat, nursing a too foamy draft, his life going nowhere, Melanie's on the upswing, even without him. What did a guy have to do to get a little credit, get his due?

If Melanie could use him, it was only fair if he got to use her a little. She owed him. It would be reasonable for him to latch on as her stock rose. She'd see that—she'd *offer* it—as soon as she got to know him better. They would be a team.

Melanie had formed the wrong opinion of him, she'd have to be shocked, shaken up, have a new world of Lenny opened up to her. What would shake a woman up? Fear, passion. That's why he had bought the ski mast and nylons, he'd scare her a little, then play to her needs for a strong man.

All well and good, but in the light of day, or even in the light of fake Tiffany lamps, the thought of getting into Melanie's apartment with his disguise didn't sound so plausible. The front of the apartment was too well lit, even at night, and the front room had a window, she'd see him standing on the stoop. Who'd let in a guy with a mask?

The back door had more possibilities. He could knock, slip on the mask at the last minute, much less chance of being seen. But what if Melanie never opened that door for anyone? Push his way in, maybe? Break a window?

Once he got in, he just needed to get Melanie in the bedroom. He'd have to work out the details of how to do that, or improvise, he was fast on his feet. It was all about the bedroom, get her there, let her see what a man he could be. Then unmask himself. Real life shock and awe.

Focus on the end result, not what could go wrong. Eye on the prize.

Lenny stared at the remnants of his fourth beer. One more for the road, a little liquid courage. The barmaid finally looked at him, and he pointed to his stein for another, gulping it down so he wouldn't get cheated. The barmaid, to her credit, brought him a fresh glass, which would have been enough to make him reconsider leaving a tip, but she put it down without a word. *Bitch.* She's *supposed* to be nice, and she can't even say hi. Fucking women.

The barmaid leaned over the bar, listening as some mop haired guy in a hideous checked shirt told her some story. *What's he got that I don't?* The barmaid laughed, her eyes animated. Lenny dismissed the barmaid, he didn't need her. *I'll have Melanie to listen to me.*

Yet he couldn't take his eyes off the barmaid, standing on her tip toes, staring in the guy's eyes like he was the greatest, and she was preparing herself for a kiss. The guy had probably never kissed a girl. Lenny had a few pimples, but the barmaid's idol was a walking commercial for acne medication. Why wasn't the girl looking at Lenny with expectation and hope in her green Irish eyes? Just like Melanie, she'd barely registered him, like he was wasn't even there.

Fuck that.

Lenny stood up quickly, his head spinning, too many beers on an empty stomach. He reached for the stool, grimacing, his bandaged hand still sore.

He plopped onto an empty stool next to the pimply guy, the barmaid not giving him a glance. The guy was still going on with his story, some bullshit about a monster truck show in New Hampshire, no way she could be interested in that for real.

Stifling a burp, Lenny said, "Hey," getting the girl's attention.

"Welcome to O'Malley's. I'll be right with you." Turning back to Pimples.

Lenny couldn't believe it. The bitch had looked right at him and forgot that he had been drinking there for over an hour just a few feet away. Really? Was he fucking invisible? "I'm from LA, we don't have truck shows, we do demolition derbies with Porsches and Mercedes."

The barmaid glanced at Lenny. "Uh, right."

"No, really," said Lenny, figuring she'd never been west of New York. "You'd love it if you like monster trucks. People trick their cars out just to bash them up."

"Sounds like a waste to me," said the girl.

Shit, she was naïve too. "Most people in LA got so much money they don't care."

"Right. Whatever." The barmaid turned back to the other guy. "Go on, Timmy. You were saying."

"Have you ever been to California?" asked Lenny.

This time she ignored him totally. Timmy's shoulders shifted toward Lenny, but Lenny didn't bother to look over, his eyes still on the girl.

"I'm going to enter as soon as I get my hemi rebuilt," said Timmy.

"Wow, that's great."

"Hey," interrupted Lenny, not believing his ears, the chick was getting a thrill about a *truck*. "How about a drink?"

She reluctantly turned her eyes away from Timmy. "What would you like?"

"The same."

The girl frowned, a look that might have been cute if Lenny wasn't so pissed. "Oh, a Bud light, right?"

"No light, just Bud. Do I look like I drink light beers?"

"Maybe you should," the pimple faced guy said, and the barmaid didn't try hard to hide a smile.

Lenny turned to him. "Fuck you say?"

Timmy set down his beer. "I said, maybe you should. What are you, twenty one, you already got a beer gut?"

Lenny sputtered, no way he looked twenty one. Automatically he sucked in his stomach. "I still can't figure out what you are saying. Maybe if you didn't talk like some redneck in training, people would understand you."

"Who you calling a redneck?"

"I said a redneck in training. You haven't even graduated yet." Lenny grinned at his own joke, Timmy too stupid to know he was being made fun of. Time to go in for the kill. "When you do make full redneck status, you can drive your truck south, like into the Gulf of

Mexico. If you can find it." Satisfied he'd put Timmy in his place, Lenny turned his attention back to the bargirl.

"How about I get you that drink?" she said.

"So you *do* remember me," said Lenny, brightening. Just like he suspected, show a woman who was top dog, a real man, and they sit up and take notice. Shock and awe. He placed his hand over hers on the bar. "I could take you for a ride, my Cadillac is a lot more comfortable than a pickup."

"Yuck. Let me go."

Lenny tightened his fingers around her thin wrist, not letting her pull away. Her eyes widened as she recognized his strength. *Shock.* Now for the awe. He held up his bandaged hand. "I got this beating up a guy at a bar. You should see the other guy's face."

The girl shied away, straining, Lenny electrified by her struggle. He grinned, letting go, his gift to her.

"Don't you touch her again," said Timmy.

"What the fuck you gonna do? Beep your monster truck horn at me?" Lenny was enjoying this, people clearing a way around them, feeling his power.

"No, this," said Timmy.

From out of nowhere came a fist, catching Lenny on the side of his head, knocking him away from the bar, only to be met by another punch from the other direction, so strong it stood him up, the impossibility of it dimly registering through Lenny's concussed brain, no way scrawny Timmy could punch that hard, there must be another guy.

The next fist smashed directly into Lenny's nose, a crack so loud the bargirl shrieked, fading to a wail like a passing siren as Lenny slumped to the floor.

THE NAPKIN, saturated, barely slowed the blood dripping onto Lenny's shirt. Lenny was past caring about the shirt, his head back, staring at the roof of the Caddy, trying to get his nose to stop bleeding. Breathing through his mouth parched his tongue, but he couldn't get enough air through his blood filled nostrils. Even the slightest pressure hurt like hell, for all he knew it was broken.

He didn't even remember making it back to his car, his head pounding after being jumped by Timmy and his friends. Lenny hadn't actually seen anyone else, but there had to have been friends, no way Timmy could have done this by himself. *It was that sucker punch, fucking coward couldn't face me fair and square.*

The last thing Lenny remembered before the punch was the look on the girl's face, her recognition of his power, seeing him in a new light. She had been afraid. Really afraid. If only he had been able to have another minute with her, he would have transformed that fear to adoration, his strength impressing her. She would have forgot all about Timmy and would have been in Lenny's hands.

Fucking Timmy had done him one favor. Lenny now had proof that he could make a woman see him differently. He just needed to take control, show his strength.

Melanie wouldn't have a Timmy to get in the way.

CHAPTER 9

GIGI DOYLE STRUGGLED to find the keyhole of her apartment door, balancing her purse and laptop case on her hip, not wanting to put either one down in the rain. She hated these weeklong work trips, she always had to bring so much stuff. Her next promotion, coming up soon, would thankfully cut her travel in half.

It was good to be home. Her back was killing her from lugging her laptop. All she wanted was a cup of herbal tea and a pillow.

She held the door open with her foot, wheeling her luggage just inside. Immediately she knew something was wrong, the apartment didn't feel right . . .

Didn't *smell* right.

The oppressive, detested odor of cigarette smoke drove her against the door, Gigi clutching at her blazer as if that could ward off the offensive smell. She'd just had this jacket dry cleaned . . .

"Mel?"

Gigi clicked on the light. Newspapers and magazines everywhere, the couch pillows haphazard, toppled wine bottles. Her favorite green sweater on the floor.

The living room looked like a tornado had blasted through. Or the scene of a struggle.

"Mel!" Scared now, her heart pumping.

Gigi froze in the doorway, desperately waiting, hoping, praying for a response, any indication that her sister was safe, that it was okay to breathe again.

Nothing but the musty cigarette smoke, blowing past her into the open air, tendrils snaking into her nostrils, making her cough, a slap in the face forcing Gigi to look at the room in a new light.

Not a tornado, or a struggle. Just Melanie's detritus everywhere. A wine glass—no, *two* wine glasses—on the floor, Melanie too lazy to even wash a glass. The wine Gigi had been saving for a special occasion. The magazines, all glossy fashion spreads, Melanie's favorites. Gigi didn't even want to look at the kitchen.

Gigi kicked off her heels and ran across the living room, knowing it was hopeless, her entire outfit would have to go to the cleaners. She uncranked the windows in the living room and over the sink, breathing through her mouth, trying to ignore the dirty dishes. She paused at the back door, considering; it didn't have a screen, so she left it closed.

The bathroom was a disaster, makeup everywhere, Gigi's new mascara left open. That by itself was almost as bad as the smoke.

The bedroom was surprisingly clean, though the bed had been slept in, one of Gigi's blouses over the closet door, where never in a million years would she throw a cotton top. Not much smell of smoke, although Gigi opened the window anyway. The relative neatness of this room compared to the others was odd, unless . . .

Shit. Gigi rarely swore, even mentally, but this merited it. She squeezed into her robe, right over her work outfit, still clinging to the hope that she could save it from the cleaners as she went back to the entry for her purse and phone. Speed dialing Melanie while belting the robe.

Voicemail. "Thanks for leaving my place a fucking mess, Mel." Gigi didn't remember if she'd ever sworn at her big sister. "And if you had a guy in my apartment, I'll never let you stay here again." Her fingers were shaking as she got ready to click off, but not before she yelled, "And you owe me a new Lancome mascara!"

IT WAS HARD TO SEE at night with the sunglasses on, but there was no way Lenny was going to uncover his swollen eye. His nose had finally stopped bleeding, although it still hurt like hell, every breath a humiliating whistle. He couldn't let Melanie see him like this. Good thing he had bought the ski mask and nylons, he'd need them more than ever.

Getting punched had lit his fuse, he was *ready*.

GIGI PEELED OFF HER WORK CLOTHES, the blazer, skirt, and blouse going right in the basket destined for the dry cleaner. Her pantyhose she threw in the trash, they'd run as she had put new sheets on the bed. She'd pulled on a pair of clean sweats, knowing they'd have to be washed again, but she couldn't bring herself to wear clothes that were already in the hamper.

Every time she bent over pain shot across her back, she had to stop carrying around that heavy laptop. The last time she had a similar pain it had lasted for over a week, she couldn't afford that now. Didn't she have a few muscle relaxants left over? She checked, yes, thankfully, she hadn't finished the prescription. She downed one of the pills with two ibuprofen, that should help.

The bedroom fixed, she surveyed the living area. Start with the hardest job, which wasn't the newspapers and magazines, but the pile of dishes overflowing the sink. She gingerly picked up the wine glasses on the way.

Next to the sink, a yellow sticky note in Melanie's quick script. 'Sorry the place is a mess. I got a really hot lead, will clean up tomorrow when you are at work.'

Gigi stared at the note. Why couldn't Mel have left it on the outside door? Yet her heart softened just a bit. Her sister's hot lead would likely turn into another dead end, just like all the others. Mel just couldn't seem to get a break. Gigi could never do what Mel did. Not only couldn't she act, but the whole crazy, random process of getting ahead in show business was incomprehensible to her. Work hard, get ahead, that was Gigi's world, that was the way things *should* be. It was working for her just fine. Sure, it was hard at times, but the more she worked, the more rewards she got, more pay, a better position. Put in the time, dedicate yourself, and good things happened.

But not for actors. Melanie had put in the time, but not much good had happened yet. A few jobs here and there, barely enough to pay the rent. Melanie would never ask Gigi for money, she was too proud, or too much a big sister, but Gigi knew Mel struggled financially. A flash of guilt over the mascara; Melanie probably couldn't afford Lancome.

Gigi pulled on her rubber gloves and went to work on the sink. Melanie's promise to clean up would likely come to naught. Melanie wasn't the most reliable, not always showing up when they were supposed to meet, not sending their mother a card on her birthday. It had been that way ever since they had been kids, Gigi always the one taking care of the little things, even doing Melanie's chores, somehow Melanie's irresponsibility feeling like her own failing.

It was the least Gigi could do, because Mel did take care of her in other ways, almost like the big brother they didn't have. It was Mel who had publicly shamed the entire clique of cool kids at school for making fun of Gigi. It was Mel who had walked Gigi to middle school when they had moved to a not so good neighborhood after their father had lost his job, a chaperoning task that would make Melanie late for the high school opening bell, resulting in detention. Melanie never mentioned it and Gigi only found out when her mother had been visited by the truant officer. Even then Melanie had lied, claiming her homeroom teacher was a creep, logging her in late because he wanted her in his detention class, immediately putting the school official on the defensive. It was years later when Gigi realized the beauty of Melanie's deception, how this particular lie also avoided suggesting that their situation was their mother's fault. The complexity of Melanie's deceit was another skill Gigi lacked; Gigi could barely white lie when a girlfriend would ask if her favorite new dress was flattering or not.

And it was Melanie who had dealt with the boy who had once put his hands on Gigi, the older boy who had been leering at her, the first boy who had paid her any attention at all. Gigi, fourteen, so unready, so shocked that any boy would even look at her, let alone want to touch her, had frozen, which the boy took as acceptance. Fortunately other kids had been around, the rough grope was as far as it got, that day at least. Gigi hadn't said a word to anyone, but Mel had recognized Gigi's discomfort immediately that night at dinner, and later had pried the truth out of her.

The next day the boy didn't show up for school. Melanie missed school that day too; Gigi, at lunch period, shocked at seeing her sister outside the middle school, Melanie just staring at the front door. Melanie walked Gigi home, Gigi knowing Mel was there to protect her, feeling guilty, but unable to say no to her big sister, not only because Gigi was scared, but because she couldn't take this away from Melanie, this responsibility, this gift.

The next day the boy showed up at school just as Melanie and Gigi walked up. Melanie said, "Wait here," and then bore down on the boy, beating the living daylights out of him, not with a fury, but with a cold hearted ruthlessness, an attack so surgical that no one moved or screamed, not even the teachers outside the school.

Although that was the only physical intervention Gigi had witnessed, there were probably more, and many other times when Melanie had come to her aid. The two of them would be together, some creepy guy eyeing Gigi, Melanie making the guy turn away with just a look. When they got older, the guys even creepier, more aggressive, making comments, Melanie pushing right back at them, her words driven with such a power that even grown men cringed.

Melanie had never spoken of these interventions to Gigi, Gigi realizing Melanie didn't want her to feel weak, or become reliant on Melanie's protection. Melanie's only allusion to it all had been making Gigi promise to always tell her everything, to never be embarrassed to tell her sister if something bad had happened, to never fear for what Melanie might do.

All that strength, and still Melanie chased rainbows of possibilities, wisps of a stairway to show biz heaven.

Gigi methodically washed. Her sister might be able to sleep with a sink full of dishes, but she could not.

LENNY DIDN'T PARK in his usual spot, not wanting to take the chance Melanie would be coming home and would recognize the Caddy from his frequent drive bys at the restaurant. After a few passes around the block he found a good space where he could see approaching cars, and by turning around, Melanie's apartment.

Her lights were lit, she was home.

One decision left, the ski mask or the nylons?

THE DISHES DONE, the living room straightened up, Gigi stepped into the shower. It was late, she'd never get the eight hours sleep she needed to be good at work, but she just *had* to wash her hair, clammy with smoke. Which meant she would have to dry it, she hated sleeping with wet hair.

The hot shower didn't have its usual effect of making her tired, she was so wired from all the cleaning. As she put away her hair dryer she noticed a pill bottle in the drawer, sleeping pills. Mel had given them to her because this particular brand had given Mel headaches. Gigi wasn't big on pills except in emergencies, Melanie seemed to live on them, pills to fall asleep, pills to wake up.

Gigi fingered the bottle, wide awake at half past midnight. One pill couldn't hurt . . .

LENNY COULDN'T DECIDE between the mask and the nylons, so he took both with him as he got out of the car. He reluctantly left the camera, the last thing he needed right now was a keepsake photo of his bloody nose. The street was dead quiet, the last dog walker long since passed, not even noticing Lenny slumped in his seat. Melanie's front porch light and living room lights had gone off a half hour ago.

Lenny stepped across the street, heading toward the back alley. While still a block away his heart leapt when he discovered that the lights in the rear of Melanie's apartment were off as well. Which meant she was in bed.

His steps quickened, the mask in one hand, the nylons in the other.

GIGI LAY HER HEAD ON THE pillow, her hair still a little wet, but the sleeping pill had hit fast, maybe her empty stomach, maybe the long day. She hadn't even bothered to turn on the tv in the bedroom to help her relax. Random thoughts flowing through her head, tomorrow was trash day, the cake she had to make for the office party, getting the car oil changed. Calling Melanie and apologizing for her mean phone message, asking about whether her lead had worked out. Buying an air purifier for her bedroom. She needed to write some of this down, she needed her lists, too much to remember. But just the thought of turning on the light was tiring, she was drifting off, so much to do, something pulling at her brain as she fell asleep, yet another task in her endless list, she'd left the windows open, she'd never done that . . .

THE WHEEZING AIR THROUGH Lenny's still swollen nose was the loudest sound in the alley. Not a light on anywhere along the back of the complex. Even though the rain had ended, the night was cloudy, giving Lenny the perfect cover. Dark, but still easy to make out the gate which led into the small yard behind Melanie's apartment. Lenny left the latch undone.

One last look up and down the alley. No one there. He turned to the apartment and was greeted with his first bit of luck: all Melanie's windows were open. Maybe she always slept with the windows open, he didn't know, he didn't care. He just took it as a sign, he was doing the right thing, maybe the gods were finally giving him a break.

A whole string of losses had weighed on him, dragging him down. It wasn't like he had fallen from some lofty perch; although he bragged about LA, things there hadn't been much better. Yet each day brought him farther from his dreams, farther from his needs. The move east. Bullshit tips about possible celebrity sightings. Smashing up his hand. Getting beat up in the bar.

Worse, possibilities dangled in front of him, only to be yanked away, driving him down, kicking him. Finding Melanie, and then getting blown off by her. Coming up with the idea of making both of them famous, and then Melanie stealing it.

Fucking Melanie. Time to show her, time to turn this all around. Having something go right, just for once.

He'd use the mask, it would be easier to take off, easier to reveal himself to Melanie. *Shock and awe.*

Lenny crouched under the living room window, adjusting the mask, the simple act strengthening him. The casement was open far enough for him to stick his head right up against the screen. With no light behind him, he knew he'd be invisible. He *was* invisible, a superhero with a mask, a cloaking power.

No one in the room, the nightlight leading his eyes to the hallway. He stepped across the pathway, into the garden. Aside the bedroom window he stopped to listen. Nothing. Even his nose had cleared up, another sign.

He peered into the room.

Much harder to see, no light, the bedroom door probably closed. Yet an unmistakable form in the bed. She was so close . . .

He stared at the form, his heart pounding. Not a form, Melanie. *His* Melanie.

His fingers felt for the screen, no way that would work, too loud. Pushing any thoughts of frustration out of his head—he was on a new path, he could feel it, there was simply no room or need for frustration—Lenny retraced his steps to the other side of the back door, all the way to the far end of the unit. Here, under the living room window, he went to work, his fingers shaking with excitement.

The blade on the pocketknife slid easily through the screen, the tearing sound no louder than a rustle of leaves. Lenny had this same type of screen at his old house, two simple press in latches holding it in place midway up. He only needed to cut a tiny slit, virtually invisible, just enough for the blade to reach the latches. Once freed, Lenny twisted the screen so it fit through the window and set it on the floor.

Still not a sound from the apartment. Lenny hoisted himself up on the sill, gritting away the pain from his hurt hand.

He was inside.

One last adjustment of his mask as he tiptoed across the living room. The hallway would be risky, the nightlight. He'd turn it off once he got his bearings.

The bedroom door was unlocked, another sign, Lenny feeling it, everything going right. He should have done this a long time ago, taking things into his own hands. Not waiting for the world to come to him, but taking the initiative. He didn't need roofies, not any more.

He bent to snap off the nightlight, then grasped the door handle.

Shock and awe.

The door opened soundlessly, the room pitch dark. But Lenny had memorized it from his earlier reconnaissance, he had fantasized for hours about being in this room. He knew exactly where the bureau was, where the chair was, and especially where the bed was.

He stood over the bed, letting his eyes adjust. Melanie was sleeping on her side, facing away from him, the covers half thrown back. It was hard to tell what she was wearing, he assumed some kind of sexy lingerie.

What did a woman that beautiful dream about?

Lenny wasn't so egotistical to think she was dreaming about him. Not yet.

Very gently he lifted the covers, now wishing he had left the light on, he wanted to see her, this other side of Melanie he hadn't seen, so vulnerable.

As slowly as he had ever moved, every shift a risk and a thrill, Lenny slipped into the bed, his clothes no barrier to Melanie's heat, yet even the heat unable to stop him from shivering, to keep his hands from shaking.

Time for the shock.

In one motion he pulled her tightly against him, spooning, his mouth on her neck, turning her, he wanted one good kiss, so caught up in it he forgot the mask. He freed his mouth, hurrying, she'd wake, he needed to be kissing her before she had a chance to react.

She was moving on her own, not really struggling, mumbling, still half asleep. Lenny pressed his mouth to hers, waiting for her response, but she just lay there. Lenny ran his hand down along her body, over her luscious breasts. She stiffened, and Lenny smiled in the darkness, she was awake.

He let his hand drift lower, his mouth still on her, his lips working their magic. She still hadn't said a coherent word.

Lenny rolled right onto her, she didn't resist at all, her lips moving, but not talking, moaning maybe. He'd been so right. The feisty Melanie was nothing but an act for the world, she just needed the right man to tame her.

She just needed Lenny.

Any minute now she'd come alive, she'd be the fiery Melanie that Lenny dreamed about.

Yet she barely moved, a rag doll.

She needed more shock. His hands sought out her crotch, and finally she reacted, her lips parting, Lenny taking that as a signal, his mouth back on her. He used his knees to spread her legs, sensing only token resistance.

This was as far as he had planned on going, but her reaction begged him to keep at it, she wanted this, she wanted a man like him, she wanted *him*. Lenny.

"Surprised, aren't you?" he breathed, his own voice new to him, a powerful growl. "Bet you didn't think I could do this."

His fingers grasped at her bottoms, pulling them down, her hips gyrating. Lenny fumbled at his own pants, trying to work the belt, hurrying, not wanting to lose this chance. Her hands moved in opposite directions, one grasping at his bandaged hand, the other pushing between them.

His pants finally free, he poised himself over her, not believing his good fortune. He hadn't even dared to dream about this, about his plan working to perfection, Melanie helpless beneath him, wanting him so badly she couldn't even speak.

Yet he wasn't ready for her, or at least the part of him that mattered. Painfully balanced on his bad hand, he willed his body to react, for his erection to appear.

Melanie seemed to wait for it too, because she had gone limp again, as limp as he was. Mocking him.

Bile rose in his throat, it was so fucking unfair, to be so close, his once in a lifetime desire before him, naked and ready, and he couldn't rise to the occasion.

So fucking unfair. Or in his case, not fucking unfair.

This was more embarrassing than the damaged hand, than the broken nose. He couldn't reveal himself to Melanie now, not in this position, as far from the alpha male as could be.

Fighting back tears, he collapsed on her, his face in the pillow. With what little dignity he had left he mumbled, "The next time you see me you'll know it was me tonight, and we'll do it for real." Not for a minute believing it himself, not wanting to have another dream shattered, but just in case.

Lenny waited a few seconds for a reply, anything, some kind of reaction, a moan, a hint of expectation, of disappointment, but all he got was the mocking silence.

He pulled her pajamas and underwear back up over her hips, like it was his idea.

He rolled out of the bed, tripping, stumbling to the door with his pants around his knees, needing to get away before Melanie heard him cry.

CHAPTER 10

T HE HARSH GRINDING FORCED its way into Gigi's dream, an oddly
welcome rescue from her nightmare. In that floating in and out state
between sleep and wakefulness, Gigi opened her eyes into semi darkness. The sound came again, louder, powerful hydraulics, a machine
of horror, yet oddly familiar.

A garbage truck.

No, that couldn't be it, she never heard trucks so loud in her quiet
bedroom. Must be the dream. Gigi closed her eyes, drifting back off,
fighting to avoid falling back into the nightmare. The crash of metal
on metal impinging on her brain, a slight hint of fresh air.

Groggy, Gigi turned her head. The window of her bedroom, open.
She never left the window open . . .

The garbage truck whined, pulling Gigi from the sleeping nightmare. Why had she left the window open? Slowly it came back, the
cigarette odor, Mel's mess, the sleeping pill.

She'd kicked off the spread and sheets in the night. Too early to
get up. Reaching for them, a new odor in the bed, not cigarettes . . . beer? Mixed with another smell, burnt, earthy.

Cringing, she reached for the light. The glare burned her vision,
tears running as she squeezed them shut, not able to focus, dots floating in her pupils, dots of light still there when she opened her eyes,
the dots transforming to random droplets on the bedspread, an assaulting stain on her usual obsessive cleanliness.

Her mouth opened, a soundless scream, too stunned to remember how to use her vocal cords. She rolled out of the bed, wildly

kicking loose from the sheets which threatened to envelop her legs.

Another clang from the garbage truck, making her jump, jarring her into action.

She forced herself to look more closely at the spots on the spread. Dried blood? Checked herself, no cuts or scratches. She'd washed the spread before she had left on the trip.

Mel.

The blood was probably days old, Gigi had been too tired to notice the night before, too out of it from the sleeping pill.

But the smell of beer, still fresh.

The mascara would be nothing compared to this if Mel had brought a man to her bed. And not washed the bedcovers.

Gigi pulled on her robe and gingerly gathered up the spread and sheets with the tips of her fingers, dumping the load into the washer dryer combo in the little closet in the hallway, pouring in extra detergent and starting the washer. She padded into the hall, no way she was getting back in the bed, she'd lie down on the sofa for a while.

Froze as she entered the living room, her favorite orchid plants overturned, dirt spattered across her pristine rug. The window screen on the floor, Gigi not comprehending, had the screen blown in? Walking closer, the scene finally registering, the violation of her apartment, her safety, her life, pricking her vocal cords to action.

She screamed.

Clasped her hand over her mouth, could someone be in the apartment?

Gigi side stepped her still unpacked luggage and fumbled the latch to open the outer door. Her fear urged her to run, her anger rising, winning. She had to know. Leaving the door open, she grabbed one of the empty wine bottles by the neck and tiptoed back toward the bedroom, peering into the open bath door. Nothing. Glanced into the spare room. Back at her bedroom, the closet door stood ajar. Gigi took three quick steps, the bottle cocked, and jerked open the door.

Just clothes.

Her adrenaline inspired bravery slipped away, her hands shaking. She dropped the bottle and collapsed against the wall, confused. Had someone tried to rob her?

She didn't have anything valuable except for her diamond studs and a few hundred dollars emergency cash, which she kept in the top drawer of her dresser. She checked, everything in its place.

Purse.

It was on the table by the door, right where she'd left it. She examined the contents, all there. She quickly walked through the living room, nothing appeared to have been taken. Maybe the thief hadn't even come in, something had frightened him off.

Gigi picked up the phone, dialed Mel, got her voicemail. "It's me, someone broke into my apartment, you didn't let anyone see my stuff, did you?" Trying not to sound accusing, yet the mess she had found meant her sister had probably brought someone over. "Just call me, okay?"

Gigi had never been robbed before, this was why she had moved to this nice neighborhood, to be safe.

She gently picked up the orchids, maybe she could repot them. The potting mix had left a dark mark on the rug, and Gigi dutifully got out the stain remover and mindlessly went to work blotting it out. She couldn't think straight, the shock of the break-in dulling her movements, and she was so very tired, why couldn't she wake up? She closed her eyes, trying to remember the night. She had taken a sleeping pill but she couldn't recall actually swallowing it. That damned pill. Her memory was filled with only vague, foggy images.

After the rug she straightened up the other fallen plants. She needed to separate herself from the mess, from the violation, get things back the way they were. She'd call the apartment manager and file a report.

As she was fitting the screen back in the window she noticed dried specks on the windowsill. She'd just washed those windows, she wouldn't have missed all this dirt. No, not dirt, it was . . . dried blood? She leaned over the sill, looking out, seeing the footsteps in the soft ground, seeing the drops of blood on the outer wall, under the window.

Like the blood on the spread.

The thief had bled here on the window, he'd bled in her bedroom, he'd been in the bed . . .

Gigi dropped the screen, the bile rising up, and threw up on her boxwoods.

*   *   *

"911. WHAT'S YOUR EMERGENCY?"

"I think someone broke into my apartment last night."

"Are you at 611 Lakeview Apartments?"

"Yes."

"Are you safe? Is the person who broke in still there?"

"What? No. I've locked everything up."

"Are you alone?"

"Yes."

"Are you certain?"

"Yes, it's a small apartment, I've checked. I—I think I may have been—I think the thief may have touched me when I was sleeping."

"You were assaulted?"

"No, I—I don't know. I can't think straight. I took some pills . . ."

"Are you on medication?"

"No, it wasn't mine, I mean—"

"Miss, are you under the influence of narcotics?"

"No, it was a sleeping pill, and something for my back."

"I'll dispatch a patrol car, the police will come. What is your name?"

"Let's just forget it, okay? I'm fine, I might have been imagining it."

"Miss, the police will come and take a statement. Are you sure you don't need medical attention? We can send a sexual assault counselor as well."

"No, please, can't this just be anonymous? I don't want my boss to find out . . ."

"Miss, all calls to 911 are recorded. If you are in immediate danger officers can be there in a few minutes, otherwise someone will come take your statement about the break-in as soon as they are available."

"I'm fine, really . . ."

"Is there someplace safe you can go?"

"I guess I could go to my sister's . . ."

*   *   *

MELANIE PICKED UP THE bits and pieces of her clothing as she made her way across the hotel suite. Fuck, what a night. The local press had tracked her down, calling and asking for a comment on the *Shock and Awe* situation, and she'd calmly played it cool, knowing it would only inflame their interest. She had wanted to go out and celebrate, and also get Jason's threats out of her head, but she didn't want to be seen.

That didn't leave too many options in Marburg, and though Boston was a possibility, she didn't want to be far away. So she'd called Tim Tazik, the photographer, who had gleefully booked a hotel room a few towns over and brought two bottles of champagne. They'd just hung out at first, watching the Tony Awards. Melanie had done a little stage, she didn't like it much, but most serious actors had it on their resume, it was just another rite of passage.

The show got boring, as most award shows did. Still, Melanie wanted to be at one someday, even as an attendee, a lot of glitz, and the publicity was hard to beat, photographers lining up to take your picture, a lot of interest in what you were wearing. She wouldn't even have to pay for the outfit, some fashion house would lend it to her, even the jewelry was borrowed.

She let Taz take a few photos, nothing showing her face, a small price to pay. Taz had reminded Melanie that she owed him more than that, and the champagne was very good, so she let things go a little further than she had intended, a lot further actually, but what the hell, she *did* owe him, and he might come in handy again. And he hadn't been half bad in bed.

Not good enough to wake up with though. While he was still snoring she extricated herself from the sheets, or what was left of them.

Outside, raining, she slipped on her shades anyway, glad she hadn't dressed up, she would have looked terrible. She walked quickly to her car, it wouldn't do to be photographed doing a walk of shame, not with what she had planned. Her career was about to take off.

She needed coffee.

Safe in the car, still feeling the champagne, she automatically checked her messages. Voicemails from last night and early that morning. Melanie smiled, the press anxious to talk to her, she must not have heard the phone ring, too hung over.

Not the press. The most recent call was from Gigi, trying to sound calm, but Melanie knew her sister's tone, she'd known it since they were kids, she could tell Gigi was scared.

Melanie forgot the coffee and drove as fast as she could to Gigi's apartment.

"YOU DIDN'T SEE ANYONE? And nothing was missing?"

"No, I told you already, no."

Melanie didn't doubt her sister that something had happened, although if you looked around the apartment you'd never know, the place in much better shape than when Melanie had left it. Except it wasn't like Gigi to make up a story.

Gigi was curled up in the corner of the couch, her legs tucked, her arms wrapped around herself. She was dressed in her work outfit, a cream blouse with a blue skirt.

Melanie put her arm around her sister. "Come on, you'll get your clothes all wrinkled. Why are you dressed up, anyway?"

Gigi, sniffling, sat up straight, smoothing down her skirt. "I have to go to work and I don't want to be late, but I have to wait for the police."

"The police? You called the police?"

"Yes, when I couldn't reach you . . . I'm sorry, I didn't mean it was your fault. But when I saw the blood, I thought someone had—been in bed with me, I called 911."

Melanie had been robbed a few times, until the word probably got out on the street that she didn't have anything worth stealing. It was just a fact of life in a bad neighborhood, shit flowed downhill. She hadn't even bothered reporting it when her car had been broken into. What were the police going to do, write a report that would get filed away?

The blood was disconcerting though. Melanie had brought a few guys over here in the past. Gus, a while back. The latest one, Jack, no, John, something like that, a few nights ago, the first night Gigi had been away. He hadn't been bleeding, as far as she knew. But they had been smoking some weed, and then the wine, shit, was he the type who would come back to rob the place? She didn't know him all that well, but he was an office guy, that's why she'd brought him here, her place not nice enough.

"What did you tell the police?"

"I didn't talk to them, just the 911 operator. I didn't give my name, but I told her I thought someone might have been in bed with me."

"Christ, Gigi, do you think you were raped?" Melanie, seeing Gigi cringe, said, "I mean, assaulted?"

"I don't know, I was so tired, the sleeping pill. But I felt sore all over, and the beer smell, a man must have been in the bed, oh, Mel, I—"

"Shh, don't worry." Melanie pulled Gigi close, forcing down her own anger, a creep touching her sister, she thought those days were long gone. If the guy she'd brought here had something to do with this, she'd cut off his balls.

"Gigi, were your clothes, I mean, did you check yourself?"

"I was in my pajamas, everything was fine."

"You said you were sore."

"Not down there, no, I meant my back, my neck."

Gigi sobbed into Melanie's shoulder, Melanie stroking her hair, trying to calm her down. If Gigi had been assaulted, something needed to be done, but Gigi would get dragged through the mud. And if she hadn't been assaulted, any intervention by the police would just be a reminder of the break-in. And the painful memory of the boy who had groped her years ago.

"Gigi, I'm sorry to do this, but tell me again what you remember. Everything."

Gigi nuzzled into Melanie's chest. "I got home, I was just so glad to be back after the long trip, when I got in the place was all messy—"

"Sorry about that. I left you a note, I was going to come over and clean, but a whole bunch of stuff happened."

"I saw the note, did you get a role?"

"I'll tell you about it later, it's all good. What happened after you got home?"

"I was mad at you. I cleaned up, it took a while. My back was killing me, I think I pulled it again, so I took a muscle relaxer. I got wired up cleaning. I didn't think I was going to fall asleep, so I took one of those pills you had left me."

"You took a sleeping pill on top of a muscle relaxer?"

"Yes, why, is that bad?"

"Not bad, but it will knock you out. You said nothing was wrong with the window before you went to bed?"

"Everything was fine. But the place smelled like smoke, I opened them all. I'm sorry, I didn't mean it was your fault, but you know I hate the smell of smoke."

"Asshole," said Melanie.

"What?"

"Not you, sorry." Melanie was thinking about John, he'd brought the weed, they'd smoked out the window, but he'd lit a cigarette after, Melanie too wasted to remember to stop him. "Keep going."

"That's all I remember, the sleeping pill hit me so fast, I fell asleep. I had some wicked dreams."

"What kind of dreams?"

"Some man was talking to me, it was all dark, or he had very dark skin, it's confusing."

"What did he say?"

"He wasn't making sense. Something about being surprised. Then he—."

"He what?"

"It's embarrassing."

"Come on, Gigi, it's me."

"He—kissed me. I thought it was one of—those dreams, you know?"

Melanie shook her head, her inexperienced baby sister. "I know, it's all right."

"Then he said something like when he saw me again, we'd do it for real."

"For real? Was this someone you knew?"

"I don't think so."

"You said he had dark skin?"

"I don't know. His face was black, but it was dark. I couldn't even see his eyes."

Melanie lay her head back on the sofa. The last guy she had brought over had been white, but that didn't mean he didn't have a black friend. "Anything else you remember?"

"Wait, the beer smell, did I mention that? And the blood. I put everything in the wash, I thought you had—anyway, I came out into the living room and saw the screen on the floor. I wouldn't have called 911 if I hadn't seen the blood on the windowsill, that's when I thought someone had been in here." Gigi sucked in a breath. "I can't let them find out about this at work, the police are going to ask about the sleeping pills, that wasn't my prescription. What if they tell my boss?"

"What, that you took one of my sleeping pills?" Melanie wasn't worried about that, but Gigi, sweet Gigi, was missing the big picture. If this made the news—and *everything* made the news in Marburg, as Melanie could certainly attest—then Gigi's name would certainly come out. Even a hint of some kind of sexual incident, even as a victim, would put Gigi in a bad light.

No fucking way Melanie would let that happen to Gigi. The police would be useless, all the evidence gone anyway, the sheets in the laundry, Gigi's obsessive cleanup, even the morning rain washing off the outside wall. And maybe nothing really had happened, just a bad set of coincidences, the thought of an assault put in motion by a bad dream brought on by sleep inducing drugs.

But the police would be here soon, and they'd want to know what had happened, they'd want to file their useless report. Whether she wanted it or not, the attention would be on poor Gigi.

Melanie absentmindedly stroked Gigi's hair. Just when things seemed to be getting on track for her own career, just when she was about to get her well deserved chance, this happened. Not only this, but the call from Jason, threatening her chances for a big break.

Jason.

Another asshole to deal with. She had to fix this fast so she could get back to dealing with Jason, and focus on her career.

Jason in her head, Gigi in her arms, their faces and bodies melding.

Suddenly it all came together, a way to protect her sister, and keep Jason at bay.

Knowing she should think it through, but not having the time, Melanie grasped at the idea. All she needed to do was shift the focus away from Gigi, just as she had shifted the focus from Lisa Vista. Shift the focus onto herself.

Still working it out, she said, "Gigi, I don't think it's a good idea to tell the police you got assaulted."

Gigi looked up, puzzled. "Why?"

"Because you aren't sure what happened. They'll ask all kinds of questions, did you have men here, about the sleeping pills. You're right, your boss will probably find out, the police will go to your office."

"But what if whoever broke it did something to me? I don't want him to get away."

Melanie pulled Gigi into a tight embrace. "Don't worry, they won't. It will be like when we were in school, remember how I always protected you from the boys? If anyone touched you, they'll get what they deserve."

After a long silence, Gigi said, "So what should I tell the police?"

"You don't have to tell them anything, I will."

"What do you mean?"

Melanie, making it up as she went along, thinking it would work, she could pull this off, it was just acting. "I'll tell them it was me who called. And . . ." Melanie looked around the apartment. Gigi had washed up the blood, but who knows what else might have been left behind. "I'll tell them that all this happened at my place, not here."

"That won't work, the 911 operator knew the address."

"I'll say I was upset, I came over here to see you."

"That's just wrong. We have to tell the truth."

Melanie's voice hardened. "Did that boy who touched you in school tell the truth?"

"That was different."

"No, it's the same. Fucking men, all liars, out for themselves. You think if they catch the man who broke in here he's going to admit getting in bed with you? They're all the same, and we'll deal with it the same way. *I'll* deal with it. This is something I know all about. You don't have to learn. I don't *want* you to learn."

"I can't lie, you know how bad a liar I am."

"You don't have to lie, just don't say anything. In fact, go to work right now. Who knows when the cops will show up."

"I don't know."

But Melanie could hear it in Gigi's voice, the relief, the faith in her big sister, who would make it all go away.

"You don't have to *know* anything. Trust me, have I ever let you down?" Melanie, already thinking through the next act of this film, seeing it in her head, the cops showing up, Melanie looking much more than Gigi like she just had sex, because of course she had. Just needing to sound a little groggy, a little messed up, which wouldn't be hard.

Waiting for the inevitable question from the police. *Do you know anyone who might have done this?*

Hesitating, then claiming it was all a mistake, or might be, just the fog of too many drinks, the sleeping pill. Officer, did I mention that I was with my friend Jason? Jason Ayers? I just can't remember everything that happened . . .

Leaving it open, nothing happened, something happened, then telling Jason that her memory might clear up suddenly if he bothered her, if he tried to derail her dreams.

She gently helped Gigi to her feet, her arms around her sister protectively. "Don't worry, I'll take care of everything." Melanie held her like that until Gigi's body relaxed. "Come on, let's get your makeup cleaned up."

CHAPTER 11

DETECTIVE STAN BROOKER spiraled the nondescript Ford sedan up the sinuous turn of the airport parking garage. The car, in ownership limbo between the impound lot and the auction block, had been confiscated from a drug dealer who got away on the drug charge but not the tax avoidance. The sedan, not what Brooker would have expected even a half assed dealer to own, squealed in protest.

Forced against the door by the hard turns, Brooker's passenger muttered, "I hate these fucking parking lots."

Brooker shrugged, not an easy thing to do when making a ton and a half of automobile go in a direction the forces of nature didn't want it to go. "Because of the turns?"

"Because I get lost in them."

That remark made Brooker glance sideways at his partner, Robert Winter. Just a quick glance, otherwise they were going to end up against a wall, which wouldn't bode well for their undercover stakeout. Brooker didn't recall Winter ever getting lost, anywhere; Winter had an unerring sense of direction.

Brooker thought about bringing it up, it was the second time in the last month Winter had said something which made him wonder if Winter was okay. Brooker was forced to let it go, because just then a man came out of the stairway off to their left, innocuous, unless you noticed that he didn't have any luggage.

Winter noticed right away, which also gave Brooker pause about questioning his health. "Could have just dropped someone off." Winter turned in his seat, craning his neck to keep the guy in sight.

"Can't stop now, too obvious," said Brooker. "I'll go up to the next level and park, we can come down the stairs."

"He slipped back into the stairway. Might have spooked him. Stop here."

Brooker didn't question Winter, hitting the brakes even though they were in the middle of the ramp. "You going down?"

"Yeah, on the ramp. Go all the way up to the top floor, just in case, work your way down the stairs."

"Hispanic, mid thirties, goatee, five six, denim jacket?"

Winter peered back into the car. "Not bad, for an old man who was supposed to be concentrating on the driving."

From Winter, that was a compliment. "Only three years older than you."

"We're both fucked then," said Winter, his eyes on the stairwell door. "More like five eight. Black jeans, dark work boots." Winter took off at a jog back down the spiral ramp.

Brooker continued on up. Old only in cop years at fifty three, Brooker *was* a little on the heavy side. He was glad he'd be walking down the stairs instead of up.

BEFORE WINTER HAD STARTED forgetting where he parked in garages, he had actually liked them for stakeouts. Generally there were only two ways in and out, the ramp and the stairwell. A larger garage could have two sets of stairs, but even then the entire lot could be covered by only six cops. Just four were needed in a garage like this one, the eight decker shared by the Boston Regional Airport and a sprawling office complex.

Only he and Brooker today, though. There wasn't enough evidence to suggest that a real criminal would be here, at least the one they were after. Winter was sure that there was *some* kind of criminal in or around this lot, there were criminals everywhere. Right now his focus was on finding who was committing a series of seemingly random muggings. The fact that the captain believed they were random meant he wasn't keen on letting Winter and Brooker spend much time on them. That the muggings hadn't even happened at this garage, or even at the airport, killed any chance for a second team to help with the stakeout.

To Winter, there were few truly random crimes. Maybe theoretically, but once you fell into the trap of thinking a crime was random, once you gave up looking for the connection that explained the motive, the opportunity, the how and why of the crossing paths of the victim and perpetrator, the easier it would be to assume that all crime was cosmic chance, a butterfly buffeted by the wind. Even the flittering direction of a butterfly could be figured out, if you knew the connection.

A car coming up the ramp forced Winter against the wall at the last turn. Unconsciously Winter checked out the driver, a middle aged woman, oblivious, chatting on a cell phone, his cop mind instantly classifying her as a civilian, which in his ex military mind didn't mean she was a non government worker, but that she wasn't a threat. The idea of randomness still in his thoughts; if she'd run over him, no one might have made the connection if she had actually been a hired killer out to get him. Even a good detective might not figure it out.

Winter slowed to a walk, checking the aisles in case the Hispanic man had beat him downstairs. Feeling good, this particular guy they had spotted might be just here for a flight, but Winter was moving, doing something. His eyes on the stairwell door, Winter casually walked through the garage, a world with its unique atmosphere of exhaust, burnt oil, and Doppler echoes. The muggings weren't about airports, they seemed to have no real connection, which is why he and Brooker were here after their shift was over. Technically the muggings were their case, but the last one had been a month ago, the victim couldn't describe the attacker, and hadn't been hurt. All of that, and the seemingly random nature, meant the case dropped lower and lower on the priority list.

Winter had mused over it, as he always did with these seemingly random crimes, and had come up with one idea. The only connection he could find between most of the victims was that they had recently had a chance at some kind of windfall. One man had returned from Vegas, one couple had flown to New York for an appraisal of an antique vase left to them in a will. A CPA had qualified for a poker tournament. That the Vegas man hadn't won the jackpot, the vase was worth nothing, and the CPA had lost in the first round didn't matter, it was the fact that all of their stories had been covered on the news beforehand. Could the mugger be stalking people who might be coming into money? Even those not in the news?

A tenuous link, but it wouldn't be the first one Winter had correctly identified, a sliver of a thread which had eliminated the excuse of randomness. Winter's success bought him some slack from the captain, but not enough to justify time, let alone overtime, on a stakeout such as this one. So Winter and Brooker gave it a shot, every few days hanging around the airport to see if they could spot a returning traveler being stalked.

Today offered an added incentive, the regional airport had just started weekly flights to Aruba, which had a new casino. The flight was due to land in a half hour.

A sharp beep to Winter's right, his hand going to his Ruger LCP at his hip under his hoodie. Too warm for the sweatshirt, even at night, but Winter hated wearing a belly band like Brooker did, using his untucked, oversized shirts to hide his gun. Winter was carrying his backup piece; his standard 9 mm locked up at the station, too bulky on a stakeout. The beep noise registering, a car being unlocked with a remote, yet no one around. The unmistakable sound of the stairwell door opening, one of those bars you had to push. The Hispanic guy came out, looking somewhat confused. He held up his hand, Winter focusing on the motion, thinking *gun*, but it wasn't a gun, it was a set of keys, the beeping again.

The guy visibly relaxed, heading for the car. He passed right by Winter, looking more sheepish than suspicious, and Winter almost laughed, the guy had forgot where he had parked, and was just using his remote to unlock the car so he could find it.

Not a bad idea, thought Winter, I'll have to remember that.

BROOKER COULDN'T FIND A parking space on the top level. Who the hell parks way up here? He was forced to go back down to seven, where there were plenty of spaces, go figure. No people in sight, nine in the evening, but he checked it anyway, walking its length, realizing that if the mugger were here hiding, Brooker would look pretty suspicious. On the other hand, if the mugger were crouched down behind a car or one of the massive support poles, he'd look pretty suspicious himself.

Brooker bypassed the stairway. He had to check the upper floor, which meant going up the ramp. The stairs would be faster, but the man they had spotted might drive out from eight, and then they would have wasted a trip. Although the guy would have to be a track star to have made it up six flights already.

Up the ramp, huffing a little, he needed to lose some weight. He wondered if he had ever got married if his wife would have helped with that. Or maybe he'd be heavier, home cooking instead of takeout. The takeout was certainly fatty, but maybe he would eat more if the food was better tasting? Another unsolvable mystery.

Not that he thought these muggings were unsolvable. Maybe they were, maybe they weren't. Winter's idea was as good as any, better, because the man had a history of pulling cards out of thin air, a magician who made randomness disappear. Until he explained the trick, which was the hidden connection, the string that yanked the card into his sleeve. Then it all made sense, and, because Winter never rubbed it in, you felt more awed than put down or stupid. At least that was true for Brooker. Some of the other detectives didn't get it, they thought it was luck, Winter's success—and Brooker's by association— as random as the crimes had appeared to be.

A clanging echo, coming from everywhere and nowhere, just as Brooker hit the top floor. Someone coming out of the stairway? He slipped behind a support pole, thankful of its girth, a plane revving up, drowning out any chance of hearing footsteps . . .

WINTER FOUGHT THE URGE TO RELAX, even though the Hispanic wasn't the guy they were looking for. Winter wasn't certain he could predict how someone who pulled off multiple assaults would act if spotted, but pretending he had misplaced his car didn't seem to be it. Besides, the Hispanic didn't fit even the vague descriptions they had received from the mugging victims. No one had gotten a good look, not that it would have mattered, eye witness accounts were notoriously unreliable. All these people carrying phone cameras around, catching evidence of infractions by cops everywhere, yet no one ever got a picture of a crime? Another mystery to solve.

He headed for the stairway, since that was where Brooker would expect to meet him, and it wouldn't do to leave your partner wondering, especially on a stakeout. Brooker would expect the worst, just as Winter would. Winter also didn't want Brooker to take all those stairs, even down, he had to get his partner on some kind of diet. Too bad the guy wasn't married. Winter's ex wife's cooking had been so bad it was better than any diet.

Winter waited a few steps outside the stairwell door, expecting the whine of the revving jet to dissipate. Lessons learned while serving in combat situations: normal background noises drowned out the footsteps of danger, everyday sounds lulled you into a sense of complacency. He'd seen men lose their lives that way, and while he had no particular feeling of invulnerability, why add to life's dangers, especially a cop's life, even one in a relatively small city?

The pilot of the jet wasn't co-operating, a frustrated drag racer. Winter weighed the risks of not having a quiet stairwell versus that of Brooker left alone in case the real mugger happened to be in the garage, and that being no contest, he opened the door.

Muffled thuds, an echoing resonance that could be anything, especially against the backdrop of the jet. Winter closed the door quietly, his hand again on his weapon. More thuds, an animalistic grunt, a yelp of indeterminate origin.

Some kind of commotion not far above, no way Brooker could be this far down so soon. Winter took the stairs two at a time yet under control, his gun in his hand by his side, not able to see up the enclosed stairway yet not wanting to spook some innocent civilians by rushing on them with a pointed gun.

Winter passed the third landing, the tumult still above him. As he turned for the next flight of stairs the door he had just passed smashed open into him, throwing him against the wall and numbing his arm as his mind registered a woman's yell from above, immediately stifled. Winter bounced off the wall as a ruddy skinned, long haired man rushed in, Winter's mind flashing to the Hispanic, this guy was much bigger, the clothes all wrong, a baseball cap pulled low, the head down. The man's momentum carried him into Winter, a quick look of surprise on his face, but not so surprised that he didn't grab for the gun, Winter not able to feel his hand, afraid to squeeze his fingers, no telling where the bullet would go, ricocheting around the cinder block walls.

The guy outweighed Winter by fifty pounds, but only thought he knew how to fight, relying on his size, moving in to smother Winter with his body. Winter *did* know how to fight, and he never gave a shit about fighting fair, slamming his foot into the man's ankles, quickly followed by a knee to the stomach, getting a grunt, the guy half bending, but he was tough, catching Winter flush in the chest with an uppercut, a wild swing Winter couldn't get away from.

Winter pushed off to create some space, at the same time swinging his still numb arm around, aiming the butt of his gun at the man's head. Missed, his hand hitting the wall, the man still reaching for the gun. Winter went with it, his hand to hand training ingrained in muscle memory, sliding around, pinning the big man to the wall, along with his gun, not what the guy expected. Winter gave him three quick shots in the kidneys, too much bulk there to do much good, but a kick behind the knee worked, hitting the right nerve, the knee buckling. Winter wrestled his gun hand free, catching the guy's head with the butt, and he went down.

Winter backed off to get him covered, he didn't have handcuffs but always carried a long zip tie. "Don't move," he ordered, but as he was reaching for the zip tie another anguished yelp from above, a woman in pain.

"Brooker!" he yelled, on the off chance Brooker was in the stairway, and to give whomever was above fear, and hope, that help was on the way. Winter took two steps up, his gun hovering on the long haired guy, lying on the landing, bleeding from where Winter had cut his head. Winter couldn't wait, the woman screaming for help. Shifting the gun to his left hand he grabbed at the rail with his right, pulling himself up the stairs.

At the next landing another big man stood behind a petite woman, his arm around her neck, bending her over the rail, her skirt pulled up, her dark hair dangling in air, the woman sobbing, the guy holding a knife, a good sized Tanto. Winter lifted the gun, awkward, he couldn't hit the fucking wall with his left hand. The assailant, crew cut, clean shaven, almost military in appearance, holding the knife like he knew what he was doing, the way Winter would have held it. Winter bringing the gun around as the man, not cowed, calmly pulled the woman's head back by the hair, the knife against her neck.

The jet screamed on takeoff, rattling Winter's teeth even in the stairway, deafening. A huge weight slammed into him, shoving him down, the edge of the hard stairs driving in his shins and then his forehead. He lashed out with his feet, hitting nothing but air, his forearm screaming in pain as a foot stomped on it, a quick impression of the long haired guy's legs. Winter fighting to hold onto the gun, not giving up even as the boot came down again, but even his resolution was no match for hundreds of pounds of force, his fingers opening beyond his control.

Winter grabbed at the boot, twisting hard, the jet still whining, the man with the knife stepping down toward him, a mountain. Winter couldn't get up, two men on him now, arms and legs and somewhere, a hand with a knife . . .

Adrenaline adding magic fuel to his training and his raw survival instinct, grabbing the ruddy guy by his hair, using it as a lever and bouncing his head off the stairs, bang, bang, bang, the cracks so loud they overcame the now fading jet. Winter feeling more than seeing the knife come at his face, twisting the handful of hair so the head was between him and the knife, he was too close, the knife only partially blocked, the tip catching Winter in the forehead, blood flooding into his right eye.

Winter twisted the hair again, the man screaming as the next knife stroke gashed his ear, rising up, crazed enough to lift the knife man, the pressure off of Winter for a heartbeat, he slid down stairs, his nose smashing into each step. No time, there was still the knife and his gun, he desperately tried to clear the blood from his eye, the pain from the cut not yet registering.

The knife wielder had fallen back on his ass. Winter pounded back up the stairs and drop kicked him in the face while holding onto the rail, getting his weight into it. The short haired man's head snapped back, but he didn't let go of the knife, so Winter kicked him again. Another scream from the woman, the long haired guy had latched onto her, her face smeared with his blood. Winter stomped on the fingers holding the knife, twisting, trying to break as many as possible, kicking the knife down the stairs as it came free. Not a word from the downed guy, which tipped Winter off that he wasn't giving up, a silent warning to leap out of the way of the man's other hand reaching for Winter's legs.

The miss left the now unarmed man stretched out, awkward, so Winter kicked him in the face again even as he turned to the woman, who had gone slack, hurt or in shock. Winter could deal with the punches, the kicks, even the knife, but not with seeing a man with his hands on a woman. He rushed forward, Long Hair trying to put the woman between them, Winter going for his cut ear, grabbing, pulling, his hands slick with blood, getting nothing, going back again, the guy screaming, telling Winter he had his fingers in the right spot. He dug in deep, yanking the guy around by the ear, pulling his arm away from the woman, spinning him just as the military guy loomed. Winter used the long haired man as a battering ram, letting go as he hit the other assailant, both of them crashing down the stairs.

Winter's eye was now filled with blood, his hands slick, he didn't know if he could shoot even if he could find the gun. The woman collapsed, he had to step over her as he flew down the steps, the bigger man pushing Long Hair off. Winter grabbed his hair again and used it like a whip to smash his head against the wall as hard as he could. Winter let him go, grabbing the rail just as the big one got up, no hair to grab on to, so Winter kicked him in the neck. The man went down, gurgling, Winter on top of him, pummeling away, a rushing in his ears, he'd taken a hit somewhere he hadn't even realized, the sharp pain from his forehead cut now registering, he might not have much time, needed to finish this . . .

Strong hands pulling him off, Winter stunned, he'd bounced that fucker's head off the wall, no way he could be back up. Winter spun around wildly, arms wrapping around him, an urgent but somehow familiar voice forcing it's way through the blood and haze.

"It's me, Winter, slow down, hey . . ."

The voice finally registering, Brooker. "Knife," croaked Winter, tasting blood.

"I got it. Your piece too. They're both down for the count."

"Woman," said Winter, still barely able to see.

"In shock, but breathing. Not cut, it's not her blood. I'll go check on her again. Just sit, okay?"

Win felt for the stairs, pulling his shirt out to clean his face. Long Hair lay crumbled at his feet, his head a mess, his body twitching in pain. Alive. The bigger guy looked unconscious. A scream behind Winter, he turned, the woman in a frenzy, biting and clawing at Brooker. Brooker wrapped his burly arms around her, the wrong thing to do, as it only made her fight harder. Winter crawled his way up the stairs, the woman probably thinking her nightmare wasn't over, Brooker another attacker. Her eyes widened as she saw Winter, another nightmare on the way, Brooker trying to be gentle, the woman having none of it. Winter held up his hand, trying to tell her it was okay, a bloody zombie crawling toward her as she was held immobile. Winter stopped, suddenly feeling useless.

Brooker whispering something to the woman, slowly winding her down, Winter hearing the word *police*. The woman shaking her head, disbelieving. Brooker let her go, but kept his arms loosely around her, a fence of protection.

"I'm going to show you my badge," said Brooker. "It's okay, I'm a cop, we're just trying to help you, don't you remember?"

The woman never took her eyes off of Winter, her arms clutched over her breasts protectively, her clothing tie dyed in blood. Brooker reached for his shield and held it in front of her face, the badge must have had some kind of power, because she collapsed.

Brooker grabbed her as she fell, guiding her to the floor, checking her pulse. "Feels okay, I think she just fainted."

"Call it in," said Winter.

"I will, let me just lock these guys down."

Winter handed Brooker his zip tie as Brooker passed him on the stairs, not upset that Brooker wasn't checking on him, the first priority was safety. Brooker handed Winter back his gun and Winter painfully followed his partner down the stairs to cover him. Brooker cautiously approached the short haired man first, staying out of Winter's line of fire. It didn't matter, the guy was dazed, completely out of it.

"These our muggers?" asked Brooker.

"I very much doubt it. All wrong, no masks, a knife instead of a gun, the assault."

"You just stumbled upon them? Randomly?"

"Very funny."

Brooker zipped up Long Hair, who hadn't moved at all, the bright blood clashing with his ruddy features. "Jesus, buddy, you almost killed this one."

Winter looked down at the prone assailant, shook his head, and stomped as hard as he could on the guy's nuts. "I hate fucking rapists."

Brooker, impassive, observed, "Technically, he's an attempted rapist, at least as far as we know."

"You going to kick me in the balls too?" asked the short haired guy. He'd come to, his voice a croak.

Winter felt good hearing the raspiness, he must have tagged the guy pretty good in the throat. He picked up the knife and used it to cut a strip from his shirt to wrap around his forehead. When he was finished he held the knife up. "Army?"

The guy sneered. "Marines."

"You're a disgrace," said Winter. "But I won't kick you."

Brooker looked from the Marine to Winter, shrugged, and kicked the Marine in the crotch.

"Fuck! You said you wouldn't kick me!"

"He did, I didn't," said Brooker.

"What was that for?" asked Winter.

"I hate attempted rapists."

Winter laughed, that was worth the price of the cut. "Call it in."

Brooker shook his head, pulling Winter up the stairs, out of earshot of the woman and the two assailants, whispering. "Listen, this looks bad. You've got your history . . . and everyone is all over law enforcement, here, everywhere, all of us, that man in custody our guys did a number on, the two shootings by the Boston cops, this won't go down well."

"Come on, they were raping her," protested Winter.

Brooker pressed on. "Not a rape. *Attempting an assault* is how it will play." Brooker jerked his hand down the stairs. "If that guy dies . . . look, man, I know you did what you had to do, this time and the other times, I would have done the same thing, but this isn't the right time for this to come out, they'll have your badge."

Winter nodded toward the woman, who seemed to be breathing normally. "She'll back me up."

"Want to bet your career on that?"

Winter sagged, the reality of the unfairness a more potent assault than the two men he had fought. "What do you have in mind?"

Brooker looked down at the two men, the woman, considering. "They were out of it when I got here and announced myself, and the woman was in shock, we can say she was in shock. You need to get out of here."

Winter was already shaking his head. "That won't work, it'll just turn the attention on you."

"Better me than you, I've only got one strike, you already have three, plus the one they don't know about, the big one, ours. They would have run you out already if you didn't clear so many tough cases, we're both on borrowed time. I can take one more hit if I have to. And I won't have to, I'll tell them I didn't do it. Some good Samaritan intervened, some stranger, he ran off as I was arriving, I was too focused on the woman to get a good look at him."

"That's a bullshit story."

"That everyone will want to believe, with the mood the public is in they'd rather believe that than hear a story about some heroic cop, they'd think it was just spin to take attention away from the fact that we almost killed them."

"*I* almost killed them."

"*We.* We're in this together, like that other time, like always."

"It'll never work. What if the Marine tells a different story?"

"What's he going to say? He had a seven inch Tanto and some civilian punched both their lights out?"

"I'm no civilian."

"Did you identify yourself?"

Winter couldn't remember. "I'm not sure."

"He'll never admit any of it anyway. And look at me, he's going to say that I beat him up? I don't have a mark on me."

Winter tried one last time. "He'll say you held a gun on him."

"On two of them, with a hysterical woman grabbing at me? I'll take my chances."

Winter gave in. Brooker was right, about everything. This whole thing had taken maybe two minutes, and yet, like a car accident, it could change his entire life. He'd owe Brooker, again, but because he'd never recognize a debt himself if the situation had been reversed, he didn't say anything. But he was keeping count.

"Let me at least stay long enough to watch these two while you call it in."

Brooker pulled out his cell phone. "No signal, must be the garage. I'll carry her out and make the call. Better she not come to and see you, you look as bad as those two. Although still fast for an old man, taking out two guys who outweigh you by a ton."

Winter touched his forehead, the pain setting in. "Not fast enough."

"How's the cut?"

"I've had worse."

"Get it cleaned up, you can't keep using the excuse of falling in the shower."

"The time I did fall in the shower no one believed me."

"See? Look what you got for telling the truth. Just help me get her up."

"Leave her," said Winter. "You're in no shape to be carrying her."

"Shit, she's like a hundred twenty pounds."

"When's the last time you did a hundred and twenty deadlift?"

Brooker shrugged. "This isn't all flab, you know."

"About that. It's time for a diet."

"You sound like the wife I don't have. I'll run out of the garage and make the call."

"First deadlifting, then running, what are you, some kind of Olympiad all of a sudden?"

"And here I was worried about you being in pain," said Brooker, heading down the stairs. He turned at the doorway. "Try not to kick anyone while I'm gone."

CHAPTER 12

MELANIE WAS DYING FOR another cigarette, her last one gone an hour ago, sticking her head out the window so Gigi wouldn't smell the smoke when she came home from work. If Melanie had known the cops would take so long to show up she could have run out to the store. Where the fuck where they, anyway? The cops were useless, what if she really *had* been assaulted?

She'd used the time to practice her lines, building on her quickly concocted scheme. It had some holes, but she could pull it off. Act a little shocked, out of it, drop a few hints, a mix of anger and embarrassment. She didn't bother with a mirror, mirrors forced you into exaggerated facial expressions, this wasn't the stage, you had to *feel* it.

Melanie had never been assaulted by a stranger. Any man who might have overcome her confident vibe and tried anything she would have kicked in the nuts or far worse. Yet she knew the anger, the same anger she'd felt when the teenage boy had touched Gigi. She could call it up in a heartbeat, give her the adrenaline rush.

She still wasn't sure what had happened to Gigi. The apartment had broken into for sure. But the story about a man in the bed, that could have been a bad dream. Gigi had seemed fine. If someone had in fact touched Gigi, and Melanie found out who it was, she wouldn't bother calling the cops, she'd take care of it herself.

Since the cops were coming, though, she'd use it to her advantage. No sense in wasting an opportunity, and she'd meant what she had said to Gigi. No reason for her little sister to get dragged into this, especially if it were nothing.

The doorbell chimed. Finally. Melanie took a moment to get into the role, and went to open the door.

MARTIN RYDER IMPATIENTLY drummed his fingers on the steering wheel while simultaneously flicking through his notes. He'd been parked in front of the Lakeview apartment complex for almost fifteen minutes, having arrived punctually. The squad car that was supposed to be here was now twelve minutes late.

Ryder was pissed not only at the lack of respect that showed him, but on how it reflected on the police department. The police, both detectives like himself and uniformed officers, were there to serve the citizens. By being late, the cops were disrespecting the woman who had called the police. The woman's time was as important as theirs was.

He bet himself fifty bucks that it would be one of the older guard who showed up in the patrol car, just putting in their twenty, hardened and cold to the citizens they were sworn to protect. Ryder fought this attitude every day, even in the detective squad. The fact that he was the newest and youngest member, still treated as an outsider, didn't help. He wasn't sure he wanted to actually be part of that club anyway.

Hell, he'd been told that one of the reasons they wanted him in Marburg was to change the culture, bring in a new, enlightened approach to law enforcement. Those were the mayor's exact words. For the mayor to have to get involved in recruiting new police officers was an indictment of the entire force.

The report didn't say anything different from the first three times he had read it. A woman, unnamed, had called 911 about an overnight break-in with a possible assault. Normally that would have led to a squad car being immediately dispatched, along with a detective. But Marburg was too small for twenty four hour detective shifts, and the woman had been rather vague about the assault, which had lowered the priority enough that he hadn't been dragged out of bed. The 911 call hadn't been transcribed into the report, and Ryder hadn't waited to hear the recording, wanting to get here as soon as possible.

His shift had just started and this was by far the best possible case he could be working on today. He would handle the assault report, if there was one, and the uniforms would deal with the break-in.

If they ever showed up.

Eight minutes later, a blue and white pulled to the curb, parking in front of a fire hydrant even though there was an open spot not fifty feet away. Ryder automatically checked his hair in the visor mirror, got out of the car, buttoned his suit coat, and walked to the squad car.

Only one cop inside, not especially surprising, the department cutting back routine day calls to one officer to save money. Ryder recognized him, a guy named Burkett, a big bellied, red faced veteran who Ryder suspected drank on the job. Burkett was on the radio, or pretending to be, just to make Ryder wait for him.

Ryder thought about tapping on the window, pointing out the hydrant to Burkett. He didn't need to park there, it was no emergency, and besides, it would do Burkett good to walk the extra steps, he certainly could use the exercise. But the uniforms didn't report to him, what was he going to do if Burkett ignored him? Suggest that Burkett write himself a ticket?

This was the kind of insolence Ryder would fix if he made it to chief.

Burkett finally finished with his likely phantom call and pried himself out of the undersized blue and white, a small consolation for Ryder, Burkett having to squeeze himself into the smaller, cheaper cars the department now used.

"Officer Burkett," said Ryder, deciding to be civil, take the high road, no need to antagonize Burkett as they were about to see the citizen.

"Ryder." Burkett hitched up his utility belt, which promptly slid back down under his protruding stomach.

"I'd appreciate it if you refer to me as Detective Ryder while we are with the citizen," said Ryder, fighting to keep his voice flat.

Burkett shrugged. "Whatever. She probably won't notice, she's likely a 10-50 anyway."

"How do you know that?" 10-50 was the local radio code for under the influence, usually referring to drugs, but Marburg police and the sheriff's office used it to also mean drunk. Ryder hated the 10 codes, another relic of the private club of yesterday's policing.

"I talked to Millie."

The possible drug aspect wasn't in the report, which bothered Ryder, but on the other hand it also helped explain why a squad hadn't been dispatched immediately by Millie, the 911 operator.

Burkett took a few steps up the walk. Ryder couldn't help himself. "You left your hat in the car."

Burkett turned, looked like he was going to say something, then pushed past Ryder on the narrow walk, forcing Ryder to half skip to avoid stepping on some flowers. Burkett took his time getting his hat out of the cruiser, and without a word pushed by Ryder again, Ryder having no choice but to follow, since there wasn't room for both of them on the walkway.

Burkett rang the bell, and when the door opened Ryder involuntarily took a step back. The woman who answered was wickedly attractive, dressed in tight yoga pants and a loose top, braless, her hair a little disheveled, sexy rather than unkempt. Mid twenties, highlighted light brown hair, barefoot. Ryder fought his urge to stare, she was that hot.

"Thank god you're here!" the woman breathed, making it sound as though two supermen had answered her frantic summons, arriving just in time to save her life. Her tone sent a message right to Ryder's pituitary gland, a rush of instant testosterone forcing him to square his shoulders. Burkett hitched up his belt so high he looked like a blimp.

"Yes, maam, miss, we're with the police, you called 911," Ryder feeling like an idiot, babbling the obvious.

The woman didn't notice, or pretended she didn't, and let them in, leading them into the living room, her ass tightly outlined in the form fitting stretch pants, Ryder silently cursing Burkett's view blocking girth.

"Maybe I shouldn't have bothered you at all," she was saying, "I was just *so* upset, I didn't know what to do."

Ryder finally made it past Burkett, just as the woman turned. She held her hand over her chest protectively, which only served to draw Ryder's eyes there. He felt, rather than saw, Burkett hitch up his belt yet again.

"That's why we're here, maam." Burkett's voice had deepened. "Why don't you just sit down and tell us what happened."

Ryder should have been leading the interview, but he was uncharacteristically tongue tied, his only coherent thought was that this woman shouldn't be called *maam*, the term just didn't fit. He stood next to Burkett as the woman sat on the edge of the sofa.

Ryder finally found his voice. "This is Officer Burkett. I'm Detective Ryder." He extracted a card and handed it to her, taking the opportunity to get a good look at her eyes. She didn't look inebriated or high. "What is your name?"

"Melanie Doyle Upton. Doyle is my real name, I go by Melanie Upton, I'm an actress."

"Please tell me about the burglary," said Burkett.

Ryder frowned, the burglary would have less priority than the possible assault. But before he had a chance to reply the woman was already talking.

"I was just so *mad* at first. Someone coming into my personal space. But nothing seems to have been taken."

"You reported a possible assault?" Ryder reached for his notepad, his eyes still glued on the woman.

Upton twirled her hair. "I didn't really say that someone *assaulted* me," she said. "I shouldn't have even mentioned it."

"Why don't you start at the beginning," said Ryder, trying to take control of the interview. He didn't remember ever being so flustered when taking a statement. Upton, while not the most beautiful woman he had ever seen, oozed distracting sensuality.

"Well, when I woke up I noticed that my stuff was all out of place, I think someone had gone through my purse, and the door was open, I can't believe I would have left it unlocked before going to bed, it's not the best neighborhood."

Ryder looked up from his notepad. "So the man might have come in the door?"

"I assume so, or he could have just followed me upstairs."

"Followed you? Was it someone you had seen earlier?"

Upton looked away, embarrassed. "That's kind of personal, do we have to talk about that?"

"If someone touched you inappropriately, it doesn't matter if you knew him or not," said Ryder. "Just tell us what happened."

"I'm not even sure *anything* happened." Her eyes dropped. Sheepishly, she added, "He might have just, you know, not been able to control himself."

Ryder was having problems controlling himself too, and the woman's ambivalence wasn't helping him focus. Something she had said finally clicked. "You said he might have followed you upstairs? We didn't come up any stairs."

"Yes, up to my apartment, I had a *really* busy day, I had taken a sleeping pill, I was a little out of it, and I'd had a few drinks—"

"I'm sorry," said Ryder, ignoring Burkett's *I told you so* look about the 10-50; a citizen admitting to a cop that they'd had *a few drinks* usually meant they were drunk. "Can we come back to the stairs?"

The woman looked confused, which on her gave off a *please help me* vibe rather than a vacuous one. "What about them?"

"There are no stairs here," said Ryder.

"Here? This didn't happen here, it happened at my apartment."

"This isn't your apartment?"

"No, this is my sister's place. I live over on Third."

Ryder shook his head, feeling as confused as the woman looked. "But you made the 911 call from here, didn't you?"

"Oh that." Upton brightened. "You see, I was so upset that I called my sister—we're really close—she told me to come right over, I didn't feel safe at my place. I wasn't going to call you at all, I've been broken into before, you know, the neighborhood, but my sister said it was the right thing to do."

"Your sister, where is she?" asked Ryder, looking around the spotlessly empty apartment.

"She's at work. She offered to stay, but I didn't want to get her in trouble, being late and all."

Ryder looked at his muddled notes, not at all like him, normally he was methodical in his questions, something he was proud of. Citizens, especially crime victims, usually tangled their stories, and only a step by step interview would serve to sort out the facts. But even he was all mixed up, he'd have to rewrite everything. "What's your sister's name?"

"Do we have to get her involved in this?"

"It's just for the report, we have to say where we responded."

"Gigi."

"Gigi Doyle?"

"Yes."

"So the break-in didn't happen here?" asked Burkett. "We need to go to where the burglary occurred, that's where you should have called it in from."

"What Officer Burkett means," said Ryder, "is that when a burglary occurs, we usually get the call from that location and that's what we need to see for out investigation."

"I don't think anything was taken," said Upton, "so there might not even be a burglary."

"It's a burglary either way," said Burkett. "You see, maam, according to the law—"

Ryder interrupted. "I'm sure Miss, I'm sorry, is it Miss?" When the woman nodded, he went on, "Miss Upton doesn't need to know the details of what constitutes a legal burglary. Miss Upton, can we return to the man? You said," he wished he had brought in the notes from the 911 call, "that you had been assaulted when you were sleeping?"

Upton looked away again. "Not exactly. Like I said, I'd taken a pill, I might have imagined it."

"But you had been with someone earlier?"

"Yes, a friend of mine."

"What's his name?"

"I don't think we have to get him involved, I can't imagine he had anything to do with this, he likes me a lot." Upton hesitated, as if reconsidering. "No, not him."

"Is this a close friend?"

Upton blushed. "We'd been close in the past, we were just getting—reacquainted. He had been out of town for a while."

Ryder's mind filling in the blanks, Upton saying nothing but implying everything. "So this friend, he could be the one you—believe touched you when you were sleeping?"

"Oh, I don't think so. He'd have no reason to—I mean, he does sometimes have a hard time controlling himself when he's with me, but—"

"He's violent?" prodded Ryder.

"Oh, no, not *that*," said Upton. "I meant, you know, his urges, male urges, men like you would understand." Upton crossed her slim legs, Ryder certainly getting the message.

"Miss Upton, in cases like these, especially when," Ryder was about to say *when there are drugs and alcohol involved*, but caught himself, "when someone doesn't remember everything clearly, it's a good idea to check all the possibilities. I strongly suggest that you go to the hospital and have a SAFE exam." Ryder used the technical anagram, he hated the term *rape kit.*

"What's that?"

"A collection of possible evidence of a sexual assault."

Upton shook her head. "I really don't think that's necessary."

"Still, it's a good idea. Just in case."

"I don't think I was raped, not really, if that's what you are thinking."

Ryder pushed on. "And we need the name of this man you were with."

"I don't want to get him in trouble, He's—pretty famous, or will be soon."

Ryder had seen this before, a rich and powerful guy, taking what he wanted, browbeating a woman into silence with his money and position. "That doesn't mean he gets to—take advantage of you."

"What's this test all about?"

"It's perfectly safe, a special nurse at the hospital will check you for—evidence of an assault." Ryder had worked only a few sexual assault cases, he didn't have enough experience to know how the victims reacted. He'd heard that it could range from anger to shock to repressed disbelief or even denial.

Upton sighed. "If you think it's best, Detective—," she glanced at Ryder's card on the coffee table. "Ryder."

"I do. And the man's name?" Ryder's pen was poised.

"I still think nothing happened. Probably. So why don't we hold off on that?" said Upton. "Like I said, I don't want to get him in trouble."

"We'll need to go to your apartment to make the burglary report," said Burkett.

"If you say so, I guess. Now?"

"After you go to the hospital," said Ryder.

"Okay, okay, if you insist," said Upton. "I'm still not sure anything happened." She wrapped her arms around her chest.

Ryder picked up the defensiveness in her posture and her voice. He had no doubt she was protecting someone.

"We'll take you to the hospital," he said. "Officer Burkett and I will then go to your apartment, with your consent, and do a search."

"Is that necessary? I told you nothing was taken."

"It's just a precaution," said Ryder. "Do we have your permission?" He really didn't need her permission if a crime had occurred, but given the vagueness of Upton's statements, it was better to be safe than sorry.

Upton hesitated. "I guess so."

"Does anyone else have access to your apartment now? Someone who might have gone there since you left?"

"No, not unless they broke in again."

"Okay, please get whatever you need."

"I have my own car."

"It's better if we drive you." Ryder wanted an opportunity to talk to her away from Burkett, maybe get her comfortable enough to tell him about the mystery man. "We'll have an officer drive you back here."

"How long will it take? I have to go to work later this afternoon."

"Not long, an hour or two." Sexual assaults were pretty rare in Marburg, Ryder was sure he could get the SAFE test and examination done quickly.

"Can we stop for some cigarettes?" asked Upton.

"You won't be able to smoke in the car or the hospital," said Ryder. "Besides, we need to—preserve any evidence."

Upton got up. "Let's get this over with."

MELANIE HAD NEVER BEEN in a police cruiser before. She was hoping that's how they'd get to the hospital, even if it meant riding with the fat cop. But the good looking detective guided her toward a brown sedan. She thought maybe she'd have to ride in the back, but he opened the front door for her.

On the drive to the hospital the detective tried to pry more information out of her, but Melanie had played her hand as planned, deftly, she thought, letting the cop suspect that something had happened, without her really saying any such thing. She needed to keep him on the fence, just in case Jason wouldn't listen to reason.

She wasn't especially worried about Detective Ryder; she'd caught him looking at her legs, her body, certain he bought the story of some mystery suitor not being able to control himself, maybe stepping over the line. Melanie had also played the helpless confused ditz, a character the cops had likely seen in similar cases. All in all, it was a pretty good performance, if she did say so herself.

She glanced over at Ryder, who was trying to drive and look at her at the same time. He was cute, probably early forties, in good shape. Melanie didn't have the thing for cops that some women did, drawn to their confidence. This one, he was different, no swagger, overly polite, bordering on nerdy. She'd had to keep from laughing as he had struggled to write notes, purposely jumping topics to keep him off balance.

The other one she'd mostly ignored. She met a lot of cops like him, trying to impress her with their uniforms, their guns. She'd been stopped a few times for speeding, a couple of possible DUI's, all of which she talked herself out of, the cops letting her off with a warning, but usually giving her their number as well, everyone playing the game.

No, neither cop would be a problem.

The hospital test could be, she should have showered, like she'd made Gigi. Would some of Taz's DNA be on her? Could they match it to anything? She doubted Taz had been arrested, but who knew, she wasn't sure what kinds of arrests led to DNA collection. And anyway, so what if they did? She could always claim she'd been with him earlier in the evening, it was true anyway.

She settled back, crossed her legs as elegantly as possible in the car, and smiled as she caught Ryder turning his head to watch.

*   *   *

"DAMN, ANYTHING COULD have happened here." Officer Burkett, hands on his wide hips, stood in the doorway of Melanie Upton's apartment.

"Have some respect, she could be a victim," said Ryder, although he had to agree. The apartment was a disaster zone, clothes, magazines, shoes everywhere, the place looked like the after affects of a college party.

"Victim? Is that what you were thinking when you were checking her out?"

"What's that supposed to mean?"

"You know what I mean," said Burkett. "She's some piece of ass."

"Watch your mouth," said Ryder, feeling his cheeks flush, turning away. "Andie will be here in a minute, don't let me hear you talk like that in front of her. Or anyone."

"Aye-aye, captain."

Ryder didn't think Burkett meant it for a minute, but he let it go for now, hearing Andie coming up the steps.

Andie, the crime tech, or as close as Marburg had to one, still in training, taking certification courses in Boston. Ryder had worked with her before, she was young but good, methodical, like he was. Today, as usual, she wore khaki pants and a blue denim shirt with Marburg PD embroidered on the chest, her blond hair in a short pony tail, a camera slung over her shoulder, her identification clipped to her belt.

"Detective Ryder," she said. "What do we have?"

Ryder told her what they knew, a little embarrassed at how few specifics he had. Andie didn't seem to notice, she was already looking into the room, peering past Burkett. "We were waiting for you before going in. The possible victim gave us permission to enter and the key."

"Okay," said Andie. "Please wait here while I secure a path for you, unless you feel the need to check the other rooms."

Ryder had already thought of that, the bath door partially closed, the bedroom out of sight. The entrance door lock was flimsy but didn't appear to have been forced. They hadn't heard a sound, and Upton had said the place was empty. Still, one couldn't be too careful. "I'd like to go in far enough to see into the bedroom, and push the bathroom door all the way open. You good with that?"

"Sure, let me just get a few shots from here. Officer Burkett, would you mind?"

"Sure honey, go ahead."

Ryder was about to jump on Burkett's condescending comment, stopped, wondering what was worse: letting a man get away with that, or stepping in, implying the woman couldn't take care of herself.

Andie saved him. "I put honey in my tea, officer. You look like an herbal tea drinker, you need some honey, is that what you mean?"

"I don't drink herbal tea," said Burkett, but he moved aside.

"Pity," said Andie, already snapping photos. "You should try some chamomile, calm you down." She moved aside. "Don't touch anything."

Ryder stepped forward, but Burkett was ahead of him, his gun out. "I got this, Detective," said Burkett, a little bluster in his voice.

Not to be outdone, Ryder said, "You clear the bedroom, I'll take the bathroom." He drew his gun, took three steps into the apartment, then waited for Burkett to get ready by the other doorway. "Go."

Ryder pushed the bath door open and stepped back, hoping Burkett still remembered enough police tactics to clear a room. The small bathroom was empty, the shower curtain wide open, not enough space for anyone to hide.

"Clear," said Burkett. "Of people, anyway. There's more shit in here than in the living room."

Which was also true of what Ryder could see of the bathroom. Burkett had been right. Anything could have happened here.

CHAPTER 13

LENNY WALKED BY THE entrance to the restaurant for the third time. He knew Melanie was inside, he'd been sitting in his car down the street for hours, and watched her go in. Now all he had to do was pull the trigger.

He'd forced himself to wait a week since he had been at Melanie's apartment. The first few days he'd hardly slept, in disbelief for not being able to finish what he had started, his manhood failing him when he most needed it. Frustration turned to anger, Melanie not responding the way he wanted, not helping, not accepting him. Then fear, the cops would show up, Melanie claiming he'd raped her. He took to hiding in the attic apartment; suffering the relentless questioning of his mother was better than being on the street. He went three days without a shower because he was afraid he wouldn't be able to hear the police pounding at the door over the running water.

When the cops didn't show up he concluded there were only two possibilities. Either Melanie hadn't recognized him, or she had and not only wasn't upset, but was pleasantly surprised. Her knowing it was him was by far the preferable of the two, so he simply stopped thinking of it as a break-in. If Melanie had known him better, she would have invited him in for sure.

Since that change in his frame of mind, Lenny relived that visit every night, during the day even, the smell of Melanie's hair, the feeling of her body. He'd rerun the movie in his head, different outcomes, getting it just right. The kiss, his hands on her, Melanie moaning . . . all of them ending the same way, Lenny the stallion,

Melanie succumbing to his power, accepting him.

Now that he'd had a taste of what was in store he couldn't hold back much longer. Not only being with Melanie, but becoming partners too. They'd be a perfect fit. He'd manage her career during the day, and they'd have their nights together. Lenny would help her get some good roles, they could move to LA. Lenny could impress Melanie with his local knowledge, where to hang out, where to eat. They'd get an apartment, no, a house, up in the Hollywood Hills or even Calabasas. Malibu was so last decade.

After waiting all week he worried that he was too late, Melanie might have already parlayed the photo from the press conference into a role. She needed to believe her opportunity came from the idea Lenny had given to her. Okay, she'd stolen it, but the result was the same.

And then there was the visit to her bedroom.

On the off chance Melanie really hadn't recognized him, Lenny needed to get her to connect him with that night, even more than connecting him with the photo idea. He just couldn't figure out the best way. Coming right out and saying it wouldn't be good, he'd have to play it cool, let Melanie draw the conclusion. Where to approach her? Getting her alone would be hard. His last attempts in public hadn't worked so well, her having to put on airs in front of everyone. He was convinced now that's all it was, seeing how passive she'd been when he got her alone in the bedroom. She was just an insecure little girl, all bluster, needing a man like him to help her bloom.

The restaurant seemed the safest bet, she couldn't very well brush off a customer.

MELANIE DUMPED THE TUB of dirty dishes in the kitchen, not caring whether anything broke. This was going to be her last day working in this shithole. She'd only come to the restaurant today to pick up her paycheck, but her asshole boss Lyn told her that she hadn't given notice, and if Melanie didn't work another week the restaurant didn't have to pay her anything, it was in the employment papers she'd signed. Like she'd read them.

She'd be out of this shitty job, out of Marburg, any day now. The calls had already started to come in, the press asking about *Shock and Awe*, a few casting call invites. It was happening.

All Melanie needed to do now was play it cool, pick and choose. And get a handle on Jason, just in case. She now had a knife she could hold against Jason's throat if he tried to mess with her. She hadn't seen him at the club or the hotel, even though he still had a room. Probably hanging in Boston, avoiding her. If she didn't see him tonight she'd call him.

She'd also been thinking about how interested the police had been about who might have attacked her. That could be a goldmine. Not for the police, but for her. What if the gossip rags got wind of a hot actor like Jason being so infatuated with her he couldn't control himself? Another card to play.

The possibilities were endless.

Feeling better now, good thoughts to get her through her shift.

Tiffany, the hostess, stuck her head through the swinging door. "Mel, customer. Says he's a friend. I put him in your section even though you're not up."

Melanie, still focused on what calls she was going to take, said, "Who is it?"

"I don't know. Remember I'm doing you a favor, Julie will be all over my ass for skipping her."

Tiffany waited a beat before disappearing back into the dining area, making it clear that she expected Melanie to kick back some of the tip to her, even though it was Julie who was getting stiffed. "Screw you, bitch," said Melanie.

Melanie was about to follow Tiffany when she realized that the customer might be a reporter who had tracked her down, or even a local agent. She took a minute to check out her hair in the safety mirror on the wall, useless, the mirror curved and scratched. Not that it mattered, she looked like shit, who could look good bussing tables?

She swung through the doors, trying not to appear eager, already thinking up a story about how she'd explain why she was still at work instead of getting ready for a show. But instead of someone important, the only new customer in her section was that loser Lenny. He was staring at her like a deer in headlights, his leg twitching as if he was going to bolt.

Melanie caught Tiffany smiling, a big joke. *'You'll get yours,'* Melanie mouthed.

Tiffany hid her hand behind the hostess station and gave Melanie the finger.

Melanie ignored Lenny. Just because Tiffany sat him in her section didn't mean she had to serve him. She stopped at her other occupied table, chatting it up, looking out for Julie, she could dump Lenny on her. Julie was nowhere to be seen, but the owner, Jake, was having a drink at the bar, watching her.

When Melanie put in a drink order, Jake, an ex mall cop who liked to push his weight around, jerked his head at Lenny. "Mel, don't leave that customer waiting too long."

"Julie is up."

"He's in your section."

"Tiffany fucked up again."

"Watch the language around the customers."

"What customers? I just see you drinking away the profits."

Jake scoffed. "I know what you're trying to do. You're trying to get me to fire you so you won't have to work your shifts to get your check. I've been onto you since the start."

"In your dreams. Just because Lyn's letting you have some doesn't mean you know me."

Jake swallowed his drink. "Just handle the customer, okay?"

Melanie was too tired to bother with him. She'd get Lenny to leave on his own.

"And Mel? If Julie really was up, make sure you kick back something to her on the tip. You can't just go around taking advantage of people."

Melanie gave him the finger behind her back as she crossed over to Lenny. Today he was wearing a black fake silk shirt, three buttons open, bling on a chain, looking like a cast off from Miami Vice. He was still bouncing in his chair, watching her every move, yet cringing as she got closer, like he wasn't quite sure what to expect. She greeted him with, "What the fuck are you doing here?"

Lenny bit his lip like a five year old who was trying not to blurt out that he had just raided the cookie jar. Melanie turned away, she didn't need this.

"What does it look like I'm doing? I'm here to talk to you."

Lenny looked his usual jerk self but his voice was different, not quite matching his demeanor, a little cocky, and more subdued than when he had accosted her at the hotel bar. "I'm working," she said.

"We could do this somewhere more private. Your place?"

"This is as close as you'll ever get to my place."

Lenny smiled. "I'll never tell."

"Bullshit. You ever get near a woman's place you'd be bragging about it to all your friends. That is, if you had any."

Lenny picked up a menu. "Then I'll eat. You gotta talk to your customers."

"You going to make another crybaby scene? Maybe I should clear anything breakable off the table?"

"You can't rattle me anymore, Mel. I know you now."

First Jake and now Lenny. "You don't know shit about me. Just give me your order, eat, and get the fuck out."

Lenny's eyes twitched. "Not a very nice way to treat a man who you've—you know."

"You don't need me to have a conversation with yourself. Are you going to order or not?" Lenny frowned, Melanie thinking something about him was off, even more than the other times she had seen him. Not that she cared.

"You owe me big time," said Lenny. "You know, the idea about the photo."

"Not that again. Get over it."

Lenny grinned, Melanie wondering what was up. This wasn't the same guy who'd run crying out of the hotel bar.

"Maybe I already am, Mel. After what we've shared."

Melanie calculated her ability to get her remaining pay if she slapped Lenny silly right then. She'd feel better for a few minutes, and even that might have been enough if she'd been owed only for a few days. But two weeks pay, she needed the cash. She leaned over Lenny, sticking her chest practically in his face, waiting for him to look down, and sure enough, he did, his face flushing.

"I wouldn't share a used stick of gum with you." She stood up, smiling sweetly for Jake's benefit in case he was still watching. "Now what would you like to eat?"

"You sure blow hot and cold. You give a guy really mixed messages, did you know that?"

Maybe he really *was* slow, thought Melanie. "Where are you reading hot anywhere?"

"So you really don't remember—." Lenny bit his lip again. "Don't push me, Mel. Or maybe I *will* tell people."

"Tell them what? You're a stalking psycho?"

"I'll tell them the truth. About the photo. About you."

"And what makes you think anyone will give a shit what you say?"

"See? You do care. I bet you got some calls already. Admit it, my idea worked. Would it hurt you so much to toss something my way?"

First Tiffany wanting a piece of her tips, and now him. Everyone wanted something from her. Melanie didn't need the aggravation, there were more important things to concentrate on. "What do I have to do to get rid of you?"

Lenny brightened. "How about dinner? We could sit and talk."

"About what?"

"About your future. Our future."

"Our entire future is going to last about thirty minutes. That's the time it should take you to eat and get out of my life."

"Why do you treat me like this? I know you aren't like this all the time. Like when you're alone."

"Like you know."

"I know you have another side. You know I can help you like I already did."

Shit, the guy just didn't give up. "There's nothing you can do for me."

"I could surprise you—again."

"What are you babbling about?"

"You're a smart girl, you figure it out."

Melanie had no idea what he was talking about. Did he mean his raving at the hotel? "I'm in no mood today, believe me. Just give me your order, okay?"

Lenny looked like he was going to say something else, but then smiled and said, "I'll have the breakfast special."

"It's too late for breakfast."

"I'm sure you can get them to make an exception for me. Is the cook a guy? I bet you can get a guy to do anything for you."

Except get rid of you. Melanie thought about it for a second, wondering if it would be worth it, see if the cook would throw Lenny out right in front of the owner. Another time it might be fun to see, but not today. "Fine. I'll get you the breakfast special. How do you want your eggs?"

"Over easy," said Lenny, drawing out the word *easy*. He laughed. "Just like the way things are going to be for you. And us."

Melanie wrote down the order. Had another thought and turned back to Lenny. "You know, if you want easy, there's someone else here who wants you bad. Better than wasting time on me."

Lenny's head spun like a top. "Who?"

Melanie flicked her eyes to the hostess station. "Tiffany, up front. She made it a point of telling me how hot you looked when you came in. She actually wanted to serve you herself."

"Did she?"

"Really. She gets off in twenty minutes. If you eat fast, you can catch her."

Lenny looked at her suspiciously. "You wouldn't shit me, would you?"

Melanie raised her hand. "I swear."

"She's not as good looking as you."

"So here I am helping you out like you wanted, and you're complaining?"

Lenny shrugged. "Maybe I don't want her."

"You know, women love a guy who gets lots of other women. It's a competitive thing. You make it with Tiffany, I'll think more of you, and maybe we can have that dinner."

Lenny's head swung back and forth between Melanie and Tiffany, Melanie feeling the need to pinch herself to keep from laughing, this was the hardest acting job she'd ever done.

"Hurry up with my order," said Lenny.

Melanie spun for the kitchen, wondering what that was all about, Lenny acting like he knew her. He had as much chance of having dinner and seeing the inside of her apartment as Tiffany did.

*   *   *

THE COFFEE MAKER BEEPED and Melanie poured herself a cup, more to keep herself busy; Gigi only had decaf in the apartment. Melanie never understood why people drank decaf.

Gigi was staring blankly out the back door window, as she had been for the last twenty minutes.

"Sure you don't want a cup?" Melanie asked.

"No, thanks."

Melanie dumped two sugars into her coffee, if she wasn't going to get the caffeine she might as well get the rush. Thought about adding a third. She grabbed the skin over her hip, not much fat there, she wanted to look good for the shoots that would be coming soon. She could afford another sugar.

She sipped the coffee on the way to the small dining table. "Why don't you come over here and sit."

"I can't believe someone was right *out there*."

"No one is there now. Come on, it's no use staring out the window."

Gigi sat across from Mel, hugging herself, disappearing into her oversized sweater. Melanie had already comforted Gigi, now was the time to get her over it.

"I feel so guilty," said Gigi.

"About what? You haven't done anything wrong."

"This whole thing is turning into one big lie."

"You worry too much."

Gigi leaned forward. "And you don't worry enough. About anything! For God's sake, Mel, this is serious!"

"There's nothing to worry about. Trust me. I've got this all worked out."

"I haven't even told the apartment manager about the break-in yet."

"No." Melanie didn't raise her voice, Gigi had to understand why instead of being told. "You can't tell them anything about this. They'll call the cops, they'd come *here*."

"But I *have* to tell them. What if the burglar is out there right now and he's planning to go after another apartment? We have to warn the other residents."

Melanie's first instinct was to suggest that it wasn't a burglar, since nothing had been taken. But the alternative, that a man had come in to harm her sister, was even worse, and she didn't want that thought in Gigi's mind.

Melanie had already called John, the last guy she'd had over to Gigi's. She'd woken him up, he was in Europe, and according to him, had been for a week. He swore he barely remembered that night. Melanie had driven them in her car, and he'd been pretty high. She hung up and immediately called his office, asking for him, and was told he was overseas. He worked for a big law firm; Melanie didn't think he'd be likely to have a burglar buddy.

Maybe Gigi had dreamt the whole thing. She could have heard the break-in, her mind filling in the blanks, weirded out by the pills. "Gigi, is there some guy who you've been interested in? Attracted to?" *Having fantasies about?*

"No, why?"

"You know, someone you might have been—dreaming about."

Gigi, incredulous. "You think I made this up?"

"No, no, not at all. I believe you. I'm just trying to see if the break-in and—what you remembered from that night were the same."

Gigi hugged herself tighter. "I was really groggy."

"So there's no one you've had the hots for? It's okay, there's nothing wrong with a little fantasy now and then."

"It didn't seem like anyone I knew."

"Okay." Melanie needed another approach. Gigi thought the guy might have been in bed with her, but who would go that far and not do anything? More likely Gigi had dreamt the whole thing, a fantasy dream about a man she knew, someone who didn't want to hurt her, a guy without the guts to ask her out. What was it Gigi thought he had said? That when he saw her *again,* they'd do it for real. Sure sounded like someone she knew. "Gigi, is there some guy you've—been hoping would ask you out? Or did some guy ask you out and you turned him down?"

"You think someone might be after me?" Gigi shrunk down farther into her sweater.

"No, that's not what I meant. Just—someone on your mind." Melanie stopped herself from adding *someone you wanted to surprise you.*

Gigi shook her head vehemently. "I can't think of anyone."

"Who was the last guy you dated?"

"Evan Schmidt. My friend Susie introduced me to him. We had dinner a few times."

"When was that?"

"Last summer."

"Jesus, Gigi, you haven't had a date since last summer?"

"I'm pretty busy. I don't really have time."

Melanie again wondered if they shared the same genes. "You gotta get out more. What happened to this Evan? Did he want more and you turned him down?"

"No, he was a real gentleman. I liked him, but he moved away. I haven't spoken to him in six months."

Melanie hadn't met many real gentlemen, but if one could be found it would be Gigi who would do it. "Okay, so probably not Evan. Anyone else?"

"No. It had to have been a burglar. That's why I've got to warn everyone."

"Gigi, *listen* to me. If you do, the police will be suspicious that my sister got broken into the same night I got broken into." *I'd be fucked,* thought Melanie. *I won't be able to leverage this at all.* "If they found out I'd not told them the truth, I'd get in trouble."

"You shouldn't have done that."

"I was protecting *you.* You really don't want this coming out at the office. A break-in, sure, that would be okay. But you told the police you might have been attacked. Do you want everyone whispering behind your back at work, there's the girl who got assaulted?"

"I don't think they would say that."

"I know you always think the best of people, but they can be mean. You remember how those boys were when you were young. You know what happened to those boys? They grew up into *men*. And a lot of women aren't any better. They'll make up stories about you. Anyone who is jealous of you, anyone who doesn't want to admit you get ahead because of your hard work, believe me, they'll do anything to take you down."

Gigi started crying, the last thing Mel wanted, she'd hoped to avoid playing hardball. But she had to get Gigi focused. She got up and wrapped her arms around her sister, pulling her close, giving her strength. Soothingly, she said, "I know you're upset, but you've got to try to think clearly. I'm going to take all of this off you. I'm going to make it so you can just forget it, like it never happened. I will deal with it. All of it."

Still sobbing, Gigi said, "What are you going to do?"

"I've already done the most important thing. Right now no one thinks anything happened here. Let's just keep it that way, okay? It will be better for you. And you'll be helping me too, by not getting me in trouble."

After a moment Gigi nodded, but Melanie continued to hold her until her sobs subsided. Melanie hated seeing her sister this way, Gigi didn't deserve this at all. Maybe the break-in had spurred the bad dream. Melanie reminded herself to take her pills back.

If Melanie caught whoever had broken in, she'd deal with him in her own way. The guy had probably thought the apartment was empty, had run off when he had seen Gigi. Or he was a pervert, peeking in windows.

"Listen. I don't want you to be nervous, but from now on, keep your eyes open."

Gigi looked up. "For what?"

"Just guys acting funny. Hanging around here, following you. Paying you lots of attention."

"You mean a *stalker*?"

"No, nothing like that," said Melanie quickly, but of course that's what she meant. "Just anyone who's acting weird, wanting to be with you." *Someone like that jerk Lenny,* she thought.

Lenny. This sounded exactly like him. Always coming back to her, even after she'd practically humiliated him. Talking like they were fuck buddies.

"Gigi," she asked casually. "Do you know a guy named Lenny? Grutz, Gruse, something like that."

"No, why?"

"Nothing. Just a jerk I ran into who's a little strange. Couldn't be him if he doesn't know you."

Besides, Lenny wouldn't have the balls.

CHAPTER 14

Robert Winter watched morosely as the catering staff at the Lexington Hotel set up the banquet room for the awards ceremony. A nasal voiced supervisor was barking orders—snorting orders, to be precise—even though the staff certainly appeared to know their jobs. All except one poor guy who looked clueless, a small boned Latino, constantly glancing to the other staff to see how to set the tables. That's how Winter would be, not knowing where the soup spoons should go, or even if there should *be* soup spoons.

Winter wasn't the only one who noticed the Latino's distress. The supervisor bore down on him like a bird of prey, or more like a waddling penguin, strutting in her too tight skirt and snappy heels across the room, the other workers skittering out of her path, sentient bowling pins avoiding the oncoming crash. Her hapless target backed up against the wall, frozen in place.

"I bet he wouldn't even look that afraid if it was Immigration coming," said a voice at his shoulder.

"Damn it, Beth, what are you doing here?"

"Nice to see you too, dear brother." She stood on her toes and kissed Winter on the cheek. Beth hadn't been blessed with the family gene of height.

"I didn't mean it that way." Winter hadn't seen Beth since, when? A funeral. For some reason he couldn't remember whose. "It's a long drive."

"I've been looking for an excuse to get into Boston, this was a good excuse."

Winter didn't believe that for a minute; Beth hated cities, even one as small as Boston, which is why she lived in some rural town in Pennsylvania. She'd come for him. "Why? No Starbucks in your hayseed town?"

Beth smiled up at him, fussing over his tie. "We do have a Starbucks, actually. And can you believe it—they're going to install something called electricity this year! But what I really came for was the Dunkin Donuts, one on every corner, it's just so cultured here."

Winter let her fuss, touched that she'd made the trip. "I hate these things," he said.

"The tie?"

"The reason for it." Winter flicked his hand toward the room. "The tie too."

"You're getting a big award, you should be proud. I know I am."

"It's all bullshit."

"I doubt they are going through all this for nothing. About time they gave you some credit."

Win gently pushed her hand away. "I don't need an award."

"How about Brooker? I hear he's getting one too. Speaking of which, where is the big guy?"

"He doesn't want to be here either. He threatened to not show up."

Beth tilted her head. "I don't get it. Some recognition can't hurt. Especially since Brooker caught some rapists, right?"

"Attempted rapists. And the word is they're going to sue the city for police brutality during the arrest."

"How can anything be more brutal than a rape?"

"That's a question with no good answer." Winter thought about telling her the truth, that it was he who stopped the attempted rapists, the two men in the airport stairway. But what would it serve? He didn't need Beth's, or anyone else's, recognition. "It's all political. The department is getting out ahead of the lawsuit, trying to put a good spin on the situation. Make the slimeballs look guilty, just out to save their skin."

"Are they?"

"Sure."

"Guilty or slimeballs?"

"Both. If they weren't, the department wouldn't take the risk." The department had wanted to be on the offensive, but chafed at giving the award to Brooker. He and Winter both had a long history of playing to the edge, and while that had been overlooked and even condoned years ago, it was a different time. But the woman who'd been saved in the stairway was related to a friend of the governor, and she'd been vocal about her savior getting recognition, even though she was a little hazy about the details of the rescue. That she'd been assaulted, though, was certain.

"It can't be all political, otherwise you wouldn't be getting an award too," said Beth.

"A bunch of us are, they went through the trouble to set up the room and everything, they need to get their money's worth."

"I'm sure it's more than that."

"Just more politics." Winter's award was for solving the series of random burglaries. His theory had been right. The burglars had been scoping out possible prey at the airport, returning from trips where they might have come into money. Another supposedly random case, not so random at all once you connected the dots. Closing a burglary case would be no reason for an award, especially for Winter, but one of the victims had turned out to be a retired law and order judge who had even more connections than the governor. The judge, a true lover of the limelight, couldn't comprehend why someone wouldn't want a public award, and that's why Winter was here.

What kind of crook was smart enough to plan and keep secret a series of high stakes burglaries, and yet didn't realize they were breaking into a judge's house? Another mystery, the mix of incredible smarts and mind boggling stupidity of crooks.

"Where's Audrey?" asked Beth.

"Ah, I didn't even bother to tell her about this. The traffic from the city . . ."

"At this time of the afternoon?"

"She's real busy, her job."

"You always make excuses for her."

This was an old conversation that Winter didn't want to have again. Beth knew that his daughter Audrey didn't like that Winter was a cop. Audrey hadn't always felt that way; Winter suspected that the last few years working with the elite in Boston had changed her.

The catering supervisor was still hovering over the Latino, her arms flailing like she held a whip, impressing upon everyone in the room who was really in charge, as if that would make them all work faster or better.

"What makes people act like that?" asked Winter.

"Insecurity. Making it clear she knows everything."

"Seems like that would make it worse, trying to pretend you're someone you're not."

"Not for everyone."

"If she's good, then she shouldn't need to remind everyone. If she isn't, she should just learn, or accept it. I can't sing, I don't go around pretending I can. It's a waste of energy."

"You're right."

"You agree with me?"

"You can't sing."

Winter smiled both at the truth and at how well Beth still knew his moods, that he'd need this lift.

"There's another reason," said Beth, indicating the supervisor. "She wants to point out supposed incompetence to disguise her own."

"How do you know she's incompetent?"

Beth turned to him. "If you had a rookie partner working with you and he didn't know the ropes, would you treat him like that?"

"God help me."

"That's because you know what you are doing, and are secure about it. You don't need to make a big show of what you know."

"I meant, god help me if I get a rookie."

Beth punched Winter on the arm. "Right."

"Speaking of partners, see if you can find Brooker, okay?"

"Where are you going?"

"To find out if I can keep that guy from being browbeaten to death in front of us."

"You can't save them all, you know."

Winter shrugged. "But I can try."

"You think she's going to assault him? Or he's going to assault her?"

"Actually, I was more worried about me. A few more minutes of watching this and I won't be responsible for my actions."

AT ANY OTHER TIME, the sight of an unsmiling Winter approaching might have scared the Latino into racing out the door, but in his current state his eyes pleaded like a puppy that had managed to get its head stuck in a picket fence.

The woman must have noticed the Latino's change in demeanor, or felt Winter's presence; she spun around. Winter got into her space, forcing her to shrink back. He jerked his head back toward the stage. "They don't seem to know how to work the sound system. Do you?"

The woman's eyes flittered away. "Of course."

Which was what Winter suspected, she'd never admit she didn't know anything. "They're going to need it for the run through."

"I'll take care of it," she said, already glancing past Winter.

"Good."

Winter waited for her to clear out before turning to the Latino. "Need some help?" he asked cheerfully, feeling better already.

"I'm not too good at setting tables. I usually just move the chairs, carry stuff."

"I'm not good at it either. Come on, let's just copy the other table settings."

Winter started to rearrange the silverware. It looked fine to him, even after seeing how the other tables were set. He couldn't figure out what the supervisor had been in such a snit about. The Latino glanced at him a few times, then settled in to his work, quiet, like Winter.

When they had finished the second table, the Latino said, "Excuse me, but I think that the sound system is broken. She won't be able to fix it."

"I know. I've been here before. It hasn't worked for years. It's a piece of shit, no one could fix it."

"She's not going to be too happy," said the Latino, but he was smiling. "That she can't get it working."

"Who's she going to admit it to?"

"Sometimes it is very hard working for bosses like that," said the Latino carefully.

"Tell me about it," said Winter.

AUDREY WINTER WATCHED her father from across the room. He wasn't with the group of cops in their dress blues near the dais, boisterous, in a good mood. No, he was in the far corner, working with one of the catering staff, setting the tables.

That her father was also in his dress uniform didn't connect him to the other cops any more than the distance between them. He was one of them, and yet a man alone, in one of the bluest collar of professions, yet still seeking out the common man, in this case, a slightly built dark skinned worker in a white hotel uniform.

Audrey leaned into the doorway, suddenly very sad, wanting so much to go to her father, yet needing the separation. Seeing him reminded her of her mother, of their family, growing up, happy, or so she thought at the time. The truth hidden from her for so long that when her parents told her they were getting a divorce—both of them sitting down, serious, an adult conversation with a thirteen year old who was half girl, half woman—she didn't believe it, it was a cruel joke from parents who never joked about important matters.

She blamed herself, she blamed each of them, only learning later that the seeds of their discontent had been growing for years, and the end, when it came, was not rife with recriminations and anger and blame, but only sadness for everyone. When Audrey had learned later that they had stayed together as long as they did just for her, she blamed herself even more.

And still not as much as when she'd learned that the only reason her parents had probably married was because her mother had become pregnant with Audrey, both her parents progeny of a time when doing the right thing meant getting married, true love not be damned, just not considered critical in the equation.

As much as Audrey loved her father, it was hard to be with him now. He acted as if things were the same, as if they'd be going home to dinner, the three of them, even though in reality that rarely had ever happened with his job. And yet those were the memories she had retained, the three of them, eating pasta and meatballs, watching a baseball game, her mother an ardent fan.

That was why she stayed away. Not because he was a cop now, but because he had been a cop then.

Now, watching him, it all came back. She could just have well been leaning on a doorway in their little house here in Marburg, a house built by her grandfather, Winter's father, a house he didn't want to leave.

A house Audrey hadn't stepped inside in years. If she could barely stand the reminders just seeing her father, how would she be able to survive the crushing memories of the home she'd grown up in?

And her father remembered everything, his mind an encyclopedia of their lives. He'd mention details about people Audrey vaguely remembered, about experiences she'd long forgotten.

A wave of friendly laughter from the men, the shared intimacy of one of the most close knit of professions. Winter didn't even look up, perhaps intent on his task, or because he was one of them, yet not one of them. Except for Brooker, his partner. It had taken Audrey a long time to warm to Brooker, not because he wasn't nice, but because he shared a closeness with her father that she no longer did, that her mother no longer did, if either of them ever had.

Neither the sharp uniforms or this room—old, yet still elegant—could mask the down and dirty nature of the cops, their bulk and brash confidence reeking of nights on patrol, hustling winos, settling arguments, causing others, their hands on their guns, wary, suspicious. In the thick of it, the garbage men of human depravity. Less so here than in Boston, but still dealing with what the elite barely took note of.

That's who Audrey worked with now, the old money of Boston, a junior investment manager with a bright future. So bright she'd been offered a promotion, yet not without its costs. Her firm had opened a satellite office in Virginia, and if she moved she'd jump two steps and a decade of paying her dues, since the wealthy in Boston wanted gray haired men as advisors, not raven haired young women.

And Virginia was where her mother Sylvia lived.

Winter had finished doing whatever he was doing and was now scanning the room. Audrey didn't think he would be looking for her.

She'd been inclined to stay away; after all, she'd heard about this award from her aunt Beth, not from her own father. But of course he wouldn't have asked her to come.

She'd hung up the phone, one of her co-workers overhearing the conversation with Beth, curious. Cops got awards? For what, giving out the most tickets?

The woman hadn't even realized the implicit put down, simply assuming Audrey would think the same way, as all her friends no doubt did. And more than anything, that remark, that assumption, was why Audrey was here.

An even more sharply dressed cop, this one wearing his hat, brushed by her. He headed toward the group of uniforms, the conversation toning down as he neared. The new arrival, who struck Audrey as being in charge, must have been querying them about something, as evidenced by their shrugs. One of the cops jerked his head toward the far wall, and the chief, or whatever he was, set off toward her father.

WINTER KEPT REPEATING uno, dos, tres, cuatro, cinco, seis, shit, what was seven? Luis, the caterer, had been reminding Winter how to count to ten in Spanish as they made sure there were enough place settings. Winter used to know how, a little Spanish was helpful on the street, but even though he'd just gone through the litany a few times he'd already forgotten. Probably just out of practice, he couldn't remember the last time he'd tried to speak Spanish, it couldn't have been that long ago. Brooker would know.

Brooker.

He looked up at an approaching uniform, definitely not Brooker, a hundred pounds lighter and looking ten years younger, even though Captain Logan probably wasn't. Winter wondered how Logan's uniform stayed so crisp even though he wore it all the time.

"Where's Brooker?" asked Logan. His dense dark eyebrows gave him the appearance of constant worry.

"Probably around," said Winter, immediately covering, it was what partners did. "Maybe struggling with his tie."

"Maybe if he lost a few pounds," said Logan.

"Yeah, I've been on his case."

"He won't listen to me. You, he'll listen to you."

"Not about this."

"Try harder. They'll bounce him for it, you know."

Winter grinned. "After getting a big award?"

"Don't push it. I mean it."

"Having a hard time holding the wolves at bay?"

Logan jerked his hand at a commotion near the stage, the press setting up their cameras. "That's the problem. To those people, *we* are the wolves."

"Maybe you better go set some traps."

"Shit, I hate this stuff," said Logan.

"We could trade places," suggested Winter. "I'll handle the press, you can have my award."

"A tempting offer, believe me. And not because I want your award."

"That makes two of us," said Winter. "Three, if you count Brooker."

"Find him," said Logan.

Logan ambled off, grumbling. Luis had finished the last table and looked up. "Is he a tough boss too?"

Winter watched Logan stop halfway across the room, in the no man's land between the younger cops and Winter.

"Not really. He's just kind of caught in the middle."

WINTER, not especially worried about Brooker, decided to check the men's room anyway. Maybe Brooker *was* having trouble with his tie. Not that he could help, but he'd sic Beth on him.

The bathroom echoed, Winter taking the time to take a leak in the old fashioned floor standing urinals. They didn't make them like they used to, where a guy could take a piss without worrying about splash back. Who said newer was better?

Outside the bathroom he turned away from the ballroom, passing back through the lobby. Still no Brooker. He stepped outside, pulling out his cellphone; he hated when people made calls in a public space.

Brooker's phone jumped to voicemail, not his voice, but the prerecorded service greeting. Winter knew Brooker rarely checked his voicemail but left a message anyway. "The entire city of Marburg is here waiting for you," he said. "If I have to pick up your award I'll make you fill out my incident reports for the next six months. Come to think of it, I'll tell Logan you are at a Sox game, and he'll make you fill out the incident reports for the entire squad for six months." That should do it, Brooker despised paperwork.

Winter couldn't face going back inside just yet, it would just make the whole event seem longer. He pulled his phone back out, he'd call Beth, ask her to come outside for a walk, they still had a few minutes. As he was trying to remember her number, Gracie, the detective department secretary, walked up the steps. She'd been with the department longer than even Brooker, she was more cop than some of the rookies, right down to the hard stare when she needed it.

"Hey, Gracie, you see Brooker?"

"Isn't he here? I talked to him over an hour ago, I called to remind him to wear his blues. He said he was just about to walk out the door." She laughed. "Although he said he'd rather be shoveling snow in January than come. Walking out the door, my ass. I swear if I hadn't called he would have blown it off."

"Huh." Brooker lived about twenty five minutes away, there shouldn't be traffic this time of day.

Maybe Brooker was going to skip out after all.

"Ah, damn." Winter tried Brooker again, still no answer.

"Are you calling his cell or the house?"

"Right." Winter tried the house, the line was busy. He and Gracie chatted a few minutes, then he tried again. Still busy. Winter had never known Brooker to talk more than a minute on a call; Brooker hated phone calls as much as he did.

"Starting soon," said Gracie. "You better get in there."

Winter nodded. "You go ahead."

If Brooker had lived inside the Marburg limits Winter would have called the desk to send a squad to rustle Brooker, it would serve him right. But Brooker lived two towns over, grandfathered into the rules requiring cops to live in the city limits. Winter called the county sheriff.

"It's Winter. I'm over at this rah rah at the Lexington. Brooker didn't show, you got a deputy out that way you can swing by his place?"

"What am I, a taxi service?"

"I'm not asking you to go personally." Winter wasn't upset, and neither was the sheriff, they went back a way, each helping the other over the years. "Logan is on my case, Brooker's getting a big award."

"I hear you are too."

"Do me this favor and you can have mine. I'll pin it on your ass."

"That's the only way it would get there, I certainly can't reach it. I'd like to help, but everyone is tied up with that drug bust down in the South End. I'd be there myself, except the press is all at your event."

Winter knew about the drug thing, he'd forgot. "Okay, no problem."

He hung up just as Gracie popped her head out the front door. "The Captain wants you. But he wants Brooker even more."

"Stall him," said Winter, heading down the stairs for his car.

"What? How?"

Winter waved to her over his shoulder. "Think of something!"

WINTER TRIED BROOKER TWICE more from the car, both times the home line still busy, the cell phone going to voicemail. No accident or heavy traffic on the way out of the city. After the second failed call Winter reached under the seat for the magnetized portable flasher, leaned out the window to snap it on the roof, and hit the siren. He was in his own car—he hated the rolling soft ride of the unmarked department cars, plus everyone recognized them anyway. A buddy had installed the siren in exchange for Winter doing a little background check on the guy's daughter's new boyfriend. The boyfriend had a sheet in Florida, the daughter, surprisingly, had listened to her father, and a possible disaster was avoided. Winter had a not so friendly chat with the boyfriend, suggesting that a return to Florida would be much healthier, and not just because of the weather.

He flicked off the siren a few blocks from Brooker's neighborhood, closely packed Craftsman bungalows harkening back to the days of factory workers where kids still played stickball in the street. No need to alarm the entire neighborhood.

Brooker's old Ford was in the narrow driveway. *Just walking out the door,* Brooker had told Gracie. Winter parked on the street and headed for the side door.

Winter rapped on the glass, looking around He'd been there a hundred times, nothing seemed amiss.

Winter knocked again, louder. The house felt empty, a sensation Winter knew couldn't be explained but was often correct. Not that he'd ever trust the feeling if he was going after a criminal. He tried the door, locked, which usually meant that Brooker wasn't home. It was hard to see through the window, the late day sun glaring against the leaded glass.

Maybe Brooker had gone to a Sox game after all, and was laughing in a beer right now.

Winter cupped his hands around his eyes and peered into the window. He knew the layout, a small vestibule, the laundry room to the left, then a short hall leading to the kitchen and living room. Something on the floor in the hall . . .

Winter squinted, it looked like the old princess wall phone, the cord's coil stretched straight, leading up to the left, where it normally hung on the kitchen wall. That's why the line was busy . . .

Winter ran around back, his heart pounding. Now he was yelling Brooker's name, something wasn't right. The kitchen window was too high to see inside, Winter frantically searching for something to stand on. Two lawn chairs sat near a large oak at the far edge of the yard, Brooker often smoked cigars there. A dog barked next door, and then another and another, extolling Winter to go, go, go.

Winter measured the distance to the chairs, they might be tall enough for him to reach the window, then thought, *fuck it*. He pulled out his pistol and used the bottom of the grip to break through one of the small panes in the door leading to the basement. He reached in and slid the latch, then broke another pane to unlock and twist the knob. His penlight got him down the stone stairs, through the obsessively neat basement, and up the wooden staircase which opened into the hall across from the kitchen, his gun still in his hand.

"Brooker?"

The door at the top of the stairs wouldn't open. "Brooker!" Winter grabbed onto the handrail, balanced awkwardly on the step, and kicked as hard as he could. The door didn't budge. Winter didn't even bother with another kick. He hunted briefly for the light switch, remembered it was on the other side of the door. He stuck the flash in his mouth and reached for his phone as he raced back down the stairs to the tool bench.

He was out of hands, still holding his gun. He hit 911, crooked the phone painfully against his shoulder, grabbed a crowbar, and was back on the stairs, ripping at the door.

"911, what's your emergency?"

Winter didn't even have proof there was one. He gasped out the address as the door flew open. Brooker was on the floor, face up, his eyes closed. A pool of blood surrounded his head, seeping into his dress blues.

He knew he should clear the house, but he needed to check Brooker. "Ambulance!" he screamed into his phone as he knelt by his partner, ignoring the 911 operator's questions as he dropped the phone, the line still open. A faint pulse at the neck, Winter's hand coming away red. The house was quiet, Winter glanced up toward the hall, no one. Brooker's gun was still holstered.

He quickly checked Brooker for injuries, Winter had too much experience in this. Just the head wound, still seeping. Winter grabbed a clean dishtowel out of the sink drawer, not sterile, but the risk of bleeding to death trumped infection. A smear of blood and some hair stuck to the edge of the counter, trailing down to Brooker.

Winter gently lifted Brooker's head just enough to slip the towel underneath, pulling it tight to bind the wound. The towel wasn't long enough to tie a knot, so he held on for dear life, for Brooker's as well as his, the fingers of one hand wrapped in the towel, the other gripping his gun, daring anyone to come down the hall.

If someone else was in the house, they'd better be sending the coroner too.

CHAPTER 15

MELANIE FIDDLED WITH THE remote control of her new television, bringing up the volume. Jason Ayers was just being introduced, and Melanie had to admit he looked good on camera. Even better for him, his genetic makeup perfectly matched the current heartthrob look for the all important X generation audience demographic.

Lesli Adams, the *New Entertainment* show host, air kissed Jason as he took a seat on the guest couch. As the live audience applauded, Lesli sat back down, showing lots of cleavage and even more leg. Melanie didn't know why the producers bothered, only women watched this show, which is why they booked guests like Jason.

"So Jason," said Lesli, "how does it feel to be on one of the top new shows this season?"

"It feels great, Lesli."

"Why do you think the show is connecting so well with viewers? Besides, of course, great acting?"

"Nice try, bitch," said Melanie to the television. "You're not his type."

Jason laughed. "We got great reviews from some of the toughest television critics, like Patrick Read."

"He rarely has anything good to say about tv in general," said Lesli.

"I know. But the writing is great."

"Speaking of which, they've created quite a chemistry on the cast."

"It's really starting to gel. Working with Michael Stevens is amazing, he can do anything."

The interviewer leaned in toward Jason. "We've been hearing about some possible cast changes."

Jason looked over his shoulder, play acting. "Oh really? Should I be worried?"

"Not you of course," said Lesli. "Lisa Vista."

"Those are old rumors."

"Well, they're back again."

Melanie paused in the middle of opening another bottle of wine.

"I have no idea," Jason said. "We don't get a script until we're about ready to shoot, so I don't know what the writers have in mind."

Bullshit, thought Melanie. Jason might be able to get one over on silicone Lesli Adams, but Melanie heard the fake glibness in his voice. Something was going on with the cast.

"One of the trade journals reported that Lisa Vista might be in a Nick Calen movie, last year's Best Director Oscar nominee."

"Well, I wouldn't know about that," said Jason. "It's been great having Lisa on the cast, I'm sure she's going to have a lot of opportunities in movies too."

Melanie thought airhead Lesli had a better chance of getting cast in a Calen movie than Lisa Vista ever would. *Shock and Awe* might have been flying high, but not because of Lisa Vista. Melanie had read the rags; Lisa was clearly not working out, just as Melanie had predicted. Maybe her stunt at the press conference a few months ago would finally pay off big time. Not that it hadn't helped already, but nowhere near enough. A lot of offers to be an extra, so many that she stopped taking them, concentrating on jobs with lines and more face time. Enough to be able to afford the new television and some new shoes, but she was still stuck in her dump of an apartment.

And she hadn't landed a big role.

Lesli turned to the audience. "So who wants to hear about Jason's *personal* life?"

The screen panned across whooping twenty year olds who looked like they were dressed for a dance club. Melanie leaned forward, she wanted to hear this too.

"We hear there's a hot woman in your life," said Lesli.

Melanie's stomach did a little flip. The rumors she'd been carefully sowing about her relationship with Jason were finally reaching daylight, all the way across the country. *Here it comes . . .*

Jason kept a poker face. Melanie was impressed, she thought he'd be a little embarrassed. Maybe he was seeing the light after all. If Melanie got cast against him, there'd be real chemistry on the set, maybe enough to move *Shock and Awe* to the number *one* new show.

"Where do you get these rumors?" asked Jason.

"Now that you're a star you're going to have to get much more comfortable talking about your love life," said Lesli. She waved toward the audience. "Why don't you reveal to all your fans today who it is? We all want to know!"

Jason was smiling, not as uncomfortable as Melanie expected. She was already reaching for her phone as Jason said, "I promise you, Lesli, as soon as I have something to share, you'll be the first to know."

Melanie muted the sound as Lesli cut to a commercial. She had her new agent, Doug Vettig, on speed dial.

Not speed answer, though. Melanie still had to go through the receptionist. *Last time,* thought Melanie. After this I'll have his direct dial. Or a better agent. Vettig probably made everyone wait just to appear busy.

"Hey, Mel, what's up?"

"Finally," she said. "You know you have the shittiest on-hold music."

"What are you, the Grammy nominating committee?"

"Not the way to talk to your clients, especially one about to earn you some big money."

Vettig's voice brightened. "You got something for me, I mean, us?"

Melanie hadn't even met Vettig, she'd only seen his heavily retouched website photo. Why someone in LA would need a fake tan was beyond her. Vettig was far from the big time, but still a step up from who she had before. "I just heard Lisa Vista is getting booted off *Shock And Awe*."

"That's news to me."

"No one called you?" Melanie couldn't believe it.

"Why would they?"

"Because I'm the one who's probably going to get the role. You know they've been thinking about it."

"Because of that press conference? Jesus, Mel, that was ages ago."

"It was a good idea then and it's a good idea now. Vista sucks, and everyone knows it."

"I told you, I haven't heard a word."

A new agent for sure. "I thought you'd be up on all this, since it's your job and all. Funny you'd be finding out about it from me."

"I know what my job is, honey."

"Don't *honey* me, Doug. This is the perfect opportunity for you to get me a real job instead of that stupid tampon commercial you offered me."

"Commercials are solid. I haven't heard about any roles."

"How about being proactive? Why don't you set the wheels in motion instead of waiting for a fucking phone call."

Vettig's voice hardened. "Let me give you a little advice, honey. I've already got you more than you ever had. From the reports I get it's clear you've got some talent. But you don't know how to play well with others. You have to pay your dues. So you just might think twice before turning down commercials, lots of actors started out that way. Commercials get you soaps, and soaps get you press and screen time, and both get you casting calls for bigger things. It's a ladder you have to climb one step at a time."

Melanie had heard this speech a million times. "I'm not much for ladders. Lots of actors get a break. Look at Lisa Vista. I would have nailed that role, no one would be complaining about any lack of chemistry between me and Jason."

"Look, Mel. You think the universe revolves around you and everybody owes you something. In case you've never heard this before: you're just one pretty face in an ocean of pretty faces."

"There's an ocean of agents, too."

"You want to go find yourself a new agent? Be my guest. I don't need another prima donna, LA is full of them."

"Screw you."

"There you go, proving my point. You think some big name director is going to take that attitude?"

Melanie's phone beeped with another call. "Gotta go, Doug. That's probably my *Shock and Awe* casting call now. Maybe they cut you out of the loop."

Vettig laughed. "It doesn't matter. We've got a contract, remember? If you get that role, I still get my cut, whether the call comes through me or not."

IT WASN'T SOME CASTING agent calling, it was Tim Tazik. Melanie was so pissed at Vettig she hit the wrong button on her phone, picking up Tazik's call instead of shunting him off to digital Siberia. She got her voice under control; she still might need him at some point. "Taz," she said.

"You're hard to reach. I want to get together again."

"I already paid you back, Taz."

"That was a long time ago. And you seemed to enjoy it."

Melanie didn't take the bait. She made a non committal *hmm* sound.

"Plus you got some publicity."

"Not enough. I thought I'd be in LA by now, and all I'm getting are calls for commercials and crowd scenes. Who knew you had to have talent to be a face in a crowd?"

"Maybe I can help you out again. There's a big fundraiser being thrown by Sam Hasting, you know, the media guy and philanthropist? It's for the performing arts council, raising money to get more production moved to the east coast. I did some family pictures for Hasting, his wife loves me, he got me a ticket. Two tickets, actually. Want to go?"

"Speaking of wives, what about yours? Why isn't she going?"

"She's in California. For a week."

Taz let it hang there, letting Melanie do the obvious math. Another tit for tat, literally. Melanie weighed the options. "Who's going to be there?"

"Everybody. All the usual suits from the production companies, lots of the top agents from New York. Plus anyone associated with every show and movie being shot around here, producers, directors."

"Hasting has that kind of pull?"

"They all suck up to him because he has streaming media channels. And he also funds off-Broadway. Most of the plays lose money, but you know how television and movie people are, they think they have to do stage too."

Melanie poured herself another wine as she considered. Taz would certainly want something in return for this. On the other hand, her agent wasn't doing her much good, and this would give her a chance to get in front of heavy hitters. As usual, she'd have to rely on herself.

"Is it dressy?" she asked.

"Black tie."

"You'll need to buy me a new pair of shoes. And I'm talking *nice.*"

"Consider it done."

"Okay. And Taz? Even with the shoes, this counts as one favor, not two."

MELANIE WASN'T IMPRESSED EASILY, but she was having a hard time not ogling wide eyed at the sheer size and elegance of Sam Hasting's home. Mansion was more like it, and she'd already overheard that it was only one of his houses. There must have been over a hundred people in what appeared to be the living room, Melanie only later discovering that she hadn't even reached the real crowd, arrayed around the hotel sized pool, filled with floating candles.

There was more bling than at a Tiffany's, and even in her best little black dress and her new Saint Laurent's ankle strap sandals—courtesy of Taz—Melanie was feeling decidedly under accessorized. She made a mental note to ask for jewelry next time she did Taz a favor.

Taz had been waylaid by Hasting's wife, and Melanie had slipped away after being introduced; she didn't think Mrs. Hasting, even with all her money, could do anything for her, not just yet. Across the room a small group was crowded around a painting; Melanie wasn't interested in art, but she *was* interested in what rich folk found intriguing.

The painting looked vaguely familiar. After the crowd drifted away, she took a closer look. It was a small pastel, signed Degas. Damn, could that be an original? The next painting, modern, just some lines, she skipped on by.

"That's a Romsky. That one is probably going to be worth more than the Degas someday."

Melanie turned to a short guy who looked even more under-dressed than she was, even though he was in a tuxedo. In her heels she could see the top of his comb over, a valiant but unsuccessful attempt to fit in with the chic crowd. Melanie immediately pegged him for a production company suit.

"Really? It looks like—I don't know, something a kid could have done."

"Yes, but Romsky did it first, so it's worth a million bucks."

"You're kidding me." Melanie tried to understand why. "If I had done it first, would it be worth a million?"

The suit laughed, his voice deeper than his stature suggested. "Nope. Because you aren't Romsky."

"Like if you're already famous and write a book it sells more than if you were an unknown and had written the same exact book?"

"Now you get it."

And she did, exactly. It was just like acting. She could play a lot of the roles that big actresses landed, just as well if not better. But she couldn't get those roles, because she hadn't *had* those roles yet. A perfect Catch 22.

A white jacketed waiter offered caviar. Melanie gave it a try, her first taste ever, and didn't understand what all the excitement was about. The next tray was better; she wasn't sure what it was—duck?—but it was delicious, going down well with her third champagne.

The suit was still there, so Melanie asked, "Do you know if Hasting bought any of these before they became valuable?"

"Some. The Romsky he got as a gift."

"A gift? Who gives gifts like that?"

"People with money. He got that one from Evangelina Stilson."

"Now you're shitting me. She's just an actress."

"An actress with two best supporting Oscar nominations, twenty movie credits . . . and a nice share of her ex husband's net worth, even with a prenup."

Melanie was fully aware of how Hollywood could lead to the

gravy train, but this was hard to get her head around. She didn't even think Stilson was that good of an actress. Is this how these other people lived? In houses like this, meeting rich guys, giving gifts worth millions?

Melanie needed to get a piece of this. Screw the ladder to the top, she'd get herself a rocket.

"How do you know all this, anyway?" she asked the comb over.

"I'm Jack Howker. I'm with Grayson Productions."

"Grayson? Don't you guys produce the *New Entertainment* show?"

"That's us."

"I watch that all the time." Melanie left out her thoughts about how they were messing up with the way they positioned Lesli Adams. "I didn't expect you'd have people here."

Howker gave her an expensive veneered smile. "We have people *everywhere.*"

Howker was probably just a suit, not involved with the production directly. Still . . . She gave him her second best smile. "Nice to meet you, Jack. I'm Melanie Upton. You wouldn't happen to know any good agents, would you?"

THE PRE DINNER SPEECHES DRAGGED ON, extolling the virtues of the arts council and how it could make Boston the Hollywood of the east. Melanie leaned over to Taz. "Why doesn't Hasting just donate one of those paintings and we can call it a night?"

Taz squeezed her arm. "Be nice," he said, his lips barely moving.

Melanie wanted to get back to working the crowd. Taz had been right, everyone was here. She already had made six good contacts, including the Grayson suit and the agent he had introduced her to. Four of the six no doubt wanted to get in her pants, an undercurrent that everyone, including Melanie, understood as they had shaken hands. One of them, the producer for a sleazy, and incredibly successful, television reality series called *The Other Woman*, had practically backed her against the wall into one of Hasting's expensive art pieces. His name was Larry Barrett, and he had regaled Melanie with the background of the series, which revolved around the uncovering and revealing of secret affairs of the rich and famous. Melanie didn't need the explanation, she knew all about the show. But Barrett was connected, this wasn't his first hit series, so she'd let him look down her dress while she pretended to be interested in his spiel.

Melanie tuned out the speaker. As she sipped yet another champagne she checked out the crowd. She recognized a lot of people, especially the talent. Melanie suspected she was one of the few guests who hadn't already made it in the wide, multilayered world of entertainment. Even those she didn't know were probably successful behind the scenes people, many worth even more than the talent.

Melanie had dreamed of this world since she was a little girl. And even in her dreams, she never had imagined it was this good, this rich, this elegant. Yet instead of being awed, she felt at home. This was where she belonged.

ONE IN THE MORNING, the party in full swing, guests still arriving. The champagne was flowing, literally; Melanie had discovered a champagne fountain near the pool house, right next to another fountain of Godiva chocolate. Coke everywhere, the dust bunnies of the rich and famous. Melanie hadn't even had to ask, total strangers had offered it up to her. Taz must have more pull than she had thought. He must have vouched for her, she could have been an undercover cop. Maybe these people just didn't give a shit about getting caught. Or could buy their way out of any trouble with the police.

A gaggle of the younger talent crowded around a tall sequined beauty with impossibly straight hair. Melanie recognized her immediately, Ashley Hanna, the pop diva, the most successful of the latest array of breathy heavily branded singers, the music business approach to canned goods and detergent. Hanna looked the part tonight, wholesome with style, the next door girl who wore a ten thousand dollar wardrobe with five times that in jewels.

Melanie appraised her professionally and gave her high marks. She had *a look,* not the same as Melanie sought, the aura of just under the surface sensuality. Hanna's was more the unspoiled fresh canvas that everyone could paint to their own inner desire. Not only men, but young women, projecting their own goals of success and fame into Hanna's persona.

"She draws a lot of attention, doesn't she?"

Howker was back at Melanie's side. Melanie didn't mind so much, he was far from the only man hitting on her. Taz was off trying to drum up business, so Melanie might have looked to be fair game. "Some of the attention she's drawing is from men who could be her father." She glanced at Howker, trying to estimate his age. "No offense."

Howker took a sip of his drink, he didn't seem bothered. "To each their own. Not my type, actually."

Melanie had heard a lot of come-ons, that one wasn't bad, but Howker wasn't *her* type, although if he could get her on the *New Entertainment* show—or not block her from an invite—she needed to play nice. "You think she had that look and someone spiffed it up, or did they create it from scratch just for her?"

Howker shrugged. "Does it matter?"

"I guess not."

An overly made up middle aged woman trying to hide her decades pushed between Melanie and Howker. "There you are, Jack. Is this girl bothering you?"

Howker's eyes darted between the two women. "No, not at all."

"Good, because you need to watch out for her, she'll grab any man not tied down. Isn't that right, Melanie?"

"Oh, Nora, I could never hope to compete with you at grabbing men."

"I take it you two know each other?" asked Howker.

"Melanie and I crossed paths at repertory. *Measure for Measure* it was. I was playing Isabella, the lead. Melanie was one of the prostitutes." Nora turned to Melanie. "It's hard being typecast, isn't it? Not that many other natural roles for you."

Melanie gave Nora her *you're so sweet* smile. "Haven't seen you around in a while. Have you had any roles since then? Must be what, three years ago now? Oh, wait, didn't I see you on that commercial for irritable bowel syndrome?"

"I must say this is the most interesting conversation I've heard tonight," said Howker. "But am I going to need a flak jacket?"

"I don't think so," said Nora. "I just saw Jason Ayers walk in. Melanie will be slithering off to glom onto him."

"What's the matter, Nora? He too young for you to try for?" Melanie was proud of herself for not turning to look for Jason.

"Don't listen to her, Jack. She and Jason have already had their thing, back before he made the jump. I doubt he'd give her the time of day now."

"Jason gives me more than the time of day. As a matter of fact, he can't resist me." Melanie was looking at Nora, but her words were for Howker. "He can be quite—forceful." She let the message sink in, planting yet another seed in case she needed it someday. Melanie watched Howker file all that away, and then, with just the right amount of feigned sympathy, added, "Oh, I'm so sorry, Nora, to be talking about sex. You're too old for that now, aren't you?"

"Come on, Jack," said Nora, taking Howker by the arm. "I need some fresh air, it's downright bitchy in here."

Howker let himself be led away, but Melanie was pleased to see a reappraising look in his eye. *There were more ways than casting calls to show off your acting talent.* Howker would no doubt file that away as well.

MELANIE POSITIONED HERSELF under one of the lights near the steps to the pool bar, where Jason would be sure to notice her; no way she was going to approach him. Jason stood in a small group gathered around Michael Stevens, the older actor waving his arm around like he was about to throw a lasso, entertaining them with some story.

Melanie was nicely buzzed, and not just from the alcohol and coke, it had been a good night. She'd owe Taz after all. Hopefully he wouldn't want to collect tonight.

Stevens's story ended with a whoop. Melanie turned on her inner charm beacon, always practicing, a little movement of her hand there, a twist of her head, looking like she was moving even though she was standing still. When Jason looked over she felt the usual jolt she got when her acting wiles worked, she'd never tire of that. Some days she thought she could make a man rob a bank just by looking at him.

Jason peeled off from Stevens's posse and made a beeline for her. Melanie waited until he had to work his way through the crowd before she turned; she wanted to make it obvious to anyone who was looking that he was coming to her.

The sudden grip on her arm was surprisingly strong. "Melanie, what the hell are you doing here?"

Melanie didn't need acting skills to be pissed. "It's a party. I got invited."

"Bullshit. No way you could get into a place like this."

"I have my ways."

Jason's eyes flicked through the crowd. "You mean you screwed your way in."

His voice was loud enough that a few heads turned to them. Melanie's ears hummed with the little break in conversation; people were listening. "Don't hurt me, Jason," she said, making a big show of pulling her arm away.

Jason was alert enough to lower his voice. "Are you stalking me?"

Melanie didn't think enough people heard that, so with just the right mix of disbelief and fear, making her voice carry, she said, "You're not *stalking* me, are you?"

Jason hesitated, then grabbed her arm again. "We need to talk."

Melanie waited a beat before allowing herself to be reluctantly led away. If any guests remembered this, and she was sure they would, it would certainly appear as if Jason were dragging her against her will.

Next to the still bubbling champagne fountain, Jason spun on her. "Come on, out with it."

"I don't owe you any explanation. But now that you're here—. Word is they are going to make a cast change on your show. If they aren't already planning on giving me that part, I want you to get it for me."

"You are one hundred percent certifiably nuts. Are you still on that?"

"Come on, they're going to make a change, and I put the idea in their head. If they had done it back then, they wouldn't even be in this position, because I was right, Lisa Vista was so wrong for that part."

"After that press conference stunt there's no way Scott James would touch you."

"You didn't say anything to him, did you? Remember, I still have those photos of us. They'd hurt you now more than ever."

"I didn't say anything, not that I care about any photos. But I will if you don't get out of my life."

Melanie relaxed mentally, but still kept her body tense in case anyone was watching. Jason *was* worried about the photos, even though she didn't have any that were especially embarrassing. Still, any photo she let out would prove they'd been together. "A whole bunch of people basically just saw you push me around. You're the one who has to be careful. You think you are flying high now, but Scott James will cut you off like a gangrened leg if he gets a whiff of you assaulting women."

"What are you talking about, assaulting?"

"Don't say I didn't warn you. Now are you going to help me with that role or not?"

Melanie watched as Jason's wheels turned. He was not especially bright but he'd be able to connect the dots. Jason's grasp on his own brass ring was still at risk. One little jostle and he'd crash and burn, and he knew it.

His mouth set as he made up his mind. Melanie gave herself a mental high five, she'd won.

"Come on, I want you to meet someone," said Jason. He pulled Melanie through the crowd, back toward the main house.

This time Melanie was smiling as she was led, giving curious gawkers an *aw shucks, he can't resist me* look, a pleasant embarrassment. Yet her heart was pounding; each step was bringing her closer to her dream. Jason was undoubtedly going to introduce her to a bigwig from the show, maybe Scott James had shown up.

She fought to lock everything in memory, she didn't want to ever forget this moment, when all her work and planning came to their final fruition.

Inside, the crowd had thinned somewhat, except for a group by the grand staircase, where Ashley Hanna was doing a Vivian Lee impression on the third step. Jason pushed through the adoring worshippers, letting Melanie's hand go just before he stepped up next to Hanna.

Hanna's eyes lit up, taking in Jason. Melanie, still on her high, was uncharacteristically a beat behind, Jason's hand moving around

Hanna's waist in slow motion. Yet even the surprise at who Jason had led her to didn't stop Melanie's internal memory recorder from imprinting the scene on her brain.

Hanna leaned in to Jason, and Melanie woke up from her reverie, from her fantasy high, from the top of her mountain, the reversal triggered by the obvious very personal familiarity between Jason and Ashley Hanna.

Jason pulled the diva close to him, but his eyes were locked on Melanie. "Ashley, this is—actually, it doesn't matter, she's not important. Melanie, I'm sure you know who Ashley Hanna is. What you don't know is that *Shock and Awe* has a replacement for Lisa Vista already. Ashley will take over the role before the end of the season."

The gaggle of onlookers clapped, climbing the steps, a real life visitation of their own shock and awe. Melanie's knees wobbled, her face failed her, not even an Oscar winner could have maintained her composure through that blow.

Jason, smiling triumphantly, watched Melanie topple over the edge into despair.

IN THE POOL HOUSE BATHROOM, Melanie slapped herself in the face. It was either that or drown Jason in the pool. *Ashley Hanna*, of all people. Making the Madonna jump to acting. And from what she had seen, no doubt sleeping with Jason.

They'd stolen her idea. The show would get it's chemistry, and they'd have Ashley Hanna *and* her fans.

Melanie slapped herself again, not because she was angry at herself. The game was rigged, and worse, it was a tease, dangling the magical jewel in front of her before yanking it away. Better she cause her own pain than stand for it to be forced upon her.

Time to change the game.

She pulled herself together, pushing through the line waiting for the bathroom. She'd scored the last of the coke she could find, and now she was wired for her mission.

She found Larry Barrett in the spa, the bubbles doing nothing to improve his bulbous stomach, yet the three women with him in their bras and panties didn't seem to mind. One had her hand on Barrett's thigh, and the other two were fighting to get a better position against his hairy chest.

Barrett wasn't too high to notice Melanie. "Plenty of room for one more," he said.

"Tell me, Larry," said Melanie. "Whose the biggest name you've had on *The Other Woman*?"

"Melanie, right? That's a hard one," said Barrett. "We've had a lot of big names."

Melanie jerked her head back toward the house. "As big as the famous ones here?"

"Some more, some less."

"Who gets the big ratings? The young ones or the older ones?"

"The younger ones, definitely. The older ones all have had their flings, it's not a big surprise to anyone."

"I have a story for you."

Barrett eyed her, focused now. "Young or famous?"

"Both."

Barrett pulled the gropers off him. "Spa time is over, ladies. I have to go to work." He waited until the grumbling women dripped their way out of the spa. "This better be good."

Melanie kicked off her shoes, hiked up her dress, and sat on the edge of the spa, dropping her feet in the water. "Tell you what, Larry. I'll make a bet with you. If it isn't, you can have me instead of the teeny boppers." The hot water felt good, she'd been standing all night. Her anger had focused like a laser, lighting her way to the game changer. Nothing would stop her now, not even the thought of having to see Larry Barrett naked.

Besides, with the story she had in mind, there was no way he'd make her pay off on her bet.

CHAPTER 16

G IGI PEERED OUT between the blinds on her back door window. Thanks to the security lights she'd had installed the small garden was bathed in light. She doubled checked the new hardened deadbolt on the back door. She'd already made sure all the windows were latched; since the break-in, she'd not opened a single one, even when she was at home and awake.

Somewhere out there, the man who had broken in to her apartment was still at large.

A dog barked and Gigi flinched, stepping back from the window. Frozen in place she imagined the worst, a man sneaking toward her apartment.

The dog barked again, a single yap. What did that mean? Gigi forced herself to step forward, gingerly lifting the blind. The backyard was empty.

She retreated to the couch, curling up under a thick blanket, as if that could keep her safe. Maybe another glass of wine. She'd been drinking more lately, it helped her fall asleep—no way she'd take any more pills. But the dreams still came. She hadn't slept through the night since the break-in, her dreams vivid, filled with the odors of that night, the stale beer, the blood.

For the first time in her life she wished she owned a gun.

Earlier that evening she'd passed the building superintendent as she arrived home. She hadn't told him anything yet, because of her promise to Mel. But she couldn't keep living like this.

Tomorrow. She'd tell him tomorrow.

*   *   *

MELANIE WAS ON SUCH A HIGH even the bumper to bumper traffic out of Boston couldn't bring down. Plus, she wasn't driving. Larry Barrett, the producer of *The Other Woman,* had provided a limo for her—an honest to goodness stretch limo—for the taping of the show. Melanie melted into the luxurious leather, every bit the modern goddess.

The limo driver, a dapper Latino dressed in a suit who held the door open for her and called her "Miss Upton," had pointed out the small bar and informed her that there was fresh ice. Sipping her second gin and tonic, Melanie hoped the traffic lasted for hours.

The taping could not have gone better. Melanie had been masterful, and Barrett, watching from the set, had told her as much. She'd hinted, insinuated, and, when it helped her case, even told the truth, all while making it clear there was even more to her story, implying she knew more about Jason Ayers, secrets reeking of lust and passion. She'd dangled just enough information—and leg—to keep the show's host Nancy Anders on the edge of her seat. To Nancy's credit, she didn't seem at all challenged with Melanie's sexuality; in fact, Nancy had given Melanie's knee a little squeeze during a break in the shooting, telling her to 'push it.' The story had all the makings of a ratings hit, it was current, touched on a popular new show, and, most important, included dirt on a big name.

Ashley Hanna.

Not that Ashley had done anything wrong. But she'd be caught up in it, and the promos for the show would be able to dangle her name out there. Even the way Nancy had introduced the segment reeked of more to come:

"Hollywood is abuzz with the hot romance of Jason Ayers and pop superstar Ashley Hanna. But things aren't always what they seem. Turns out Jason may like the spotlight with Ashley, but when he wants real romance, he returns to his ex. Here she is, tonight's Other Woman, Melanie Upton!"

Melanie had given Nancy a little hug. When she sat down she did her leg cross, waited a beat, then said, "Nancy, I appreciate you inviting me on, but maybe it is Ashley who should be here, and I should be the one who's upset. After all, she's the real other woman!"

Nancy, using a wonderful conspiratorial voice that Melanie made a note to learn, said, "We heard there were fireworks at a recent party you all attended."

Melanie had remembered not to glance at the monitors to see how she looked, it would appear that she wasn't looking directly at Nancy, a sure sign of deceit to the viewers and unprofessionalism to casting directors. "I can't believe Ashley showed up, she must have known I'd be there."

"We've also heard that Jason was very angry, there's actually this video . . ."

On a big screen behind the set, a video from the party, a little choppy, but clearly showing Jason pulling Melanie along, and, clear as a bell, Melanie saying, "Don't hurt me!" Melanie was pleasantly surprised they had dug this up, she hadn't seen it. The actor side of her brain was criticizing her tone, maybe she should have emphasized the word *hurt* a little more? But it did the trick.

"Is he always that forceful?" asked Nancy.

Melanie had made a little fluttering motion with her hand over her breast, *hot.* Shifting her voice to make it sound like she couldn't believe it either, she had replied, "He just can't resist me. He wants me so badly he once had to practically break down my door to get to me."

Nancy leaned forward, wide eyed. "What *happened?*"

The director hadn't revealed to Melanie the exact line of questioning, telling her they wanted to see spontaneous reactions, but Melanie was well prepared for this. Even if she hadn't tipped Barrett off to this story, Melanie would have worked it in the way a politician delivered talking points no matter what the question. "I was at home watching the Tony Awards, you know I've done some theater, right?—and well, I guess I'd fallen asleep, and then, you know, there's *someone in the room with me.*" This last part whispered. "I was a little groggy, and not knowing at the time who it was . . ." She'd let her voice drift off.

"That sounds pretty serious!"

Melanie had raised her eyebrows. "That's what the police thought!"

"You filed a *police* report?"

"Did I say that?" Melanie had covered her mouth in mock dismay. "Seriously, it's kind of a game, you know, we're all good now."

Nancy, smelling the ratings, had pressed on. "Does this happen often?"

Melanie had allowed her tone to turn a little wistful. "Well, it's been hard for us to be together as much as he'd like, with the shooting schedule, and all."

"We hear that Ashley Hanna might get the role on *Shock and Awe* that everyone was buzzing about you getting, are you disappointed?"

Melanie had been prepared for this too. "Oh, that show has twists and turns, you never know how long a character will last. I mean, if they are really going to go soft and cuddly, Ashley will be great, but can she do edgy?"

"So how *does* Ashley Hanna fit into all this?"

"That's a good question, isn't it? Maybe you should ask her!" Melanie loving the idea, wouldn't that be the icing, the famous Ashley Hanna being pressed about Melanie Upton.

All together, deftly done, if Melanie did say so herself. She'd study the tape later, in real time and in slow motion, to see how she looked. She was good, but realistic enough to know she could be better.

Melanie could practically hear the voiceover lead-in promoting the show: *Does Ashley Hanna know about Jason's other woman? Hear the shocking details tonight!*

No matter how they'd play it, Melanie would be in the spotlight—and she'd have a claim that would one up even Ashley Hanna. Everyone would be dying to know: Who could possibly draw the attention of new heartthrob Jason Ayers away from the wonderful Ashley Hanna?

Melanie Upton, that's who.

The more vehemently Jason or Ashley denied it, the more viewers would think it was true.

The story was so big that Barrett planned to move up the schedule, airing it as fast as they could get the editing done. The show staff had done well by Melanie, treating her like a star, like she was the big news. Melanie would remember that, invite them all to a screening someday.

The soundproofing of the limo drowned out the traffic. Melanie could get used to this, her own limo, a personal driver who stocked the bar with her favorite drinks. She was so close . . .

It would be a tightrope to walk for a while, to be sure. Laying just enough information out there about Jason to stay in the spotlight. She'd likely get one big shot, and she couldn't afford to blow it. Soon it would be her time, she'd be the hot commodity, on everyone's lips. All she had to do was parlay that into the payday, climb aboard her rocket, and kick those one step at a time, pay your dues ladders to the curb.

Melanie was getting a buzz on, the drinks on an empty stomach, she'd been too wired to eat. The buzz grew more persistent. Her phone. Could it be another casting call already? Why not?

Not a casting call. Gigi.

Not a real letdown, Melanie happy to share. "Hey, Gigi, I've got great news."

"Mel, I'm really worried."

"What? What's wrong?" Melanie alert, something in Gigi's voice.

"This whole situation—I can't stop thinking about it, I can't sleep, I can't anything."

"You mean the break-in?" Melanie asked.

"Of course the break-in, what do you think I'm talking about?"

Melanie wasn't ready to come down from her high. Even for Gigi. "You're blowing everything out of proportion."

"And you're not taking it seriously."

"Why? Did something happen?"

"No. I just think I need to tell someone in case he comes back here. Do you know how I'd feel if it happened to someone else? I wouldn't be able to forgive myself."

That was so like Gigi, Melanie should have predicted this, she'd just had too much on her mind. "You don't have to worry, I'm taking care of it."

"You've dealt with the police but that doesn't take care of the apartment complex. I saw the building super today—"

"You didn't say anything, did you?"

"No, but I should."

"Don't say a word. We talked about this, you don't want people at work to find out about it, and I've already told the police it was me."

"Maybe you shouldn't have done that."

"Too late, it's done, so just keep quiet about it." Melanie softened her tone. "Please."

"I'm really afraid . . ."

"I'm coming over. Don't do anything until I get there, okay?"

"Okay—"

Melanie didn't give Gigi a chance to change her mind. "I'll be there as soon as I can," Melanie said and hung up.

NOW IT WAS THE FRONT WINDOW Gigi peered through, anxiously waiting for Melanie. As soon as she stepped into the apartment Gigi felt much better, throwing her arms around her sister. "I'm so sorry, I'm so sorry!"

"Hey, it's alright. Everything's going to be fine."

"I'm just not used to being afraid again. I'd almost forgot how bad it was. I haven't felt this way since—"

"Shh. You really need to stop thinking like that. You're a strong woman on the inside, you can be strong on the outside."

Gigi reluctantly pulled away. Mel was the strong one, not her. "Can I get you some tea?"

"Sure."

"What kind would you like?" Gigi said over her shoulder, glad to be doing something useful instead of staring out the window.

"Whatever you have."

Gigi busied herself with the water, setting out some mugs on the small island as Melanie sat. That same dog barked and Gigi flinched, her hands shaking so hard the mug rattled against the counter.

"Jesus, Gigi, you need to calm down."

"What if he comes back?"

"I'll kick his ass."

"But you aren't here all the time." Gigi tried to keep the desperation out of her voice.

"What brought this on? You need to tell me if something happened."

"No, just—. I'm *scared*."

"I'm not going to let anyone hurt you."

"But what if he breaks in again? What if he attacks me when I'm going to my car? Or coming in the apartment?"

"Gigi, the chances of that happening are no different now than they were before. You think you're the only person whose apartment got broken into? I can't tell you how much I've spent fixing my busted door, they've broken in so many times."

Gigi fought back her first thought, *That's why I spend all this money on rent, so I can live in a better neighborhood.* She recognized what Mel was trying to do, bolster her with tough love. It wasn't Mel's fault that she'd been defiled.

"It's not just the break-in, it's—Mel, he may have *touched* me."

"I thought you said nothing happened that night?"

"I don't know anymore. I can't think straight. I can't even sleep in my bed, you know? I keep feeling him in the room. In the bed."

The teapot whistled, making her jump again. All at once she started to cry.

Melanie reached her arm around, cradling her, Gigi melting to the touch. Hard as Melanie could be on the outside, the cool veneer, Melanie had always been warm to her; it was as if Gigi could tap into the good part of her sister's raw emotional heat. She did feel safer, and she'd pity anyone who was on the receiving end of that heat, since she'd seen how Melanie could transform it to wrath.

Maybe not that much pity. Whoever had broken in didn't deserve pity.

Gigi straightened up. "Let me get your tea." She carefully poured the water, half expecting a new sound to make her jump. "You said you had some news?"

Melanie lit up. "I do! You know that show *The Other Woman*? I just came from a taping, I'm going to be on it."

"What? Isn't that about affairs? You're not married . . . wait, Mel, are you having an affair with a married man?"

"It's not just about married people. Just, you know, a secret lover."

"Who?"

"Remember Jason Ayers? He's been—after me again. But he's on this new series—I know you don't watch much television, but he's going to be big, and he's been dating Ashley Hanna."

"Ashley Hanna? The singer?"

"Can you believe it? He has Ashley Hanna, and he can't keep his hands off me. You have to keep it a secret, okay? Until the show airs."

"Gee, Mel, who am I going to tell?" And why would she want to?

"It will be out soon enough. I'll be famous. It's the break I need."

Gigi couldn't understand why Mel would see dirty gossip as a break, but Mel probably had a plan. "I'm glad for you, I guess," she said. "When is it on?" Trying to be polite, this wasn't how she was hoping to see Melanie on screen.

"Soon. Once it does, things will finally start coming together for me, I know it. I just needed a break, I deserve a break. Jason is it."

Gigi hadn't seen Jason in years. She remembered him mostly because Jason was one of the few of Mel's many men her sister had actually referred to by name.

"What's Jason think about all this?"

Melanie flicked her hand. "Don't worry about him. He'd do the same to me if the roles were reversed. It's a tough business."

"I'm glad I'm not in it." Gigi didn't have her sister's toughness or her confidence. It had always been that way and would never change. Sometimes she couldn't believe they were sisters, Melanie so beautiful, so self assured. Their bodies and features were actually pretty similar, yet their personas a world apart.

Gigi drank her tea, not sure how happy to be for Mel. It's what she wanted, making it big. They were so different in what they wanted as well, Mel reaching for the limelight, Gigi happy in the shadows.

The shadows made her think of the back yard, the need for the security light. The fear descended, icy fingers grabbing at her. If she felt this way with Mel here, how was she going to be by herself?

"Mel, about the super. What if I don't tell him exactly what happened, but just say that I saw a prowler? Maybe they could start some patrols, have more lights installed."

"The less you talk about it the easier it will be."

"Not for me."

Melanie sighed. "Okay. If it will make you feel better, tell him—tell him just what you said. You saw some guy lurking around back. That's it."

Gigi brightened. "I'll feel better, just by doing that." She *had* seen a prowler, or she thought she had, so it would be like telling the truth. All she had to do was leave out the part about him being inside, not outside. Maybe she could just leave the super an anonymous note.

"But remember, if the police come talk to you—I doubt they will, but just in case—just tell them what we agreed, okay?"

The super was one thing, the police totally different. "I don't know if I can lie to them. You know I'm not good at lying."

"It's easy. I was upset, I called you and came over. Which was true, I was here later. Focus on that part, the truth. That's all you have to say. It will help you feel better. The more you repeat that nothing happened here, the more you'll believe it too."

"But something *did* happen."

"Listen, Gigi, I didn't want to bring this up, but—." Mel's voice softened. "Remember those boys who were after you, the one who put his hands on you? How often do you think about them?"

Gigi grimaced. "Not very. It was a long time ago."

"That's not it at all. You don't think of them because I took care of the situation. Just like I'm taking care of it now. Pretend it never happened."

"I can't pretend. I'm not an actress like you."

"Then just keep repeating that it didn't happen here, or that you imagined it. Like a bad dream." Melanie touched Gigi's hand. "I'm not trying to make light of this. If something really bad *had* happened, we'd be handling this differently. But nothing did. You're going to be fine. You *are* fine."

Gigi wished she had her sister's strength. What would Melanie have done that night? Probably jumped out of bed and kicked his ass, just like she had said. Trying to sound more confident than she felt, she said, "Okay. I'll try."

"Good. Now, one more thing. If someone from the press should contact you—"

"The press? Why would the press want to talk to me?"

"Not about you. About me. Once that show airs, word may get

out, you know, about what I reported—not what you reported, what I reported. About a break-in. People may start to mix the two stories up, me being in a jealous relationship, some kind of assault."

"Why would they do that?"

"Gigi, I can't control the press."

"Is that what this is all about? Publicity for *you*? You told the police you were assaulted so you can get on *television*?" Not knowing where the insight came from, perhaps their shared genes, perhaps the glittering excitement in Mel's eye, perhaps Gigi's own shared responsibility.

"It's not like that. I was trying to protect you. I would have helped you anyway, you *know* that. But if I can get a little something out of it, why not?"

Gigi was still grappling with the implications of what Mel was doing. "You seem pretty happy about getting attention too."

"I've always had your best interests at heart. And I've always looked out for you. Haven't I?"

Gigi couldn't deny that. "Yes, I suppose you have."

"Well, why question me now? All I was saying is that if the press comes after me I can handle it. Would you want to deal with them? Or the police?"

"Mel, please, there must be another way for you. You don't have to do this. We can still tell the truth, you can get them to cancel the show—"

Melanie grabbed her arm, Mel's voice shifting, a voice from Gigi's past, filled with the same wrath as when Gigi had been touched in school.

"Gigi, don't cross me up here, okay? I got enough people I need to jump over without you adding to it."

Gigi couldn't meet her eyes. What had Mel got herself mixed up in? Fighting back tears, she mumbled, "Whatever you say."

And just like that, Gigi was a part of it. The realization was as scary as her fear of another attack.

Melanie's grip relaxed, her touch now one of protection. "Do you want me to stay tonight?" The big sister once again.

Gigi couldn't face the idea of being in her bed. She wasn't that strong. "I'll take the spare bedroom. You can sleep in my room."

CHAPTER 17

Lenny stared wistfully at the new Canon camera body in the display case. Too many megapixels to count, to even matter, but speedy in low light, exactly what he needed. That was the camera he was supposed to have, the one he *should* have had by now. Yet he wasn't here to buy, he was trying to sell one of his lenses. He was broke.

He was always broke. He hadn't had much money in LA, but he got by, he knew where he could always make a twenty if he was desperate, grabbing photos he could sell. The B list in Hollywood, shit, the C list, the almost not-on-a-list, was better than the A list in Marburg or even Boston. Not that he could afford the gas to get into Boston.

Absolutely nothing had worked out for him. He'd found it impossible to build up a reliable network of informers who could tip him off to the few celebrities worth shooting. Maybe that's what he needed to do, start an informant business. But there weren't enough photographers to sell tips to, even if he had the informers. Why would there need to be more photographers if there weren't a lot of celebrities?

Just his luck. He had landed in a place with little competition, and still couldn't score, since there was nothing to compete over.

Even worse, his personal life sucked. He was still stuck living with his mother and Tom, both of them increasingly on his case to get a real job. Like he wasn't busting his ass. As for ass, he hadn't gotten any in forever.

What pissed Lenny off the most was that he had almost made it.

He had almost found a way out, a jump so big in his life he wouldn't even be in this shop, drooling over a camera, he could have chucked the whole photography gig and become Melanie Upton's manager. That plan had been ruined when she had stolen his publicity idea—which would have worked for him, because it was working for her. Lenny searched the internet every day for mention of Melanie, her name coming up steadily even after the fervor over the press conference had died down. Melanie photographed at a fancy Boston club, on a yacht, at parties. He'd seen her in a regional commercial for a chain of boutique clothing stores. There were even rumors of her being considered for a movie role. She'd get out of this rat hole of a city soon and he'd be left behind.

The last time he'd seen Melanie she'd blown him off again. To make it worse she hadn't acted any differently after his night with her, more accurately, his few minutes with her. She didn't seem like the type to just let that slip by. At the restaurant he'd expected her to either scream for help or quit her job right there and walk out with him.

Instead Melanie did neither. She either hadn't known it had been him that night, or was too high and mighty to admit that he'd been in bed with her.

He'd broken into her apartment for nothing.

Melanie must have had a good laugh, making him think that bitch hostess Tiffany at the restaurant wanted to hook up with him. Tiffany had made him look like a fool when he'd asked her out, as heartlessly cold as Melanie.

"Can I help you?"

The camera store clerk was young, her hair pulled back in a ponytail, wearing a green polo shirt with the name of the store on the chest. Not that she had much of one. Her pale skin looked like she was spending time in the darkrooms that no one used anymore, drawing attention to the bright red bumps of her acne. She peered at Lenny through out-of-style pastel-rimmed glasses. Lenny shook his head to clear the image, she was a nerd right down to her beige khakis, a walking advertisement that the airlines could use to get people to fly to California.

"I know you sell used equipment," he said. "I have this nice telephoto I'll let you have for a good price."

The clerk examined the lens, turning the focusing ring, holding it to the light. "It's in good shape. But this is an old model, everyone wants a faster lens. The only people using these are beginners without that much money."

She said it casually, not a put down, but that's how it felt to Lenny. "It's a good lens," he argued. "I've taken photos with it that I sold for thousands." Which was bullshit, but how would she know?

"I'm sorry. There's just not that much demand for mid zoom lens. We can offer you seventy five dollars."

"Seventy five bucks? Are you crazy? I spent over five hundred for it, and that's with a professional discount!"

The nerd was shaking her head. "It has the old style image stabilization. I'm afraid it just isn't that valuable."

Lenny grabbed the lens back, their hands briefly touching, reminding him how long it had been since he'd touched a woman. She wasn't his type, too plain. She probably hadn't had a date in years. Still . . .

"Maybe we could talk about it, you know, over a drink?" he ventured.

The blonde pressed her hands over her chest, perhaps protecting herself from Lenny's outburst. "Are you asking me out?"

Lenny shrugged, trying to look like he didn't care one way or another, but unattractive as she was, a woman was a woman. "Whatever."

"I'm sorry, I'm not allowed to date customers."

"We don't have to call it a date," said Lenny, fingering the camera. "We could call it a business discussion."

"But I'm not attracted to you," she blurted.

Just his luck, a woman who probably hadn't hooked up in ages, or maybe not at all, was blowing him off. He was trying to think of a suitable put down for her when the shop door bell dinged.

The clerk's eyes rushed away from Lenny. "Mr. Tazik! My favorite customer!"

Lenny recognized that name. Tim Tazik. The photographer who had made Melanie Upton famous. The photographer who had done what Lenny had planned, who was as complicit in stealing Lenny's idea as Melanie was.

"Hi, Jenny. How's my favorite camera expert?"

"Just fine, Mr. Tazik."

"I keep telling you, call me Taz, everyone else does."

Lenny hated him at first glance, and would have even if Tazik— wait, *Taz*—hadn't stolen his idea. Taz gave off a casual, confident air, the little gray in his hair more sophisticated than old. Tazik's eyes swept past Lenny like he wasn't there.

"Let me guess," Jenny said. "You're in the market for a camera. The new Canon."

"As a matter of fact I am."

"Really? I was just kidding."

"You're probably psychic." Tazik unleashed a ten thousand dollar set of veneers on her.

Lenny wasn't going to give up Jenny's attention without a fight. "I have it on order," said Lenny. "I'm a pro, I've got a guy in New York who gets me deals."

Jenny wrinkled her nose. "I thought you were selling?"

Lenny waved his hand. "Just old stuff, need to make room." To Tazik he said, "I'm Lenny Gruse, you may have heard of me."

"Can't say I have, what kind of work do you do?"

"Mostly celebrities, I just moved to Marburg from LA."

"Pretty slim pickings here for that."

Lenny played it cool. "I won't be around long, I've got something big in the works. In the meantime, I've got contacts, there's always stuff happening worth shooting. How about you?"

"Like you said, there's always something to shoot. Why'd you leave LA?"

Lenny glanced over at Jenny and lowered his voice. "Personal reasons, if you know what I mean."

Tazik grinned. "I get it. Some lady. I hope she's rich, because it'll be hard to make the same kind of money here as you did on the West Coast."

"It hasn't been easy," Lenny admitted. "There's a lot of back-stabbing in this town."

"Really? How so?"

"People steal your ideas."

Tazik frowned. "What's there to steal? I mean, no offence, but there aren't that many unique ideas for pictures, unless you are doing fine art, and that market is so fickle."

"There's always a hook. I've had some that have made me a bundle. Being in the right place at the right time, getting a certain look. But here I made the mistake of telling someone one of my ideas, and then—*bam*—another photographer did exactly what I had been planning."

"Could be a coincidence," Tazik said. "Ideas are just floating out there for anyone to tap into. It's not who has the idea, but who takes it to the bank."

Lenny couldn't believe it, Tazik was practically admitting he'd stolen his idea. "You speaking from experience?"

"As a matter of fact. Let me show you." Tazik pulled out his cell phone. "I have a little side interest, celebrity tattoos. You might say, that's an old idea, it's been done. But not the way I envisioned it, not the same old here's why so and so got a tattoo and what it means. Instead, I've put a book together that combines pictures of body parts of different people to create one completely inked person. I pitched it to a publisher, they loved it, the book is being released next month. The buzz is so good I've started work on the next edition. Look."

Lenny watched Tazik flip through the photos, interested in spite of himself. It was a good idea, maybe he could find a way to use it. "I see you shoot mostly women," he said.

"It's all women. I might do a guy book, but, hey, women are prettier, right?" Tazik winked at Jenny.

"Good excuse to get to know them, too," said Lenny, already thinking it would be a great way to snare women, better than his current approaches. He'd also heard that women with tattoos were easy. "You can get a little action on the side."

"Let's keep it clean," said Tazik.

Lenny glanced at a blushing Jenny, who was the last person he'd expect to have a tattoo, especially like the samples Tazik was showing off. That one, for example, way up on a women's slim thigh . . . something about it familiar, a distinctly African vibe.

Lenny reeled as the picture flicked by. *It couldn't be.* "Hey, those are good, can I take a longer look while you do your camera shopping?"

Tazik shrugged and set the phone on the counter. "Sure. Come back in a few weeks, Jenny is going to carry the book, right?"

"Can't wait to see it," said Jenny.

Lenny ignored them, skimming back to the photo of the tribal tattoo. He *knew* that tattoo, a sinewy black whirlwind flowing upward. He'd seen it on the video of Melanie, the one he'd found on the internet, the one where she'd been showing off her legs. Tazik had mentioned coincidences, this couldn't be a coincidence.

"You do most of your shooting around here?" Lenny asked.

"What? Yes, mostly, why?"

"No reason."

That clinched it. Who else but Melanie would have a tattoo like this in Marburg? How had Tazik managed to get Melanie to let him take this shot?

The press conference, that was it. Lenny had to fight the urge to smash the phone. Tazik had not only stolen his idea, but Melanie had paid Tazik off just the way Lenny was hoping *he'd* be paid off. Lenny bet Melanie had let Tazik look at much more than just her thigh.

Lenny squeezed the phone, wishing it was Tazik's neck. He'd get back at Melanie, he'd get back at both of them. The tattoo stared at him like a snake, slithering into his brain. He studied the photo, every inch, if there was some way to turn it against Melanie . . .

The image was date stamped, recent, just a few months ago. Something about the date stuck in Lenny's head. Shit, that was the night he went into Melanie's apartment, the night he had . . . no wait, it couldn't be, not if she was with Tazik that night. Lenny fiddled with the phone, trying to see if he could pull up the actual time stamp of the photo, maybe it was taken earlier in the evening . . .

"Something wrong?" Tazik asked.

"What? No. No, nothing's wrong." Lenny reluctantly swiped past the picture of Melanie and handed the phone back to Tazik. "Just not used to your phone. Nice work, and I should know."

Lenny stumbled out of the store, stunned, feeling the eyes on him, not caring, he needed air, he needed to think.

*   *   *

MELANIE HELD THE PHONE away from her ear. Her agent, Doug Vettig, was screaming, ruining her nice champagne buzz.

"Christ, Melanie, what were you thinking?"

"About what, Doug? You finding it hard to keep up?"

"Keep up? Like seeing you make a fool of yourself on that ridiculous show *The Other Woman*?"

"You wouldn't have thought it was ridiculous if *you* had booked it, you're just jealous. I had to do all the work. I can't believe you are going to get a cut from my appearance fee."

"They're going to *pay* you?"

Melanie flicked the phone onto speaker, lowered the volume, and poured herself more champagne; Vettig could scream all he wanted now. "Thousands. Come to think of it, maybe as much as you've ever earned me."

"I get you real work, not gossip shows."

"Real work? Please. Work for lemmings. Anyone can get that, I deserve more. You know I can act."

"So can a million other women. And acting isn't spreading innuendos about Jason—"

"Just stating the facts."

"—and Ashley Hanna, of all people. Are you just nuts? Everyone *loves* that girl. And Jason's thing with her, it's so Hollywood adorable, they eat that shit up."

"You mean Jason's thing with me."

"Melanie, wake up. You're the wicked witch in all this. You make a third wheel sound like fun."

"Doug, what do you care? You'll settle down when the calls come in and the big cha-ching starts ringing in your ears."

"You don't get it, do you? You think all the people Ashley Hanna knows, the people who crafted her princess image, are going to take this lying down? They're going to drag you though the mud. No one will touch you."

Melanie tried to remember how to flick through her contacts without losing the call, not that it mattered, Vettig was dead to her anyway. Where was the number for that agent she'd been introduced to at the party? There, Marvin Stanlish.

"You still there, Melanie?"

"Yeah, yeah, Doug, I hear you. You're making a big thing out of nothing. The publicity always wins in the end."

"Not for you. You think people are going to love you if they think you're taking Jason away from Ashley?"

"You sound like a teenage girl. Jason and Ashley! Does that make your heart go pitter patter?"

"You need to stop playing games. This kind of bullshit will roll off them like teflon, but it'll ruin you."

"Any kind of publicity is good publicity, isn't it? I need to do whatever I can to get my name out there. I've got to put myself above the crowd."

"That's *my* job. *You* need to do what I tell you and pay your dues."

Melanie dripped the last of the champagne into her glass. "I told you, I'm not one for dues."

"Do you know how hard it was for me to sell you before this latest fiasco? Every time I mention you to a casting director they say you're a diva, trying to grab the limelight. You're nothing more than a glorified extra. You have to work your way up. If you want to put this behind you, you're going to have to lay low for at least a year so people can forget about the old Melanie. And then you need to come out as the new Melanie, the sweet, friendly, quiet Melanie. Like Ashley Hanna."

"A year? Are you fucking crazy?"

"No, I'm dead serious. You're a liability, no one's gonna touch you. I couldn't get you a porn film now."

Melanie didn't know why she was arguing, they had a contract, they were stuck with each other. Unless . . . "If I'm such a bother, we could always decide to part ways."

"*Finally* we agree on something. I don't want to ruin my reputation with whatever new crazy ideas you try."

Melanie brightened, some good may have come out of this call after all. Doug just didn't get it. "No problem. Have your secretary, if you have one, that is, send me the paperwork. I'll be out of your life. But don't come crying when I get the big contract."

"I won't be holding my breath. Although I get my cut on anything you earn before you sign. And that means whatever you got from *The Other Woman*."

"You're right, don't hold your breath. Or hold it until you drop dead, I don't care." Melanie clicked off. She spun her contact list past Stanlish, she'd get to him next. But first she had to call Larry Barrett. If Doug Vettig was no longer her agent, maybe they'd cut her appearance fee check directly to her.

Let Vettig choke on that.

CHAPTER 18

MELANIE HADN'T EXPECTED the phone to start ringing the day after the airing of *The Other Woman*, but when a week went by with nothing, she began to worry. Had Vettig been right after all? Had she been blacklisted?

The show promo had been exactly as Melanie had envisioned, and though her critical eye noticed a few things, her appearance had been more than good enough. Shit, even a producer or casting director who thought she was making it all up would have been impressed with her acting chops. Either way, *something* should be happening.

She checked the ratings of the episode of *The Other Woman* she had appeared on; their highest ever. So that wasn't it.

A registered letter arrived from Vettig, a one page form canceling her contract. Maybe Vettig was getting the calls, and wasn't telling her out of spite? He'd mailed the letter too early, and now couldn't change his mind. She hadn't signed yet, and so he still had a responsibility to her, right?

Melanie could see Vettig being too proud to admit he was wrong. Well, she practically had a new agent; she'd spoken with Marvin Standish, who said he'd take her on once she'd officially split from Vettig.

Ten in the morning, she smoked a quick joint to get in the right frame of mind, smooth away any hint of desperation in her voice. Better prepared, she dialed Standish.

"Marvin? Melanie Upton. I got the paperwork, it's done." She hesitated a breath, putting a little ooze in her voice. "I'm yours."

"Good, good."

"Listen, Vettig may be holding back on me, you know, anything recent."

"I'll take care of him. I saw the show, you were amazing."

Melanie suspected Standish was being too complimentary; he wanted her just as much as she wanted him. But what the hell, she deserved a little appreciation. "Finally, someone who gets it. Vettig told me I was gonna have to lay low for a year after that show."

"He just doesn't know how to work it. He's probably gotten lazy out in La La Land."

"I'm looking forward to seeing you work some magic," said Melanie, meaning it. "What do you want me to do?"

"Just for the records, I need a copy of Vettig's letter. And we need to do some paperwork of our own."

"That's easy enough. What else?"

"We need new publicity photos. The stuff you have is okay, but you need an edgier look, more street. We want people thinking you're the real deal, a genuine chick from the other side of the tracks who even the most wholesome man can't resist, not some actress who's been made up to be rough and tumble. You get me?"

Melanie did. Without coming right out and saying it, Standish was telling her she could keep working the Jason angle, that she could play up the idea of the woman so hot she was enough to pry Jason away from the straight Ashley Hanna. That Standish didn't mention it directly only meant he was covering his ass in case it went south. She didn't blame him, she would have done the same thing.

"When do we start?" she asked.

"Let's not waste any time. This afternoon around three okay?"

"Sure."

"Text me your address, I'll send a car."

Melanie had a better idea. "Have it pick me up at the Hilton here in Marburg. And Marvin?" She took the last hit on the joint. "Make it a big white limo, okay? Let's get some attention."

Standish laughed. "I like you already."

*   *   *

LENNY HAD BEEN BACK and forth between the restaurant, the club, and the Hilton so many times over the last few days he was getting dizzy. Melanie had to show up somewhere. He'd considered taking the chance of going to her apartment but he was afraid he'd be noticed. The hotel still seemed like the best bet.

Lenny had reluctantly concluded he had no future with Melanie—until he'd seen her on *The Other Woman*. She'd woven a bullshit story implying she'd been practically assaulted by Jason Ayers—not a bad strategy, he had to admit—although it was a little risky. But Melanie also had the gall to claim it happened the night of the Tony Awards, the night Lenny had broken into her apartment *and* the same night she had been with Tim Tazik. How the hell would she have had time to see Jason?

Lenny couldn't for a minute believe that Melanie suspected it was Jason who had crawled into her bed. Lenny didn't think Jason had the guts, he looked like such a wimp. No, Melanie was just using Lenny *again,* him being in her bedroom giving her the idea for the whole *Jason can't keep his hands off me* story. Maybe Tazik had a part in the planning as well. One big publicity idea, everyone getting their piece except for Lenny. Even Jason would do okay, his name now bigger than it had ever been.

Lenny wasn't going to let them get away with it. He needed something fast; his mother hadn't given him a dime in weeks, and Tom was making noises about Lenny chipping in for food. Melanie was Lenny's last chance.

Plus this meant he had something to hold over her. She'd *have* to toss him a few bucks. Hook up with him too.

Melanie would need to keep the Jason story alive, and so she'd want to be seen where Jason was staying. Which meant the Hilton.

Lenny parked in the Hilton staff lot, pretty inconspicuous amongst the other older model cars, but where he'd still have a good view of the guest lot. Not much going on, so quiet that even with his windows half open Lenny couldn't help from dozing off until a rapid tapping made him jump. A robotic-looking police officer was peering into the car.

"You have a bed to sleep in?"

Lenny was instantly wide awake. That Melanie was blaming Jason for the break-in hadn't stopped Lenny from being spooked every time he saw a cop. "Sorry, officer, I'm supposed to be meeting someone here, they must be running late. I've been working nights and I'm just exhausted. They should be coming any minute now."

You can't stay here. You don't have a staff parking sticker."

"Couldn't you give me a few more minutes? I'm not in anybody's way."

"What's your business here?"

Lenny lied. "My ma is sick, I have this night job, but I need something else during the day, you know, to help with her medical bills. This guy I met washes dishes at this hotel, he said he could introduce me to the kitchen manager. I'm just looking for some honest work."

"I don't recognize you, you from Marburg?"

"We just moved here a few months ago, we're over on Hamilton Street."

The cop hesitated, Lenny thinking he was going to ask for ID, but instead the cop said, "I'm back this way in twenty minutes. If you're sleeping in your car or not gone by then I'm going to write you up. Understand?"

"Yes sir, thank you, sir."

The cop walked off through the guest lot, Lenny watching him in the rear view. Still no Melanie. When he saw the cop come back Lenny started his car and cruised the block a few times until he saw a police car pull out of the Hilton. Just as Lenny turned into the lot again he spotted Melanie getting out of her Toyota. She was wearing a peach colored tank top with dark blue skinny jeans, striding confidently along in strappy heeled sandals, Lenny thinking she looked hot, as always, the chic top softening the look of the skin tight pants. Her arms needed a little more toning. Lenny would get her to work on that, it was the kind of advice she needed from him.

Before Melanie had a chance to reach the back entrance of the hotel he cut her off with the Caddy and popped out, discreetly pulling at his shirt to hide the wrinkles.

"You're like a virus," said Melanie.

"Hello yourself," said Lenny, not even upset she was her usual bitchy self. "I want to talk to you."

"Get in line. Or better yet, don't."

Melanie had still given no indication she was willing to admit anything at all about the night he had been with her. Could she be playing him? Lenny glanced around, looking for witnesses. Was she working with the police, setting him up? Where was that cop? "I saw the show," he said carefully.

"You and a million other people." Melanie skirted around the Caddy.

"I got to say, you are good," said Lenny, truthfully. "Jumping into the public eye by implying Jason Ayers practically assaulted you. Too bad it's all a lie. We both know you couldn't have been with Jason that night."

That stopped her. Melanie squinted at him. "You don't know shit."

"As a matter of fact, I do."

"As usual, I have no fucking idea what you are talking about."

"Do you want me to spell it out?" Lenny was sweating, this was it.

"I don't want anything from you. Except to be left alone. Remember the last time you were here? My friend the bartender? Keep bothering me and I'll have him take care of you."

So she was going to keep playing that game. Lenny tried a different approach. "You owe me." Lenny saw Melanie about to object and kept going. "Not the photo idea, I'm over that. But you got to admit, you'd have never made it to *The Other Woman* if I hadn't put the publicity idea in your head."

"You want to go around claiming credit for my success, I don't give a shit. Just don't bother me."

"Believe what you want. Just remember I helped get you there, and I can pull you down just as fast. I'll tell them you weren't with Jason."

Melanie barked out a dismissive laugh. "Who's going to believe a nobody who hangs out behind a dumpster in a hotel parking lot?"

"I wasn't hanging out here, I was waiting for you."

"I could walk into that staff entrance right now and come out with three guys who'll swear you were. You know why? Just because I asked them to. That's the difference between me and you. People will do what I want, and people will cross the street if they see you coming. No, that's not it. They'll drive their car up on the sidewalk to run you over if they see you." Melanie was halfway to the back entrance.

Lenny had plenty of experience with harsh words from women, but Melanie was wearing him down. If only she wasn't so hot, and such a perfect meal ticket. One or the other he'd be able to maybe walk away from, but the combination was irresistible.

"I can prove you weren't with Jason."

Melanie stopped, her hand on the door. She half turned to him, the small motion lifting Lenny's spirits, like he'd scored a point. More than one.

"What do you want, Lenny?" she said, a surprising weariness in her voice, like she'd grown tired of playing a part.

Lenny gave her his best smile. "Let's be a team. Me and you. I can help you. And I'm not embarrassed to admit you can help me. You're smart, you know how this game works. We can do better together than fighting with each other."

"I'm not fighting you, I'm ignoring you. You got nothing I want."

"I told you, I have proof you weren't with Jason."

"So you're a blackmailer now?"

Lenny's heart leapt, she'd practically admitted she wasn't with Jason. "Such a harsh term, Melanie. For your future partner. We might have more in common than you think."

"What planet are you from? I'm moving up, you think I'm going to carry your weight too? Go find someone else to run your con on."

"You aren't as far ahead of me as you think. And you'll be the next Tonya Harding if I tell the world what I know. I got a friend at Channel Ten. How are you going to feel if you're lying in bed tonight, watching your fancy tv, and you're the lead story on the news, charged with making up that story about Jason?"

"Get out of my life, asshole." Melanie went through the glass door.

"Think about it!" Lenny called after her. "Me and you!"

Melanie flipped him the bird and kept walking.

MELANIE WALKED THROUGH the lobby of the Hilton, glancing briefly at the bar. She needed a drink after seeing Lenny, a drink and a shower. But she was at the hotel only so people would remember seeing her around, they'd spread the word for sure. If she was really with Jason she'd have a key to his room, she wouldn't be hanging around the bar, although she could say she was just having a drink before he got back. Unless Jason was in his room, then she'd be screwed.

Too many moving pieces . . .

After making sure the front desk staff had noticed her Melanie waited until no one was by the elevator and got on alone. She didn't have access to the Executive Floor, so she hit a few random buttons. She got off at two, switched elevators, and rode down to the gym and pool level.

No one was in the hall, good. She took the stairs and walked out the side entrance. As far as everyone in the lobby who had seen her was concerned, she was up in Jason's room.

Melanie snuck a peek around the corner of the building. Lenny's ugly Cadillac was gone. She hurried to her car and drove out of the Hilton lot, heading for home.

Lenny had bothered her more than she had let on. Certainly there was no way he could have any proof that she wasn't with Jason that night; the only person who could claim that was Taz, and being supposedly happily married, he'd never say a word. Melanie couldn't imagine Taz and Lenny hanging out, swapping stories about women they'd slept with, but she'd have to find out if Taz had let something slip along the way, maybe Lenny had heard a rumor . . .

But Lenny had sounded so damned sure of himself, like he had something on her. Had he seen her go into the hotel to meet Taz? She and Taz hadn't even hooked up in Marburg, how would Lenny even know where they'd been?

Unless he'd been following her, she didn't put it past him.

Melanie parked in the litter strewn lot behind her apartment building. She had to get out of here, away from the run down building, the musky smell of the fumes from the Indian restaurant, her ancient car. She was so close to escaping everything she despised. It was bad enough not making it big, but being forced to live barely above a street person was degrading, she deserved better.

Things were coming together, she just needed a little more time. Always a realist, she knew her path to becoming a star was a little tenuous, wasn't everything? She'd set it all in motion, this was probably the best chance she'd ever get in her life. That jerk Lenny was right about one thing: if her story about Jason came undone, she'd be a laughing-stock. Yet she couldn't imagine how Lenny could really have proof about her not being with Jason.

Still, Lenny threatened to blow her entire carefully crafted story wide open. She had to find out what he knew and figure out a way to shut him up. Not in the way he hoped, even she wasn't that desperate. She wouldn't be his partner or his meal ticket, and certainly not his girlfriend.

Inside her apartment Melanie poured some wine, plopped on the couch, and flicked on the television, looking for a mindless show to calm her down. *Television . . .*

What had Lenny said? Something about watching her fancy tele-vision. How did Lenny know she had a new tv?

He couldn't have. He'd said *sitting in bed, watching television.* Melanie's bedroom wasn't big enough for a tv, not like Gigi's . . .

Melanie sat up so quickly she spilled the wine all over her silk blouse. Like one of those pictures you squinted at and it turned into something else, she finally understood what Lenny had been babbling about. All those cryptic comments to her about knowing who she really was, about what they'd shared. Gigi's break-in, some guy who'd touched her, some perverted stalker who seemed to know her, who said that the next time they saw each other they'd do it for real . . .

Lenny smugly sure Melanie couldn't have been with Jason that night, because Lenny believed *he* had been with Melanie, in her apartment. An apartment with a television in the bedroom.

Gigi's bedroom.

Gigi hadn't imagined anything, it hadn't been a bad dream, it hadn't been a druggie looking to rob the place, it had been *Lenny*, he'd broken in, thinking he was at Melanie's apartment.

Lenny had laid his hands on her sister.

The wine had seeped through her blouse, clammy on her skin, a blood red stain. Melanie literally saw red. Not wine, but Lenny's blood.

Lenny asshole sleazebag, she was going to fucking kill him.

CHAPTER 19

MELANIE HAD BEEN IN THE Hilton parking lot so many times she might as well have lived there. Where the fuck was Lenny? He'd been cropping up like an ugly pimple until she needed to find him. He'd been here yesterday looking for her, she was certain he'd be back at some point, but so far, nothing.

She exited the lot and headed out of town on one of the back roads, she needed to think. Not that she hadn't been all night. She was ninety nine percent convinced that Lenny had been the freak who had assaulted Gigi. It all made sense, his comments, his attitude. The asshole must have followed her to Gigi's at some point, thinking it was where she lived.

Melanie wouldn't have thought Lenny would have the balls for a break-in, let alone trying to climb in Gigi's bed. *Her* bed.

She'd get him for that.

If she'd been in Gigi's apartment that night, she would have beaten the shit out of him. Gigi simply didn't deserve this, and Melanie was going to make it right, just like she always had, protecting her sister. If Melanie hadn't been staying at Gigi's, none of this would have happened. Not that it was *her* fault either.

Still, Melanie had to be sure. She needed to get Lenny alone, pry the truth out of him about Gigi. Even if he had nothing to do with the break-in, Melanie still needed to find out what proof Lenny thought he had about her not being with Jason that night. If Lenny had date stamped photos of her and Taz she'd be screwed. Melanie wouldn't put it past Lenny to have hung out at a hotel all night, waiting for Melanie to come out to get a walk of shame shot in the morning. If that went public, no one would believe her story about Jason, a story she really needed to ride until the roles started coming in. Publicity was so fleeting, if she got caught in her lie she'd flame out before she even had a chance to blaze.

The old saying was that bad publicity was better than no publicity, but in her case it would be the kiss of death. Melanie shuddered at the possible headline: *Ashley Hanna consoles heartthrob Jason Ayers after desperate actress fabricates despicable assault story.*

Or worse: *Publicity seeking photographer colludes with actress to blackmail America's sweethearts Jason Ayers and Ashley Hanna.*

Melanie wasn't going to let that happen.

As it was, she hadn't charged Jason with anything, not really, she'd just tossed out the idea, and it had taken wing, the insinuation more powerful than her yelling rape. At every opportunity she'd said nice things about Jason, each utterance leaving just a hint of doubt, but most important, making it clear that Melanie was *somebody*, she had that special sauce that drove men wild, that women wanted to emulate. Her ticket to stardom.

All of her plans in jeopardy if she couldn't find Lenny.

Driving on the quiet road with her knees, she flicked through her phone. Lenny called himself a photographer, he must be online. What was his last name? A horn behind her blared, Melanie ignored it. Something with a *G* . . .

The horn blared again, Melanie sliding over, letting the asshole past, giving the car the finger, not even looking at the driver, still intent on her phone. She started to type *Marburg photographers*, misspelling as gravel crunched under her wheels. Frigging Lenny, he wasn't even here and he was driving her off the road.

Melanie pulled the Toyota to the shoulder, got the search ready, but at the last second changed her mind. She didn't know a thing about internet records, but who knew what could be found from her search history. She didn't want a record of any connection to Lenny.

She spun the car around and headed back to Marburg. After one quick run past the Hilton—no Lenny—she continued cross town to the library. It only took a quick tuck of her hair under a Red Sox cap, sunglasses, and a slouch in her step to transform her into just another local.

She'd been in the library once, acting out a reading for some little kids, an embarrassing gig she'd taken years ago when she thought that was what actresses did to learn their craft. Nothing inside had changed, the same unnatural green hues, the same magazine racks. A few elderly types sat at the public computers. No one even looked up.

Melanie googled *Lenny photographer Marburg*. He popped up, surprisingly, on the first page, maybe he was more well known than Melanie had given him credit for. Lenny *Gruse* . . .

Lenny had a website, Melanie clicking through his portfolio. He wasn't half bad. Not as good as Taz, but Lenny's shots felt more real, less posed. Probably because he'd been waiting behind a dumpster to ambush the subjects . . .

She made sure there were no shots of her. There weren't, in fact, nothing that she recognized from Marburg at all, no local actresses or backgrounds.

No address listed, Lenny obviously didn't have a studio. Melanie copied the contact phone number onto a yellow sticky sitting by the computer, cleaned out the browser search history, and left.

Back in her car, she rolled down the windows and lit a smoke. What now?

Get Lenny alone. If she was going to pry information out of him, she'd need some privacy. No way she could do that in the bar at the Hilton, too many ears, and who knew what Lenny might say or do.

Melanie didn't want him at her apartment either. Nothing that would tie them together, just in case he did try to pull some stunt, like bring the press along to get his own publicity, claiming he was her muse, or—shudder—her lover.

Lenny probably didn't know where she really lived. She could call him, ask him to meet her at her place, then see where he showed up. If he went to Gigi's that would be one more piece of evidence that he'd been the one who'd broken in. But not conclusive, and what would she do? Beat him up in front of Gigi's neighbors? Call the cops?

Hello officer? It didn't happen at my place across town like I claimed, and it wasn't Jason Ayers as I implied, it was this greaseball Lenny Gruse, and it was my sister he got in bed with, not me.

They'd lock Melanie up along with Lenny.

No, she'd have to deal with this on her own. As always.

Lenny wanted a meal ticket, but more than that, he wanted Melanie, that was pretty clear. He wasn't the first guy who she'd tied up in knots, she recognized all the symptoms. Most of them she'd ignored, unless she needed something. Lenny had nothing she needed, or so she had thought.

Still, she could use *his* need . . .

Melanie tossed her butt out the window. Underneath assorted junk in the glove compartment she found what she was looking for, a prepaid cell phone. A married guy she'd been seeing in Boston, a source of great coke, had given it to her, telling her to use it to call him so his wife wouldn't know, he had one as well. Melanie had pretended it was a brilliant idea, not bothering to mention she had a collection of them, practically every married guy she'd been with having the same idea, like they'd all graduated from the same school of adultery.

The battery was dead, so she rooted around for a charger, plugged it into the cigarette lighter, and punched in Lenny's number. Some of that good coke would be really good right about now.

LENNY LAY IN HIS hard narrow bunk bed. Sweat dripped under his tee shirt. He couldn't go downstairs to the one room with air conditioning, because both his mother and Tom were home, and he didn't want to face the cross examination about the job hunt he'd pretended he'd been on. He'd gone out, but only to find Melanie, and had snuck in the back door and surreptitiously dashed up to the attic in his bare feet.

He'd switched his phone to vibrate and it lay on his chest where he'd be sure to feel it, yet he couldn't resist constantly checking to see if he'd missed a message. Melanie would call, he was sure of it.

A few hours earlier he'd panicked, it suddenly dawning on him that Melanie probably didn't have his phone number, he'd never gotten that far with her. But she was smart, she'd figure out how to contact him.

He hoped.

To pass the time he flicked through the shots he had of Melanie on his camera, too few of them. The first two he had taken, in the restaurant when he'd first discovered her, just her backside, so hot. A few others he'd managed, quick snaps, his camera on the strap, wide angle. Junk photos, no way to sell them, even when Melanie became really famous, but Lenny could fill in the blanks, they were *his*.

He'd have more soon enough.

Melanie had stopped for him at the back of the Hilton; beneath all her high and mighty bluster she knew she needed him. He had leaned into her psychologically, and for the first time since he had spoken to her, she had blinked.

She was obviously afraid of what he could do, she had to be desperate to keep her story going about Jason. He knew it, and she knew he knew. All the dancing around would end, sooner or later. She'd give up. And even better, give it up.

The more Lenny thought about it, the more he realized how fragile Melanie's situation was. Sure, she'd been on *The Other Woman*, she'd played her card and so far she was ahead. But she was bluffing, and though the rest of the world might be buying her story, at least enough of it, Lenny had proof of her deception. That he couldn't exactly produce the Tazik photos or admit Melanie couldn't be with Jason because he himself was in her apartment didn't bother him at all. The important thing was that Melanie realized he knew her secret, and she'd always wonder. If he had to he could threaten to go to the police, they'd get the photos from Tazik. Then what could Melanie do?

Melanie needed Lenny just as much as he needed her. More, because she had more to lose. If Melanie walked out of his life today, Lenny would be no worse off than he was before. Melanie, though, would be screwed. Hard as it was to make it as an actress, Melanie would have a tough time getting cast in amateur theater if word got out about her made up assault story.

If Melanie didn't play ball, Lenny could ruin her entire life. He didn't have any friend at Channel Ten, but no doubt one would be easy to find if he needed to. Reporters were even more bloodthirsty than actors.

As the afternoon wore on he kept adding to the list in his head of what he'd demand from Melanie. A contract as her manager, to be sure. A retainer; he'd tell her he needed to focus on her exclusively, he wouldn't have time to be chasing down celebrity photos.

And most of all, a little time in the sack, the ultimate proof of her acceptance of his terms. She'd slept with that Tazik guy for a lot less.

The next time he got Melanie in bed he wouldn't be sneaking around in the dark, wearing a mask. She wouldn't be able to pretend or deny he was there.

He fingered the last of the roofies in his pocket, always handy. He wouldn't need them for her, he'd probably never need them again.

Lenny dozed off, smiling, letting it play out in his head, making the movie come out exactly how he wanted.

The buzzing phone jolted him awake, his camera crashing to the floor. No name, just a number he didn't recognize.

"Hello?"

"Hey, Lenny, it's Melanie."

As if he wouldn't recognize her voice. "I knew you'd call."

"I want to talk. About everything."

Given what he'd been dreaming about, it wasn't hard for Lenny to read a lot into that word, *everything*. He was wide awake, sitting up in the bed. "Sure. Your place?"

There was a pause, then Melanie said, "I don't know. There have been a lot of press following me around. I think until we get things straightened out between us it might be better if we aren't seen together. You were right about the Jason story, I need to keep that alive, so I can't be seen with another man. Not now."

Lenny got it. "That makes sense." As long as Melanie was willing to see him, he didn't care where. Although not here, no way he'd bring her to Tom's attic.

"Unless you think you should come to my place?" Melanie's voice was hesitant, deferential.

She was looking for his guidance already. "Nah, not now. We'll have time enough for that."

"If you're sure. It's pretty quiet."

"You never know who might be sneaking around. Better not risk it." He certainly knew how easy it was to spy on her apartment.

"If you say so." There was another hesitation. "You're right. We better get out of Marburg, too many people know me here. And if we're getting together, could you bring your camera? I need some new photos."

"Sure." Lenny was already reaching for the strap.

Melanie's voice shifted. "If things work out, maybe we can do a few *au natural*."

"Like Tazik did?" Lenny cursed himself, he didn't want to sound petty, especially now that he practically had her. So what if she'd been with Tazik? That was the past, she wouldn't need Tazik any longer.

"You've seen those?"

Melanie sounded more curious than angry, so Lenny said, "Something like that."

"I'll let you shoot something better. Much better."

Lenny grinned. This was more like it. "We're going to be great together."

"I hope so. But Lenny, we still have some things to work out. I've got a very complicated plan in motion and we have to make sure we're on the same page."

"I get it, I do."

"Just keep it quiet until we have a chance to talk, okay? Don't tell *anyone*." Melanie's voice turned hard, so sharp that Lenny couldn't tell if it was an act. "If you do, and you can't give me what I need, I'll humiliate you worse than you can imagine. I swear I'll take you down with me."

"Hey, don't worry, baby, this is Lenny Gruse you're talking to."

"I still don't know you. You'll have to—prove yourself."

Lenny tightened. Was that a crack about his inability to perform in her bedroom? "Don't worry," he said. "I've got what it takes. But we'll have to be public at some point, that's going to be part of the deal."

"One step at a time. I'm prepared to do my part."

Lenny relaxed, Melanie sounded like she was on board. He was still confused as to why she hadn't brought up the whole bedroom situation, but maybe she didn't want to piss him off. Or she really didn't know. Or care.

"Where should we meet?" he asked, already pulling off his pants, he needed to get in the shower.

"You know Greenhill? East on the expressway toward Boston about ten miles. When you get off the exit go through the town and cross the railroad tracks. There's a very private little place there called the Greenhill Motel."

Lenny didn't want to admit he barely knew his way around Marburg. It sounded easy to find though. "Why way out there?"

"I told you, we have to do this privately. Plus I know the desk clerk, he can get us a room for nothing. Unless you want to spring for a room?"

"Uh, I figured, you know, you must have some cash coming in from—"

"What, we're having a date and you want me to pay?"

"That's not what I meant."

"It takes a while for the checks to show up. Anyway, like I said we can get a room for free. And I mean it, before I get in bed with you professionally I need to see if—if you are good doing it for *real*, you know what I mean?"

There it was again, another veiled reference to his temporary impotence. Or maybe he was just being sensitive. "Sure, sure."

"Good. When you get to the Greenhill, don't go in, the manager might be there, and the guy I know won't recognize you, so you just can't go telling him you're expecting a freebie. There's a parking lot out back, just wait for me back there if you don't see my car. You know my car, right?"

"The blue Toyota, sure. Melanie, we got to get better wheels."

"If things work out right, we won't be driving ourselves around any more, limos all the way."

That sounded just fine to Lenny. "What time?"

"How about ten tonight? I got to go somewhere before that."

"It better not be another date." Lenny tried to keep his voice light.

"Not that kind," said Melanie, and she hung up.

MELANIE STARED OUT of her grimy windows at the even grimier

street, the din of crashing pots and pans from the restaurant below so loud she could barely hear the television. Not that she was listening. She'd been standing in the same spot for an hour, her eyes unfocused, using all her faculties to figure a way out of her problem.

The situation with Lenny was even worse than she had thought. Lenny had certainly seen the photos Tazik had taken of her in the hotel that night she'd slept with him. She'd been too drunk to remember exactly what was on them, a vague recollection of laughing as Tazik showed her some and held back others, implying he'd captured more of her than she'd ever let be photographed.

She'd deal with Taz later. Even if he had recognizable nudes, who was he going to show them to? They'd been shot in a hotel bed. How would he explain that to his wife? No one would care anyway, half the actresses in Hollywood had nude photos floating around, and the other half wished they had a body good enough that people would want to see them naked.

Taz wouldn't be a problem.

Lenny, on the other hand, was a mine field. He could screw with her a dozen ways.

And the whole thing with Gigi. Melanie had hoped that Lenny would let something slip on the call, but he'd been cagier than she had expected, not admitting that he knew where she lived, or rather, where he thought she lived. She'd pushed it as far as she could. Any more he'd get suspicious, and she might never learn the truth. The phone wasn't the right way, she had to be looking at his face.

If Lenny didn't get his way, she had no doubt he would play his trump card, he'd claim Melanie had made up the whole Jason story. She could deny it, claim Lenny was just trying to get some publicity, although she'd have to be especially brazen to pull *that* off, since it was what she was doing too. Lenny could say it had been his idea all along, the photos at the press conference, the whole game. Who knows who he had already blabbed to about his connection with her.

Who has seen her with Lenny? Some people at the club, at the restaurant, at the hotel. Nothing that couldn't be explained; Lenny just one of many guys hitting on her, although the bar scene where'd he broken the glass dish—maybe she'd have to talk to the bartender about that. It was another reason why she'd picked an out of the way place to meet Lenny tonight, the fewer people who saw her with him, the better.

An especially loud smash from the restaurant below, a pot crashing to the floor. That's what she needed, something to smash Lenny's head in if he was the one who had broken into Gigi's apartment. And even if he hadn't, smash his head anyway, scare him off.

Would that work? Melanie considered bringing someone along to meet with Lenny. The bartender at the Hilton, he had a thing for her. The bouncer at the club. Shit, she could think of ten guys who'd be happy to beat the crap out of Lenny just to make her happy. Even Taz might be willing to do it.

Too complicated. The last thing she needed was some other asshole who felt that she owed him.

Maybe she could talk Larry Barrett into getting Lenny some kind of gig, pay him a few bucks, make him feel important. Shut him up. She'd have to figure out a way to explain why. Even more complicated. Plus Lenny wouldn't settle for that, just as she wouldn't if she were in his shoes. If she had what Lenny had to hang over someone's head, she'd milk it for everything. She didn't even blame Lenny for that part, it was just the way things worked. You used what you had, or you got nowhere.

No, she'd have to take care of this herself. Find out what Lenny had, and if it was something that could come back to bite her, destroy it.

And find out if Lenny was guilty of the break-in at Gigi's. And especially if it had been more than a break-in. If it had, she'd make him pay.

She wished she had a gun to threaten Lenny with. She had no doubt she could scratch his eyes bloody, kick him so hard in the balls he wouldn't be able to walk for a week. She'd done all of that to men before, and more. But a kick in the nuts was useless as a threat, it wouldn't stop Lenny from turning on her the minute he got his voice back.

Another crash from below, a tray of silverware, cymbals reverberating in her head. Silverware . . .

In her tiny kitchen she pulled open the cabinet under the sink. A wide eyed mouse stared at her, either too surprised or not afraid to move. Melanie threw a scouring pad at it, then rooted around amidst the clutter of kitchen detritus left behind by previous tenants, frying pans, plastic cups, there, a kitchen carving knife.

She held it up, waving it theatrically. One look at that and Lenny would wet his pants. He thought he knew her, he didn't know shit. She'd convince him she was a nut job, that she'd cut him open. She wouldn't even have to act.

CHAPTER 20

AT EIGHT THIRTY Melanie was back at the Hilton, this time walking in the front door. She was wearing a bright blue plunge cut dress and a new pair of Jimmy Choos, courtesy of Tazik, who'd paid off. The dress had been a gift from some other guy. Blue wasn't her color so she'd never worn it, but it was time for people to start remembering her.

Melanie did her usual pass through the bar, lingering a little longer, getting a comp drink from her bartender friend, giving off the vibe that she was waiting for Jason or had just come from his room. After throwing back the rest of the drink she drove to the club. She gave the bouncer's arm the usual squeeze and walked in, feeling the eyes on her, she never tired of the rush.

Fiona was at the bar, two guys in leather hitting on her. Fiona seemed to be enjoying the attention. Melanie caught her eye, Fiona's face tightening, Melanie catching the hidden message. *I like you, girl, but if come over here flashing your cleavage at these two guys I'll rip your heart out.* Melanie gave Fiona a smile, she had more important things on her mind than stealing some bikers from a bartender.

Melanie made a quick walk though the entire place. At the front bar she let a group of middle aged men buy her a drink and chat her up, telling them she was on her way to meet her boyfriend, just stopping to say hello to a few friends. From any other woman the men might have taken this as a brush off, but the way Melanie was dressed and the way she looked had them all convinced—*of course* she had a boyfriend. Melanie made sure they got her name and then slipped out, the bouncer still spinning his keys.

Back at her apartment she stripped off the dress and shoes and quickly slipped into jeans, black sneakers, and a man's shirt. She stuffed her hair under a Bruins cap, changed her mind—people might remember a hockey cap in summer—replacing it with her worn Red Sox cap. Half the people in Marburg wore those, men and women.

Melanie doubted all this secrecy was necessary, but she'd been a little sloppy with Lenny, and now that she suspected what he could do to bring her down, she had to create as much distance from him as she could. The last thing she needed was for Lenny to claim he'd concocted the whole Jason story with her, followed by people popping up who had seen them together, like she and Lenny were dating.

Just thinking it made her cringe.

In the Toyota she popped in a CD and took a final look around the back lot, deserted, as usual, even the restaurant staff didn't park back here.

On the way to Greenhill she rehearsed how she'd work Lenny. The most important thing was finding out about Gigi, but if she started with that she'd never learn what else she needed to know. She'd have to control herself, build up to it, find out about the photos, how incriminating they were, if there were copies, what else Lenny knew, whether he could prove anything. Only when that was accomplished could she trap him into admitting whether he was at Gigi's.

With *her*, she reminded herself. If Lenny had broken into Gigi's apartment, he had thought he was at Melanie's. That was how she'd work it, she'd hint around that she wanted more, why had he left so soon . . .

Just another acting job, it shouldn't be that hard. In fact the more she thought of it as a role the easier it would be, nothing personal, it wasn't about her or Gigi, just a part to play.

Until she found out the truth.

The knife lay on the seat next to her, dull, no reflections from the streetlights giving it away. She should slip it under the seat; if she got stopped by a cop it would be hard to explain, but it gave her comfort. The time she'd beaten up the boy who had groped Gigi she hadn't brought a knife, she'd used her fists, her fingernails, her teeth. Maybe it was a good thing she hadn't had a knife that day, who knows what she might have done.

But scaring off and punishing a teenager was one thing; a grown man, even a loser like Lenny, was something else. He outweighed her by fifty pounds at least. So she'd bring the knife.

The exit to Greenhill was dark, no cars getting off. She drove slowly through town, everything seedier than she remembered it, if that were possible. The place was a dump, an old manufacturing town with no factories running. The main drag was lined with fast food restaurants that hadn't been remodeled in years, interspersed with boarded up stores and vacant lots. It was hard to imagine a city of almost five million people was less than an hour away.

The Toyota bounced across a set of rails, except there was no bad part of town, the entire town was across the proverbial tracks. Melanie knew the motel because she'd once been offered a hook up there with one of the first men who promised her he'd help her make it big, years back when she believed that shit. She'd pulled into the lot, taken one look at the motel and drove right back out, her instincts telling her that any man who wanted to meet up with her at a dive like the Greenhill couldn't have much going for him in his head or his pocketbook.

But she remembered enough about the place to know it was a good spot to meet Lenny. If nothing had changed, and it was hard to imagine it would have, the back of the Greenhill was bordered by a vacant lot and an old industrial warehouse. She could flash the knife at Lenny if she had to and no one would be around to see.

She drove slowly past the front of the motel, an old fashioned neon light promising vacancy, no doubt the place practically empty. A few stores along the street, all closed. Beyond that, old houses, some with lights on, mostly upstairs, working stiffs going to bed early.

Melanie pulled the Toyota into an apartment complex lot. An old guy was getting out of his car, he didn't even glance her way. Melanie waited until he disappeared into the complex. She sat there for a few minutes, even though she wanted to be early to meet Lenny, running her fingers over the tip of the knife. It wasn't especially sharp, but Lenny wouldn't know that.

Melanie got in role and slipped out of the car. From the backseat she pulled on a thin leather jacket, dropping the knife in the pocket.

A door slammed somewhere in the complex, but no one came

toward the parking lot. Melanie headed back toward the motel, a whisper in the darkness, a black spider on her way to ensnare an unsuspecting prey.

LENNY GOT LOST looking for the Greenhill Motel even with the help of his phone GPS. He was squinting through the windshield, searching vainly for signs, the streets so close together he missed the turn. The houses didn't even have driveways to turn around in, cars parked on the streets, even on the small front lawns.

Was this really where Melanie wanted to hook up?

No more after this. Lenny was tired of this shit, getting jerked around by Melanie. He'd make it clear tonight who was calling the shots. They'd meet at her place next time, he certainly knew how to sneak in the back without getting caught by the press. Lenny laughed, *he* was the Marburg celebrity photographer, or used to be, that gig was thankfully over. Soon he'd be walking in the front door of Melanie's apartment, maybe even have some photographer shoot pictures of *him* for a change. *Manager Lenny Gruse on his way to see Melanie Upton.* Or better yet *Melanie Upton Lands Lenny Gruse.* She'd be known by her association with him, not the other way around.

He finally got the Caddy on the right route. Even though the GPS was flashing he drove right by the Greenhill Motel without noticing it; he was looking for a new chain building, not an ancient inn. Maybe it was romantic inside, that's why Melanie had picked it. She'd said she knew the desk clerk. Lenny would have to find out why, he didn't want to be comped by some old boyfriend of hers.

Melanie had so much to learn about how he wanted to be treated.

Lenny turned around again, giving himself one last look in the visor mirror. He hadn't shaved, women loved that two day beard look. He'd worn his best dark blue silk shirt, black jeans, short boots. The shirt was open three buttons, showing off a little chest hair and a gold chain, understated, he wasn't a pimp. He'd stolen some of Tom's cologne, not the best, but he'd run out of his own.

Looking good.

A small sign said *Parking* and he pulled around the back of the motel. The lot was bigger than he expected, a half dozen cars clustered by the back entrance of the motel, lit by a dim spotlight over the door. Across the lot another bunch of cars parked near what looked like a warehouse, illuminated by an even dimmer yellow floodlight.

A figure in a baseball cap was leaning against one of the cars by the door. Lenny started to park but the figure crossed in front of the Caddy and tried to get in the passenger door. Lenny had the doors locked and the figure peered into the window.

"Are you going to let me in or what?"

Lenny responded slowly, not expecting to see Melanie in a baseball cap and a leather jacket, he was hoping for something sexy. He hit the unlock button and Melanie slid in.

No slinky dress, but she still looked fine, her legs slim in the tight jeans. Melanie looked at him and Lenny was hoping she'd lean over for a kiss, but all she said was, "Did you tell anyone?"

"No. Not yet. Where were you tonight?" That wasn't how he wanted the evening to start, already jealous, and still a little pissed that she hadn't dressed up for him, what was that under the jacket, some kind of man's shirt? Who gave her that?

"Not that it's any of your business, but I was at my sister's."

Lenny pulled into a parking space and shut off the engine. "You have a sister?"

Melanie frowned at him. "I thought you knew."

Lenny shrugged. "It's news to me."

"We see a lot of each other, she lives right near me."

"At Lakeview?"

Melanie's faced changed, a hardening, an intensity Lenny had never seen in her before. The look was so severe he cringed back against the door. He'd felt disdain from her, but never anything like this. What had he said? Was she really that pissed just because he didn't know she had a sister?

"What?" he said.

Melanie turned away from him, looking through the windshield, nothing there but darkness. Even in profile she was alluring, that perfect nose, her slim figure. Lenny had seen a lot of beautiful women, lusted over hundreds, but he'd never wanted one as much as he wanted her.

And now he'd pissed her off. He tried to think of what to say. He was so smooth with women, everyone except Melanie. He'd have to fix that. She just twisted him all around.

Melanie seemed to be composing herself, Lenny praying he hadn't messed up, women were so sensitive.

Melanie finally turned back to him, her face relaxed, but the steel still in her eyes. "Nothing," she said. "Just family stuff. Hey, about those photos . . ."

"Are we going to go inside?"

"Let's get this other thing straightened out first. I don't want to be talking shop in there, you know what I mean?"

That was more like it. "Look, Melanie, like I told you, I'm impressed by what you are doing. The whole Jason thing, it's working. But you got to play it just right, you don't want to come out of this looking like some desperate third wheel now that Ashley Hanna is in the picture."

"So if you are so impressed, why are you holding this over my head? Threatening to blow my story?"

"I didn't mean anything by that. You just kept jerking me around. I just wanted to get your attention, take me seriously."

"I want to believe you, I do. But you got to admit, I don't have much to go on."

Lenny leaned over toward her, he wanted to take her in his arms and console her, but she spun on the seat and set her back against the far door, out of reach, her legs tucked under her lap. "I don't want to ruin your story. But you got to let it go at some point, you have to become known as someone other than Jason Ayer's other woman."

"Gee, I never would have thought of that! You're *so* smart."

Just when Lenny thought he was softening her up, Melanie fell back into her bitchy mode. "It's talk like that that pisses me off, makes me say things I might not mean."

"Like having proof I wasn't with Jason?"

"I've seen the proof alright. I didn't really mean I'd use it. Unless you forced me to."

"So you don't have it?"

"I've seen it." Lenny knew he sounded like a little kid, but Melanie turned his crank.

Melanie's voice softened. "Lenny, if we are going to work to-gether—*be* together—we need a little honesty here."

"You answer me a question first and then I'll tell you."

Melanie sighed theatrically. "Okay."

"What's with you and Tazik?"

"*That's* what's bothering you?"

"You said honesty, right?"

Melanie crossed her arms over her chest. "Fine. I slept with him because he took those photos at the press conference. Is that what you wanted to hear?"

Lenny swallowed hard, his gut twisting. He had assumed as much, but hearing Melanie admit it was tough to take. "That should have been me," he said. "I gave you that idea."

"Tazik is nothing to me. I'm here with you now, aren't I?" Melanie cocked her head. "Is that why you thought I wasn't with Jason? Taz showed you the pictures he took that night?"

Lenny nodded glumly. "He said he was doing a book on tattoos. I recognized yours from a picture I saw on the web. Plus, you know, you wouldn't have had time to be with Jason."

Melanie gave him an enigmatic smile. "Me being with more than one man in a night you mean?"

Lenny looked away, he couldn't face this now, not if he didn't know how she felt about it. "Something like that."

He thought Melanie was going to press him, but instead she said, "I was pretty drunk that night, do you have copies of the pictures? Taz never showed me."

"Yeah, you were out of it alright." It made sense now, her reaction in the bed, she must have been stoned. He softened, maybe *she* was the one who couldn't perform that night. "I don't have copies, Taz showed them to me on his phone." He thought of something. "Hey, he said he was going to do a book, no way he'd use camera shots for an art book. Did he use a better camera? Or did you promise him a real shoot?"

"You're sitting outside a motel with me, and that's what you want to talk about? Another guy?"

"If we're going to be partners you have to listen to me when it comes to your image," argued Lenny. "This is what I can help you with."

Melanie dropped her eyes into her lap, her voice hollow, resigned. "Tell me exactly what you mean by partners."

Lenny had been thinking a lot about this. "First, it's the business stuff. Think of me as your manager. I'll give you guidance on your publicity, what roles you should take."

"I already have an agent."

"You need more than an agent. You're going to be a *star*. You need someone to manage all the details. You want to waste time doing paperwork, going to meetings? You're going to be acting, doing interviews."

"And I expect you want to be paid for all this."

Lenny was ready for this too. "You'd have to pay someone, why not me? I can manage all your money too. You want to be worried about all that while you're on television, in movies?"

"I guess so," said Melanie, her voice subdued.

"It'll work out, you'll see." Lenny hesitated, waiting for an argument, but Melanie just kept looking in her lap. He forged ahead. "And if we are going to be working so closely together, you know, I think it's only natural that we are together all the time." Shit, that sounded so lame. She needed a forceful guy, he'd seen proof of that.

"About that." Melanie finally looked up, her eyes still not matching her vibe. "If you and I—get together, we have to keep it quiet, at least for now. I have to keep the Jason thing going for a while, you said yourself it was a good play."

Lenny felt a flush of heat, she was his for the taking, this was as close as Melanie would ever get to saying it, at least right now. "Sure, but we can still hook up, like here, tonight. You know what I mean?"

Melanie glanced around the parking lot, then stretched catlike against the door, slipping her hands into the pockets of the jacket, the leather separating to reveal her chest. Lenny felt her eyes on him, really looking at him, but it was just an impression, his own eyes were focused elsewhere.

"Maybe if you had played your cards right that night you were with me, we wouldn't have to do this, sneaking around at a motel." Melanie's voice was a sigh, a promise.

Lenny wasn't thinking straight, it was all happening just as he planned, he didn't care what Melanie was wearing, he didn't care about the dark motel or the baseball cap or the man's shirt. "Melanie, about that night, you know, in the bed, I just wanted to show you what I could give you . . ."

Melanie's lip quivered, she sucked in a breath Lenny could hear. "Shit, shit, shit," she said, her eyes glazing over. "Why did it have to be you?"

"I just wanted to change your opinion of me, surprise you. Hey, it must have worked, you're here, right?"

She stared at him for a long time and then slowly slipped out of her jacket, a striptease just for him, the leather pooling in her lap. She moved across the seat, getting on her knees, leaning over to him, close, Lenny hadn't been this close to a woman in forever. Her musk filled his nostrils, the brim of her cap hit his forehead and fell off, her face filled his vision, her eyes wide open, magnetic even in their hardness. Lenny felt the heat, he'd *won*, he'd impressed her, he didn't have to apologize, the break-in hadn't been a mistake after all . . .

""My sister's name is Gigi," whispered Melanie.

"What?" croaked Lenny.

"Gigi. This is for her."

Lenny held his breath as she leaned in, he prayed she was going to kiss him. Her body pressed against his, her hand blissfully dropping to his crotch. A sharp pain, she was grabbing him, too hard, he squirmed, another sting, even sharper, Lenny's eyes widening in shock, she was too rough, his hands flailing, trying to force their way between them, but his muscles didn't respond, his whole body weak, she was sucking every bit of his energy. Melanie pushed relentlessly down, down, Lenny not comprehending, his expectation of pleasure confused by the excruciating pain, his mouth finally opening to scream. Melanie covered his mouth not with hers but with her hand, the pain unbearable, jagged invasions repeating over and over, rising up into his gut, Melanie's eyes inches from his, so big, how could her eyes be so big, he was falling into them, numbed by her beauty, numbed by her touch. She must have come closer, his vision filled with her very pupils, nothing but blackness.

*   *   *

MELANIE LOOKED OUT over the reservoir, slivers of dancing reflections from the streetlights far across the water on the causeway. The water lapped against the wall below her, the only sound except for an occasional car passing on the other side of the reservoir.

She used to come here in high school. The far reaches of the reservoir on the outskirts of Marburg, a small road, barely wide enough for a car, pounded through the woods from decades of kids looking for a place to smoke their first cigarette, light their first joint, have their first kiss. She'd done all of that here, and more.

No one here tonight, and it didn't look like anyone had been around for a long time. The beer bottles were dusty, the condom wrappers crushed. Melanie felt suddenly very old, high school kids these days didn't sneak around, they hooked up at parties in front of everyone else, it wasn't a big deal anymore.

Acts that ten years ago were shocking, acts that would get you all kinds of publicity. Easier days. Look what she had to do just to get on television now.

She should have felt some remorse over Lenny. Perhaps it was that she had protected Gigi and gotten revenge; Melanie had taken care of things as she always had. Lenny would never bother her sister again. Gigi wouldn't have to know anything other than she was safe. Melanie would find a way to convince Gigi of that without telling her the details. Gigi was just too sensitive to learn the truth.

Lenny had given her no choice. He was never going to let go, he would always be her albatross.

Melanie had pulled out the knife from the jacket pocket, Lenny so full of himself he hadn't even noticed. She hadn't planned on killing Lenny, just scare him, but once he admitted he'd been in the bed with Gigi, that he'd put his hands on her, she had to punish him. Just waving a knife and warning him not to do it again, or getting him to admit he was sorry, was not enough. She wanted to hurt him, cut his balls, but she lost control even while her mind was sorting through her options. How can you threaten someone to not do what they were *already* guilty of? Gigi had been so out of it, Lenny might have raped her . . . and to make matters worse, Melanie had tried to make light of it to Gigi.

She'd stabbed him deeper than she had realized, the blood gushing out from his leg, Lenny stunned, staring at her in disbelief, not fighting or trying to escape, frozen in her deadly embrace. And once he was bleeding Melanie was stuck, what was she going to do, call an ambulance? Say she was defending herself? Make an anonymous call from where, her own phone? How would she explain why she was there? And if he survived, he'd bury her for sure, the photos he had seen would be nothing compared to this.

In the end she had held him down and watched him bleed, feeling no remorse, she was just doing what she had to do. Even if she could have found a way to free herself, he had defiled Gigi. That she could never forgive.

Maybe she'd always known it would end like this, that one day she'd have to pay a horrendous price in order to make it big. If it hadn't been Lenny, it would have been someone else she'd have to step over. Perhaps that was why she had had taken the knife, a part of her deep down inside aware of the steps she might have to take.

And Gigi. She would always have to protect Gigi.

She swung Lenny's camera around over her head by the strap, casting it out into the deep water, the splash satisfying. She'd pulled the memory card out earlier, breaking it into pieces, letting the bits of plastic slip from her fingers as she had driven back toward Marburg. She'd seen nothing incriminating on the memory card, even in the few shots of her, interspersed with hundreds of photos of other women, the desperate attempts by a desperate man to connect to beauty. If Lenny had backups her pictures would be lost in the sea of anonymous bodies.

Melanie stripped off the shirt, there was blood on it. Standing in just her bra and jeans, she formed the shirt into a pouch, filled it with a large rock, wrapped it up and tossed it in the water, watching it sink. It was too dark to see if there was blood on her jeans, she didn't want to take the risk, so she stripped those off too, as well as her sneakers, lashing them together by the laces and flinging everything into the dark abyss.

Melanie stood there in her underwear, not feeling the rocks dig into her bare feet, her senses immune to the chill breeze. As a teenager she been in this very same spot with even less clothing, it didn't faze her in the least.

Lenny's cell phone also went into the reservoir after she'd smashed it with a rock. Then the knife. She'd taken all his money, eight dollars, he didn't even have a credit card, loser. She'd go back home, put the blue dress back on, and hit the club once more. If she needed an alibi, which she doubted, people would remember seeing her at the club.

Nobody would care about Lenny. She certainly didn't.

Melanie gave one last look at the reservoir, thinking of simpler times, then turned away and walked to her car to get on with her life.

CHAPTER 21

MARTIN RYDER WAS ABOUT TO brief Captain Logan when Logan's phone rang. Logan held up his finger in a wait gesture to Ryder and picked up the phone, which pissed Ryder off. Logan couldn't possibly know that the call was more important than his report.

"Logan." The Captain put his feet up on the corner of his messy desk, disturbing Ryder even more than the interruption, the casualness of the entire department evidenced in Logan's repose.

"My detective is here now to give me an update," said Logan. "I don't think we have any breakthrough yet?" Logan looked quizzically at Ryder, who shook his head. "I'll make sure he copies you on everything. Appreciate any help you can give us." Logan leaned back, his chair creaking, Ryder half hoping he'd fall over. "Right. How's Judy? Give her my best. We'll see you at the Rotary meeting. Hey, did I tell you about the wild turkey I bagged with Lewis? Biggest bird I've ever seen. Next year, come with us, we got a spot." Logan swung his feet off the desk, his boots thumping. "Okay, Larry, we'll be in touch."

"Sheriff McAndrew?" asked Ryder.

"Yeah. Offering his help in the stabbing you are working."

"We can handle it." Ryder tried to hide the disdain from his voice about McAndrew; he really didn't have anything against the sheriff, but he hated all the good old boy bullshit. It wasn't likely that McAndrew, or even Logan for that matter, would go hunting with Ryder, even if Ryder hunted.

Logan grunted. "Never turn down help. And he's not going to step on your toes. He could probably take jurisdiction if he wanted."

"I thought we had Greenhill?"

"Only because it's an unincorporated town. Technically it would be under the Sheriff. Or the State Police, who knows. But there was a deal cut a hundred years ago when Greenhill contracted to use the Marburg Police. No joke, back when the police were on horses. The deal didn't exactly spell out who handled major crimes. I don't even know if they still pay the city or what."

"Either way I can handle it," repeated Ryder. He hadn't been lead on a homicide in Marburg and wanted the case.

"Tell me where we are," said Logan.

Ryder looked at his notes, but didn't need them. "Victim is named Lawrence Gruse, aged twenty four. He had no identification—no wallet—but there was an insurance card in the car where the victim was found in the name of Patricia Gruse, the victim's mother. The car was registered to her. Both the victim and his mother moved to Marburg earlier this year from California. They're living at a house belonging to Tom Harris—Patricia's boyfriend. Harris has no record. Neither does the victim or the mother. Cause of death is multiple stab wounds to the upper leg, groin area, and lower torso. One of them hit a femoral artery, Gruse likely bled out."

"Bled out in the car? He didn't try to get help?"

"Looks like it. We're waiting on a toxicology report, see if he was drunk or high, he might not have even known what was going on. We found three capsules in his pocket wrapped in foil, a few empty glassine envelopes, a half dozen empty baggies that may have held marijuana. Everything is at the lab."

"Knives are usually personal."

Ryder said, "Could be a crackhead." Any crackhead who got his hands on a gun typically sold it or traded it for more drugs.

"Witnesses?"

"No one we've found, even though he was parked pretty close to the back entrance of the motel."

"I know the place, pretty dark."

Ryder looked back at his notes. "Only three guests registered. The place isn't exactly a metropolis. One checked out, we're tracking him down. The others are an elderly couple. They claim they were asleep. We're looking at them, but probably nothing there."

"Employees?"

Ryder wished Logan would just let him give his report in order, he knew what he was doing, Logan jumping around like a three year old. "Two, together all evening in the lobby watching a movie. Didn't hear a thing. They say people park in the back all the time even if they aren't coming into the motel." Ryder hesitated, maybe Logan would be helpful after all. "You say you know that place? That back lot. Drugs? Prostitutes?"

Logan shrugged. "Could be. I haven't been to that part of Greenhill for years. Used to be a good fish place on that main road, before you cross the tracks. Don't remember any reports about the motel. You should check."

He thinks I'm an idiot, thought Ryder. "I did. Only three reports in the last five years, all minor. One guest skipped without paying, another stole a television, I guess that was before they bolted them down. The third an arrest of a guest, possession with intent, but he wasn't dealing there, that's just where they caught him."

"Better check it anyway," said Logan.

"I am. But the victim, Gruse, appears to have been very short of cash."

"Could have been duped, new guy in town, thinks he's scoring some dope or coke, gets robbed. No wallet, you said."

"Or cell phone, although he has one in his name. We didn't find it at his house, and the number rolls to voicemail. We're pulling his phone records. Nothing obvious on his computer, he was a part time photographer, some emails about selling photographs."

"Porn?"

"Selling porn photographs or porn on his computer?"

"Both."

"Twenty something guy living in an attic apartment at his mother's boyfriend's place, what do you think?"

Logan's eyes hardened. "I don't need the tone, detective."

Ryder bit his tongue, he was letting Logan get to him. "Sorry. Porn on his computer, yes, nothing apparently underage. The photographs he was selling were celebrity shots."

"In Marburg?"

"Probably explains why he wasn't rolling in money. We haven't gone through all his photos yet, but a lot of them seem to be celebrities."

"Anyone have it in for this guy?"

"We're still checking. We can't find many people who know him. Kind of a loner, or just finding his way around."

"You getting the help you need?"

"Cindy is doing the records searches, I'm doing the interviews. With some help from Burkett, a few others."

Logan shook his head. "Be careful where you send Burkett alone. He's a little rough around the edges."

Everyone here is, thought Ryder. *Even you.* "He's canvassing mostly."

"What else you working?"

"The stolen car thing, the Geary brothers chop shop. Those cousins dealing out of the back of Antonio's pizza. Still looking for their source. A few burglaries. That assault case, or possible assault case, the break-in over at Third. A few others, nothing major."

"Drop everything except the homicide and the assault," said Logan. "Give the pizza drug thing and the whole Geary package to O'Dowd. Split the burglaries up to the senior officers—no, better yet, give them to Hendricks, he's next in line for a shield, let's see how he manages a ton of shit at once."

That was fine with Ryder. He didn't even mind keeping the Third Street burglary, or whatever it was. He'd been just about to do a follow up with the good looking victim when the Gruse murder had hit.

"This killing. Could be random," mused Logan.

Ryder didn't want to go there. Most murders were solved within a few days or not at all; crimes of passion, the husband calling it in, the gun on the counter. Or after the neighbors reported constant fights. Obvious drug deals. "Still a lot to check," said Ryder, not wanting to give it up, a closed homicide would look good on his record.

"Still, I want Winter to work with you on this."

"Jesus, Captain." Ryder couldn't keep the displeasure out of his voice.

"No, not Jesus, just Winter. He's good at this shit, even more so if it's random."

"Nobody wants to work with him."

"Nobody wants to work with you either," said Logan. "Winter had a partner for ten years, you couldn't hold one in Derry and you can't here either."

"All good reasons to explain those."

Logan held up a hand. "Save it. I'm not going to have only one detective on a homicide, I wouldn't even let Winter do that, and he's cleared plenty. I told you, don't turn down help."

Ryder snapped his notebook shut. It was bad enough he had to use that Neanderthal Burkett to do footwork, and chafe under Logan. Now he'd have to work with Winter.

Maybe even a homicide case wasn't worth this.

WINTER PARKED BEHIND the Ford in Brooker's driveway. Every time he stopped by to visit he thought about asking if Brooker wanted him to drive it around, it wasn't good to let a car sit. He couldn't remember if he had asked. Today for sure.

He knocked on the side door and let himself in, the way of old friends. In the kitchen a black woman was at the sink, washing dishes, she turned as the door opened, startled. Winter paused, Brooker's nurse.

"Sorry," he said. Winter couldn't remember her name. "I'm a friend of Brooker's . . ."

"I know, Detective Winter. We've met a few times." The woman dried her hands on a dishtowel. "Can I get you anything? Mr. Stan is in the living room."

Winter was bothered by the fact that he couldn't remember her name, he was usually pretty good with names. Had they really met a few times like she said? He thought just once. She looked familiar enough, the very dark skin, close cropped hair, slim, looking elegant even in a white nurse's smock and soft sneaker-like shoes.

"No, I'm good. I just stopped by for a minute." Winter stood there, oddly embarrassed, not accustomed to seeing someone in Brooker's house. Brooker had never married, and Winter couldn't recall him ever mentioning bringing a woman to his place. "I'll just go in, then."

Winter found Brooker in the living room, the television turned down low, some kind of nature program, Winter surprised at that, Brooker was mostly a sports guy. Huh.

Brooker clicked off the television and got up from the easy chair, Winter gesturing him to sit down. "Gotta move around," said Brooker, but he sunk back in the chair. He jerked his head toward the kitchen. "Maria is on my case about it all the time."

Maria, that was her name. "You still need a nurse?" said Winter. "Something happen?"

Brooker waved his hand. "Nah. She just comes a few times a week, follow up. Makes sure I'm taking my meds."

Winter was about to comment on that when Maria appeared. "I brought coffee," she said, setting two mugs down on the coffee table. "Decaf, that's all Mr. Stan can have." She gave Winter a stern look, as if he might have some No-Doz hidden in his pocket to slip into the coffee.

She left. Winter sat on the sofa, noting the coffee she had put in front of him was black, the way he drank it. Brooker's was half milk, the way he took it, Maria seemed to know a lot. Winter took a sip, he hated decaf and knew Brooker did too. "Decaf?"

"You get used to it," said Brooker.

Winter toyed with the mug. "Decaf, nature shows, making sure you get exercise, take your pills. Sounds more like a wife than a nurse."

Brooker glanced at the door. "Could do a lot worse."

That wasn't what Winter expected to hear. He wasn't sure how to respond. Brooker flushed, which took a lot, he was a ruddy guy, always had that drinker's glow, even though he wasn't an alcoholic.

Brooker let him off the hook. "She's been good company, I'm going nuts cooped up here."

"You'll be fine once you get back to work."

"Might be a while," said Brooker. He took a sip of coffee. "Or not at all."

Winter's head snapped up. "What?"

"The department is in no hurry to bring me back, what with the lawsuit still hanging out there."

"I told you I should have taken the heat on that."

"They would have buried you. Even without a lawsuit. You've

had three strikes so many times it's a miracle we've made it to extra innings." Brooker looked out the window. In a more subdued voice he said, "There's another thing. Damn doctors might not give me clearance. Unstable angina, all that shit. Next time it might be worse than me just passing out and banging my head in the kitchen."

"You just need to lose some weight, get some exercise." Brooker actually didn't look that bad.

"Now who sounds like a wife."

Winter pushed his coffee away. "Stan, don't do this to me." The thought of not working with Brooker was unfathomable. "Does Logan know?"

"Not yet. I went to my personal doctor. Why?"

"Logan is putting me on something with Ryder. I thought it was a one time thing, but . . ."

"You think he's trying you two out together?"

"He better not be. Ryder's—a little stiff."

"He's an asshole," said Brooker. "For a guy who wants everything by the book he'll do anything to get ahead."

"Ah, he just a little stiff."

Brooker frowned. "You said that."

Winter looked away, confused. Had he? First he forgot Maria's name, now he was repeating himself. He reached for the coffee, remembered it had no caffeine, and put the cup back down. "Just get better," he said. "You leave me stuck with Ryder and I'll put you back in the hospital for real."

Brooker leaned forward. "Watch your back with Ryder. There may be another reason beside bringing new blood into the department that he's here."

"To keep his eye on whether we're all following modern police policies?"

"Or to keep his eye on us specifically. Now just you."

Both men mulled over that. Winter said, "Logan would have to be in on it."

"Ryder could be watching him too."

"Ryder doesn't seem like an Internal Affairs guy."

"Who knows? Maybe they've got new blood too. Anyway, just keep it in mind. Don't let him see so much of—our way of working."

Winter grinned. "I don't know how to work any other way."

"That's what I'm afraid of. The world is changing. Soon cops like us won't fit in at all. I've at least got an excuse to quit. What the hell would you do?"

Winter couldn't imagine not being a cop. He expected to be working well past his twenty. "Maybe modern police techniques really are better."

"You've seen Ryder, what do you think?"

"Now you're getting me depressed."

"What's Logan got you two on? The Greenhill homicide?"

"You know about that?"

"I have a heart problem, I can still read the papers. Drug deal?"

"Not sure yet. I just got briefed by Ryder. Say what you want, he's organized. I didn't see the paper, what did it say?"

"Not much. Adult male found dead in a car behind the motel. I read it in the *County Weekly*, must have just made the edition, not much detail."

"You're sicker than I thought, reading the *Weekly*. That paper even have sports scores?"

"High school. You know, some of those kids aren't bad."

Winter didn't know if Brooker was serious. Pro sports Winter enjoyed, he couldn't imagine watching anything less than that, even college games bored him. "Victim lived here in Marburg, is a recent relocation from Los Angeles with his mother. Had some kind of freelance photography business. No record. Still waiting on toxicology, but no marks on his arms, no paraphernalia in the car or his house. Might have been scoring some weed, but why go all the way to Greenhill for that?"

"Might not know where he could score locally."

"Like just about any street corner or hotel? Another thing odd, he was stabbed multiple times, around the groin."

Both men shifted in their chairs. "Ouch," said Brooker.

"My sentiment exactly. Weird place to get stabbed for dealer taking off a customer, and what dealer does that, anyway? Even if someone lured him there, wanted to rob him, okay, but stab him in the nuts?"

"In the nuts?" Brooker was still squirming in the chair.

"Close enough. Caught him low, he was sitting in the driver's seat, what killed him was his femoral artery getting sliced. Normally I'd think it was personal, especially a knife, but the M.E. said he might have got the groin stab wounds during a struggle."

"Still could have moved around, called for help."

"There was no cell phone, although we know he owned one. Probably stolen. Ryder thinks the victim might have been high, got cut, passed out, whatever, just bled out."

"You don't think so."

Winter shrugged. "Too early. Ryder just wants to get it closed, he's looking at dealers and robbery assaults where the MO was a fake drug sale."

"I don't recall any of those around here."

Winter grinned. "There haven't been any. But it'll keep Ryder busy, out of my hair."

"Admit it, you think he's an asshole too."

"I'm giving him the benefit of the doubt."

"Unless Logan sticks him with you."

Winter got up. "That'll make Logan the asshole. And maybe you too, if you don't get back to work. Just get better, okay?"

CHAPTER 22

WINTER HAD A HARD TIME finding a place to park near the house where Lawrence Gruse had lived. More cars than Winter would have expected to see, the economy finally improving. He could double park and stick his police tag on the dash, but didn't want to inconvenience anyone driving through.

Winter finally found a spot a few blocks away. He walked back, through a neighborhood interchangeable with dozens of others around Marburg. Old houses all in a similar style, New England capes, distinguished from each other only by color and now and then a small porch addition or a car port. He knew the area—there weren't too many parts of the city he wasn't familiar with—although couldn't recall having been on this particular street.

It was warm but he wore a sport coat, mostly to hide his gun. He hated showing up at a victim's house in his usual summer attire of an untucked shirt, even though this wasn't the next of kin notification. He'd have worn a tie for that. Winter usually dressed casually—Marburg had a dress code for detectives but it was mostly ignored—but thought it disrespectful to not at least wear a jacket when visiting the mother of a victim.

Martin Ryder was waiting for Winter in front of the house, in a suit and tie, better dressed than anyone else in the department. Ryder was leaning against an aging Crown Victoria parked half on the sidewalk. Winter grimaced, for a guy who was supposedly by the book, Ryder wasn't especially considerate. It would be a pain for cars to maneuver around the huge Ford. Winter might have let it go, but

Ryder glanced at his watch, a not so subtle comment about Winter being a few minutes late.

"If you'd found a legal parking space instead of blocking the street I'd be waiting for you," said Winter.

Ryder dusted off his pants. "If I had one of the newer cars I wouldn't have to block anything with this tank. And I didn't want to be late."

"Just be ready to move it if a truck needs to get through here."

"They can go around."

Just a few minutes together and Ryder was already pissing Winter off. Brooker was right, Ryder was an asshole. Winter let it go. "You've been here already, right?"

"I did the notification. House belongs to a guy named Harris. No record. Pretty well off until he lost his job, his wife, and his big house across town, he's been living here less than a year. He just started working part time. The victim's mother, Patricia, doesn't work. She's probably here; the only car they had was the Cadillac her son was found in, and we still have that."

"How did she take it?" asked Winter.

"About how you'd expect. Maybe a little too focused on where this leaves her."

"Her son the breadwinner?"

"If he was, we haven't found out how."

"The boat?" Winter jerked his head toward a large sport fishing boat with a Yamaha outboard taking up most of the small driveway. Winter didn't know much about boats except that they were even more expensive than they looked, and this one appeared new.

"Belongs to Harris. He had a few of them, had to sell them off for the divorce settlement." Ryder glanced at the house. "Tell me again why I'm back here? We searched the house and Gruse's room, and his computer is at the station with tech."

Winter went up the walk. "I just want to get a feel for the guy." He also didn't know enough about Ryder to trust his search skills.

"He was probably just trying to score some dope," said Ryder.

Winter turned around. "Let's not say that in front of the mother."

"I'm not an idiot," said Ryder. "But I did ask her about whether her son was partaking. It's procedure."

Winter rang the bell, wondering where Ryder had learned his procedure. He'd certainly not ask a mother a question about drugs so directly during a notification.

The woman who answered the door wasn't quite what Winter expected. She just didn't look local, her hair too made up, her tan too real, her makeup too expertly applied. She was dressed well, a silky blouse with pearls, a pleated skirt, heels, almost an executive look, but something was just a little bit off, like a woman trying to look monied and just not getting it right. Her eyes were red, maybe from crying, but her makeup wasn't smudged.

"Mrs. Gruse? I'm Robert Winter, with the Marburg Police. I believe you've met Detective Ryder."

"Do you have information on Lenny?" she asked. Her eyes were wide, her voiced laced with drama.

"A few things, can we come in?" asked Winter.

The woman led them into the living room, Winter taking in as much as he could before she turned around. Mismatched furniture, a small television on a stand, machine made wool rugs, a few photos on the walls. Not really messy, but not extra neat either. Winter got the impression of a divorced guy, getting the odds and ends furniture, recently acquiring just the hint of female touches, yet from a woman who didn't give off the homemaker vibe.

Patricia Gruse sat on the sofa, her eyes drifting toward a half empty wine glass next to a mostly empty wine bottle. Winter couldn't blame her, she just lost her son. He was trying to figure out a polite way to say she should just go ahead and drink in front of them when Ryder spoke.

"Mrs. Gruse, we just have a few more questions about your son."

Winter winced, jumping in, "After we give you an update on our investigation. Is it okay if we sit down?"

"Of course. Can I offer you something to drink?" Her eyes flicked to the wine again.

"No thanks," said Ryder.

Winter didn't want anything, but he figured it might make her more comfortable to drink. "Some water would be great. I can get it myself, if that's okay."

"Sure. The kitchen is that way."

Winter didn't want to leave Ryder alone with her for long. "I'll be right back. Perhaps Detective Ryder can start with where we are." He gave Ryder a look, hoping he got the hint not to interrogate the woman right off the bat, then stepped into the kitchen. Like the living room, in that never never land between clean and messy. Some mail on the kitchen table, Winter flicked through it, all addressed to Tom Harris except for a Verizon bill for Lawrence Gruse. The Harris mail looked innocuous, junk circulars, bills. Winter grabbed a water glass from a shelf over the sink, and used the sound of running water to mask his opening of drawers and cabinets. Not much in the way of dinnerware, contributing to his initial impression of a guy re-establishing himself. A few meds in the top drawer, mostly OTC, one prescription bottle for an anti-depressant in the name of Patricia Gruse. Nothing that looked like it belonged to Lenny or any indication of drug dealing or addiction.

He took one last look around, nothing jumping at him, and went back into the living room as Ryder was saying, "We are in the process of seeing if there were any witnesses when your son was attacked."

Gruse looked up at Winter, who made a show of taking a drink as he sat down, and as he expected the woman reached for her wine, now that she didn't feel she was drinking alone.

"I just can't believe this," said Gruse. "I thought Marburg would be so much safer than LA. And I hoped Lenny could find a nice girl."

"I'm sorry," said Winter. "Can you tell us what brought you out this way?"

"My boyfriend, Tom, we'd met when he traveled to the west coast. It just got to be too much back and forth for him, he wanted me to come live here so we'd be close."

Winter wondered if that was after the divorce or what caused it, but didn't say anything. If Harris looked to be involved with the Gruse murder in some way he'd find out later. "And your son, he came with you?"

"Yes, Lenny lived with me in LA. It's so hard for young men these days to get a steady job, with the economy, you know. He's a photographer, he can live anywhere."

"He took pictures of celebrities?" asked Ryder.

"Mostly. He was very good, although it doesn't pay much, there is a lot of competition. He was looking for something steady, and then do the photography on the side." She paused. "That's why he was living here, keep his expenses down."

"So he must have spent a lot of time with celebrities," said Ryder.

"I guess so. He certainly took enough photos of them."

Winter knew where Ryder was going, celebrities meant drugs, maybe Gruse was dealing. It wasn't a bad idea, but he didn't like jumping to conclusions. "We're going to take a look at Lenny's photos to see if they might help us out."

Gruse frowned. "I thought you said it was a robbery?"

"We need to look at everything," said Winter gently. "Just in case."

"You think someone came after my Lenny?" Gruse's hand went to her pearl necklace. "Am I in danger?"

"I don't think so," said Ryder. "But the sooner we close off possibilities the better."

"You'll keep me safe, won't you?" Gruse was looking at Winter, not Ryder.

Winter leaned forward. Contrary to popular opinion, police work was much more after the crime than preventative, but instead he said, "The best way to keep you safe would be for us to find out what happened to your son."

"Do whatever you have to do," said Gruse.

"Thank you. We'd like to look at Lenny's room again, if that's okay with you."

"It's upstairs."

"Detective Ryder knows the way, there's no need for you to come up," said Winter. He wanted to leave her to her wine, not looking over his shoulder. "We'll stop back when we're finished."

Winter followed Ryder up to the second floor, but turned into the bathroom on the landing instead of continuing on. "Just be a sec," he said. This bathroom was a mess, empty after shave bottles, stringy hairbrushes, a grungy towel on the shower rack, the shower door grimy. Two cans of Monster in the trash. Winter suspected it was Lenny's bath, no makeup, no women's items. The medicine chest was filled with aspirin and B12 supplements, no prescriptions.

In the short hall Winter passed an open bedroom door. A king sized bed, made up, with two closed doors. Two bureaus and a long dresser with a makeup mirror, two jewelry boxes, brushes. Patricia and Tom's room. Winter stepped in, checked the bath, the closet, the dresser. Cursory, more to get a feel.

Ryder waited impatiently on the narrow staircase to the top floor. "We didn't need her permission."

"I know. Sometimes it doesn't hurt to be polite."

Ryder continued on up. "What would you have done if she'd said no?"

"She wasn't going to."

"How do you know?"

"Mother losing her son, what do you think? She wants to understand why, she wouldn't question anything we want to do. Later maybe, if we don't come up with much, but not now. Besides, if she'd said no, you could have read her the law." Not what Winter would have done, but he knew that's the way Ryder would handle it.

They had to duck to enter the top floor. It was not really a traditional attic, just a small dormer at the front of the house accessible by a plywood door. The room was full of boxes, a second plywood door leading to another room. Two squat dressers were crammed against one wall, the top drawers partially open. A single bed against another wall, more like a cot, two suitcases stuffed underneath. A folding table holding a few disconnected cables sat under the only window. An old shelving unit was built into the last wall, filled with camera equipment.

"We found the computer on the table," said Ryder. "Nothing much in the drawers, clothes mostly. No jewelry at all. He didn't have a watch on him."

"Not many young people wear watches any more," said Winter. "They all have cell phones."

"I do."

"To someone Lenny's age you're an old man," said Winter.

"Speak for yourself."

"I am too. I don't sweat it." Winter was looking at the camera equipment. "Any idea what this stuff is worth?"

"We took an inventory, Cindy is checking prices. Stuff looks old."

"Or just well used. He was a photographer." Winter barely knew which end of a camera to hold, he didn't even like getting his picture taken. "Are these all digital?"

"I think so. We pulled all the memory cards, the tech guy has them. We can look through everything back at the station."

"You find backups?" Winter remembered reading about a photographer who had lost half his livelihood because his camera was stolen and his backup was lost in a fire. Something about always needing more than one backup.

"We assume they're on the computer. We'll check."

Winter sat on the bed and looked around, trying to get a sense of Lenny. It was a pretty depressing room; Winter lived frugally but his place seemed like the Taj Mahal compared to this. He wondered what it would be like, a mid twenties guy, living with his mother, confined to a small attic room belonging to a stranger. *Maybe not a stranger,* he thought. Lenny must have met Tom in Los Angeles. He'd check on that. Tom scoring dope from Lenny? It felt weak.

"It doesn't exactly scream drug dealer," said Winter. It had more a feel of a hard up guy with no prospects.

"Still could have been buying. Or just getting his feet wet, setting up shop."

"This look like a guy who would be carrying a wad of cash, worth being held up for?"

Winter got up, idly looking through the drawers, not expecting to find anything, not really many places to hide stuff. Remembered the article about the photographer who lost his backup. Lenny's photos must have been important to him, would he keep them all in one place?

He pulled out his cell phone and dialed the station, getting switched to Dan, the tech guy. "I'm out at Lawrence Gruse's place, the photographer homicide. Question for you, how many backups do photographers keep?"

"Usually three," said Dan. "For important shots, four. One on the original memory card. The memory cards are prone to problems, plus they get reused, so they get copied to a portable hard drive, a computer, and on line."

"Did you get a chance to look at anything yet?"

"We're working through it. Lots of images, tens of thousands. Quite a few recognizable celebrities, Hollywood types."

"Any backups missing?"

"What do you mean?"

"Are there any shots on the memory cards that don't show up on the computer? Or in the online backup?" Winter was wondering if Gruse had a special stash of photos, pictures he kept hidden. Girlfriends, personal images.

"We don't have access to the cloud storage, we have a subpoena going for the site where he stored his work. I haven't checked the computer yet to see if the photos match, it could take a while. You want me to do that?"

"Yes. And if there's no will . . ." Winter glanced at Ryder, who shook his head. " . . . then the photos belong to his next of kin, I think. That might be his mother if the father is not in the picture. If that's the case we could get her permission to hack it, she might even know the password. Call me if you see anything missing."

"Hard to know what isn't there."

"I know. I'll be by to see them. And have Cindy take a look, she might follow the local celebrity scene, she might recognize someone." Cindy was the department criminologist.

Winter hung up, thinking about the backups. The bathroom? Not if Lenny was afraid of fire or theft. The car.

"Did you search the Caddy?" asked Winter.

Ryder said, "No drugs, although the dog got a hit on some weed. And we can't hack the cloud, we need to wait for the subpoena. Lenny's father could have a claim on them, if we found something without his permission or before the court ruled on the intestate it could ruin the legality of the search."

"We'll let the lawyers figure that out," said Winter. "In the meantime, I want to take another look at the car."

"We didn't miss anything," argued Ryder.

Winter suspected Ryder might miss a tornado. "Probably not. Let's check anyway."

*   *   *

THE CADDY WAS MORE of a mess than Gruse's room, the floor of the backseat a veritable dump on wheels. Winter ignored the junk and the obvious places for a drug stash; Ryder was on that kick and he would have gone over them carefully. Winter wasn't buying the drug angle, not yet, although the location of the killing still bothered him. What was Gruse doing there? He'd gently asked the mother as they had left, she'd had no idea, nor did she know any of Gruse's passwords or who his friends were. Winter saw that she had started on another bottle of wine and left her alone, ushering Ryder out when his questions kept coming back to drugs. If there was a drug angle they'd have more luck coming at it from the other way, the dealers. Winter knew who all the major—and most of the minor—dealers were in and around Marburg.

As Winter sat behind the wheel of Gruse's car the cracked leather seat bit right through his shirt. Winter was having a hard time getting a handle on Gruse. Guy goes from taking pictures of big celebrities in Hollywood, ends up in Marburg, living with his mother, driving her older model car—probably lived in it, if the junk in the backseat was any indication. Winter wondered if Patricia Gruse would ride around in such a mess, with her manicured nails and nice clothes. Gruse's clothes had looked pretty normal for a twenty something, mostly jeans, a lot of black, a little outdated maybe? Winter wasn't up on Millennial fashion, something to ask one of the younger cops.

Winter tapped his thigh, considering. There were only so many places in a car where you could hide a large quantity of drugs or even a gun. A small memory card, that was another matter, it could be anywhere. Probably needed to be kept dry, although it could be in a baggie . . .

Ryder was eyeing him from the doorway of the impound garage, probably hoping that Winter wouldn't find anything. Winter had an urge to yell for Ryder to get an evidence bag, just to pull his chain, pretending he'd discovered a brick of smack that Ryder had missed, it would be worth seeing the look on his face . . .

Dan had said the memory cards got swapped out. Gruse would want to be able to get his hands on them easily, they wouldn't be under the spare tire or in a wheel well. What could you get your hands on quickly in a car?

Winter opened the door and knelt on the floor, feeling under the dash, nothing but wires. Ryder came over as Winter was checking in the glove compartment.

"We looked there."

Winter ignored him, flipping through the owner's manual. He hadn't seen a fuse box. The owner's manual said there was one under the hood and another under the back seat. Weird place, but Winter checked it anyway, struggling with the seat cushion. The fuse box held just fuses.

He sat back in the driver's seat. Maybe he'd been wrong about the car, Gruse might have another place to stash stuff, but where? Winter lay his head back, thinking. Not a safe deposit box, too complicated. There was a garage door opener clipped to the visor. Winter pictured the house, the driveway, the boat. Harris didn't have a garage . . .

Winter unclipped the opener and pried off the battery case. No batteries, but three thin memory cards.

He resisted the impulse to wave them under Ryder's nose.

CHAPTER 23

WINTER, RYDER AND DAN COLE, the tech guy, crowded over the computer monitor in Cole's small office. Cole was young, still trying and mostly failing to grow a soul patch. He'd helped Winter on a few prior cases and Winter was impressed with his skills and especially with the fact that Cole wasn't condescending to Winter over his limited familiarity with technology.

"Before we get to the photos I want to show you this," said Cole, pointing to an array of icons on the screen. "Gruse had an organizational system. These are all folders, identified by the name of a person. Inside each folder he put the photos of that subject."

"Some of the folders don't have personal names," said Ryder.

"Right. That's good news and bad news. He also has folders for where he took the shots, or some other distinguishing characteristic about the grouping. For example, this one, *Clubbing,* has photos of celebrities out on the town. This one is for *Premieres*, this one *Up and Coming Actors,* and so on. Most seem to have been taken in and around Los Angeles, and are dated when he lived there, so that makes sense."

"Is that the good news or the bad news?" asked Winter.

"Good if you know where you want to find a photo based on a topic or location. Bad if you want to answer your question about what pics might not be backed up. If Gruse had a photo of an up and coming actor, but the photo was taken at a premiere, he'd duplicate the photo so it would show up in both folders."

"Waste of space," said Ryder.

"Space is cheap," said Cole. "The alternative is setting up a database, which he also has, but it isn't up to date. The problem is that he often changed the file name when he duplicated the photo, so we can't just use easy ways of comparing what photos might be missing. Once I get a better handle on his naming convention, I can write a small program, but I might miss a few."

"That's fine, give us what you can," said Winter. He pointed to one of the folders. "Incognito?"

"Just celebs who are out and about, but wearing dark glasses, caps, trying not to be noticed."

"How about this one," said Ryder. "Hot stuff."

Cole grinned. "Wondering when you'd ask about that." He clicked on the folder, the screen filling with thumbnails. "I think he meant hot in a publishable sense, and not porn, if that's what you were thinking."

"I wasn't thinking anything," said Ryder.

"Sure, whatever. Anyway, it's mostly actresses, dressed up, sexy looking, that sort of thing." Cole clicked through some of the images. Winter didn't watch much television and hadn't been to a movie in years, but even he recognized some of the actors and actresses, mostly the older ones. Most of Gruse's collection, however, was younger subjects.

"How many pictures?" asked Winter.

"Tens of thousands. He's been doing this for a while."

"Waste of time," said Ryder. "We don't even know what we're looking for. It's not like he's going to have a photo showing the person who stabbed him."

"Not in the act, but who's to say he doesn't?" said Winter. "Gruse let someone in his car, good chance he knew who it was." He turned to Cole. "Can you see if he has any photos categorized under Greenhill?"

"I already checked, no. He does have a Marburg collection, all from the last few months."

"Let's see those."

Cole switched to another set of thumbnails. "What are we looking for?"

"We don't know yet," said Winter. "Something that stands out."

"Or a photo titled *My Killer,*" scoffed Ryder.

Winter ignored him, Ryder still pissed because Winter had found the memory cards. Looking through the photos was a long shot, but still had to be done. And they could come back to the photos if a name popped up anywhere in the investigation. *Names* . . . "Can you sort them by the ones that have names?"

"Sure." Cole's clicked the mouse around, too fast for Winter to follow. "Looks to be over a thousand folders with names. Some of the folders only have a few photos, others have lots. Look here, Inge Harris, she's on two television series, there are hundreds of shots of her."

"How about the Marburg photos? Any of those have names?"

"No . . . it doesn't look like he classified those. At least not on these memory cards. Wait, let me check the computer." Cole switched to a different screen. "We made a duplicate of Gruse's laptop drive, we'll use that for the searches. Doesn't look like any named photos there either."

Cole flipped through the pages of images, most shot on the street, Winter recognizing the backgrounds: Main Street, some of the stores, the Marquee club. The great majority of the shots were women, candids, some at odd angles, as if Gruse had taken them without aiming.

"Guy was a stalker," said Ryder. "Maybe that's who killed him, someone he creeped out."

Winter didn't dismiss that, it was as good a theory as any, although he'd never heard of someone who'd been stalked committing a murder. The husband or boyfriend of a woman being stalked, maybe. He filed it away as a possibility to be looked into.

Cole switched back to thumbnails. "Anything in particular you want to see?"

"Is there a folder marked personal?"

"None. Any personal shots could be mixed in with the rest though."

"Still, a photographer with no personal shots? His friends? His mother?"

"Maybe those are on his phone," said Cole. "Selfies."

Winter said, "Who takes pictures of themselves?"

"Everyone," said Cole.

Winter really didn't get it. A different generation. He didn't feel old, but things had changed. "Are the Marburg photos categorized at all?"

"Not that I can see. All in one folder. Wait." Cole did some more clicking. "Huh. The number of photos in the Marburg folder on the computer and on one of the memory cards is the same, so it looks like a backup. But on this other memory card the Marburg collection is smaller." Cole pointed to the screen. "Some different dates, too."

"Show us those," said Winter.

These thumbnails had a different feel to them, some out of focus, others showing only profiles or subjects from the back. Still mostly women.

"Not as good," said Cole. "Rejects maybe."

"Then why keep them?" mused Winter.

"Good question," said Cole. "And not only keep them, but have them all together on one card." He flipped through the pages.

"A lot of asses," said Ryder. "Guy had a think for butts. I told you, stalker."

"But these people aren't recognizable," said Winter. "Someone thought Gruse had a photo of their butt and stabbed him because of it?"

"They might not have known he only had a rear shot," offered Cole. "Could be recognizable in other photos."

"Great," said Ryder. "We can spend days trying to match butts to faces."

Cole said, "We could do it by comparing the clothing."

"Let's try to narrow it down another way first," suggested Winter. "But that's not a bad idea at all."

"Hey, go back," said Ryder.

Cole recalled the page, and Ryder reached for the mouse. "Let me, you guys are too slow." He paged through a series of the images.

"Now who's the stalker," said Winter. The pictures were mostly women's rear ends.

"Thought I saw someone in the background in more than one shot," said Ryder. "But it just looks like the photos were taken close together."

"Maybe that's it," said Cole. "Gruse caught a picture of a crime being committed in the background. Like in *Blow Up*."

Winter and Ryder looked at him quizzically. "Don't you guys watch old movies? Famous picture."

Ryder rolled his eyes, and Winter shrugged. Another long shot, but Winter had seen stranger connections that explained linkages in seemingly random crimes. "Put it on the list," he said.

They all turned at a knock on the door. "You men looking at porn?"

"Hey, Cindy," said Dan. "No, just more of the photos I showed you before."

"Sure, sure," said Cindy, coming over to look. A subtle floral scent wafted through the room, Cindy's perfume. She was a petite woman, close to Dan's age—Winter was terrible with ages, especially younger women, they all just seemed *young*—and wore her hair funky. Today it was a silvery blond; her hair color changed more than the weather. Her earrings dangled as she peered at the screen. "These are from Marburg," she said.

"You can tell that from looking at women's rear ends?" asked Ryder.

"*I'm* focusing on the backgrounds. Look, that's taken outside of the Starbucks on Main Street, and this one is near The Café." She handed Winter a stack of papers. "Gruse had an account at Marburg First Bank. We don't have access yet, but my friend there told me it had less than a hundred dollars in it."

"She shouldn't divulge that information," said Ryder.

"It's actually a he, and he didn't give me the exact amount, he just confirmed the account, and I asked him if it was a lot, and he said no, and then we went back and forth and I figured it out."

"How would you feel if that was your account privacy being violated?" argued Ryder.

"If I was dead? I'd be past caring," said Cindy. She turned to Winter. "Anyway, here's the list of Gruse's phone contacts, we just got it from Verizon. The actual texts and historical call log will hopefully show up in a few days. This is just the most recent back up of his contact list. I've also listed the few dozen or so numbers he called from his recent call log."

"Great," said Winter. "Can you cross reference the phone numbers in the contact list to addresses?"

"Already started. Look at the last page, those are the loc
bers. A lot are cells, it will take a few days to get addresses for ↴
On the landlines, all we have now are the physical addresses. I dia
get a chance to put in all the names, but I thought you'd want this
right away."

"Good work," said Winter. Some of the addresses he recognized,
a few stores and restaurants, an office building. He picked up a pen
off of Cole's desk and started ticking off addresses, then handed the
list to Ryder. "I'll take the ones I marked, why don't you cover the
others."

Ryder hesitated, then took the pages. "If I have the sheets, how
will you remember which ones you have?"

"Only half a dozen names, I'll remember."

"I'll be jumping all over the place," said Ryder. "Let's split it up by
geography, save some driving."

"Better if I talk to the people I know," said Winter. "When we get
more we'll do it that way, and give some to the uniforms. If there's a
small chance we could be talking to the killer, we should go easy. Just
say that we're talking to everyone who knew the deceased, routine."

Ryder appeared about to object, but Winter was halfway out the
door. "Thanks, everyone. Let me know if anything pops."

RYDER WAITED UNTIL Winter and Cindy had gone, then said to Cole,
"Can I get a copy of those Marburg shots? Maybe I'll notice something when I'm out checking out these names."

"Sure." Cole opened a drawer, unpacked a new thumbdrive,
slipped it in his computer, and as the files were transferring said, "You
think the killer's picture might be on here?"

Ryder wasn't sure about the killer, but there was a photo of someone who looked familiar. The back of someone, anyway. He hadn't
mentioned it to Winter, what was he going to say, he had recognized
a woman's butt?

"Wishful thinking, if you ask me," said Ryder. He still thought it
was a small time drug deal gone bad. Gruse was probably scoring
some weed, got taken for a dupe, and was stabbed for his trouble. The

robber might not have even meant to kill him, just flashed a knife, and it got out of hand. He grudgingly had to agree with Winter, though, why would a drug dealer bother? Unless it wasn't a dealer, but just a thief pretending to be, that would explain the out of the way location . . .

He'd check out Gruse's contact names, but when that was finished he'd make another stop. After all, he still had the other case, the break-in possible assault. Melanie Upton. He needed to take another look at her rear end.

To see if it matched the photo he'd just seen on Gruse's memory card.

CHAPTER 24

MELANIE FLICKED THROUGH the photos that Standish's photographer had emailed, her new publicity shots. Not bad, better than what she had before. Standish's photographer—a spike haired, heavily inked guy who looked more like a gangbanger than an artist—knew his craft, keeping her loose during the shoot, making subtle suggestions, nothing pushy. The results weren't exactly how Melanie had pictured her early career brand, but in the shots she oozed a street vibe that would play well with her other side of the tracks Jason love story.

Six o'clock, she was getting hungry, nothing in her apartment as usual. She was getting tired of delivered pizza and Chinese, but she hated eating out by herself, plus it didn't fit the image she was trying to portray. Successful actresses didn't dine alone. Gigi was on the road again, and since Melanie had quit the restaurant job she had to not only think about where to eat but pay for her food, forgetting how expensive it cost to stay alive.

She considered Taz, decided not to overdo that, he might get ideas of something permanent, and she was about done with him, there was nothing more he could do for her. Maybe she'd go to the Hilton, charge a nice lobster to Jason's room, wouldn't that be a kick.

A knock at the door. Melanie ignored it, probably a drunk or lost delivery guy. She must have left the downstairs door propped open. The knock came again, insistent.

"Who is it?" she yelled out, not bothering to get up from the sofa.

"Miss Upton, it's Detective Martin Ryder of the Marburg Police."

Shit . . . they knew about Lenny already. Melanie glanced toward the window, then closed her eyes, what was she going to do, jump from the second story?

She was surprised at her own reaction, no panic, instead sliding to the floor like a rag doll, seeking comfort in her favorite position, propped against the front of the sofa. It was no use, a wave of depression pressing her to the floor, she just couldn't get a break.

Fucking Lenny Gruse, torturing her from the grave.

Melanie still had her phone in her hand, she slowly swiped through her publicity photos again, so close, she'd been *so close* . . .

"Miss Upton?"

Melanie lay her head back, suddenly very tired. She'd been on a high for weeks, an adrenaline rush spurred by the sight of a mountain top suddenly in reach. Even having to deal with Lenny nothing more than a blip, it was all behind her, she could focus again on the prize.

Now this.

No way to pretend she wasn't at home now. If it hadn't been the cops she could just tell them to go away. If she didn't answer they'd be suspicious or kick the door in.

Not that it mattered, they had to know. She should have planned it out, not acted out of rage, but hearing Lenny admit he'd been in bed with Gigi had been too much. She'd punished him where he deserved it. It wasn't her fault he'd bled to death.

Fucking Lenny Gruse.

Melanie took a last long look at her favorite of the new photos, a straight on shot of her looking directly into the camera, makeup so artfully applied it was invisible, an urban street glare that dared anyone to hold her eye, and yet so intense it was impossible to turn away from.

A look that said, *Don't cross me.*

Fuck Lenny Gruse, fuck the police. She'd do what she did best, she'd figure something out. Or go down fighting.

She pushed herself to her feet. "Just a minute, I'm coming."

At the door she paused, picturing an audience on the other side. It wasn't a door, but a curtain. She was on stage. All she had to do was get in role.

Melanie cracked the door. Only one man there, Ryder, the good looking detective who had slyly checked her out when driving her to the hospital. No one else, no uniformed police. Would they really send just one cop?

A faint glimmer of hope ran through her, which she immediately disguised by saying, "I remember you." Knowing that Ryder would puff up.

And he did, a little flush to his cheek, the hint of a smile.

"Miss Upton," Ryder said. "I'm sorry to trouble you but I wonder if I could have a few minutes?"

Melanie's adrenaline flowed back with a vengeance, her mind racing. Ryder sounded especially polite, asking instead of barging in, were the cops trying to trick her? "Well, I was just about to jump in the shower—." She let it hang, to see how pushy Ryder would be.

"I promise you, this won't take long."

Melanie pretended to think about it, waiting him out. Sure enough, Ryder broke first.

"I was passing by," he said. "On my way back to the station. I thought I would give you an update on the break-in."

Melanie fought the urge to fully relax, this could still be a trick, maybe they suspected her but didn't have proof. Were the cops smart enough for that? She hadn't been too impressed by Ryder, she'd snowed him easily enough about the break-in. Unless he'd figured something out . . .

She slid back the chain, turning her back on Ryder as if she didn't have a care in the world. "I thought you would call first, I might not have been dressed appropriately." Not that she was, wearing just a long loose man's shirt with no bra, barefoot. The shirt barely covered her underwear. She knew without looking that Ryder was ogling her.

Melanie dropped into the middle of the sofa, pulling her bare legs up under her. Ryder looked around the room, the only other seat piled high with clothes. Melanie wondered if he'd try to squeeze next to her on the couch.

Instead he stood awkwardly, apparently trying to keep his eyes off her legs, and not succeeding very well. Melanie, on her home turf, feeling the balance of power lean her way. "You have some new information?" she prodded. "It's been a while. I've been wondering why no one has told me anything."

"I'm sorry about that. We performed a thorough investigation of the immediate area around your neighborhood and found nothing of significance. We also interviewed several people in the restaurant downstairs, as well as your neighbors. No one remembered seeing or hearing anything out of the ordinary that night."

Ryder sounded like a robot, as stiff as he had been the first time he had interviewed her, nothing to tip her off to what he was really after. Melanie focused on his movements, his hands, his eyes. "You think a man coming to my apartment would be out of the ordinary?" She gave him a hint of a smile, just the right amount of coy.

"No, I didn't mean to suggest that."

"Because I do have guests, now and then," she continued. "I mean, you just came walking up the stairs. Would you being here be considered out of the ordinary? It's not like you have a police uniform on, you could just be a man visiting me, you think someone would have noticed?"

Ryder's eyes darted away briefly. "You never know."

"I have lots of friends who visit. Like the man I mentioned to you."

"Yes, about him—"

Melanie rolled over the cop. "I mean, he's been here many times, of course."

"You still didn't tell us his name."

"I don't want to get him in any trouble. I doubt it was him. Really." Melanie gave her hair a ditzy twirl. "I mean, I don't think it could possibly be."

"If we knew who he was, we'd be better able to investigate," said Ryder. "We could show his picture around."

Melanie pretended to consider. "I'll think about it."

"You can't withhold evidence from an investigation," said Ryder, back in his cop voice.

Melanie scowled at him. "Are you telling me I'd get in trouble if I don't tell you details about my *personal* life? I'm the victim here, remember?" She crossed her arms over her chest, as if protecting her innocence.

"That's not what I said."

"It sure sounded like it."

"You led us to believe that nothing may have even happened, that you were a little—foggy."

"I wasn't drunk."

"You had taken some pills."

"That doesn't give anyone an excuse to take advantage of me."

"So are you saying that's what happened?"

"I told you I'm not sure. Bits and pieces come back to me."

"The man you were with earlier that night, have you seen him since?"

"Yes, of course, why?"

"Because—if he was the man who assaulted you—if you were assaulted—it will be hard for people to believe he committed an assault if you have been together after the fact."

"I told you, I don't think it was him."

Ryder shuffled, his hands in his pockets then back out. Melanie would have been enjoying jerking him around if she hadn't been worrying about Lenny.

"You're not giving us much to go on," he said.

"Look, I'm just saying it like it happened," said Melanie. "I don't remember much. If I do, you'll be the first to know." She waited a beat, then added, "I still have your card." Like she slept with it under her pillow.

"Well, *something* happened. Your physical exam suggested—"

"Do we have to talk about this?" asked Melanie. "It's very embarrassing." Ryder reddened, off balance, as she had hoped. "You've already been through my apartment, touching all my personal belongings . . ."

"We conducted our investigation as per proper police procedure."

"Are you saying you didn't touch any of my belongings?"

"Only those that were necessary."

"And who decided that?"

"The crime tech, and to some extent, myself."

"And what exactly did you find? No one ever told me that."

"We found—we didn't find anything probative either way."

Melanie fought to keep from rolling her eyes. Instead she gave Ryder another hair twirl. "I'm afraid I'm just a simple girl, Detective Ryder. I didn't even finish college. I don't understand that word."

"Probative. It means there isn't evidence that would prove anything either way. That you were assaulted."

"Or that I wasn't."

"Exactly."

Finally, Melanie thought, some good news. They couldn't prove she was assaulted, but couldn't prove she wasn't. She'd still be able to point that gun at Jason's head if she needed to.

Melanie waited, if Ryder was here about Lenny he'd work his way around to that somehow. She certainly wasn't going to help him. So far everything the cop said had been bullshit, he could have done this over the phone. Which left only two possibilities. He was here to trick her into saying something about Lenny, or he was hitting on her.

She could test at least one of those possibilities. She stretched out her legs, watching Ryder out of the corner of her eye, and sure enough his head swiveled to the couch like a puppet on a string. Uneasy as she still was about the reason for Ryder's visit, she had to suppress a giggle. Ryder staring at her legs certainly seemed *probative* of his real intent.

RYDER FOUGHT TO KEEP his eyes off of Melanie's legs, mostly unsuccessfully. The woman was a vixen, and Ryder suspected she knew it. He wasn't buying her *I'm so simple act*, everyone knew what probative meant, didn't they?

Still, he knew assault victims, especially those under the influence, often didn't remember all the events clearly. She might have been assaulted, she might not. He'd have to look into this case some more; her hesitancy to give up the name of her lover, for instance, was odd. Or maybe not. Ryder didn't have much experience with famous people, if the man she'd been with was in fact famous. There might be a good reason she was protecting him. Or maybe the mystery man had paid Melanie off.

He glanced around the room, it didn't seem much different than when he had searched it. The television, that was new. But so what? He doubted anyone could be bought off with a tv, they were pretty cheap these days.

He realized Melanie was waiting for him to say something, she was probably wondering why he was even here. He was wondering himself. He felt awkward just being in her apartment, she'd been right, he'd looked through her things, her personal belongings, her clothing. He did that all the time at crime scenes, but this felt different, an intrusion.

He was more confused about the possible assault than when he had arrived. He also couldn't figure out how to ask her if she knew Lenny Gruse. *Hey, I think I saw a picture of your ass on the camera card of a homicide victim, can you put on some tight jeans and turn around for me?*

Instead he mumbled, "Thank you for your time, Miss Upton. I want to assure you, we will keep at this. We're going to catch the person who broke into your apartment." Ryder said the words, but wasn't sure if he believed them, because he wasn't sure if anyone broke in at all. "If you remember more, please call me anytime." He cringed, that sounded like a line. "Or the main line at the Marburg Police, they'll pass the information along to me."

"Oh, I'll call you personally," said Upton. She uncoiled herself from the couch, standing, Ryder feeling good he managed to keep his eyes on her face.

He walked to the door, feeling Upton behind him, half in his space, half ushering him out, her presence a magnet.

A thought came to him, he turned, and she almost bumped into him, she was that close. "A friend is thinking of becoming an actress, she was wondering where she could get some publicity photos?"

For the briefest second Ryder thought he saw a flicker in Upton's eyes. Annoyance at another question? Surprise?

"Not many good photographers around here, you have to go to Boston."

"Is that expensive?"

"It can be. I don't pay any more, but someone starting out would have to."

"Any local photographers who might be cheaper?"

Upton clutched her shirt to her chest, as if she suddenly was aware she was partially dressed. "There's a guy named Tim Tazik, he's pretty good, reasonable."

Ryder waited for her to keep going, talk about photographers, mention Gruse, but she just looked at him. He couldn't press it, she'd given him a name. He'd sound like he was fishing, and if she asked him why, he'd sound like an idiot, and the last thing he wanted was to sound like an idiot in front of her. He'd had enough of that in high school, half the reason he became a cop was to get some respect. The fact that a lot of women liked cops was a bonus.

He turned to go, at a loss. Worse, he'd never got the chance to see her butt in tight jeans.

MELANIE HAD BEEN READY to ditch the cop, just another guy trying to get in her pants. He was good looking enough, but she was beyond needing his help, it wasn't like she was going to be in Marburg much longer. Plus she needed to keep Ryder primed in case she needed to push the Jason assault button, that wouldn't work very well if she slept with him. She needed Ryder to think she was a decent woman, not some floozy.

Until Ryder asked about photographers, an alarm going off in Melanie's head, why the hell did he ask that? No way it could be a coincidence, did they think she was that stupid?

She'd blurted the first name that popped into her head, Tazik. She couldn't very well say she didn't know any photographers, and she sure as hell wasn't going to mention Lenny. If the cops talked to Tazik, and he let something slip about her being with him that night at the hotel . . .

Melanie wanted to see if Ryder pressed her, but he just turned to go. She needed to find out what else the cops knew, the uncertainty would eat at her. Needed an excuse to pump some information out of Ryder . . .

Her stomach twisted, and she brightened, going with more than just her proverbial gut. "Hey, are you hungry?"

CHAPTER 25

WINTER DECIDED TO HIT the addresses on the outskirts of the city first and work his way in. He took the loop highway around to the east side, rush hour over, not much traffic until he got caught up behind a pothole filling crew, cringing every time loose tar crackled through his wheel wheels. By the time he reached his exit the twenty minute drive had doubled, souring his mood.

Once off the loop road Winter cruised along a narrow street lined with industrial businesses, car and truck repair shops, a parking depot for the sanitation department—the city's gathering point for any vehicles running on diesel, the fumes seeping into the car. Winter liked the earthy smell. It reminded him of his father, always working on the family cars, not as a hobby, but because they couldn't afford to pay professionals to fix them. At any given time one of the cars wasn't running right, especially in the cold winters, leading to morning scrambling to figure out how to get to school and work.

He rolled down the window, for some reason he felt closer to the beat of the city that way. The addresses from Gruse's contact list didn't ring a particular bell; he'd marked these for himself because he knew the area. Not only was it one of the higher crime neighborhoods, but Marburg's bigger drug hauls had taken place here, a million places to hide a literal ton of anything.

The first stop was a bust, an electronics store, the windows spray painted with white drooping letters announcing a going out of business sale. Winter pulled to the curb. Whatever sale they had was long over, a metal pull grate covering the doorway, the window displays empty. He'd passed the place in the past, but seemed to remember it being a different business. Nothing remarkable about it, Winter guessing it could be a front for a small time drug dealer, but it didn't have the right feel, not enough foot traffic in the neighborhood. He'd ask Cindy to check and see if any arrests had been made at this address, although he suspected she was already on that.

Winter drove along the street, slowly, his cop eyes registering the undercurrent. Three guys in overalls smoking outside a car repair shop gave him an unhurried glance, barely pausing their conversation, telling Winter there was nothing there. A block later, two men in jeans, eyeing his car while pretending not to, virtually shouting to Winter something was going on, especially as they stopped talking to one another, involuntarily foolish, it wasn't like he could hear from fifty feet away. Winter didn't recognize them. If he wasn't working this homicide he would have stopped, dug around, but not now. He'd come back in a few days, if they were still there he'd push it.

He used to have a few good sources in this neighborhood, including a mechanic who wasn't above not asking many questions about the source of cheap parts for a rebuilt Hemi. Winter had let him slide once in exchange for good information on a chop shop, which had led to some give and take. But the source had retired to Florida or North Carolina or someplace else warm, which to Winter sounded like everywhere else but New England.

A few old houses now appeared between the factory buildings and parking lots, some with more weeds than the industrial buildings, others so manicured they appeared to have been dropped in from another planet. More people on the street, no sidewalks, kids that should have been in school. Winter couldn't remember ever being allowed to play outside if he was kept home from school for being sick. One kid here and there he could understand, but groups of them? Street home schooling?

The world was changing, and Winter couldn't run fast enough to keep up.

The second stop wasn't much better, a used tire dealer, Winter struggling in his pidgin Spanish to ask about Gruse. No one knew anything, or maybe they did, and just didn't understand his questions. Winter wasn't surprised no one spoke English; this was the Dominican part of town, most of the customers wouldn't either. Winter made a note to himself to check the tire condition on Gruse's car, maybe that's why he had called this shop.

Winter shrugged off his hoody before getting back in the car, way too hot. He pulled his shirt out over his pants, unclipped his holstered gun and put in on the passenger seat. He leaned against the car, the clanging of rattling metal, air compressors and a smooth bachata rhythm all melding into a background melody to his musings. Who kept an electronics shop and a used tire dealer in his phone contact list? Or maybe it was the recent call list? Winter had been in a hurry to hit the street, he'd forgot which category these addresses came from. If they had been recent calls, that would make sense, Gruse calling around for information, computer parts, tires. If they were on his contact list, maybe Ryder was right after all, some kind of drug hookup, Gruse a small time dealer.

Winter got in the car, started to turn around to go back to the loop road, remembered the nasty asphalt work, and instead took the more direct but normally slower route through the residential section. The industrial buildings melded into triplex apartments and tenements, people on stoops. It had been that way as long as Winter could remember, the apartments without air conditioning, never cooling down, even at night. The stoops *were* the neighborhoods. No one needed a newspaper here, information flowing up and down the streets like runoff after a thunderstorm.

Winter got a lot of stares, a white guy in a Latino neighborhood. It didn't bother him, he was the interloper here, he was news. At a stoplight two kids on the corner, no more than twelve, stopped showing off for each other on skate boards to give him a street glare, part challenging, part icy, part boredom. Winter knew they were waiting for him say something. Even though they had the stare almost down pat—a depressing thought—they still had a lot to learn.

No one was behind Winter, he let the light go through the entire cycle, red to green and back to red, giving them a stare in return they'd never master, not only because it was unlikely they'd become cops, but they might not live that long. The fact that he could tell this about two kids who were just hanging around a corner was another depressing thought, about them and him.

They broke first; they had the nascent toughness but not the patience.

The smaller one, wearing knee length nylon basketball shorts and a tee shirt with the name of a band Winter had never heard of, said, "Hey five-oh, aren't you going to ask us why we're not in school?"

Winter wasn't surprised, it was always the little guy who did the talking. "No, I was going to ask you why you're wearing a shirt with someone else's face on it."

"Shit, man, everyone does that."

"I have a whole drawer full of tee shirts, I don't have a single one with some stranger's face."

"He's no stranger, he's famous."

Maybe he was. Winter wouldn't know, he liked music, but it was another thing he couldn't keep up with.

The other kid—also in a tee shirt, this one plain—tall and so thin he could almost hide behind the street sign post he leaned against, spoke in Spanish to the shorter boy, then in an incongruous Boston tinged accent, said to Winter: "Can you catch anyone in that thing?"

"Depends on what they're driving," said Winter. A small pickup truck pulled up behind him. Winter leaned out the window and waved it by. "Something like that," he said, indicating the rusty Nissan, "sure. Something with more muscle, maybe."

"What you got in there?"

"A V-6 with a bolt on turbo."

"No shit."

"No shit," said Winter. "You like cars?"

The tall kid shrugged, toeing his board, pretending to be disinterested, but Winter could see him eying the car. Sure enough, after a moment the kid asked, "You put it in yourself?"

"Nah. I like to drive them, not take them apart. I know a guy." Another car pulled up behind them, a throaty roar of a dual exhaust, Winter glancing in the mirror at a tricked out Camaro. He waved that one by as well, a young white guy at the wheel, Winter catching a glance of a leather jacket and lots of bling.

"How about that one?" asked the shorter kid, more a challenge than an interest in cars.

"Easy," said Winter.

The younger kid scoffed, but the taller one said, "How do you know? He could have the V-8 with *two* turbos."

"I can tell."

"How?"

"Anyone with that much muscle wouldn't need to be showing all that flash."

The car kid's eyes changed, as if he was reconsidering Winter. "You're pretty smart for an old man."

Winter jerked his head toward where he was heading. "You know the custom shop over on Mill Street?"

"Not our block," said the shorter kid.

"I know it," said the other boy. "They got all those wheels in the window, that big poster of a Brembo brake."

"That's it," said Winter. "Guy who owns it did my turbo. His name is Joseph. If you want, go see him, tell him Winter sent you. If you don't call him Joe, he'll show you a bolt on."

"He a white guy?"

"Does it matter? Cars don't care who's driving."

"You mean I just show up?"

"And you give him my name."

"He owe you or something?"

"Just a friend. Don't need to owe friends."

The short kid looked unconvinced, but Winter could see the taller boy considering. Winter shifted his voice, like he didn't care one way or another. "If you're interested enough, he might even find you something to do, you might learn a few things."

The light changed to green, Winter took his foot off the brake. The kid would go or he wouldn't. Who knew? Someday he might be bolting on turbos instead of hanging around on a corner, especially with a friend who would get him in trouble. Winter sensed the shorter kid was already a lost cause.

The tall kid said, "Aren't you going to ask us why we're not in school?"

Winter grinned. "Probably for the same reason I skipped too. I'm not *that* old." He gave them a nod and drifted through the intersection.

*   *   *

WINTER'S THIRD STOP was at an old L shaped strip mall with a bank
that had changed names five times, a pharmacy, and an old Mam-
moth Mart that had been converted into a series of small offices. He
remembered the place as a kid, the first big discount department
store, a cavernous building where you could get plastic lawn furniture,
toys, cheap tools and even cheaper clothes, his mother outfitting him
and his sister both. The kids trying on clothes in the aisles, no dress-
ing rooms, then rushing off to the toy aisles, not to buy, but to play.

Winter had picked this address because it had been listed only as
The Plaza, which is what the shopping center was called. Back before
the days of computers, he'd once helped the bank manager with a
cash shortage problem, which had turned out to be not a theft but a
clerk with dyslexia who kept giving out either too much or too little
money, the customers who got too much not complaining. Today
they'd figure it out before the end of the shift.

Winter parked in front of the office suites, that was the best bet.
The original large windows were still there, revealing a conference
room and some offices, mostly empty.

The lobby was small yet had the high roof of the original store,
open beams, air conditioning ductwork, which from the noise it made
was also the original installation. A young woman in an unnatural
shade of red hair sat behind a modern looking glass desk, bare except
for a multi-button phone, looking more bored than the street kids.
Winter thought she would have brightened at his approach if for
nothing else than to break the monotony. Instead, she was focused on
her gum chewing, her eyes sleepy.

Winter nodded a hello, indicated the large phone setup. "How's
this place work? Everyone have the same number?"

The girl didn't seem to care that Winter hadn't even introduced
himself, like people came in all the time asking the same question.
She finished popping a bubble and said, "There are three lines.
Someone calls, I answer Marburg Business Park, they give me a business name, I connect them through."

"The calls can't go through direct?"

"Nope."

"Huh." That didn't help Winter much. "So you wouldn't know
who called what number."

"We get lots of calls. That's what we do."

"I didn't see many people through the window," said Winter. "Not many suites taken?"

"You looking to rent?"

"Not really. Why so many calls if no one is here?"

"A lot of them are empty all the time. Mostly small companies that need a street address for credibility. It sounds more professional, I pick up the phone instead of a recording."

Winter hoped she did better phone than conversation. "Which business uses the number ending in 4321?"

"Why do you want to know?"

Winter showed her his badge. The girl seemed more impressed with her gum. "I'm trying to find out if a certain person called a business here."

"You should ask them."

"It's complicated," said Winter.

"Two companies share that number now. An architect and The New Look Agency."

Winter didn't think Gruse would be hiring an architect. "Who are they?"

"A modeling and talent agency. They're the only ones here that get lots of visitors."

"Someone back there now?"

The girl nodded. "Jerry."

"Can you call him for me, see if he's available?"

"Do I have to?"

"Don't like the guy?"

"He's a sleazebag."

Winter wondered if Jerry knew how his receptionist was marketing him. "Okay if I just wander on back?"

"Don't say I didn't warn you." She lazily waved over her shoulder. "Back that way, at the end of the hall."

Winter went down a dimly lit corridor, passing mostly closed doors on either side, some without even a name. The suite at the end was an exception, a classy looking gold sign bearing the agency name, a glass door which chimed as Winter entered. Inside, a nicely decorated waiting area, coffee tables filled with fashion magazines, the walls covered with huge posters of models, close ups of faces, sultry looks mixed with vacuous stares. Winter thought the receptionist could give them a run for their money, at least in the bored look department.

A guy about his age bounded out of the back room, dressed in a bright blue silk shirt, too tight black pants, half boots, and a comb over that made Winter cringe. Even if the receptionist was wrong about Jerry being a sleazebag, he was doing a good job of at least looking the part, especially when his capped smile froze in place when he saw Winter.

"Can I help you?"

"My name is Winter, I'm with the Marburg Police."

Jerry held up his hands like Winter was holding a gun. "I assure you, officer, all the women here are old enough, or they have parental permission."

"What exactly do you do here?" asked Winter.

"We're talent representatives for models and actresses."

Winter indicated the photos on the wall. "Your clients?"

"Not exactly, they're established models, just setting the tone. Give the girls—women—something to shoot for."

"I see," said Winter, thinking that if it was his business he'd have his real success stories on the wall. He wasn't here to deal with slimy guys selling dreams, but maybe he'd pass on a word to vice, just in case. "I'm trying to get a line on a photographer who might have called you."

"Lots of photographers call. What's his name?"

"Lawrence Gruse. Probably went by Lenny."

Jerry shook his head. "The name doesn't ring a bell. Is he with a studio?"

"I don't think so. It would have been a few months ago."

"Was he calling me? Or for one of the girls?" Jerry seemed to realize what that implied, quickly adding, "A lot of the women don't give out their personal number, they use our number on their websites and in their portfolios. It's more professional. Anyone who wants to hire them for a shoot, or even for a casting call, is supposed to go through me anyway."

"You get paid for that?"

"Fifteen percent of any jobs they get, it's industry standard. And a small amount each month for the phone service."

"So Gruse could have been calling to hire a model?"

"If he's a photographer, sure. That's how it works."

"If I needed it, could you give me a list of your clients?"

"Sure, it's no secret. You could just look on our website, they're all listed. These women aren't hiding, they're trying to become famous."

ON THE WAY DOWNTOWN, Winter tried to start building a picture of Gruse. He didn't have much, but wasn't bothered. It always took a while, and he was careful not to fall into the trap of drawing conclusions too early, people were more complicated than they seemed. That didn't mean that the answer couldn't be simple, like Ryder's idea of Gruse being the victim of a thief posing as a drug dealer, but before Winter went down that path he wanted to get a better feel for Gruse.

The places Gruse had called could mean little, the crumbs of a phone history that combined to form nothing definitive. Gruse could be a part time drug dealer or just a guy scoring recreational dope. Or neither, his death having nothing to do with drugs.

Winter parked on Main Street, in between his next two stops. He'd passed The Marquee club, knowing it was closed, late morning, but walked back anyway, the owner was often there during the day doing liquor inventory. Winter cut through the side alley, ignoring the door with the rear entrance sign, and instead climbed the loading dock and pounded on the metal garage door. No one answered. After a minute or two he did it again with the same result. Winter would check back tonight when the club was open.

Back on Main, past his car, a few blocks down to The Café restaurant. He hadn't eaten here in a while. The food was okay, Winter more of a diner guy. The owner, Jake, had slowly shifted The Café upscale, the menu filled with salads Winter couldn't pronounce. But once inside the solid aroma of good old fashioned meat being grilled reminded him it was close to lunchtime.

A pouty young brunette hostess who looked like she was practicing the look needed to get on Jerry's agency wall gave him a well practiced smile. "Table for one?"

"Actually, I'm looking for Jake. Friend of his."

"He was just at the bar a minute ago. If you wait there he'll be back."

Winter thanked her and made his way through the tables, the place doing better than he remembered, those fancy salads must be selling. Jake was just coming out of the kitchen when Winter reached the bar.

"As I live and breathe," said Jake, shaking Winter's hand. "I thought you were dead."

"That welcome get you a lot of customers?"

"I wouldn't say that to the paying ones. You, you get to eat free, anytime."

"How's the boy?" asked Winter. Jake, who had worked for a contract agency that provided security to shopping malls, had once been in the unfortunate position of being called by a store manager to pick up two shoplifters she had caught. Nothing odd about that, except the shoplifters had turned out to be Jake's sixteen year old son and his friend. Jake had no choice but to call the police, and Winter had got the call. Winter had quickly figured out it was a one time thing, or could be if it got rerouted. Winter had talked to the store owner, who turned out to be a friend of Brooker's, and had worked out a deal everyone was happy with. Jake had never forgot what he viewed as a favor and Winter viewed as nothing more than the right way to handle it, and ever since Winter had never paid for a burger.

"He's good, good, he graduated community college, he's going to transfer to UMass. Hey, you hungry?"

"I could eat. Unless it's all green."

Jake waved his hand. "That's for the tourists. I'll get you a steak, medium, right?" Without waiting for an answer Jake stuck his head back in the kitchen. "Two New York strips, medium." He came back out and pulled out a stool for Winter, waving the bartender over. "You working? Or can I get you a beer?"

"A beer sounds good, but I'd better not. They're cracking down on freebies too. I'll pay for the steak."

"So if you were at my house, and I tossed a few steaks on the grill and offered you one, you couldn't eat it?"

"Sure I could."

"Consider this my home. I practically live here. Shit, the world is falling apart and they're worried about a cop getting a free meal."

"Tell me about it," said Winter. "Next they'll be making me wear a tie." He nodded to the bartender. "Just water."

Jake pointed to his empty tumbler and the bartender filled it from a pitcher under the bar. Jake tipped his glass. "Fortunately I can drink on the job."

"Must be nice," said Winter, looking around the restaurant. "You're doing okay."

"Pretty good. The food is the easy part, it's getting good help that's the problem. This one can't work weekends, that one can't work nights, another one doesn't like to work with so and so, it gives me a headache. On top of that, most don't last more than a few months."

"Serves you right, being a hard driving tycoon."

"If by hard driving you mean I ask them to take orders, be polite to the customers, and deliver food. Most of them consider carrying a tray hard work. You just stopping by to check in, or did you really come to eat?"

"Looking for some information on a guy who called here a bunch of times. His name is Lenny Gruse. Know him?"

Jake rubbed his stomach. "No. Maybe a friend of one of the staff. They aren't supposed to, but they get calls here. Can't figure out why, they're on their cell phones every minute, even when they're supposed to be working."

Something clicked in Winter's mind, Lenny calling a modeling agency, a restaurant. What had the agency guy Jerry said? The girls don't give out their personal numbers. Maybe Lenny was calling around, looking to find someone? "You got any models working here? Actresses?" he asked.

Jake laughed. "Why do you think no one lasts long? They're *all* models and actresses. Or want to be. That summer theater is great for business but sucks for keeping staff. They get stars in their eyes, quit after getting their first role."

"The guy I'm looking for was a photographer. Maybe he was trying to reach one of them."

"Could be. Sometimes a guy comes in, sees a cute waitress, calls to try and hook up."

"Who takes the calls?"

"Main line rings at the hostess station. Hang on." Jake caught the eye of a passing waitress. "Tell Kate to come back here please." Jake watched the waitress walk away, noticed that Winter had noticed, and shrugged. "I look at my own menus, what can I say?"

"Maybe something about only eating at home?"

"We have a few who will tempt any man with a pulse. I think some of the customers come more for them than the food."

"A restaurant owner who has attractive staff," said Winter. "What a novel concept."

Kate arrived just as their steaks did. "My friend here, Detective Winter, is looking for some information on a guy," said Jake.

"His name is Lawrence Gruse, Lenny," said Winter. "Called here a few times."

"We get lots of calls for reservations," said Kate. "I can check the system, see if he ate here."

Winter was thinking about Gruse's tiny apartment, his lived in car, his small bank account. "Maybe not a customer. He could have had a friend here."

"A friend without their own phone?" Kate sounded like that was an impossibility.

"One of the dishwashers maybe," said Jake. "We've got a few, you know—"

"I don't need to know," said Winter, heading off Jake admitting he had illegals working off the books. To Kate he said, "Maybe a guy looking to connect with one of the waitresses he didn't have a number for?"

"We get almost as many of those calls as we do reservations. Not likely they'd give me their name. It's not like anyone would call them back, some loser trying to hook up by phone."

Winter looked at Jake, who said, "Told you."

"If he was calling to try to get with a waitress, he was probably here at some point," said Winter.

"What did he look like?"

Winter pulled out his old flip phone and found a photo of Gruse that Cindy had stored on it for him.

"Jeez, they still make those?" said Kate, squinting at the small fuzzy image. "I don't think I've seen him. Have you asked Tiffany?"

"She's the other hostess," explained Jake. "She's out today."

"She's got an audition," said Kate.

"She told me she was sick," said Jake.

Kate winked at Winter. "So do I when I have an audition."

Jake spread his hands. "See what I have to put up with?"

"I'll come by at some point and see Tiffany," said Winter. "And try to bring better photos."

"Get a new phone," said Kate.

"Yeah, yeah, everyone tells me that," said Winter. He waited for Kate to head back to her station and then took a bite of his steak. It was pretty good and he said so.

"Yeah, fuck those greens," said Jake.

A HALF HOUR LATER, outside the restaurant, Winter blinked in the bright sun, wishing he had said screw it to the rules and taken the beer. The steak had been spicy, a good spicy, but calling for a cold one. In the end he'd tried to pay for it, but Jake had said he couldn't accept money if there wasn't a bill, and since there wasn't a bill, what was Winter paying for? Winter had left the money on the bar, a big tip for a glass of water, Jake couldn't stop him from doing that. Cops got free coffee all over the city, maybe all over the country; Winter couldn't remember the last time he'd paid for a cup. Was that off limits too these days? Ryder would know, but he'd be damned if he was going to ask Ryder. Ryder probably paid for his coffee, his sugar, *and* his creamer.

Winter felt the beginning of a thread on Gruse, a guy looking to meet models, calling around. It could be nothing, a new photographer in town, getting established. Or just some average guy who noticed an attractive waitress. As Kate said, it happened all the time.

He started back toward his car, stopped, looking up and down the street. Didn't he have another address to check out? He mentally ticked off his stops, he was usually good at names and numbers, but was drawing an uncharacteristic blank. Was it six addresses or seven?

He shook his head, getting old, he'd have to start writing things down. Shit, pretty soon he'd need reading glasses.

CHAPTER 26

THE STARBUCKS ACROSS THE STREET from Winter was packed, a long line inside visible through the window. Winter idly wondered if they gave cops free coffees; the few times he'd gone in a Starbucks had been to use the john. He was more Dunkin Donuts than Starbucks, maybe it was an age thing. The Starbucks customers all looked young, but on the other hand, who else would be sitting outside drinking coffee in the middle of a workday?

Winter didn't know if Gruse had called Starbucks, but it wouldn't hurt to show his picture around at the coffee shop. He'd just learned that guys often called restaurants to try to hook up with waitresses they'd met, why not Starbucks?

Winter's phone rang. He answered without checking to see who it was. He didn't give the number out to too many people, if he got a call, it was from someone he wanted to talk to. Usually.

"Detective Winter, it's Cindy. I've been going through Lenny Gruse's photos with Dan. We've been trying to sort them in different ways, see if we can find patterns. We think we have something. A lot of the women only appear to show up in a few pictures. But others are all over the place, sometimes dozens of shots of the same woman in different locations. Dan thinks maybe Gruse was stalking them."

Winter leaned against a street sign. "Or he just had more opportunities to photograph those women."

"Maybe. It's weird. Some of the photos are full on shots, close ups, like the women wanted to be photographed. Others are just taken on the street, at odd angles. Dan thinks Gruse might have been walking around, taking pictures of women without them knowing, with his camera on a strap and just shooting away."

"Would he be able to focus? Or know what he was shooting at?"

"Dan says Gruse could have set the focus beforehand. And he could have deleted any photos that didn't capture anything. Dan's working to see if he can recover some of the deleted shots."

Winter was still looking at the Starbucks. "You said you recognized some of the backgrounds in the photos. Can you group them that way? Pull all the shots that are taken near a Starbucks, for example?"

"Sure."

"Do that. I want to see if Gruse was calling around, trying to connect with women who he'd met while they were working. Or a particular woman. Concentrate on restaurants, bars, coffee shops. Cross reference it to Gruse's phone list."

"Got it."

"If you find any that match, make some copies of the best photos. Same goes for any women who show up a lot. We can try to identify the women, and see if they know Gruse."

"No problem. You want me to send them to your phone?"

Winter was thinking of the hostess Kate's comment about his old technology. "My screen is too small. Call me when you have something and I'll stop by the station for prints."

He thanked Cindy and rang off, punched up Ryder. "Any luck?"

"Nothing. One lady at the dry cleaner thought she recognized Gruse, but she was also sure she'd seen my niece and nephew who are on my screensaver, and they've never been to Marburg."

"She the only person working there? I mean, the only person a customer would have come in contact with?"

"I don't know, why?"

Winter explained his idea about Gruse maybe trying to hook up. "We need to start asking about who talks to the customers."

"Man, don't make me go back there, that old woman will bend my ear. And what do I ask her, is there someone else good looking who works here instead of you?"

"Just keep it in mind going forward, find out who works out front. We'll go back if this idea pans out. Cindy and Dan are trying to identify spots Gruse may have photographed women. We'll have a lot more places to hit soon."

"Still doesn't mean anything, if you ask me. What, you think some woman who Gruse photographed on the street was so mad at him for taking a picture she killed him?"

"Gruse might have been doing more than just taking pictures. Let's stick with it for a while."

"He had a lot of photos, what if there are a hundred women?"

"Then it will be longer than a while."

"I still think it's drugs. I'm going to work that angle instead."

Winter pinched the bridge of his nose. Brooker better get better soon, he couldn't take much more of Ryder. To mollify Ryder he said, "Anything's possible. Nothing stopping you from doing both. Go by the station later, Cindy will print out pictures of any women who Gruse might have stalked."

"Can't she just send them to our phones? Easier than carrying a bunch of photos around. You're not still doing that, are you?"

"Of course not," said Winter. He hung up, feeling like a Neanderthal. Had another idea, called the station again. "Cindy, see if you can find any record of women reporting being stalked by an unidentified photographer out where Gruse lived in LA."

"That might be a long list," said Cindy. "Being Hollywood and all."

"I know, but try anyway. And do it the other way around as well. Take all of the women Gruse took pictures of out there—the ones we have names on—and see if any of them reported being stalked."

"I'm not sure if California has a statewide database of police reports."

"Then try to list all the woman as best you can by city. Send each jurisdiction their list—actually, send them the entire list, with the women in their cities marked off. Logan has a contact or two in LA, they can help. Also see if there are unsolved rapes or homicides, especially after women reported being stalked or witnesses later saying the victims had mentioned a photographer around."

"That will take a while. But I'll get on it. You think Gruse may have stalked women there and attacked them?"

"Just pulling at strings." He was about to hang up, thought about

Ryder. "Hey Cindy? If Ryder calls in, tell him you found a few photos of a woman that look like they were taken outside of the dry cleaner."

"You want me to lie to him?"

"You're looking at photos, right? Call it artistic license."

WINTER HELD THE DOOR OPEN for two teenage girls who were adroitly carrying coffees while texting. The line at the Starbucks counter was seven deep, so he drifted toward the back to wait. Along the far wall a red-haired woman with a ring in her nose was kneeling on the floor, stacking bags of a coffee with a name Winter couldn't pronounce. She appeared to be in her late twenties, making her the oldest worker in the shop.

"Be done in a sec if you want something on this shelf," she said without looking up.

"That coffee any good?" Winter asked.

"Beats me. I drink herbal tea. But we can't keep this one in stock."

"Huh." Maybe Winter needed to expand his coffee horizons. "I'm with the Marburg Police. Have you seen this man in here?" He pointed his phone toward the woman, feeling slightly embarrassed at the small screen.

The redhead didn't seem to mind. She looked at Gruse's photo, idly touching her nose ring, which gave Winter another idea, maybe they could identify the women by jewelry.

"I don't think so. I mostly work in the back, you should ask at the counter."

Winter didn't want to wait. "Could you do me a favor and pass this around?"

Her green eyes narrowed on him. "I'm not going to get anyone in trouble, am I?"

"Nothing like that," Winter assured her. Unless of course they happened to be the person who stabbed Gruse. "We're just trying to get some information to help him out, he was the victim of a crime."

The redhead stood up. "Better than stacking coffee." She took

Winter's phone and slipped behind the counter. A series of head shakes told Winter he wasn't going to learn anything here.

The redhead returned his phone. "Sorry."

"No problem, thanks." Winter took one last look at the unpronounceable coffee and actually considered buying some, until he noticed the price, fourteen ninety five for a small bag. It couldn't be *that* good.

Instead he headed back to his car. He hadn't learned anything about Gruse but he did discover one piece of information: apparently this Starbucks didn't offer cops a free coffee.

AT THREE O'CLOCK Winter pulled into the parking lot of the Marburg Way, a modern chrome and glass throwback diner, everything made to look old except the prices. Not Winter's favorite place, but he'd been there often enough, one of the few twenty four hour spots open on his route home.

Tired of having witnesses squinting at his phone, he'd run into the office with the intent of getting some large photos printed and to see how Cindy was progressing. She didn't have much news for him but she did have a present—a tablet. Winter had eyed it warily, much like a stone age man might have studied a car. Cindy joked that it wouldn't bite—Winter wasn't convinced, but allowed her to patiently show him a few basic moves. She had loaded up pictures of Gruse as well as photos he'd taken of women working at restaurants and shops throughout Marburg. Winter actually recognized a few faces, especially now that he had a frame of reference for where he had seen them. He gingerly took the gadget.

Before going into the diner, Winter practiced on the tablet. He managed to get the photos on the screen and swiped his way through the collection, looking for patterns. He had some experience with stalkers, they tended to focus on a type, blondes, or petite women, even goths. Yet the women in Gruse's photos were all over the map, tall, short, every color hair possible in nature and from a bottle, well dressed, in ratty jeans, the entire gamut. The only thing they had in common was that they were all young and attractive. Maybe Gruse was just looking for models after all. Or he was a lonely guy. Or both.

Cindy had organized the photos by location, and Winter pecked until he found the Marburg Way diner folder. He recognized one of the waitresses, a brunette with eyes that seemed too big for her face. The photos appeared to have been taken covertly, as if the camera had been set down on the table. The surreptitious nature of the images made them cringe worthy, Winter feeling a little sleazy just looking at them.

The diner wasn't too busy. Winter spotted the brunette working one of the tables, so he bypassed the counter and slipped into a booth.

The waitress carried her tray to the kitchen, emerged a few seconds later, and without breaking stride picked up a mug and a pot of coffee on her way. At Winter's table she set down the mug, poured the coffee, and smiled.

"You're here early," she said. "I usually see you at night."

Winter was surprised, he didn't think she had ever served him. Her chrome name tag said, *Mandy*. "My job," he said.

"Don't tell me, let me guess." Mandy tapped her chin. "You're a fireman, right?"

"No, I—"

"At one of the clubs downtown? You're a bouncer?"

Winter must have frowned, because she kept going. "The late shift at the mill?"

"I'm with the police."

"Oh. You got me, I wouldn't have guessed that. You don't *look* like a cop."

Winter got that a lot, it didn't bother him, it often helped. "How did you know I drank coffee?"

"Just because I don't know where you work doesn't mean I didn't pay attention," Mandy said.

Winter fumbled for the tablet. "Have you seen this man?"

Mandy did her chin tap as she looked at Gruse's photo. "I don't think so. We get a lot of customers."

Winter didn't want to tell Mandy her picture was on Gruse's camera, which meant Gruse had to have been at the diner. Instead he prodded, "Let me show you another picture of him." He swiped across the screen, overshot, had to go back.

"Nope, can't say I have. But that doesn't mean he wasn't here."

"You seem pretty observant."

Mandy gave him that smile again, her doe eyes widening. "*You* I remember. Him—I wouldn't give him a second glance."

WINTER MADE FOUR MORE stops at locations Cindy had identified. At the first two the women in Gruse's photos were not working, but Winter showed the picture of Gruse anyway. He considered asking for a shift schedule, but it would require too much explanation, and someone would certainly get their nose out of joint and demand a warrant. Winter would go down that path later if he had to, although he wasn't sure he had enough probable cause yet. No one remembered seeing Gruse, and Winter made a note to come back to both places later.

At the third stop, yet another Starbucks—Winter wondering how Cindy had figured out this was a different store from the one downtown, since they all looked the same—Winter spotted the woman right away, deftly pouring shots of espresso with both hands. She didn't look at all like Mandy or any of the other women he had been trying to find; she was a bit older, her nose a little crooked, her body nondescript in her green apron. But when she looked up to hand a customer his drink her eyes flashed, her whole face brightening, a look that said, *I'm so happy to serve you!* Winter's first inclination was that she knew the customer, but when she turned on the smile for the next person in line he realized it was a practiced look.

And suddenly a piece of the puzzle dropped in place. Gruse's type wasn't blondes or brunettes or redheads, it was a *look*, a hard to put your finger on expression, a glance that made the person they were speaking to feel special. This woman had it, the pixie Mandy had it, as did the hostess at Jake's restaurant. Winter had noticed that skill in actors and actresses, the ability to turn an expression on and off while still making it seem natural. He'd go back through Gruse's photos later with this in mind.

The woman behind the espresso machine didn't look like she was going to get a break, so Winter stood in line and ordered a regular coffee. If he had any more coffee shops on his list he'd waste half his day pissing. When his drink was ready the woman called out, "Tall black," and gave Winter the special smile when he picked it up.

"Excuse me," Winter said, holding up the tablet, which he was finding surprisingly useful. "I'm a cop, and I'm looking for information on this man. Have you seen him here?"

Someone yelled, "Grande latte, extra hot!" The woman glanced at the tablet as she repeated the order. "Should I have?"

"I'm pretty sure he's been in here." Winter had studied the angles while waiting. He figured Gruse had been sitting in a small corner table when he had taken her photo, the counter blocking all of her below the neck.

"Can't say I remember," she said. "I only get a quick look when I hand out the drinks. Did you ask at the register?"

"Not yet, I will."

"Next time tell them who you are before you order, they'll give you regular coffee for free. If you're really a cop, that is."

Winter grinned. "You doubt me?"

The woman was already launching her prize winning look for the next customer as she said, "Cops wear uniforms or suits."

Winter glanced down at his tactical pants and boots. He'd have to get way more than just free coffee to make him wear a suit.

AT THE FOURTH STOP—a loud juice bar called Wholesome Drinks—two young women of indeterminate teenage years sitting at the bar mooning over a college aged boy squeezing oranges overheard Winter asking about Gruse. One of them, a blue eyed dimpled blonde, asked to see the photo. Winter spun the tablet their way, and they both agreed they had been stopped by Gruse one day in the Marburg city park.

"Creepy guy."

"Why do you say that?" asked Winter.

"He was hitting on us."

"I bet you get that all the time," said the juicer.

"But we didn't want it from him," said the blonde, pouting.

"He was giving us some bullshit line about taking our pictures, making us famous," added the other girl.

"Maybe he could," said the juicer.

"Please," said both girls, simultaneously.

Winter prodded them a little more, but they couldn't tell him much. They thought Gruse had been a creep with a prop camera, nothing more. They'd never seen him again.

Winter took their names anyway.

AT THE STATION, Winter and Ryder hunched over Cindy's desk as she ran her pencil down a list of names. "None of the women you talked to today who you got names from are in Gruse's contact list. I even checked his incoming and outgoing calls—his phone stored almost three months' worth, he actually didn't get or make a lot of calls—and used a reverse directory to see who each number belonged to. No hits. If he knew these women, he wasn't in contact with them by phone."

"Great, a drug dealing stalker," said Ryder.

"Did you notice anything else about the women you talked to?" asked Winter. He didn't want to color Ryder's perception with his own idea about what the women might have in common.

"It's amazing how many women want to be famous," said Ryder.

"What do you mean?"

"See these?" Ryder pointed to three names on the list. "Two want to be models, the other one an actress. All three of them used the word *famous* about ten times."

"Half the staff over at The Café want to be in acting as well," said Winter. "I don't understand the appeal."

"Young girls see these glamorous, rich women on television shows, in the movies, hanging out with hot guys, going to ritzy galas, what part don't you understand?" asked Cindy.

Winter groaned. "Not you, too."

"Just saying."

"So Gruse could just have been using the photographer story to meet women, promise them publicity . . ." said Winter.

"Or maybe he was a real photographer with connections," said Cindy. "I've googled his name, his photos have appeared in online celebrity blogs, entertainment websites, even some print publications."

"Or both," said Winter. "That would explain the stalker shots." His picture of Gruse was filling in, a guy who had just relocated to a much smaller city than flashy Los Angeles, who didn't get or make many calls. Perhaps lonely, a little depressed. Not much money. It wouldn't be a stretch to think he'd use his photography as a way to meet women.

Cindy tapped her screen. "We still have more photos to sort through, especially the ones where it's not so obvious where they were taken."

"Prioritize any full on shots, where the woman looks like she wanted to be photographed," said Winter. "Just feed everything to us as you get them. We can be back on the street first thing in the morning. Tonight I'm going to hit a few of the clubs too."

"I still think it's a waste of time," said Ryder. "Do any of these woman look like they'd kill a guy for taking their picture?"

Winter had once arrested a pigtailed, pudgy sixteen year old girl who hadn't outgrown her baby fat but had beaten her brother to death with a fireplace poker because he told her she looked like a Cabbage Patch kid. Winter didn't think murderers had a look. On the other hand . . . "The women who wanted to be famous, can you show me their photos?"

Ryder took the mouse from Cindy and clicked on the photos. "A blonde, a brunette, and, what color is that, anyway? Purple?"

"I'd call it dusty grape," said Cindy. "I think it looks kind of cool."

"They don't look at all alike," said Ryder.

Not the hair color, or their skin tones, or their general features, thought Winter. One of the women wasn't looking directly at the camera. But the other two gave off a—*feeling*, a vibe—a glint in their eye, a communication through their features that appeared deliberate. Almost as if they knew they were being photographed, or *expected* to be photographed at any time. Now that Winter knew what to look for, this indefinable look jumped out at him in some of the shots. Not all, but enough that he noticed. Was it this look that made them attractive, or was it that they were attractive and some just happened to have the look? "Let's keep track of how many of these woman Gruse photographed who wanted to be famous, models, actresses, singers."

"That might be most of them," said Cindy.

"Let's do it anyway." Winter still wasn't ready to voice his idea that Gruse was searching for a certain look. Especially since Winter couldn't exactly define what he meant. He'd also seen too many investigations go down the wrong path because someone along the way had jumped the gun, like the search for a white van the DC sniper was supposedly driving.

Winter slipped the tablet out of his oversized cargo pocket, he wanted to ask Cindy to help him reorder the images.

"Since when do you have a tablet?" asked Ryder.

Winter gave him a surprised look, his own attempt at acting. "You're not still showing photos on that tiny phone screen, are you? This is much better."

CHAPTER 27

RYDER COULDN'T MAKE SENSE of Marburg's archaic investigative software database. He had arrived at the station before his shift to work the drug angle, wanting to avoid wasting any more time showing Gruse's photo around. For the past hour he had been hunched over his desk computer, searching in vain for a way to sort drug arrests by location. The software he had used in Derry would have spit the answer out in a few seconds.

Everything was old here, even though Marburg was a much larger city. When Ryder had transferred to Marburg he'd assumed that a larger city meant bigger budgets, but instead he'd discovered older computers, older software, even older detectives. Ryder often felt like he had entered a time machine; one day he might wake up and find out that the motor pool had been replaced by horses and buggies. He knew the policing procedures would be outdated—that's mostly why they brought him in—but he hadn't expected the shortcomings to extend to basic software tools.

He gave up on the department database. Maybe he would ask Cindy, she seemed on top of everything—but he was still miffed she had sent him on the wild goose chase back to the dry cleaner, where as he feared, he had a very long and fruitless conversation with the elderly lady. That had to be Winter's idea, the old school cop practical joke. Ryder hated practical jokes.

He switched to CJIS, the Massachusetts Criminal Justice Information System. Ryder felt more comfortable with this system, although it was limited to arrests only and didn't track open investigations like a local department database would. Gruse had no record, but maybe one of the employees at the motel where Gruse had been stabbed did. Ryder punched in the names, and lo and behold, Hank Evers, the night clerk who Ryder had interviewed, had an arrest for possession of a controlled substance, oxycodone. Ryder would pay Evers another visit, find out if Gruse was trying to score or look for a source.

Ryder moved the cursor back to the search field. One by one he typed in the names of the women Gruse had photographed who had been newly identified. Sure enough, one of them, Terri Cerese, had been arrested for possession of marijuana. The fact that she was in the system at all meant that it had to be more than one ounce, and was likely a second arrest; first offenses would be sealed and off the books after a successful probation. Cerese could be a dealer.

So Gruse had been killed in the parking lot of a seedy motel where a user worked, and Gruse had at least one photo of a woman who might be a dealer. That seemed a more fruitful line of investigation than the meandering Winter was doing. Ryder would interview Cerese; he didn't trust Winter to pursue the drug angle. Winter's methodology was as out of date as Marburg's software.

Ryder clicked off, feeling like he had accomplished something, and left the bullpen. A couple of other detectives were there, no one even saying good morning. Ryder just wasn't part of the club yet.

Cindy stopped him as he passed her cubicle. He did a double take; her hair was purple today. "Detective Ryder, I may have something for you."

Ryder suspected another wild goose chase that would keep him from pursuing the drug angle. "What is it?"

"Did you know the victim in your assault case was just on tv?"

"So? She's an actress."

"She was a guest on *The Other Woman*."

"And?"

"And on the show she said, well, she implied, but she might as well have said it, that Jason Ayers—you know who he is, right?— assaulted her. That's your case, isn't it?"

Ryder could feel his mouth opening and closing like a fish gulping for air. "She what?"

"She told the interviewer that she was hot and heavy with Jason

Ayers, and that even though Jason supposedly is with Ashley Hanna, *the* Ashley Hanna, he can't keep his hands off of her. Off Melanie, I mean. She said he came into her place one night—"

"She fucking lied to me!" Ryder couldn't believe it. Melanie had told him she didn't remember much about the assault, he had it in his frigging *notes*, and now she was on television telling the world who did it? He was going to look like an idiot.

"Who lied to you?" asked Captain Logan.

Ryder had been so focused on Melanie he hadn't even seen Logan approach. Winter was right behind him. "It must be a mistake," Ryder said, ignoring Logan. "You must have heard it wrong."

Cindy shrugged. "Okay, don't believe me. I'll get a copy of the show for you."

"What show?" asked Logan.

Ryder couldn't see how to avoid telling him. "Melanie Upton—the possible assault victim at Lakeview? She told us she didn't remember much about the attack, or even if she had been attacked. Cindy claims she saw Upton on a television show identifying who assaulted her."

"I'm not *claiming* anything," said Cindy. "It's what I saw."

"*What* show?" repeated Logan.

"*The Other Woman*." Cindy must have noticed the blank stares, because she said, "Don't you all watch television? It's a show about celebrity relationships. They interview a woman who is involved with a man who is supposedly in a committed relationship."

"That gets someone on television?" asked Logan.

"It is if the people in the relationship are famous," explained Cindy. "And Ashley Hanna is famous."

"Who's she?" asked Winter.

Ryder had pushed Cindy aside, he was trying to find a YouTube of the show. "She's a singer," he said distractedly. "She's dating Jason Ayers, he's the next Mark Walburg, he's starring in a new series." When no one responded, Ryder looked up, Logan and Winter were staring at him. "What? Everyone knows that."

Winter was grinning, which pissed Ryder off. So he kept up on the news, why was that funny? "The show is being filmed here in Marburg. You've at least heard that, haven't you?"

"She named Ayers as her attacker?" asked Logan, incredulous.

"Well, yes and no," said Cindy. "It was more of an implication. Melanie says Jason might look like he's with Ashley but it's Melanie he can't keep his hands off of. He even had to force his way into her place."

"Why would she not tell us if she knew it was Ayers?" asked Logan.

"That's what I mean to find out," said Ryder.

"She might be covering for him," said Winter. "If he's as famous as you think he is. You being up on the celebrity gossip and all."

"I can't help it if I know what's going on in the world," muttered Ryder.

"Let's see, a few wars, a plane crash last week, a terrorist attack—not to mention the Sox might win the pennant again. Oh, yeah, I forgot, some guy named Jason Ayers is dating a woman named Hannah."

"Ashley Hanna," said Cindy and Ryder simultaneously.

"Cut it out," said Logan. "But the question is a good one. Why would this woman Upton cover up who her attacker was?"

"Maybe she got paid off," suggested Winter. "Or Ayers has something over her."

Ryder couldn't find a clip of the show online. "I'm going back to see her right now to find out. If she names Ayers, we can get a warrant for his DNA."

"No, you aren't," said Logan.

Ryder had already headed for the door. "What?"

"This woman already lied to you. She might be playing you, playing all of us. Let's watch this show first, get our line of questioning straight. Then someone else will do the interview."

This is bullshit, thought Ryder. "It's my case."

"I haven't said it wasn't. But you're pissed, hell, I would be too. Maybe it's a misunderstanding, but if she lied to you, you don't want to go in there with an attitude."

"I know what she told me," said Ryder, adamant. He didn't even need his notes. He'd talked to Melanie twice, shit, she had even wanted to have dinner with him, an invitation he'd refused, although he'd been really tempted, she was that hot. Not once had she implied anything about Jason Ayers.

"And I know what I heard," insisted Cindy.

"When was it on?" Ryder asked Cindy. If Melanie had done the show *after* she spoke to him, maybe she'd remembered something about the assault later. But why hadn't she called? She said she would call . . .

"I'm not sure. I Tivo-d it. I'll get the date. A week or two ago, maybe?"

Logan said, "Let's get a copy of that show."

Ryder tried again. "I want to re-interview her."

"Later," said Logan. "Let's get another take, compare notes." Logan looked at Winter. "You talk to her."

Ryder bit off a groan. Not Winter. First the Gruse case, and now this. Ryder would never get to make a name for himself if Logan kept letting Winter hone in on all his good cases. "I can handle it," he gritted.

"It's just an interview," said Logan. "Bring Winter up to speed. Since you guys are already working the Gruse case together, what's one more? Who knows, maybe you two were destined to be a team."

Fat chance, thought Ryder. I'll go back to dead end Derry first.

CHAPTER 28

WINTER LINGERED IN Cindy's cubicle after Logan and Ryder had left, Ryder no doubt off to catch up on his celebrity gossip. Winter wasn't looking forward to working another case with him. The guy was stubborn, and now Winter was getting a sense he was a closet hothead too, a bad combination. Brooker had warned him that maybe Logan was trying to team Winter up with Ryder. Winter hadn't wanted to believe it. He'd have to cut the head off that snake soon.

In the meantime, he'd have to suck it up and do the Upton interview, if for no other reason to get it out of the way and remove one more Ryder interaction.

Winter was aware of the Upton case but not the details. Ryder had given him a brief background. Winter thought of one thing he could do right away that Ryder probably wouldn't consider. To Cindy he said, "Your friend at the bank, the one you asked about Gruse? Can you see if this Upton woman had an account there?"

"Sure. You thinking she got paid off by Jason Ayers to keep quiet about the assault?"

"Or didn't. Maybe Ayers promised her something, she didn't get it, she goes on television to put some pressure on him. Or he pays her, she wants more." Winter sat on the edge of Cindy's desk. "Do me a favor. Close your eyes, think about the show you saw. Don't try to remember the words, just give me your feeling. Did she say Ayers did it?"

Cindy did as he asked, moving her neck side to side. After a minute she said, "No. She didn't connect the dots, you know? But on the other hand, she certainly made me *think* he did it. Or did something."

"Did she sound like she was making it up?"

"She *is* an actress, so who knows?"

"An actress?" Models, singers, actresses . . . some kind of connection? It would give Winter another way to approach Upton, see if she knew Gruse. "Can you call your friend at the bank?"

Winter half listened to Cindy as she made the call, trying to think of a possible connection between the Gruse homicide and the Lakeview assault. He nudged Cindy over and tried to find the file on the Upton assault, giving up after a few seconds when it was obvious that Cindy had struck out.

"She doesn't have an account there."

"It was a long shot anyway."

"Who says I don't have more banking friends?" Cindy was already dialing.

"Wait, before you do that, do you have a photo of the Upton woman?"

"I can google her. Here, quite a few."

Cindy enlarged one and went back to her call. Winter took one glance at the photo and thought, Hmm...there it is, *the look*, Upton seemed to know he was looking at her. No, that wasn't it, she knew that *anyone* would want to look at her. Like a magnet. Winter had seen that look in person a few times, he'd always thought it was meant for him. That was ego, he now realized. This woman, and the others he had known, could call it up at will.

Winter wasn't as special as he had thought. He felt a little sad, his memories of those women in his life shifting from a pleasant vibrancy to a shade of gray.

Cindy held her hand over the mouthpiece. "This favor might cost me," she said.

Winter got the hint. "Third row seats behind the dugout to the next Sox Yankee series," he said. "Or a night at the Presidential Suite at the Copley." He been offered both of these by people he'd helped out in one way or another.

"He's not into baseball," said Cindy. Into the phone she said, "Hey John? How's my favorite Patriots fan?"

Winter groaned. This was going to cost him box seats to the Patriots opener. He had wanted those for himself.

WINTER GRABBED A COFFEE in the break room and found Ryder at his cubicle in the bullpen. "Upton recently got a big deposit in her checking account," Winter said. "Where do you think that came from?"

Ryder didn't look up from his computer screen. "And how did you come by this piece of information?"

"Does it matter?"

"It does if we need it in court."

"We're not going to use it to get a search warrant. You already searched her place. Unless you think you missed something?"

"She's a victim, not a criminal."

"I thought you were pissed at her for lying to you."

Ryder finally looked up. "I am. But we need to do things by the book."

"Just trying to help." Winter waited him out, sipping at his coffee. Even he could tell it was bad, again making him wonder about that expensive Starbucks blend.

Ryder wrote something in his notebook. "How big a deposit?"

Winter hid his grin behind the coffee cup. "I don't know exactly, we'd need a warrant for that." He waited a beat, then added, "But it was five figures."

"That's a big range," argued Ryder.

"Let's assume the low end. Did Upton look like she got a lot of ten thousand dollar jobs?"

Ryder got up, stretched. "Probably not. You could ask her, seeing you are going to be talking to her."

"It could be a payoff. Maybe her friend Ayers got scared, thought she might actually nail him for attempted rape."

"That's kind of a stretch, don't you think?"

"Just looking at possibilities. Maybe you should talk to Ayers."

"I already had it on my list," said Ryder, gathering up his notebook and slipping into his jacket. "Cindy told me that most of the cast and crew from that tv show they're filming are staying at the Hilton. Ayers probably is too. I'm heading over there right now."

"If it's okay with you I'll tag along and you can fill me in more on the Upton case. I can hang out in the lobby and show Gruse's picture around while you're with Ayers."

THE HILTON HADN'T been remodeled since bright pastels were in style, but it was still the best hotel in Marburg. The regular bar was dark and roped off, closed at this early hour, but in the middle of the lobby the daytime café was open, down three steps, surrounded by a wall of planters with fake greenery.

Winter pointed to the café. "I'll be down there if you get in any trouble."

"Funny," Ryder said.

A few late risers were at the buffet grabbing the last of the eggs. Winter almost warned them; he'd eaten here a few times, and the eggs were definitely to be avoided. No staff were in the café, so Winter hung out by the buffet. The bacon called to him and he snuck a few pieces; it was hard to ruin bacon. A waitress came down the steps carrying a tray and started to clear a table.

Winter ambled over, pulling out his tablet and clicking on Gruse's photo. He'd clipped his badge to his belt. "Excuse me, I'm with the Marburg Police. Have you by any chance seen this man?"

The waitress, her hair in a bun, pulled a cloth napkin out of the apron she wore over her dark blue Hilton skirt, drying her hands as she looked at the tablet. "I'm not sure," she said. "Would he have been here for breakfast? I just have the morning shift." If she'd noticed Winter swallowing the last of the bacon she didn't mention it.

"I don't know exactly."

"It's just a breakfast buffet during the week. The lunch staff comes on at eleven."

"Thanks," said Winter. "I'll try later."

The waitress tilted her head toward the bar. "There are some guests in there, they've been staying here a while, they might know."

"I thought the bar was closed?"

"They're just watching tv."

Winter glanced at the other patrons, figured them all for tourists, and decided to try his luck. Ryder wasn't in the lobby, maybe he had found Ayers. Winter slipped past the thick rope into the dim bar. In the far corner, five guys dressed in jeans and tee shirts were watching highlights of last night's baseball games on a television mounted on the wall. Winter crossed the room and watched a replay of a replay from a West Coast game, an ultra slow motion of a tag at second.

"Told you, he was safe," said a lean guy wearing a gray workout jersey.

A man in a red Angels baseball cap said, "Let's wait for another angle."

Sure enough, another replay, two of them, Winter wondering how they could have so many cameras able to catch plays at second but never one where he needed it for a murder investigation. If someone ever got stabbed at second base he could solve cases from the bar.

"See, safe," said the guy in the workout jersey.

"Maybe," admitted the Angels fan. He caught sight of Winter and asked, "What do you think?"

"I think I'm glad I'm not an umpire," said Winter. "All those cameras looking over my shoulder."

All the men nodded agreement. They watched another replay, and then Winter said, "I'm with the local police, and I'm trying to find information on a guy who might have been in this bar." He offered up the tablet, let them pass it around the table.

"He do anything wrong?"

"No, not that we know of. I'm not trying to jam him up."

"I don't think I've seen him," said the Angels fan, passing the tablet along. No one else had either. "Want us to keep an eye out for him?"

"Thanks, but he's passed away," said Winter.

"Shit, that sucks."

Winter thanked them and turned, then thought about the Angels cap, a rarity in New England. "You in from California?"

"We all are," said the man in the cap. "We're with the *Shock and Awe* crew."

"Is that the tv show they're filming here?"

"Yep."

Winter pulled out a chair from the next table and straddled it facing them. "You know the cast members?"

"Sure, why? You looking for Michael Stevens's autograph?"

"He's in the show?" Winter had seen movies with Stevens.

"Yeah, although he pretty much stays in LA, flies out every so often for the location shoots."

"Not him. But a woman in my office, she has a crush on some actor, Ayers?"

"Don't they all," said a sad looking older guy with a soul patch and a droopy moustache.

"Sid's feeling his age," someone said, and they all laughed.

"I'm good friends with Jason," said the guy in the jersey. "We grew up together, right around here."

"You and Ayers are from Marburg?"

"Jason is. I'm from Northfield."

"No shit," said Winter. Northfield was two towns over from Marburg. "I've got cousins there. How'd you meet Jason?"

"We both ran track, I met him in the regionals one year. He ended up dating one of my friends."

"Guy was getting all the women he wanted before he even got on tv," said Sid.

"You'd do better if you'd shave off that dirt under your mouth."

"You've got one too, Carlo," said Sid.

"Yeah, but it looks good on me." Carlo, the guy in the workout jersey, said to Winter, "Jason and I were out of touch, but we've been catching up since we got on the same show. I do his stunts. He's cool, hangs out with the crew."

"Something you won't see Stevens do," said Sid.

"Got that right," said Carlo. "Anyway, I can get an autograph for your friend. Or bring her by some night there's a Sox game on, Jason usually invites us up to his suite to watch the game, she can get a photo with him."

"If she's cute that's not all she'll get," said Sid.

"Ayers does okay with the ladies, it sounds like," said Winter.

"We all do," said Carlo. "Except Sid. Lots of women want to, you know, be around the show."

Winter said, "I don't watch much television, but my office friend I was telling you about, she said she saw some show where a woman claimed Jason has the hots for her?"

"Yeah, we all heard about that," said Carlo. "It's bullshit."

"Jason's been with Ashley Hanna," said Sid. "This month, anyway."

"Why do you think it's bullshit?" asked Winter. "If Jason is so—in demand?"

Carlo leaned back in his chair. "Jason told me about that woman—she lives across the tracks. She claimed Jason hooked up at her place. Shit, I know that neighborhood, we used to go to bars there when we were underage to drink. It's a pig sty. Jason wouldn't be caught dead over there. He doesn't even like staying in this Hilton, he's more of a Four Seasons guy, you know what I mean?"

Winter nodded. "But maybe if he had a history with her . . ."

Carlo was already shaking his head. "I'm telling you, if Jason wanted some action, he's got women lining up to give it to him. He doesn't have to go over there."

"Maybe she came here," mused Winter. "Any of you guys know what she looks like?"

"We didn't bother watching the show," said Carlo. "Just some sorry assed chick looking for publicity. We get them all the time."

"I don't," said Sid morosely.

RYDER THOUGHT HE'D GET some pushback from the front desk about privacy, but the clerk not only told him Jason Ayers was a guest, but that he was likely in his room, a suite on the Executive Floor. Ryder guessed it was no secret anyway. As he was crossing to the elevator his phone beeped; a message from Cindy with a link to a video of *The Other Woman* show. Ryder sat in one of the lobby couches and clicked on it, wondering if Cindy had committed some kind of crime by sending him a link to what must have been an illegally recorded show, and even whether he should be watching it. He'd need to look that up.

In the background he could hear Winter laughing it up with some guys in the bar, Winter no doubt sneaking a drink while on duty. It was bad enough he was stuck with Winter on the Gruse case, and now he had to drag him along on the Upton investigation. The ride over had been a nightmare, Winter peppering him with all sorts of out of the blue questions about Upton, and then jumping to Ryder's interviews with the women Gruse had photographed. Ryder could barely follow along, Winter's mind was all over the place, even repeating questions, a lack of mental discipline that mirrored his unregulated investigatory style.

If this Gruse case didn't get closed soon he had a bad feeling he was going to be stuck with Winter. If that happened he'd try to get Winter bounced out of the department. He'd already seen a number of instances where Winter had broken the rules, or at least the spirit of them. No doubt his style of policing included many more infractions. Winter probably still roughed up suspects to get confessions.

Ryder watched the intro of *The Other Woman*, Melanie Upton looking as good on camera as she did in person, oozing sensuality. Ryder fast forwarded through the parts where Melanie wasn't on camera, keying in on the section where she got dragged by Jason at some party. The part about the possible assault was vague; Melanie never really came out and said it was Ayers, but she had just been talking about him, it was hard not to make the link. And nothing about it not being consensual. Still, she implied that *something* bad had happened, which was more definitive than what she had told Ryder.

The video identified the date of the show, which was well before he had last seen Upton. Which meant that Upton had known all this when Ryder had visited her in her apartment. He clicked off the video, sure that she had lied to him, or at least had left much unsaid.

In his experience, witnesses, especially victims, often had confused memories of crimes. Melanie Upton hadn't appeared confused, but she had seemed ditzy at times. Maybe she just wasn't too smart? Or couldn't keep track of what she said when?

He'd pin her down, once he convinced Logan he needed to interview her again. He didn't trust Winter to figure it out.

Ryder got on the elevator and pushed the button for the Executive Floor, but the light didn't come on and the door stayed open. He pushed it again, then noticed a small sign which told him he needed a key card. Muttering, he went back to the front desk, where the same skinny clerk was clacking on a keyboard.

"You didn't tell me I needed a keycard to get to the Executive Floor," said Ryder.

"I'm sorry, sir, I didn't know you were going up. You just asked if Mr. Ayers was a guest."

Ryder figured Winter would have slapped the kid for being so dense, but he kept his cool, if for no other reason than to not respond like Winter. "I need to get up there."

The clerk hesitated, Ryder daring him with a stern look to ask if Ryder was a frequent guest or whatever it took to get access to the paradise of the Executive Floor. Finally the clerk pulled a card from a drawer and handed it to Ryder. "This will get you access. Should I call Mr. Ayers and tell him you are on your way up?"

Ryder didn't have any reason to surprise Ayers, but he wasn't going to wait for an invitation. "Wait until I'm in the elevator."

The card worked, Ryder stepping out into a small lounge with a self serve bar filled with soft drinks and munchies. That's what they needed to protect with the key card?

Ryder knocked at the suite. Ayers opened the door, Ryder recognizing him immediately even though Ayers was wearing a hotel bathrobe, his hair tousled, his eyes bloodshot. He had one of those permanent three day beards that Ryder envied because it looked so natural.

"You the cop?" said Ayers. Without waiting for an answer he went back into the room, leaving the door open.

Ryder considered that an invitation and followed him in. The suite was bigger than he expected, a living area with two couches, a big screen television, a desk, even a bar.

"Get you anything?" asked Ayers, pointing toward the bar.

"No, thanks."

"How can I help you, Officer—?"

"Detective Martin Ryder."

"This is about Melanie Upton, isn't it?" Ayers plopped down in one of the sofas, rubbing his temples.

To Ryder he seemed more tired than worried. "Mind if I sit

down?" Ayers pointed to the other sofa and Ryder took out his note-book. "She's implied—"

"Melanie Upton is a liar."

"About what?"

"About everything. About me touching her. About me being in a relationship with her. I'm with Ashley. You know who Ashley Hanna is? You think I'd mess that up for someone like a Melanie Upton?"

Ryder could understand, Ashley Hanna was a big deal, really pretty in a Barbie doll kind of way, perfect features and hair, but to Ryder she seemed a little—plastic. She didn't have Melanie Upton's spark. On the other hand, Ryder knew first hand that Upton wasn't always truthful. "I saw this clip on the show, you and Melanie at some party. You looked like you were grabbing her."

Ayers was shaking his head. "That's bullshit. I think she crashed the party just to find me, she wanted me to get her a part on the show. She threatened to tell everyone we were a couple and that I had—acted inappropriately. I told her no one would believe her, and to prove it I showed her I was with Ashley. If anyone is a victim here, it's me. And Ashley too—she's really upset by all of this."

Ryder took a few notes, fascinated in spite of himself, this guy was sleeping with a famous pop star. He didn't look so hot right now, what did he have that Ryder didn't? Ayers probably didn't even know how to use a gun. Maybe he'd interview Ashley Hanna, see if she liked cops. "We could straighten all this up easily, if you give us a DNA sample." Upton's SAFE kit had shown no obvious signs of force, but did have male DNA. The problem was that there was no one to match it to, other than the felon database, which was negative. If he could get Ayers's DNA, and convince Melanie to name Ayers . . .

"Some woman makes a half assed insinuation and I have to prove my innocence? It wouldn't look good for my reputation if I gave DNA. You know how many woman go around telling people they're sleeping with famous men?"

Ryder didn't know what to make of that, it could be possible. But he doubted many of them called the police and reported it. Or did they? He'd have to check, maybe not around Marburg, but in a big city like LA? "If we find out that you paid Miss Upton some money to not say anything—"

"I'd never give Melanie Upton a dime." Ayers seemed wide awake now, his face flushing right through his stubble.

Ryder made a point of jotting something in his notebook, trying to see if he could get Ayers to sweat, let something slip, but Ayers appeared to be genuinely angry. Ryder didn't really have much else to pursue at this point, not unless Upton named him directly, which made Ryder all the more interested in going at her again.

Ryder stood. "I may be back with more questions." And hopefully more leverage for a DNA sample.

Ayers didn't get up. "Anything to get that bitch off my back."

RYDER FOUND WINTER waiting for him in the lobby, chatting up a different front desk clerk, an attractive middle aged blonde whose blue hotel uniform looked downright chic on her. Just Ryder's luck, he got the pimply faced kid, Winter connected with a beauty. Ryder waited impatiently while Winter finished his conversation.

"How did it go?" asked Winter, as they walked to the parking lot.

"Ayers denied everything," said Ryder.

"What a surprise. I didn't have much luck either, with Gruse, I mean. But I ran into a few guys who know Ayers—they're on the show crew. They claim that Ayers didn't need any Melanie Uptons in his life."

"Yeah, him having Ashley Hanna and all," said Ryder.

"I'm going to stop back tonight when the bar is open, ask about Gruse. And hit the other clubs too. Cindy should have more names, you can work the street while I go do the Upton follow up."

"I'd rather come with you to interview Upton."

"Better not," said Winter. "You heard Logan. Don't worry, I won't step all over you. Let me talk to her, you can tell Logan I forgot to ask some important questions, so you need to go back at her yourself."

Ryder cocked his head. "You'd do that?"

Winter got in the car. "Why not? It's your case. Drop me off at the station so I can get my car. And tell me what else Ayers said, so I'll know what to leave out of my talk with Upton."

CHAPTER 29

THE BACON HE'D PURLOINED at the Hilton had made Winter think about food, and even though it was still mid morning he hit the McDonald's drive though as soon as he had picked up his car at the station. All day breakfast, a dream come true for a cop . . .

Winter had asked Cindy to set up a time with Melanie Upton. He would talk to her, but he had no interest in muscling in on Ryder, which is why he wouldn't push back if Ryder complained to Logan that Winter didn't do a good job on the interview. The case was full of drama queens. Ryder could have it.

In the meantime he could try a few more places where Gruse had taken photos of women. Cindy was on a tear, doing an incredible job of identifying backgrounds, the woman was indispensable. If half the detectives had her doggedness there wouldn't be any open cases.

Three of the full frontal photos had been taken at Marburg Park, so Winter headed that way. He found the spot easily enough, the bandstand visible in the background. The main walkways from the street entrances crossed here, an easy place for Gruse to spot subjects. In the photos the women were captured mid stride, not posed; they could have been shot without the women knowing.

Winter made two more stops, a local coffee shop and a bakery. The women who had been photographed nearby didn't work there. He wasn't discouraged; investigations often went like this, even with his experience he never knew just where the next piece of the puzzle would fall into place. Often he wondered if cases would have been solved earlier—or not at all—if he had spoken to Person X before Person Y, or had asked a different question.

It wasn't a total loss, the bakery woman had given him a free coffee bun.

RYDER BARELY GLANCED at the list of locations he was supposed to visit before tossing them on the passenger seat. More busy work from Winter on the Gruse investigation. He still didn't understand Winter's obsession with identifying the women Gruse had photographed. Did Winter really believe one of them killed Gruse? And would just admit to it?

Gruse was his case, after all, and damned if he was going to let Winter jerk him around. Ryder would have to listen to the Captain, but so far Logan hadn't said a word about having to identify the women Gruse had photographed. Winter would probably bend Logan's ear about it, but until then, Ryder wasn't going to waste any more time. Besides, the Upton case had turned out to be much more interesting than the Gruse investigation. It wasn't a homicide, but he could make a name for himself clearing the Upton assault—it would certainly get more airtime than the murder of Gruse. That was unfair, but it was the way of the world.

If Jason Ayers was innocent, he'd be grateful to Ryder for clearing his name. Maybe grateful enough to offer Ryder a gig as a consultant on *Shock and Awe*. If Ayers was guilty—not a good outcome for becoming a consultant, but Ryder would be in the papers—then Melanie Upton would be the grateful one. Either way, Ryder would come out ahead.

Logan told him he couldn't talk to Melanie. But no one said anything about her sister Gigi. He'd get this case solved before Winter found a way to steal all the credit.

WINTER'S TIRES RUMBLED over the railroad tracks, reminding him of the times he had crossed as a kid on his bike. There had been no crossing gates then, and he hadn't worn a bike helmet. Back then no one did, just as no one had safety seats or shoulder harnesses or airbags. A lot of his friends had lived on this side, and if his grandfather had not married a woman whose parents happened to own a lot on the other side of the city, Winter would probably have grown up here too.

Though the streets grew increasingly run down as he drove, Winter never really thought of them as seedy. Yet he could understand how a visitor would think so; the older model cars, the tenements, ancient air conditioners hanging precariously out of double hung windows. No Starbucks here, no juice bars, not even a large grocery store. Marburg had some nice sections, but it wasn't an affluent city, yet the difference in the neighborhoods was obvious all the same.

Would Jason Ayers come here to meet with Melanie Upton? Ayers's high school friend Carlo didn't think so, but Carlo admitted he had hung around this part of town with Ayers growing up.

Cindy had called Winter and given her Upton's address and the time Upton had said she'd be available. Winter knew the street, he'd been down it before, just as he had most of Marburg's streets. Even when he didn't remember the name he would know the street as soon as he turned on it, it was how his mind worked.

He purposely took a slightly roundabout way, getting a handle on changes in the neighborhood. Some of the buildings had new tenants, a few of the houses had different colors, but the place still felt the same. Not quite poor, but not middle class either, filled with people who were either on the way up or the way down.

Not much traffic, so it was easy to hear the revving motorcycle pulling into an alley next to a grungy bar called Marv's. Winter recognized the bike's high back leather seat stitched with a silhouette of a naked woman. Winter had chased the bike's owner out of town a year ago, a lowlife named Sal Tully who'd been beating on his girlfriend. There was no proof, and she wouldn't press charges, but everyone knew it, and the woman's six year old had pulled Winter aside and told him as much. The six year old wasn't Tully's, and neither were his three other half siblings, but just because the woman didn't have good luck picking men didn't mean she deserved to be beat up. Not that any woman did; a man abusing a woman was Winter's definition of the ultimate scumbag. Winter obviously hadn't been clear enough, because Tully was back, and still sporting the very identifiable bike adornment, the stupid shit.

Winter turned into the alley, blocking Tully's exit. The bike was still revving for no reason, Tully just sitting there, Winter recognizing him even from the rear, curly hair tied back in a ponytail, a worn leather vest, a lightning bolt on his neck. Tully didn't turn around, he probably couldn't hear Winter's car over the bike engine. No one else was in the alley, although the space between Tully and an old garage was lined with motorcycles.

Winter was about to get out, had a better idea, and nudged the car forward. His gun was on the seat next to him and he edged it out of the holster. When he was almost up against Tully's rear wheel he waited until Tully was in full rev, then leaned on his horn. Tully almost flew out of the seat, jerking his head around, his hand slipping off the clutch as Winter had hoped, and the bike lurched forward, knocking over one, two, three bikes and then crashing sideways into the garage door, Tully's right leg trapped under his own bike.

Winter tucked his gun under his shirt as he got out of the car. Tully's bike had stalled, the biker trying to free himself, but part of the garage door had pinned it in place. Winter shifted his body so that he'd be in position when the back door of the bar opened, and sure enough, four guys in leather burst out.

One gave Winter a hard look, the other three ran to their bikes, ignoring Tully. Winter kept his eye on the beefy guy staring at him, his reaction would determine what happened next.

"Shit, Tully, what'd you do to my ride?"

"I didn't do nothin', it was that cop."

Winter shrugged. "Didn't touch your bikes. Tully drove over them."

Tully was still struggling on the ground, flecks of dirt and grease in his beard. "You made me, you snuck up behind."

"You forgot the part about me blowing my horn," said Winter. "You were in the way, I just wanted to get by."

The beefy guy looked from Tully to Winter. "That right, Tully? You drove over our bikes because he blew his horn?"

Winter didn't recognize the beefy guy, but he knew their colors, a fringe club associated with a small Boston gang. Not legit, but not big time either, larcenies, some drugs. Tully wasn't wearing their colors.

"It's not my fault, Stan. Somebody help get this bike off me."

Stan, the beefy guy, ignored him. Stan looked to be the guy in charge, so Winter said to him, "I told Tully last year I didn't want to see him around again. I thought there must be a problem with his ears, but he heard my horn just fine."

"He do something wrong?"

"He beats on women. One in particular I know, but I wouldn't be surprised if it's a habit."

"This woman, she something to you?"

"Nope. Just a citizen." Winter knew the biker would understand, a citizen was under Winter's protection, not someone part of the biker universe.

Stan's eyes narrowed on Tully, then glanced at his crew. "Your bikes okay?"

"My mirror's busted, and the muffler will need to be chromed."

"I'm sure your friend Tully will pay for the repairs," said Winter. He could see Stan calculating, balancing the cost of attracting police attention on his crew against backing Tully.

Stan said, "He's no friend of ours from now on. You good with that?"

Winter understood the message, Tully would get no refuge with the bikers. Bikers weren't all the same, just like cops and any other group, but most of them had a thing about not getting physical with women. "I am if I don't see him around again."

The biker nodded at Winter and said, "Get him up. Tully, time to give you an escort out of town."

RYDER HAD AGREED to meet Gigi Doyle in a small city park a few blocks from her office. She had asked him not to come to her office, claiming she didn't have much privacy. Ryder had no real reason to insist, nor did he want to work past his shift to interview her in the evening.

The park was just an empty lot between two buildings on a busy street, but it had a wall waterfall, an oasis in a sea of office buildings.

Ryder arrived early, sitting at one of the metal bistro tables in the corner away from the waterfall where he could watch the entrance. It wasn't yet lunch time, the park was empty except for two elderly men playing chess.

A young woman entered, dressed in a dark blue jacket and matching skirt, her dull hair cut to her chin. She wore small framed glasses and carried a gray shoulder bag. At first Ryder didn't think it was Gigi Doyle; this woman was demure, almost mousy, but after a moment she approached Ryder, her steps tentative.

"Detective Ryder?"

Ryder stood up and shook her hand. "Yes. Miss Doyle?"

"That's right." She sat down, clutching her bag in her lap, her back stiff.

Up close, Ryder could see the similarities to her sister, the same cheekbones, eye color, a soft nose. They actually looked pretty much alike, but they couldn't have been more different in appearance; where Melanie was confident and alluring, Gigi was shy and reserved. Melanie would look right at you, Gigi hadn't met his eyes yet. Ryder had no idea what Gigi's figure was like, covered by her loose jacket and long skirt.

"Thank you for meeting me," said Ryder.

"I don't have much time," she said. "My boss called a meeting for right after lunch—"

"Don't worry, this shouldn't take long. And we can always continue at another time. I just have a few questions about your sister."

"You spoke to her, didn't you? Shouldn't she be here?"

"We have spoken to her, and probably will again," said Ryder. "We're trying to find out who broke into her place." Doyle fiddled at the strap on her bag. "There's no need to be nervous."

"I'm just not used to talking to policemen."

"Am I that scary?"

Doyle finally looked up, confused, maybe not sure if Ryder was serious. An uneasy smile flittered over her mouth for just an instant. "No, I'm sorry, I didn't mean—."

"I know. Your sister was on this television show, and she said, well, she implied, that Jason Ayers might have been the man who broke into her apartment. It wasn't clear if she was speaking about that same night, although she does mention a police report—"

"I didn't see the show."

"Really? Your sister was on television, and you didn't watch it?"

"I don't watch that much tv. I travel a lot for work, and by the time I get back to the hotel it's late and I just eat and go to sleep. Even when I'm at home I don't watch much."

"But you know about the show?" Ryder was taking notes.

"Mel told me. What are you writing down?"

"Just a few notes to remind me about our conversation." Ryder hesitated, he'd never shown a civilian his notes, but Doyle was so nervous he turned the small book toward her. "See? Just your name, the time and place we met. Then I noted that you were aware of the television show and didn't watch it. That's all." He was glad he hadn't added the part about her being nervous, but would later. "Has Melanie been on television before?"

"She's done a few commercials, I did see one of those. She's a very good actress."

"You ever thought about being an actress yourself?"

"Me? No, I never had any interest. Besides, Mel's so pretty."

"The two of you look alike," said Ryder. He meant it, although he really wouldn't have called Doyle pretty.

"I guess so. But she's older—not that she looks older, and, I don't know, more confident and willing to take risks. I like a nice steady job, acting is hit and miss."

"Do you know a lot of Melanie's friends?"

"Not really, we're in different circles. Why?"

"We're just trying to find out if maybe one of her friends committed the break-in. Or an acquaintance. Did she know Jason Ayers well enough that he might have been familiar with her place?"

"You mean her apartment?"

"Yes."

"Well, maybe, from when they were dating."

Ryder was just about to jot a note, he looked up, surprised. "Your sister is dating Jason Ayers?" That's what Melanie had said on *The Other Woman*, but it's not exactly what Jason Ayers had just told him.

"Well, yes, I mean, I'm not sure what their exact relationship is right now, I don't talk much with Melanie about her—personal life.

But Jason grew up in Marburg. He and Melanie have known each other for a while, they are both into the whole acting thing. I mean, it's not that big a city, right? I know she used to see him, I'm not sure what their relationship was—"

"You said they were dating."

Doyle clutched her bag strap so hard Ryder thought it might snap. "I was using the term loosely. I know they went out, I even met him once or twice, although that was a few years ago."

"Did you ever see Ayers at her apartment?"

"No, I've actually only been there a few times." Doyle watched Ryder take a note, and then said, "I'm not going to get anyone in trouble, am I?"

"Don't you want the person caught who did this?"

"Of course, but what if—"

"What if what?"

"Nothing." Doyle looked at the waterfall, biting her lip, her voice barely audible over the sound of the flowing water. "You think Jason did it?"

"We don't know yet. Did your sister ever mention anything about Ayers being rough with her?"

"Get rough with Melanie?" Doyle looked back at Ryder, incredulous. "I don't think so."

BECAUSE HE HAD STOPPED to deal with Tully, Winter was going to be late for his appointment with Melanie Upton. He had forgot to take Upton's number with him, so he tried calling Cindy to notify Upton, but Cindy's line went right to voicemail. Winter hated voicemail more than he hated phones.

Even though he was late, he cruised slowly past Upton's apartment, wanting to get a sense of how an intruder might come in. He'd read Ryder's notes—rigid as he was, the guy took good notes—but wanted to see for himself. Upton's apartment was above an Indian restaurant, a separate door facing the street which likely led to stairs. Unless there was a separate entrance in the back, it was probably an illegal rental, but Winter couldn't always keep the building codes straight, a lot was grandfathered in. Two windows faced the street, another on the side overlooking an alley which led to the back of the building. The other wall was shared with a furniture refinishing business, so no windows there. An intruder coming in from the front would have to climb through a window over the restaurant, unlikely. The side was a possibility, but would require a ladder.

Across the street from the restaurant was a dumpster and an empty lot, then another row of buildings, a tenement, a plumber. The restaurant doors were open, Upton's windows were closed.

Winter eased his car into the alley, which opened into a relatively large parking lot, empty except for a single car. The restaurant had a back entrance, but Upton's apartment did not. Two second story windows on this side, one smaller than the other, probably a bath. There was no fire escape ladder.

He parked in the lot and walked back around to the front of the building, avoiding the condensate dripping from an AC unit in the bath window. Next to a wooden door, a homemade embossed label stuck on a mailbox in the wall read *Melanie Doyle Upton.*

The door looked solid enough, with a deadbolt, but it was propped open with a wedge. Winter let himself in, the hallway dark and humid hot. He left the wedge in the door and creaked up the steps.

No deadbolt on this door, just a keyed lockset. Winter knocked. Though Winter had seen Melanie Upton's photo and had watched part of *The Other Woman* show on Ryder's phone, he was still unprepared for the visceral energy she exuded in person. The first thing that struck Winter were her eyes, full and bright, with a hint of green. A bit taller than average height, somewhat brown hair. She was wearing a form fitting athletic top with skin tight jeans and no shoes.

"You must be Detective Winter," she said, friendly, but not shaking hands. If she was upset about him being late she didn't let on.

"You always leave that downstairs door wedged open?" Winter asked, following her into the apartment. To his left the door to the bathroom was open, the air conditioner on high, but not enough to cool even the small apartment. A sofa in the middle of the room sat facing the front windows, on the side wall a newish big screen television. A large air conditioner box sat on the floor, unopened.

"Sometimes. The landlord is too cheap to put in a buzzer." Upton cleared a pile of clothes from the only chair in the room, and said, "Here." She sat on the sofa, tossing the clothes over the back cushion.

"Sorry it's so hot," she said. "I just bought the AC units. A friend of mine put the one in the bathroom, but this one," she kicked the boxed unit, "hadn't arrived yet. I had to order it online, can you believe the stores in town are out of AC units, in the summer? Isn't that when people need them?"

Winter nodded. "It's like trying to buy winter gloves in February, all the spring clothes are out."

"*Exactly*," said Upton. "Anyway, now I'm having a problem getting someone to install it. The local store says they won't since I didn't buy it from them. I *would* have, if they had any in stock. It's too heavy for me."

Winter grinned, she was turning on the subtle charm for him. If she were a few decades older, she might have batted her eyelashes. The fact that she didn't told him right away that she was probably a pretty good actress, he didn't doubt this was a woman who could get a guy to do anything. He played along, and it *was* hot . . .

"I can probably give you a hand."

He waited to see if she gave him an exaggerated, "Oh, *could* you?" or some other bullshit, but all she said was, "Thanks, I'll get a knife to open the box."

"I got one," said Winter. He pulled his lock blade out, opened the box, slid out the air conditioner, and scanned the quick start sheet. He'd done this before, they were all the same. "Can you open the window you want it in?"

"I may need help, it gets stuck."

She crossed by Winter, closer than she needed to, giving him a nice view of her rear, intentionally, he thought, as she opened the window. Winter said, "You're in luck, you won't need a bracket." Upton looked over his shoulder, appearing to be interested, a little in his space. If she was nervous about a cop being in her apartment she didn't show it.

Winter manhandled the unit into place. "You might want to shove some foam insulation along the top and sides, but this will work for now. Where's your circuit breaker box?"

"In the kitchen alcove."

Winter found it, there were just three fifteen amp breakers. "You might not want to plug too much other stuff in when this is running," he said. He turned the unit on, waited for the compressor to kick in, and when he was satisfied the breaker wasn't going to blow he sat back down.

"Thanks," said Upton.

"No problem." Winter had taken a good inventory of the apartment as he had worked, the refrigerator on its last legs, and the small toaster oven had seen better days. If Upton was getting cash from Jason Ayers to keep quiet about the assault, she wasn't spending it here on anything other than air conditioners and a television. Of course, she could be buying lots of clothes, or have a coke habit . . .

"What happened to the other detective?" asked Upton. She curled her feet up under her on the sofa.

"He had to take care of another case. I'm just helping him out." Winter waited, giving Upton a chance to ask the question every victim always asked, 'Did you catch him?' But Upton didn't say a word. "I saw you on a television show."

Upton raised her eyebrow. "You don't strike me as a man who watches *The Other Woman*."

Winter held up his hands. "Guilty. I saw a video of it, on a phone screen. And not the whole show."

"That was my first big break, that show. I've been doing grunt work for *years*."

Upton made it sound like a decade, and maybe it was, Winter didn't know when actresses started out. "How'd it happen?"

"You know what the show is about, right? They heard about me and Jason, and he's got that fake publicity thing going with Ashley Hanna—"

"Wait, Ayers isn't really seeing Ashley Hanna?"

Upton tossed her head. "Well, they make sure to be seen together, it's good marketing. Half the relationships in Hollywood are like that, couples show up together, especially if their publicists can make a good story out of it. But Ashley—she's not Jason's type, you know what I mean? She fits the persona they are building for him now, sure, but that's not who he really is."

"And you know this because you know Jason?"

Upton smiled. "Sure. We've been—close, on and off for years. Not always exclusive, although we did that too. That's why this thing with Ashley doesn't bother me, Jason is just doing it for his career. It's actually good for Ashley too, she's so storybook, and Jason looks the part."

Winter had no idea what Ashley Hanna looked like, he was more interested in Ayers. "When you spoke to Detective Ryder, you said that someone had broken in?"

Upton shrugged. "I'm not sure, I was a little out of it. He told you about the sleeping pill, right? And I'd had a few drinks—I wasn't driving or anything. Just some wine. I was really wired, then I crashed. Anyway, I woke up, I felt that someone had been here, but it was all so hazy, and now that it's been a while, it's even harder for me to remember. I'd been with someone earlier in the evening, and I might have just—confused the two, you know?"

"Jason?"

"Look, I really don't want to get him in trouble. He's got a good thing going on the show, I wouldn't want to ruin it for him."

"When you were with Jason earlier, that was here?"

"No, at his hotel. He doesn't keep an apartment in Marburg anymore, he moved to LA. He's just in town for the location shoots."

"And you think he may have come here that night?"

"Anything's possible. Jason is—we've had a hot and heavy thing, I can give him what he's not getting from Ashley Hanna."

Winter was impressed with her ability to not provide details yet make it clear what she was implying. "Does he have a key to your place?"

"No, but he's been here plenty of times. And . . . I might have been so out of it I forgot to lock the door."

"We spoke to Ayers, he denies all of this."

Melanie laughed. "Of course he does. It's part of the game. What's he going to do, make it public that he was sleeping with me? But I've been with him, a lot." She nodded toward the bedroom. "You guys can do DNA, right? I'm sure Jason's DNA is all over the place."

Winter prided himself on never trying to assume how an inter-

view would go, but even he was surprised. Upton seemed oddly un-
concerned about—everything, the assault, even Ayers lying about it.
It was a big game they were all playing. And yet, if Ayers had assaulted her . . .

"On the show, I saw a clip of you at a party, it looked like Ayers
was grabbing you pretty hard."

Melanie looked away. "He can be a little rough. Sometimes." Her
eyes came back up, right into Winter's. "Sometimes I like it."

Now it was Winter's turn to look away, this was too much information, even for a cop. "Why did you call the police?"

"I don't know." Upton absently scraped her fingernail against the
sofa cushion. "It felt so real . . . and I'd been broken into before. I
mean, if some man was in here, that's pretty scary."

Winter let it sit, but Upton didn't add anything. "If a man came in
without your permission, and touched you in any way . . ."

"I know, I know. But like I said, I might have imagined it, or it
might have just been Jason, and I really don't want to screw up what
he's got going."

Winter thought he was pretty good at reading people, but Upton
was giving off confusing signals, a mix of self protectionism but also
denial. He'd seen the denial before in sexual assault victims, especially if the attack had been committed by a friend. But something
else was going on, and Winter didn't quite know what it was.

What wasn't lost on him was her acceptance of Ayers using the
Ashley Hanna story for publicity, and her own dropping of Ayers's
name on the show that by her own admission was her big break. Everyone using everyone else . . .

He wouldn't have to leave anything out of the interview in order
for Ryder to get another shot at Upton, there were so many avenues
to pursue, all of them probably dead ends. Unless . . . "Miss Upton, if
you tell me right now that Jason Ayers assaulted you, we can proceed
on that."

Upton twirled her hair, looking in her lap. Finally she said, "I'm
not sure I can do that."

"You can't, or you don't want to?"

"Does it matter?"

"Is anyone stopping you? Are you afraid?"

Upton shook her head, "No. I don't think it will happen again."

"If you change your mind," said Winter, "or feel clearer about that night, you should call us." He got up to leave. "And don't prop that door open downstairs. You might want to get a deadbolt up here, too." Both were obvious, steps assault victims would have already taken, more mixed signals for Winter.

"Okay, I'll do that." Upton uncurled herself from the sofa. "I'm not sure I'm going to be around here much longer. I've been getting a lot of offers, hopefully I'll be heading west soon."

Winter didn't think he was going to get much more out of her. He'd seen women afraid of the men who had assaulted them—Tully's girlfriend, for instance—but Upton didn't appear afraid of Ayers. He tried one more approach. "If Ayers did something to you, we need to know. But if he didn't—you shouldn't go telling people that he did. Especially on television. Understand?"

"I never said he did, not really."

Winter decided to let it go. If Upton kept pushing Ayers as the man who assaulted her she'd have more to worry about than his warnings; no doubt Ayers would get a lawyer and sue her for defamation. And if he didn't sue her, that might mean he was guilty . . .

There was still the issue of the deposit in Upton's account, but Winter had no good way of asking her about that. She certainly didn't look like she was rolling in money, the air conditioners couldn't have cost that much. "We might want to talk to you again," he said.

"I don't know how much more I can tell you. And I may be out of town a lot, casting calls, New York, LA."

Winter was thinking about that as he reached the door, casting calls, actresses. He turned and said, "Can I ask you something? I'm working on another case, there's this guy, a photographer, he was taking lots of pictures of actresses." Winter had left the tablet in the car, so he couldn't show her the good photo, so he had to use the one on his phone. "Lenny Gruse, he's a photographer. Maybe you've heard of him?"

Upton pursed her lips. "I don't know, it's hard to tell from that. There are a lot of photographers, and even more guys *pretending* to be photographers."

"They hit on you?" asked Winter.

"You would not *believe*," said Upton. "I've learned to ignore them, it's all background noise." She wrinkled her lip, lifting one shoulder in a half shrug. "Guys like that, they don't even register. I don't remember them."

CHAPTER 30

WINTER SPENT ANOTHER HOUR showing Gruse's photo around, with no luck. He headed back to the station to force himself to write up some notes, which he hated doing. He wanted to go home and take a nap because he was going to be out late that night, hitting the clubs. Logan never gave him a hard time about keeping a strict schedule when he was on a case; Cindy had to remind Winter to put in for his overtime.

Winter found Ryder in his cubicle, probably not only writing his notes, but preparing a presentation for Logan. Maybe he could think of a way to get Ryder to do his notes for him . . .

Winter leaned his forearms on the short cubical wall. "Well, you should be happy. I left you plenty of reasons to go back and interview Melanie Upton."

Ryder looked up. "You left something out?"

"I didn't have to, she did. She says he did it, she says he didn't do it. That something happened. Or didn't."

"*Something* happened. The SAFE kit . . ."

"That just means she had recent sex—it could have been before the assault. And now we know she was with Ayers earlier that evening."

"She *told* you that?"

"That was one of the few things she was clear about." Winter filled Ryder in on the interview.

"I interviewed Gigi Doyle today, the sister. You know what she said? She said that Upton and Ayers had a thing going from way back.

Or had an on and off again thing, starting way back. I wasn't sure what to make of that, although I can't figure out why Doyle would lie about it." Ryder drummed his keys, not typing, just clicking out a cadence. "Ayers was pretty adamant about not—wait." He moved the mouse, reading off the screen. "Son of a bitch. Ayers denied paying Upton, and he denied he attacked her. He said, 'She crashed the party to get me to give her a part on the show.' But he never said how well he knew her *before* that."

"So what do we have here? A real assault? Or a lover's quarrel?"

"Or both."

They both thought about that for a while, then Winter said, "Upton could be sleeping with Ayers in hopes of getting a part on the show."

"Or Ayers is *making* Upton have sex with him and promising her if she does she'll get a part."

Winter was glad Ryder was stuck with this one. "Upton seems more interested in the publicity she's getting from the assault than about catching who did it, which would only make sense if it was Ayers."

"Even if he knew her, he's still guilty if he forced his way in, did something to her when she was under the influence."

"I know. You can sort it all out." Winter thumped on the top of the wall. "I'm going to go home and sack out for an hour or two, I want to show Gruse's photo at the clubs tonight, and go back to the Hilton bar. And since I just told you the details of my interview with Upton, can you write it up in your notes?"

WINTER HAD NAPPED, changed, eaten, and had two cups of coffee. Feeling refreshed, he left his house just after eight. Not quite dark yet, but the days were getting shorter, which meant people would be hitting the clubs earlier in the evening. On his way to the Hilton he stopped at a dance spot called Kahoots, a 70's throwback, or maybe they just hadn't updated it since then. No one knew Gruse. Three other clubs went the same way; Winter wasn't expecting much, just trying on the off chance he'd get lucky, killing time until the Hilton got busy.

The Hilton was packed, the news about Jason Ayers must have brought out the celebrity seekers. Winter pushed his way through the crowd to the bar. Between martini shaking and draft pulls, he found out that the two bartenders were part timers brought in to handle the crowd, they didn't know anything. Winter wished he could jump up on the bar and shoot into the ceiling to get everyone's attention, like in the old westerns, that would save time.

Instead, he made a circuit, trying to put himself in Gruse's frame of mind. Where would he stand to be on the lookout for women to photograph and also approach? Winter found the spot, at a table just off to the side of the entrance, behind a row of the ubiquitous hotel fake greenery. Through the palm fronds anyone coming in could be checked out, but they'd likely be looking ahead at the bar. Once inside, the location provided a perfect view of the bar area and most of the tables.

Across the room, Winter spotted four younger women at a booth, early twenties maybe, the type Gruse might be interested in. A good place to start.

Up close, they were younger than they had appeared, but who could tell these days. All four were dressed to the hilt, bare shoulders, plunging necklines, lots of makeup, short outfits. Two were texting, the other two people watching. On the table was a shared tapas platter and four colorful drinks.

Winter had barely identified himself when one of the women, a doe eyed brunette with hair to her waist, said, "We're not drinking alcohol, officer." Which only served to confirm to Winter that they were even younger than his revised estimate.

"Relax, that's not why I'm here. Just don't go sit at the bar, okay? Do you all come here a lot?"

The long haired girl said, "Mostly since they started shooting *Shock and Awe*."

That led to some laughter, and Winter held up Gruse's photo on the tablet. "Ever see this man here?"

The four huddled around the tablet. "He's not with the show, is he?"

"No. He might have had a camera, offering to take your picture?"

Four shrugs. "Not a guy we'd remember. Now if you happened to have a picture of Jason Ayers . . . Hey, you wouldn't know if he's here tonight, would you?"

Winter fought the urge to tell them he'd seen Ayers at Chucky Cheese, which is where he'd want these girls to be if they were his daughters. Instead he left them to their celebrity vigil and tried a few more tables, with the same result.

He leaned against one of the few open spots at the bar, alone in the sea of partiers. He found it slightly surprising that he hadn't yet found anyone who recognized Gruse. The four girls at the booth were watching everyone who came in. Surely they'd have noticed a guy with a big camera. *Not a guy we'd remember* . . . that reminded Winter of Melanie Upton's response to his question about Gruse. She said she wouldn't have remembered a guy like Gruse either. Maybe a common female defensive mechanism against the desperate male.

Upton—men would certainly remember her. She'd said she had met up with Jason Ayers at this hotel. Winter wasn't getting anywhere with Gruse, so he pulled out the tablet again—he was getting addicted to the gadget—and clumsily found the video of *The Other Woman* show. He looked around, decided the bar was as a good a place as any, and nudged the man next to him. He was talking to another guy, but spun his stool to face Winter.

Winter held up the tablet. "Ever see this woman here?"

The guy, wearing a suit jacket with no tie, tan khaki's and loafers, didn't even ask who Winter was or why he was asking. "Sure, she's here a lot. Right, Steve?"

Steve, outfitted by the same blue jacket and tan slacks tailor, leaned over to look, but the video had ended. Winter started it up, tried to fast forward, realized he didn't remember how to do that. "I'm kind of new at this."

"Let me," said Steve, and took the tablet, got the video going.

"Right there," said the first guy.

Steve did something to the screen and the image froze on Upton.

"How'd you do that?" asked Winter.

"Tap this icon. Her, oh, yeah, I remember her. She's—." He looked up at Winter. "Wait, you're not her old man, are you?"

"No, I'm a cop. Finish what you were going to say."

Steve glanced at his friend, shrugged, and said, "She's hot. Even better in person. George and I were just talking about her, as a matter of fact. Hoping she'd be here tonight."

"She usually with someone?"

"That's the weird thing," said George. "Never. She comes in, even when it's slow, has a drink, leaves. Barely talks to anyone."

"You mean she wouldn't talk to you," said Steve.

"Not just me. I've seen plenty of guys hit on her."

"You here a lot?" asked Winter.

"We're sales reps for a metals fabricating company," said George. "We're through here every few weeks."

"You see anyone else tonight you recognize?"

Steve looked over the crowd. "The usual bartender isn't on tonight, big guy with an earring. I think your video woman knows him—at least she talks to him. The other bartender too, skinny guy with red hair. Other than that—they're filming some kind of tv show in town, we've seen some of the crew." He pointed to a booth. "Maybe those guys?"

Winter thanked them and bumped his way across the room. Five men and two women were crowded in a booth for four and a small table that had been pulled alongside. Winter identified himself.

"Some kind of problem, officer?"

"No, I'm just wondering if you've seen this woman." Winter held up the freeze frame of Upton.

"That's Jason's squeeze," said one of the women, her spiked pixie dyed black and silver hair sticking out like she'd seen a ghost. The woman sitting next to her, this one with a pierced nose, nudged her in the ribs. "What?" said Pixie. "It's not like everyone doesn't know."

"We don't want to get anyone in trouble," said one of the men, crossing his arms, showing thick biceps that pressed against his ribbed pullover.

Winter changed tactics. "You with the television crew?"

Thick Arms said, "Contractors. We help set up for the location shoots."

"Okay. Look, I'm just following up on something. I spoke with this woman, she said she'd been here, I just needed to find out if anyone had seen her."

"Sure," said the woman with the nose ring. "She's here all the time, because, you know, the cast is here."

"Oh, jeez, just say it," said Pixie. "She's here because Jason is here."

"I hear he's pretty famous," said Winter. "You see them together a lot?"

No one said anything, and after a moment one of the guys said, "As a matter of fact, I don't think I've ever seen them together."

"Here or on the set?" asked Winter.

"Anywhere. She's never been on the set, at least when I've been there, but I just do the initial setup."

"I'm there all the time," said Nose Ring. "I handle the equipment scheduling. She's *never* been on set."

"Of course not," said Pixie. "They have to keep it quiet, you know, because of Ashley Hanna."

"I've never seen her either," said Nose Ring.

"Me neither," said the beefy guy. "And I've been looking."

Everyone laughed, Winter joining in. Just a bunch of hardworking locals. "You from Marburg?"

"I'm from Boston," said Pixie, "but these lowlifes are local."

"You're from Braintree, not Boston."

"It's close enough," said Pixie. "Not the sticks."

"Hey, *I'm* from Marburg," said Winter.

"Then grab a chair and have a beer with us," said the big guy in the ribbed shirt. "Unless you're on duty."

Winter's shift had technically ended five hours ago. "Sure."

A HOUR AND TWO BEERS LATER, Winter had managed to gather a few additional tidbits from the show contractors. They all recognized Melanie Upton. And the all assumed she was seeing Jason Ayers. Yet no one had actually seen them together.

Odd, but maybe explainable, the whole Ashley Hanna angle. Winter filed it away, he'd fill Ryder in on it tomorrow. He wanted to make one more stop.

The Marquee had been closed the last time he'd come by, but now the place was hopping, a long line at the door to Marburg's only real higher end club. Winter bypassed the line, the bouncer recognizing him, letting him through the rope with a nod.

"Anything I should know about?" the bouncer asked.

"Nah, just talking to a few people. I may show you a picture on the way out, okay?"

"Sure."

The club was busier, louder, and even younger than the Hilton bar, a brain numbing repetitive beat shaking the floor. Winter glanced at the front bar, packed, he'd have to yell to make himself heard. He skirted the dance floor, heading for the back bar. Here it was marginally less deafening.

One of the bartenders, a thin shouldered blonde in all leather, looked familiar. Winter stood at the end of the bar until she noticed him. She held up a finger, and after pouring a cocktail came over.

"Help you, Detective?"

Winter held up the tablet. "Seen this guy?" He was trying to remember the bartender's name. Fiona? No, that was another one. Brandie, that was it. "Brandie?"

She smiled, he had got it right, her smile fading when she saw the photo of Gruse. "He's been here a few times, hitting on the ladies."

"Isn't that what clubs are for?"

"Sure, but this guy—he was always staring, you know? Creepy. Always by himself."

"He ever bother anyone? You get any complaints?"

"No. And I would have heard, the owner tries to keep the place safe. Should I be looking out for him?"

"No, he won't be a problem," said Winter. "Thanks. Hey, while I have you," he pulled up Upton's photo. "You know her?"

"Sure, Melanie Upton. She's a regular. Although I haven't seen her around much lately."

"She come in alone?"

"I think. But it's hard to tell, she's here five minutes and guys are all over her."

"They try to pick her up?" asked Winter.

"She lets them buy her drinks. I never got the sense she was looking to hook up." Brandie looked wistfully at Upton's photo. "If I looked like her, I'd probably never have to pay for another drink in my life."

WINTER DIDN'T GET HOME until well after midnight, but he was too wired to sleep. He lay in the old lounge chair, the sports channel on mute, the overhead light in the kitchen bleeding out into the living room. The chair had been his father's favorite, the arms long stained from sweat and condensation from the countless beer bottles that had rested there, just as Winter rested one now.

It was odd, he thought of his ex-wife Sylvia every time he sat in that chair, even more than his father. He actually thought of his father more than his ex wife, but the chair brought back memories of one of the few topics he and Sylvia had argued about, his furniture. Winter and Sylvia had moved into the house after his parents had passed away. She had wanted to throw out the furniture, not because she didn't like his parents—they actually had got along great—but because she wanted to make the place feel like it was hers. Winter had acquiesced on everything except the recliner, even after needing two rolls of duct tape to cover the tears. He smiled, a little sadly; the fights hadn't been the cause of their divorce, they just had different dreams, she wanted *stuff*, not just furniture, and he wanted . . . to fix things, to rid the world of troublesome people, get answers for families who needed resolution, not some pablum about a random crime.

Like this Gruse case. Seemingly random, a poor guy in the wrong place at the wrong time, a confluence of unforeseen factors leading to his death. Just some average Joe, maybe a little desperate, down on his luck—but who hadn't felt that way, at one time or another? Trying to pick up women, and what guy hadn't been there, too. Winter had never roamed around with a camera pretending to be a photographer, but guys would try anything.

Winter sipped at his beer, the television casting a dancing glow on the mostly bare walls. Sylvia had done all the decorating, and had taken most of the photos and all of the art; Winter had replaced very little in the intervening ten years. Someone seeing a mishmash of furniture and blank walls, a guy alone on a lounger, would immediately think *divorce*. It was a pretty obvious connection. Some connections weren't so obvious, and yet, in his experience, often there *were* connections, you just had to find them.

He was increasing bothered by the Gruse murder and a sexual assault occurring within a few months of each other. Marburg wasn't the safest place; its violent crime rate was about twice the national average, but it wasn't exactly Chicago or even Boston. It got its share of what Winter thought of as transient crime, criminals passing through, robberies at all night convenience stores. Most of those were solved, the thieves too high or stupid to know about where the security cameras were. The outlying hotels, run down, always an issue, drug deals. That was the logical supposition for the Gruse murder, as Ryder thought.

Yet the attack on Gruse seemed—personal. Why stab a man, who seemed to have no money, in his run down car? In the groin area, no less. A man who liked taking photos of pretty women. Then there's a pretty woman who is involved in a possible assault, which is about as personal as you could get.

Two seemingly unconnected crimes, a possible coincidence, and yet . . .

Winter had already stumbled on one connection; both Gruse and Upton had been at the Marquee. That alone meant nothing, Winter had been at the Marquee as well; some cop could just as well have shown the bartender *his* photo and made the same connection, and yet as far as Winter knew, he hadn't previously met either Upton or Gruse. Although he'd heard all about six degrees of separation.

Winter finished the last of his beer and reclined the lounger all the way so he could stare at the ceiling. The blank ceiling was a canvas, a universe, anything could happen there, any two experiences or people could be connected. It was a game his father had taught him, listening to the Sox on the radio. They couldn't afford to go to the games, and when there wasn't one on tv, his dad would tell him to picture the field on the ceiling, so and so on first base, second, the outfielders, the batter. All of the players standing totally separate, yet in a flash they could be uniquely connected, the pitcher to the batter via the ball, then the defense, the outfielder picking it up, the throw...nothing but connections, the ball serving as a connect-the-dots. And yet if you didn't know the underlying rules, the story of the game, you wouldn't see the connections, it would all appear to be just crazed random actions.

Winter no longer thought about baseball as he stared at the ceiling, but instead thought about cases. He placed people up on the ceiling, unrelated at first, just like the fielders, until the play unfolded, then the connections became apparent, even between players the ball didn't touch, because they were part of the field, part of the play, crucial to the game.

He did it now, on one side of the ceiling placing Gruse, with lines going to a bunch of women, some of whom they'd identified, some still nameless. These women all had connections to Gruse, even if the connection was just that he had photographed them. Perhaps later Winter would discover that some of those connections consisted of more than just being photographed.

On the other side of the ceiling he placed Melanie Upton and Jason Ayers. There was a linkage between the two of them, although the nature of it was still to be determined. For now all that mattered was the connection. Winter had come to realize that you could find a linkage and then look for a reason for it, or find a reason for a linkage and then find the linkage, but if you tried to do both at the same time, the possibilities were so endless you got nowhere.

A big empty white space separated the Gruse and Upton cases. Winter thought about the women Gruse had photographed: young, attractive, especially alluring. That description certainly fit Upton, and it wasn't just his opinion; he'd already met both men and women who felt the same way about her. Even Ryder appeared to be smitten. Upton could just as well be on the Gruse side of his ceiling whiteboard. Had Gruse taken a photo of Melanie Upton?

Winter shifted the lever on the lounger and raised the seat. The tablet was on the table next to the chair, he spun through Gruse's photos, looking for a photo of Upton. Nothing. He'd have to ask Cindy and Dan to show him the rest of the photos, he just had the frontal shots. And also find out if Upton was on Gruse's call list.

He reclined the lounger again, settling in, refreshing his imaginary connection planetarium on the ceiling. He shifted his attention to the Upton side. Upton didn't seem to be in any big hurry to name Ayers as her attacker. Maybe she really *had* been out of it, so high she couldn't remember. Instead of pointing the finger at Ayers, she'd pointed away from him, and yet all her denials kept coming back at the actor, a crooked finger. Perhaps she was torn between naming him and not naming him. Could an actress be blackballed? Winter would have to find out about that.

The deposit in Upton's account could be a payoff from Ayers to keep quiet, or . . . nothing at all. Would Ayers pay Upton off just because of a false accusation? If word of that got around, Ayers might fear that other women would try the same ploy. But what if Upton had some kind of proof of the Ayers assault, and used it to blackmail Ayers for money? That would explain the deposit.

What kind of proof could she have? A video? A photograph? That made Winter think of Gruse again. Did Gruse take videos? Who had shot the video of Ayers pulling Upton at the party? Had Gruse taken that?

Winter bolted upright without remembering to push the lever, which only served to roll him off the side of the chair. He grabbed the side table to save the tablet. He didn't need his ceiling diagram now, a possible set of lines had connected in his head.

Gruse was a stalker, at least a photographic one. He stalked women just like Melanie Upton. Could Gruse have been stalking Upton, and taken a photo of Ayers breaking in to Upton's apartment?

Ayers seemed to have the most to lose in the whole deal. And Upton had said he had a temper. No, that wasn't it, she said he could be *rough*. If Gruse had some kind of photographic proof of Ayers being at Upton's apartment, and Ayers found out about it, he might have been trying to get it back from Gruse. If Ayers had in fact paid off Upton, he'd probably be willing to pay off Gruse as well. Ayers couldn't take the chance meeting Gruse around Marburg, the crowd waiting for him at the Hilton was proof of that. It might explain why Gruse was at the Greenhill Motel, a meeting place suggested by Ayers. Maybe Ayers was threatening Gruse with a knife and things went south.

Winter's house phone was still in the kitchen, an old style princess model, mounted on the wall. He picked it up and was halfway through dialing the station to leave a voicemail for Cindy when he remembered it was Friday, she wouldn't be in the office tomorrow, and neither would Dan. He'd go in himself. Cindy would have an active file on both cases, and Winter could see if Upton's number was on Gruse's call list. He could also look through Gruse's photos to see if there was a picture of Upton.

Or he could call Cindy in the morning, talk her into some overtime . . .

Nothing else to do tonight, so he went back to the lounge chair. He'd unwind watching some sports highlights. The leather, long since molded to his body, welcomed him like a glove.

He drifted off to the murmur of talking heads discussing playoff possibilities, with the nagging suspicion that he'd forgot something.

CHAPTER 31

SATURDAY MORNING, the station quiet, missing the normal hum. The night shift had come and gone, the day shift out, as were the two detectives on schedule this weekend. The light on the coffee pot was lit, meaning Cindy was already there. The opportunity for overtime, plus the celebrity nature of the Upton case, had been enticement enough to drag her in on a weekend.

This wasn't Winter's scheduled weekend, but he never cared when he was on a case, especially when he felt something might pop. It also didn't change how he dressed; he wore his usual tactical pants, this pair a deep green, his polo shirt untucked. The polo shirt was his one capitulation to modern clothing, the new tech fabrics multi season comfortable. The station was stuffy, as always, the old air conditioning system not able to keep up with the additions that had been slapped on through the years.

He got his coffee and wandered over to Cindy's desk. Today her hair was a shade lighter than his pants, but no less green. He'd seen her in so many different colors of hair it looked almost normal on her.

"Thanks for the OT," she said.

"They probably don't pay you enough anyway," said Winter.

"You got that right. But the perks, wow, this incredible office, for instance."

"What have you got?" asked Winter. When he'd called Cindy that morning he'd explained what he was looking for, a possible connection between the Gruse murder and the Upton woman.

Cindy rotated her screen so he could see. She'd pulled up the Gruse photos, dozens of small icons. "I couldn't find any images of Melanie Upton. I studied shots of her from her agent's website, and also stills from *The Other Woman* video, so I think I'd recognize her. But there are so many photos in Gruse's collection that are shot from the side, even from behind. I think he had a thing for rear ends, or maybe it was the only shots he could get. She *could* be in there, but I might not recognize her."

"Anything on the phone number?"

"No. Upton's number is not in Lenny's contact list, or in his call log. We got the full history from his cell phone carrier. There are no calls to or from Upton's cell at all. And she doesn't appear to have a landline."

"I didn't see one in her apartment." Winter tapped the screen. "How many local women haven't we identified?"

"There are two answers to that," said Cindy. She switched to a spreadsheet. "This column is the photo image number. The second column indicates whether the photo shows the face. We've identified about half the women whose faces are visible, which leaves us with about fifteen more. The others will be difficult—there wasn't much background to go on. I've got a list for you." She scrolled down the screen, the image numbers rolling by. "These are the shots where we can't see the face. Me and Dan have grouped them where the pictures appear to be of the same woman. So that's the second answer to your question, we don't know how many."

"Best guess?"

"I think fifty, Dan thinks more."

"When I saw Upton, she was wearing these really tight jeans and a workout top, like you'd wear at the gym, not the loose kind. I thought it kind of weird, who wears a workout top with jeans?"

Cindy gave him a look. "You need to look at some fashion magazines. It's more common than you think, and they're called skinny jeans."

"I was thinking, maybe that's the way she dresses all the time?"

"She's a woman, *and* an actress. She probably has lots of looks. Not everyone dresses in the same outfit every day."

"Hey, I wore the tan pants yesterday," said Winter.

"Just saying. But I see your point. I'll look for pictures of women in skinny jeans."

"And ask Ryder what he saw her wearing. He's seen her twice now." Winter wasn't too surprised that there was no direct Gruse and Upton linkage; just because he had pictured a possible connection didn't mean there was one. He'd keep looking though . . . "Speaking of Ryder, I know he's not on, but since you're here working, give him a call and ask about the clothes."

"Actually, he is working. Not on Gruse, on the Upton case. I've been monitoring the web for any mention of Upton, it was Ryder's idea. She's getting a lot of mentions, mostly because of *The Other Woman* show. And just about any time Ashley Hanna is in the news—which is all the time—there's always a line about Jason Ayers and Upton. Anyway, this was posted yesterday." Cindy pulled up a YouTube video.

Winter squinted at it. "Can you make it bigger?"

"I can, but it gets grainy, it was shot in low light with a camera phone."

"I've seen this, Upton and Ayers at the party."

"You haven't seen this version. Look, it's a different angle. You can see them talking, they look pretty close, off in the corner. Then something happens, he looks angry. See when Ayers grabs Upton's arm? She looks like she's in pain. He's forcing her."

"Can't hear what they are saying over all that music."

"We have the audio from the other video, at least some of it. She said 'You're hurting me.'"

Upton had told Winter she liked it rough. He didn't think this was what she meant. "Who took the video?"

"The YouTube user name is Celebrity Sighter."

"Can you find out who that really is?" Winter was wondering if it might be Gruse.

"Not easily. This is the only video uploaded under that name. It might be a random person at the party."

Or Melanie Upton, thought Winter. "Does Ryder know about this?"

"I sent it to him a little while ago. He wants to see Ayers again right away, but I can't confirm that Ayers is in town. My friend at the

Hilton isn't working today, and the woman who answered the phone might have thought I was a celebrity seeker."

"Aren't you?"

"Ha-ha."

Winter wanted to get back on the Gruse murder, now that nothing apparent had panned out on the linkage between the cases. "Give me that list of Gruse photos, I'll try a few more places. I'm going to Shelly's Seafood restaurant to meet my daughter for lunch. It's close enough to the Hilton, I'll try to find out where Ayers is. I might get more out of them in person."

Cindy transferred another batch of unidentified images to Winter's tablet, along with a list of guesses as to where they were taken. As she handed it back to him she said, "When you are there, if you happen to see Michael Stevens, you'll get me an autograph, right?"

RYDER HATED WORKING unassigned weekends, he had his own schedule he liked to keep, nice and orderly. His shift was normally one full weekend a month, and two half weekends, one Saturday, one Sunday. It was one of the things that had made him choose Marburg over Springfield, his other option when he left Derry, the larger force meant more consistency, none of the scheduling at the whim of the shift commander.

Today he was mad enough he didn't care what day it was. Ayers had lied to him, just as Melanie Upton had. This case was full of liars with no respect for the law. Even the front desk clerk at the Hilton had led him astray about access to the Executive Floor. Time to set them straight, starting with Ayers.

Ryder took the time to put on a suit, a light worsted gray worsted wool with a red Hermes tie. The ties were a little too rich for his salary, but he liked knowing that the distinctive pattern was recognizable to anyone who knew clothes. You never knew who you might meet, always better to look good.

*   *   *

AUDREY WINTER SCROLLED through the speed dial list on her car phone, the numbers flicking in bright blue on the center multi function screen. The name she punched up went right to the answering machine. If she didn't know it was her father, Audrey might not have recognized his voice, slurred from an old fashioned outgoing message cassette. It was the same machine that had been in the kitchen since she'd lived there, and that had been—twelve years ago. It was a miracle the answering machine still worked.

Knowing her father, he'd probably not replace it when it finally broke, or if he did, it would only be at her insistence. Though she didn't see him often, she took some comfort in being able to contact him to check in. She was the one who made him get a cell phone.

It was why she'd set up these scheduled lunches, otherwise she knew that between his job and hers, they'd never see each other. An hour apart, yet they could have just as easily been on opposite coasts.

She still hadn't broken the news that she'd been offered the promotion in Virginia. Her father would say all the right things, he'd want her to go, but she knew he'd be sad, and she'd worry about him. He had no other family around.

The lunches had been good for both of them. She could forget for a little while that he was a cop, in a dangerous world of criminals and drugs and assaults. The one great thing about his dislike of cell phones was that he wouldn't be checking messages constantly during the two hours they spent together. And it rubbed off on her, practically the only time she wasn't on the phone was when she was with him.

Unfortunately, she'd picked up her phone earlier this morning . . .

Audrey pulled up another number, called the station. The operator switched her to the detective squad, a woman picking up the phone right away, a voice Audrey knew. "Hey, Cindy, it's Audrey Winter, what are you doing there today?"

"Your father has me working."

"Good working or drudgery?"

"Time and half working, which means good working."

"Do you happen to know where my dad is? He's not answering his cell. I wanted to see if he can meet a little earlier."

"He doesn't always remember to turn it on. He's on his way to the

Hilton. I can get dispatch to call him, but he might be in and out of the car, he had a few stops to make."

"Great, thanks. I'll head over there and try to catch him. Don't work too hard."

"Hey, Audrey, when you're at the Hilton, keep an eye out for Michael Stevens . . ."

RYDER HALF HOPED the pseudo-polite desk clerk was on duty so he could teach him a little respect, but instead it was the attractive blonde who Winter had spoken to. Ryder brightened, things were looking up. He flashed his badge and introduced himself.

"I'm here on official police business," he said. The woman, a little older than Ryder had first thought, but holding her age well, didn't seem that impressed, so he changed his approach, leaning on the counter. "I interviewed Jason Ayers here in relation to an important case I'm working on, and I have some follow up questions. If you could give me the card for his floor, I'd appreciate it."

"I believe I saw Mr. Ayers leave the hotel, but I will ring his room," she said. She picked up the phone, punched in a number—Ryder noticed she hadn't bothered to look up the room—and after a moment shook her head. "I'm sorry, there's no answer. I'd offer to call the show publicists for you, but they are only here during the week, they've checked out already."

"But Mr. Ayers did not?"

"No, his room is on a long term reservation."

"Is he around on weekends?" Ryder should have called ahead, he'd missed his spinning class for this.

"I can tell you I have seen him before on a Saturday. And he wasn't carrying a bag this morning. He might have just gone out for brunch."

Ryder wondered if actors carried their own bags. He couldn't picture Michael Stevens hauling suitcases through the airport. Maybe Ayers wasn't a big enough name yet. "Don't you have brunch here?"

The desk clerk's smile was forced. "Only on Sundays."

Ryder took that to mean it wasn't very good, which was too bad, he liked a good brunch. "Maybe I'll just wait a bit. If you see him, tell him I'm in the café."

He stopped at the lobby newsstand, bought the *Globe* and an iced Starbucks from a little refrigerator, and descended the three steps into the café. A waiter started to come over, maybe to tell Ryder he had to order something to sit there, but Ryder glared at him, flashed his badge, and took a table where he could watch the front door.

Twenty minutes later Ryder was out of coffee and out of paper to read. He stretched, decided against another coffee—too much sugar in those cold brews—and wandered back to the news kiosk to browse through the magazines. He'd give it another twenty minutes, then get the blonde at the desk to give him a call when Ayers came in, he'd softened her up enough.

The magazine selection was lousy, not even a health mag, and he decided to call it quits. Before he had taken two steps a woman came in the front door, his favorite kind of attractive. In shape, that buttoned up, pulled together look, chic instead of stark. She was a little on the short side, but a petite short, as opposed to a dumpy short. She even knew how to dress, Ryder guessing upscale designer all the way, elegant black slacks and low heels with a soft blue top and an unstructured jacket. Her hair was so nicely done it didn't look made up, Ryder immediately pegging her from the city. She looked to be late twenties, a perfect age for him . . . the morning might not have been totally wasted.

He buttoned his jacket, lifting his tie slightly. She'd see the pattern, and if she knew fashion as he expected she did, she'd recognize it immediately. The woman looked around the lobby, caught his eye, lingering just a bit—she'd noticed him. He feigned disinterest. The woman crossed the lobby to look in the café, glanced at her watch, and headed to the newsstand.

Up close, she was even prettier than Ryder had thought, she had the whole package. Probably well off, she may never have met a real cop. Ryder knew from experience that lots of upper class women had a thing for men who were different from the high society private school types who never got their hands dirty. He was a detective, he could offer the best of both.

She obviously wasn't meeting a guest, else she would have stopped at the front desk. Ryder picked up a magazine as she perused the front page of yesterday's *Wall Street Journal*. They were the only two customers in the small newsstand. Casually, Ryder said, "You must be waiting for someone."

The woman gave him a half smile, something between amused and polite. "You figured that out?"

"I'm a detective," said Ryder. "A real one, actually."

The woman put down the paper and picked up a magazine. "Are you now."

"That's right." Ryder considered showing her his badge, or unbuttoning his jacket so she could see his gun, decided it would be too obvious this soon.

She flipped through her magazine. Without even looking at him directly she said, "All dressed up for something?"

Ryder puffed up, she'd noticed. "I mostly deal with hardened criminals, tough guys. But it's important to fit in at every level of society, and also uphold the reputation of the law." He let that sink in, then added, "That's one of the reasons they asked me to come to Marburg."

"Really?" She finally looked right at him, intrigued.

Ryder gave her his best matter of fact tone. "These smaller cities, the police department can get set in their ways. If no one steps in to introduce modern practices—I'm sure someone like you would understand—it's like dinosaurs, not adapting to the changes around them."

The woman pursed her lip. "Dinosaurs?"

"The old school." Ryder thought he had her pegged: upscale, elite. "Unprofessional."

"I see. Thank you for enlightening me."

Her eyes brightened, Ryder believing he had formed a connection. Just as he was about to shift to a more personal discussion, she said "Excuse me," and waved to someone over his shoulder, Ryder belatedly realizing that's who she had been reacting to. He turned to see Winter, of all people, crossing the lobby, looking his usual undone self.

The woman left Ryder standing there and gave Winter a big hug, Ryder, stunned, pissed, Winter was way too old for her . . .

Winter didn't seem at all surprised to see Ryder there. "I see you've met my daughter," he said.

Ryder dumbfounded, mumbled something incoherent, but Winter was focused on the woman. "What are you doing here? I thought we were doing seafood."

"I'm sorry, I have to go to the office, so I was hoping we could do an earlier quick lunch. I'll come back next Saturday."

"Unless you have to work again. They push you too much."

"Dad . . ."

Winter looked over at Ryder, who was still standing there with the magazine in his hand. "Ayers not in?"

"No. I was waiting a while to see if he came back."

"We can ask Linda at the desk to phone you when he does. No sense in hanging around here."

The woman—Ryder still didn't know her name—put her arm through Winter's and guided him away. After a few steps she turned back to Ryder. "Detective? You might want to do some research on dinosaurs. They managed to live for over a hundred million years. Peacocks, by comparison, are a flash in the pan."

Ryder tried to smile, but he wasn't sure if his muscles were working. He heard Winter ask, "What was that all about?" but her answer was lost in the clicking of her heels on the tile floor.

CHAPTER 32

Melanie fumbled through her shoe boxes, looking for that strappy pair of heeled gladiator sandals to go with her skinny jeans. She was in a warrior mood, needing to go on the offensive. A new outfit would be nice, as would more shoes. She'd burned through the appearance fee she'd earned from *The Other Woman*—not nearly enough, given the ratings they must have got—and even though her name had appeared in virtually every story about Ashley Hanna, Melanie was feeling too much like an afterthought. She needed to be *the* story, and Hanna the jilted one. So it was time to get back in the public eye. First stop, the Hilton; she had stayed away long enough, the world needed to see her around Jason. Maybe she could trick him into coming to her apartment, work out a way for Taz to catch it on video . . .

At least her apartment was cool. All courtesy of that detective, Winter. She thought she'd handled him well enough, but he was one to be careful of, all that friendly chatter, he wasn't as simple as he seemed. It wasn't an act with him; she knew actors, and Winter wasn't acting, he was just more than he appeared. Not a man to be bullshitted, which is why she had chosen to answer his seemingly innocuous questions tangentially. She had almost slipped when Winter had asked about Lenny Gruse, Winter making it sound unrelated. Ryder had asked about Lenny too, not directly, but still . . . two cops, it couldn't be coincidental.

Yet if they had something on her, they'd certainly be hauling her into the station, not hinting around for a date or installing her air conditioning. Maybe it *was* unrelated, small city policemen with small minds, all of them figuring since she was an actress, she must know all the local photographers. Like when someone from New York found out you were from near Boston, and they said, "Oh, you must know so and so," as if she lived in a backwater town in the dark ages.

She'd keep a finger on the cops, just to be sure. Ryder, he'd be easy to play; Melanie was sure he was over his anger that she'd misled him, and besides, a little emotion in the mix was a good thing, she could use that.

She found the gladiator sandals, strapped them on, checked herself in the mirror. Perfect.

RYDER COULDN'T BEAR the thought of running into Winter and his daughter again, so he left the Hilton by the back entrance. He still couldn't believe the pretty woman was Winter's daughter, they couldn't be less alike. And what was that crack about dinosaurs and peacocks? The dinosaurs were extinct, just like her father and all his kind would be.

Maybe she had been adopted . . .

An old blue Toyota slipped past into the back lot, a woman driving, Ryder turning to look. He recognized her immediately, Melanie Upton. She was probably going to see Jason Ayers. So the front desk woman had lied to him. Ayers must be in, or on his way, why else would Upton be here?

Ryder thought about stopping Upton to talk, but he didn't really have a good question to ask, and besides, he'd already been blown off by one woman today, he couldn't deal with another one, especially if she was on her way to see her boyfriend.

Cindy had called him earlier and asked what Melanie Upton had been wearing when he had interviewed her. He remembered very clearly, but had been a little vague with Cindy. He'd sound like a pervert if he described Melanie's outfit—or lack of it—in detail.

Cindy said Winter thought Gruse may have photographed Upton, implying the two cases were connected, which sounded ridiculous.

Winter had Cindy looking through Gruse's photos, trying to find women in skinny jeans.

Which was exactly what Melanie was wearing right now, Ryder admiring her very attractive rear end as she disappeared through the back door of the hotel.

RYDER WAS SURPRISED to see Cindy still at the station, she must be dragging out her overtime. The old school—the *dinosaur*—way of taking advantage of the system must have rubbed off on her, or else she just figured she could get away with it, no one would notice. No respect for the job, right down to her irreverent hair color.

"Any luck with Ayers?" she asked.

"He's out." Ryder had been in such a hurry to leave the Hilton he'd forgotten to ask the front desk clerk to call him when Ayers returned. Or when Ayers was finished with Melanie Upton. "Does Winter really have you here on a weekend looking through Gruse's photos?"

"Yes, why?"

"Nothing."

"Did Winter catch you at the Hilton?"

"Yeah. He's out for lunch with his daughter."

"Did you meet her?" Cindy gushed. "She's great."

"I saw her. What's her name?"

"Audrey. She works in Boston."

"I figured as much. She didn't look local."

"What do you mean by that?"

"Nothing." Ryder couldn't let it go. "She seems kind of—defensive, about her father."

"Don't see why she should be. Proud maybe."

"He's just a cop, same as me."

Cindy gave Ryder a long look. "Not to make any kind of comparison, Detective, but Winter is not just a cop. He's an incredible cop."

"Of course you'd say that, you work for him."

"I work for all of you. He's broken cases that everyone had given up for hopeless. He's special."

Ryder didn't see anything special about Winter, other than his flouting of the rules and dress code. "We all get lucky now and then."

"It's not luck. Or if it is, you should all have it. Read his case files, if you don't believe me."

Ryder shrugged. "My files sound pretty good too. Anyone can sound good in a closed case file."

"Don't read his, read the files from the other detectives whose cases he solved. Not just in Marburg, sometimes even cases in Springfield and Boston. Detectives he doesn't even know come looking for him to get help."

Ryder couldn't remember another cop ever asking him for help on a case, a good case, anyway. "Like what?"

"A few years ago they found this homeless guy dead at the bus station in Boston. Not too uncommon, he died from acute alcohol poisoning. The dead guy didn't have any identification, he was a John Doe. They got some dental, but didn't have anyone to match it to. Anyway, in Florida someplace, a real estate developer disappears after going belly up in the stock market bubble. Turns out his investor was a drug lord laundering money through the real estate. Everyone figured the real estate guy had run off to South America, or had been killed by his gangster partner. Winter figured out that the dead homeless guy was actually the missing real estate developer. He drunk himself to death."

Ryder was intrigued despite himself. "How'd he figure that out?"

Cindy tapped the computer. "It's a long story, read the file. The point is, the two cases didn't even remotely look to be connected, and yet Winter found the link. Across states, mind you. You know how rare that is? I'm telling you, he's special."

Ryder drifted away, still thinking it had to be luck, Winter somehow stumbling on the connection. But at his cubicle he pulled up the case histories, maybe because of what Cindy had said, or because he had just met Winter's very attractive daughter.

Ryder found the case file. Not surprisingly, given Winter's casual attitude, it wasn't written in formal cop speak, the written language every cop used without even being trained. Sentences meant to cover your ass in case events turned out differently than they had appeared at the time the notes were taken, or if they had to be used in court.

Ryder wrote his case files up after the facts were pretty nailed down, which is why he kept a separate set of working notes. He suspected most cops did the same thing.

What was surprising was that Winter's notes were absent the usual subtle bravado which implied that the detective had been a veritable Sherlock Holmes to solve the crime. Ryder had read cases that were open and shut from the minute the crime had been committed, but where the detective's notes had sounded like he'd been superman, instead of being handed a security video showing the criminal act in living color.

The case was complicated, but the notes laid out the connection, which was easy to see after the fact. Ryder saw a few places where Winter might have caught a lucky break. The homeless guy was always near busses on their way to Florida, for instance. Any detective might have noticed that.

Ryder read through a number of other case files, some written by Winter, some by Brooker, the old fart who was out on sick leave and hopefully to be forcefully retired. Ryder found files from other detectives, a dozen from Logan about cases Winter had worked on as part of inter agency task forces, three with the FBI. Ryder had never worked with the FBI, he'd heard they were a pain, but it could get you noticed.

Ryder had to admit there were a lot of closed cases, tough cases. He didn't like Winter any more than he had before, but obviously the guy had a knack for connecting unseen dots.

And he had a really pretty daughter.

WINTER WAS WHISTLING as he went into the station, he always felt good about spending time with Audrey. She had a good job, a real career, and he hated for her to have to break away from it for him, but was happy when she did. He wished they didn't work her so hard so he could see her more often . . .

A beefy cop named Daniels was coming out as Winter went in, they nodded to each other, Daniels holding the door for Winter. Winter stopped, something about doors . . . he was forgetting something.

Doors, a guy guarding a door . . . Shit, he'd forgot to show the photos to the bouncer at the Marquee.

Daniels, still holding the door, frowned at him. Winter mumbled, "Sorry," and went past. How had he forgot that? Maybe he'd have to start taking notes like Ryder.

Nah, that wasn't going to happen.

Inside, Cindy said, "Give me your tablet, I have some more photos for you. And we just got a call from Linda at the Hilton, she says to tell you that Ayers is in the building."

"You mean Elvis," said Winter.

"Costello?"

"Don't pretend I'm that old."

"I'm not pretending. And this Linda, she a special friend of yours?"

"You're not the only one with contacts at the Hilton," said Winter, admitting nothing. "Does Ryder know?"

Cindy jerked her head toward the detective squad room. "I just told him. He's back there."

Winter found Ryder in the hall, pulling on his jacket. "Ayers?"

"Yeah. I'm heading over now to brace him about that new video." Ryder hesitated. "Want to come along?"

"I should just get a room there," said Winter. "But sure."

WINTER HAD NEVER been on the Executive Floor of the Hilton, it was pretty nice. Even the hall carpets were plusher. Ayers had a multi room suite, and from the look of it, he did his share of in room partying.

Ryder was taking the lead on the questioning, which was fine with Winter. It was Ryder's case. Winter had been a little surprised when Ryder had asked him along, maybe Logan had pressured him into it.

Ryder, his jacket still buttoned, tapped his phone and said, "Mr. Ayers, you have to admit this video doesn't look good for you."

"It's all out of context," said Ayers. If Ayers was worried about the cops, he wasn't trying to impress them with his outfit. He was wearing loose sweatpants, a muscle tee, and loafers with no socks.

"Well, give us the context then. Otherwise we'll go ask the people at that party."

Ayers glanced away, then said, "Look, I admit I was closer to Melanie than I might have let on. It wasn't like we were dating, we'd just hook up. But it was over between us a really long time ago. A year or two."

"That's a long time?" asked Ryder.

"Shit, you know how many women I hook up with in a year?"

Winter was walking around the suite, trying to get a peek into the bedroom. "Miss Upton has implied it's more recent than that."

"She's full of it," said Ayers.

Winter would have kept quiet at that point, just given Ayers the silent, disbelieving treatment, but Ryder kept prodding. "If you have something to tell us, Mr. Ayers, you best do it now, before we find a witness who says otherwise. At that point it goes beyond he said, she said."

Ayers shrugged. "Ask anyone you want. Like I already told you, Melanie is doing this all for publicity. You think that new video just showed up out of the blue? Melanie must have staged the whole thing."

"You saying she made you grab her?"

"Don't be ridiculous. She'd playing everyone, don't you see? It's a big act."

Ryder flipped a page in his notebook. "Why don't you give me a few names of the people at the party, we can talk to them, see if your story checks out."

Winter had finished his circuit of the room. Other than the messy bed, clothes thrown everywhere, three empty champagne bottles, and a heap of Starbuck's cups in the trash, there wasn't much to see. He leaned against the bar. "Why don't we start with Ashley Hanna."

Ryder glanced at Winter, nodded. "That's a good idea. I'm sure she'll back you up, right Mr. Ayers?"

"Of course she will. But I wasn't with her the night Melanie claims to have been assaulted." Ayers pointed a finger at Ryder. "Wait a minute. Melanie put you up to this, didn't she?"

"Put us up to what?" said Ryder, miffed.

"To talk to Ashley. That way Melanie can leak it to the press that the cops were questioning Ashley about me and her. It would play right into her story."

Winter saw Ryder about to argue, so he cut in, "We can avoid the—negative publicity—if you can just give us someone to talk to who knows where you were the night Miss Upton was assaulted."

"I can't believe I have to prove my innocence against an unfounded accusation. You know what kind of problem you are causing?"

Ryder said, "I'm sure you don't want us wasting our time and yours on this accusation by Miss Upton if it isn't true. As soon as this gets cleared up, the better it is for everyone."

Ayers looked away. "The bitch is killing me," he muttered. His eyes darted from Winter to Ryder. "Look, you understand, I got all kinds of women coming on to me, especially since the show hit the top of the ratings. And Ashley, man, I'm telling you, every time there is another story about me and Ashley, I get women crawling all over me."

"Sure, sure, we get it," said Ryder. "They want to know what you got, how you managed to snag Ashley Hanna."

Winter winced, but Ayers pointed at Ryder. "You got it. I'm getting more action than Michael Stevens. In fact . . ."

"What?" prodded Ryder. He put down his notebook. "Just between us guys."

Ayers looked around as if someone else might be listening. Then he leaned toward Ryder. "You know why I couldn't have assaulted Melanie that night? The night she said she was watching the Tony Awards with me? Because I *was* watching the Tony Awards on tv, but with another woman. Suzanne Mance."

"Wait," said Ryder. "Isn't that Michael Stevens's live-in girlfriend? The woman he had a kid with?"

"Exactly," said Ayers. "*Now* can you understand why I haven't told you? I'd get creamed by Stevens, he has a lot of pull. Not to mention it would screw up my thing with Ashley." He looked back and forth from Winter to Ryder. "You guys got to keep this between us."

Ryder glanced at Winter, who shrugged, non committal, he wasn't going to promise Ayers anything, and hoped Ryder was smart enough not to either. "Maybe if we talk to Suzanne . . ."

"Sure, I can make that happen. She's in LA but I can get you her private number, you can call her direct. No need to make it public, right?"

"Everything we do is confidential," said Ryder. "Unless of course some charges are filed and it goes to court."

"That won't happen," said Ayers. He picked up the hotel notepad, scribbled, and handed it to Ryder. "You can call her right now, so you don't think I prepped her or anything."

Winter was sure if Ayers needed Suzanne Mance as an alibi he would have already warned her, but unless Ayers was an idiot, he would have chosen a different woman as his alibi. Or maybe he was really smart, finding the one person who'd have no reason to lie about Ayers's whereabouts, since it would obviously put her in a really bad situation.

"Maybe you could step into the bedroom for a few minutes," said Ryder. "We'll call her right now, clear this up."

"Sure, anything," said Ayers.

Winter stopped Ayers before he left the room. "One other question, it's not related, but since we're here . . . I'm working this other case, there's this guy," Winter was pulling out his trusty tablet, "he seems to be tied into the acting scene, he's a photographer." He showed Ayers Gruse's photo. "Do you know him?"

"I don't think so," said Ayers. "He doing shots for the show?"

"Not that I know of," said Winter. "But he used to be in LA, now he's here, I thought maybe you might have crossed paths."

Ayers sounded indignant. "Shit, I've crossed paths with almost as many photographers as I have women."

CHAPTER 33

WINTER HATED RIDING SHOTGUN, so he'd convinced Ryder to let him drive his personal car to the Hilton, Ryder grumbling all the way about how unofficial it looked. Ryder appeared less perturbed on the way back to the station, filling Winter in on his conversation with Suzanne Mance. He sounded downright star struck.

Winter never understood the general infatuation with famous people, especially actresses, but he had to admit, Mance was good looking; he'd seen her in a few movies. "Did she sound surprised you were calling?"

"Maybe a little. I couldn't swear to it that Ayers hadn't tipped her off. She backed him up about being with him the night of the Upton assault. She said she was in Boston for an interview and she and Ayers hooked up in some romantic little inn. Should be easy enough to check out. I think she's in love."

"So much in love she'd lie for him?"

"Who knows," said Ryder. "Maybe I should fly out to LA, interview her in person."

"Yeah, try that out on Logan, see how far it gets you."

"If she's Ayers's primary alibi, and Upton clearly identifies him as the man who assaulted her, then we'll have to get a statement."

"If and when Upton does that," said Winter, "and I'm not sure she will, then we'll just get a subpoena for Suzanne Mance to appear here. That by itself might change her story."

"She probably wouldn't have to comply with a subpoena across state lines."

"If she's so into Ayers, she should be willing to come voluntarily."

Ryder said, "If she's telling the truth, then Ayers is off the hook for the assault."

"I don't get these Hollywood people. You said Mance is Stevens's live-in girlfriend. And yet Ayers is sleeping with her, all while he's supposed to be dating Ashley Hanna, and at the same time, Upton is claiming Ayers is with *her*."

"The way the other half lives, I guess," said Ryder.

Winter glanced over at Ryder. He was looking out the window, almost dreamily, making Winter think Ryder was envious rather than making a moral judgment about the other half. "Ayers got pretty worked up when he was talking about Upton. His history with her might have been more recent than he let on, or more intense."

"Maybe they can't stand each other but they're addicted to each other. And all this talk about other women is just that, talk."

"Could be," said Winter. "If Upton is suggesting she and Ayers are involved, but not making a false assault charge, she hasn't really done anything legally wrong."

"Right. She could be fabricating the whole thing just to get a job, as Ayers said."

As Winter pulled into the station lot, Ryder asked, "Why did you show Ayers the picture of Gruse?"

"Why not? Gruse took photos of actresses, Ayers is an actor. As good a connection as any. We just found out they're all sleeping together. Maybe they all get their pictures taken by the same photographer."

A STICKY NOTE ON WINTER'S computer screen from Cindy directed him to look at a file folder, so Winter dutifully clicked on it. Inside were other folders of images, each labeled with a style of clothing, *skinny jeans, yoga pants, tights, leggings, skirts, skorts* . . . Winter had no idea what a skort was.

He began at the top, and up popped Gruse's photos of women in tight jeans. Winter started to work through them, stopped, and since there was no one else in the detective room except Ryder, called out, "Hey, come look at these pictures."

Ryder rolled over a chair—Brooker's, which made Winter feel guilty he hadn't spoken to Brooker in a few days. "These are the photos of unidentified women Gruse photographed," said Winter. "Organized by clothing." He clicked though the images one by one. "The last time I saw Upton she was wearing these really tight jeans. Did she have something like that on when you saw her?"

"Let me think. Um, the first time she was wearing yoga pants with a pullover top, like a sweatshirt but not as thick." Ryder hesitated. "The second time she had on a man's shirt."

"With yoga pants again? Or tight jeans?"

"Just the shirt."

Winter wasn't following. "I mean, what else did she have on? A skirt? Jeans?"

"I told you. Just the shirt."

Winter kept his eyes on the screen, he wished he had a witness for this, it was priceless. "Did you put that in your notes? *During the interview, the subject wore only a man's shirt?*"

"I can't help it that's how she answered the door."

"Okay. But you should ask Cindy to see if there are any photos of women only wearing a man's shirt. Just in case." Winter would want to hear that conversation; Cindy would grill Ryder mercilessly. Winter resumed clicking through the photos, feeling Ryder steaming, knowing he would have been all over Winter if the roles had been reversed.

"Hey, stop there," said Ryder.

"Can't be her," said Winter. "She's got pants on."

"Fuck you. That one looks about right, same build, same hips."

"You can tell that from the back?" But Winter didn't disagree. The next two photos were of the same woman, walking down a sidewalk that could have been anywhere, but was probably in Marburg by the date stamp. The next photo was obviously of a different woman, bright blonde, so Winter clicked over to the yoga pants folder.

About halfway through the images Winter pointed. "Her."

This was a side shot, the background blurry, but the subject reasonably sharp. Even in profile it was clearly Upton.

"Son of a bitch," said Ryder. The next five photos were all of Upton, the pictures apparently taken from across the street. The last one showed her from behind, but on an angle. "Go back to the skinny jeans."

"Wish we could put them up at the same time," said Winter.

"Easy, let me." Ryder took the mouse and placed the images side by side, skinny jeans and yoga pants. "It's her."

"You sure? I see the similarity, the hair color and length, the body."

"I'm sure," said Ryder.

"Let's see if there's anything else." Winter ran though the rest of the folders, but they couldn't find another similar photo. "Huh." He tapped the screen. "I have an idea. A few of them, actually. What if Gruse was following Upton around, taking her photo. Maybe not stalking her in a traditional sense, but just doing what he does. He follows her home, or stakes her out there, and he happens to take a picture of Ayers going in the night of the assault. Gruse tries to blackmail Ayers, and it goes south, Ayers kills him."

"That's a stretch," said Ryder. "Gruse taking a photo of Upton, okay, I buy that." He jerked his hand toward the screen. "He's got hundreds of women, it would be more of a surprise if he *didn't* have a photo of her because she's so—attractive."

"There are other possibilities," said Winter. "Upton and Ayers might have still been hot and heavy. Ayers could have found out that Gruse was stalking her and tried to warn Gruse off, they get in a fight."

"That's even more of a stretch. I know what you are doing. I've heard you're obsessed with imaginary connections."

"It's not an obsession, and it's got nothing to do with imagination. The connections are either there or they're not."

Ryder said, "Your theory doesn't quite fit with Ayers's story of not being interested in Upton."

"He's lied before. And if he killed Gruse, he certainly wouldn't be pointing out how close he was to Upton if she was the reason he did it."

"Ayers doesn't strike me as a guy who would kill someone," said Ryder. "Why would he? He's got Suzanne Mance, Ashley Hanna, *and* Melanie Upton. Even a stuck up Hollywood actor has to see how lucky he is. No way he'd screw up all that over some guy taking pictures of a woman he's sleeping with."

"Okay, try this. Gruse is stalking Upton, and she gets in a fight with him."

"And what? She kills him? You know how many men probably follow her around, come on to her?"

"Wait a minute," said Winter. "Weren't you the one who had that idea? That Gruse was a stalker?"

"That was before you were connecting it to Upton. Besides, it's the woman being stalked who usually gets hurt, not the stalker."

"Maybe they had something going."

Ryder looked at Winter in disbelief. "There's no way *that* woman," he pointed to the screen, "was with Gruse."

"We don't know that. We deal with people every day, but we don't know anything about them, really. We see them mostly in times of stress. We don't know what's going on in their lives, what makes them tick, what reasons they have for doing anything. Not with just a glimpse. It's like Gruse's photos, just a snapshot." Winter was thinking about Upton being an actress, about how she had tried to play him. "And sometimes we're only seeing what they want us to see."

"Next you'll be telling me it was Gruse who assaulted Upton, and she somehow confused him with Ayers."

Winter hadn't thought of that, but it was a possibility. "One thing we can do is run Gruse's DNA against Upton's SAFE kit. That will tell us whether they were together the night of the assault."

"It's a waste of time," said Ryder. "These cases aren't connected." He rolled his chair back out of Winter's cubicle. "I'm going home. Monday I'll get back on the drug angle. I'm expecting the lab report on what was in those capsules we found in Gruse's pocket."

Winter stared at the image of Upton on the screen, tuning Ryder out. He needed to get back to his house, stare at his ceiling. Upton, Gruse, Ayers.

A lot of dots to connect.

CHAPTER 34

Winter spent most of Sunday in his lounger, staring at the ceiling, mulling through possible connections between the Gruse murder and the Upton assault. There was now a clear connection between Gruse and Upton through the photographs, but that was no proof of a criminal link. It would have been different if Upton had been the only woman Gruse had photographed, or if his hard drive had been filled with her images. She actually appeared less often than many of his other subjects.

Still, it *was* a link, and while Winter wouldn't jump to any conclusions, it was worth thinking about what other connections there might be. Gruse and Upton both went to the Marquee night club, but so did just about every other Millennial in town. Neither Upton nor Ayers had admitted knowing Gruse, but Gruse might know someone connected to either one of them, an agent, a publicist. Winter used his imaginary pencil to draw blank boxes next to Upton and Ayers, connected by a dotted line to Gruse.

Jealousy was a common enough motive for murder, especially one so personal as the Gruse stabbing. Ayers didn't seem like the jealous type, he was cheating with a cheater himself. Yet the Ayers/Upton relationship appeared complicated, as emotional relationships often were. That would explain Ayers's interaction with Upton that had been caught on film.

Gruse and Upton did seem an unlikely couple, but Winter had seen stranger relationships.

Unless Gruse had something Upton wanted . . . That made Winter again think about a photo: Gruse with evidence of Ayers assaulting Upton. Would Upton sleep with Gruse to get such a picture? That would give Ayers a possible motive to kill Gruse; to get the photo himself.

If Ayers hadn't known about such a photo, but had found out about Upton and Gruse—maybe Ayers was one of those men who slept around, but couldn't deal with their girlfriends doing the same.

So it was certainly plausible that Gruse and Upton had something going on. That idea was worth pursuing. He'd go back to some of the places where Gruse had been seen, try to find out if Upton had been there as well, put them together in spots other than the Marquee.

Now and again Winter fell asleep, sometimes waking with a new insight, other times just needing to get up to get a drink or stretch. By late afternoon he was tired of not moving around, so he went down to the basement and fiddled with a broken dehumidifier. He concluded the compressor was shot, hauled it up the stairs and into the back of his old pickup, and drove it to the dump.

At Sears, Winter was told that they wouldn't have dehumidifiers back in stock until spring, even though the weather promised to be hot and sticky for another month at least. That reminded him of his conversation with Melanie Upton, about stores not having the proper seasonal merchandise, and *that* reminded Winter of Upton's response when he had asked her about Gruse. Upton had said that guys like Gruse came on to her all the time. The woman at the Marquee had said Gruse was creepy. Maybe Gruse had become infatuated with Upton, which would have led to the stalking, and perhaps Gruse catching a photo of Ayers. Or Gruse had something else on Ayers, or even Upton.

Gruse, Upton, Ayers.

FIRST THING MONDAY Winter put in the request to match the Gruse DNA to Upton's SAFE kit. He was wired from mostly sitting around on Sunday, but had no place to direct his energy.

He checked in with Sal Tully's ex girlfriend to make sure she wasn't being harassed by the biker. She came to the door with one kid of indeterminate sex on her hip and a wide eyed boy grasping her leg; the two kids didn't look like each other or like Tully. Winter was a cop, not the morality police, that was none of his business.

She was surprised to see Winter but grateful. "Whatever you did, he hasn't been around again," she said. She pushed a wisp of ragged hair behind her ear, giving him a small smile.

Winter wondered at the plight of people whose bright spot in their day was a visit from a cop. "You still have my card? You call me if he bothers you."

"I don't—I threw it away. I thought you only wanted me to call you to—," she glanced down at the boy, who might have been old enough to understand, "—you know, get something in return."

That pissed Winter off as much as Tully. "Some cop do that to you?"

She shook her head. "No, really. But you know, I hear things."

Winter gave her another one of his cards. "Don't be afraid to call me. You want to check me out, just ask around. If you ever hear about a cop asking for those kind of favors, I want to know about it. Or if Tully comes back."

She nodded, holding the card, the door still open, as if she still expected Winter to come in, demand some recompense. He couldn't think of anything else to say, so he left her like that.

Over the next few days Winter cruised the town, touching base with a few of his contacts, not quite informers, just locals who had good eyes and even better ears. Winter wasn't asking specifically about Gruse—pointed questions made his contacts feel like informers, and that's not how they saw themselves either. Instead, Winter just soaked it all in, stories of break-ins, assaults, whispers of drug deals, all mixed in with a lot of nothing, talk about potholes and the weather and sports.

He showed the photo of Gruse wherever he thought Gruse might have gone. Cindy was pulling together the last of the numbers in Gruse's call list, but the pickings were getting slimmer, a camera store, a pawnshop.

If Ryder had been showing Gruse's photo—Winter had no doubt that Ryder wasn't bothering—he would have probably mapped the city into a grid and assigned search coordinates to underlings while he sat in his command cubicle on his phone getting updates. Instead, Winter bounced from place to place, more or less geographically, his priorities dictated more by his experience than a regimen. He had previously scoured everywhere he could think Gruse might go near his mother's house, and aside from Gruse being recognized as a customer who bought cigarillos at a 7 Eleven, Winter had come up empty.

THURSDAY WINTER WAS WORKING the Irish side of town, more or less. More or less in that there were Irish all over the city, and more or less because this neighborhood was no longer all Irish. Yet all the signs were here, the Catholic churches, St. Patrick, St Brigid; the street names, Murphy, Kennedy; the bars, Cullen's, Shawn's Tap.

Winter bypassed most of the bars. These were full of locals, mainly men stopping in for a pint after work, shooting the shit. Winter doubted Gruse would hang out in such a bar; he'd be unwelcome and feel it immediately.

A spittle of rain hit his windshield as he pulled into O'Malley's. Winter had been here once, reasonably priced beer and food, and also waitresses, all of which were likely to be on Gruse's personal menu.

Winter had worn his hoody—the day being unnaturally cool—and took advantage of it to cover his head until he dashed inside, the rain picking up. Mid afternoon on a weekday, the place was almost empty, one old guy on the end of the bar with a beer and chaser, two middle aged women in a booth sharing a salad. They both looked up at Winter as he came in, their eyes lingering, Winter picking up a subtle invite. He headed for the bar.

The girl pecking at the register looked way too young to be serving, a poster child for an Irish tourist agency, straight blond hair, bright green eyes, freckles.

Winter waited until she'd finished whatever she was doing, then introduced himself. She gave him a genuine smile and said her name was Kathy. Winter showed her Gruse's photo.

"He was here once," she said, her smile vanishing.

"Give you a problem?"

"You know guys." Her eyes tried to hold Winter's, failed.

"He bother you?" Winter looked around. "You here alone?"

"My dad's in the back. This is his place."

"Your dad help when guys get a little drunk, toss them out?"

"We don't get many drunks here. It's mostly families, people come to eat. The bar is more for looks."

She really hadn't answered Winter's question, so he said, "This guy was an exception? He got drunk?"

"A little."

Winter waited her out, she might be old enough to serve beer, but he bet she had a youthful sense of self control, which meant she didn't have much.

Sure enough, she asked, "He claiming something?"

"No, that's not it. Look, if he got drunk and your father shoved him out the door, good for him. He's got to protect you, and his business." Winter let that sink in. "I'm just looking for information on the guy."

"It wasn't my dad," said Kathy.

"What happened?"

"Your guy, he might have been a little drunk, but I swear he only had a few beers here, we really watch that. Anyway, he's being a jerk, interrupting me—I'm talking to another customer—bragging about being from California, telling me he's going to take me for a ride in his car. Then he grabbed my arm."

Winter had been in enough bars to fill in the rest, especially the parts Kathy had purposely skipped over. "This customer, a friend, maybe? He helped you out?"

Kathy pursed her lips. "I don't want to get him in trouble."

"Then don't give me his name. Just tell me what happened."

"My friend told the creep to take his hands off me, and one thing led to another, and you know, there was a fight."

Winter figured a lot had been left out of that too. He'd do some checking and circle back; he didn't want to blow his investigation if it turned out that Gruse had been stabbed by Kathy's boyfriend over a bar fight. "Your friend, did he know this guy?"

"No. He would have told me."

"The guy left on his own?" Winter was trying to find out if

Kathy's friend had followed Gruse out the door to finish whatever had started.

"Pretty much. Maybe he got a little help, he was groggy and his nose was bleeding pretty bad. I had to clean it up off the floor and it was all over his shirt."

"When did this happen?"

"A few months ago."

"Are you sure?" That would be odd, a bar fight carrying on for months, Kathy's knight in shining armor mixing it up with Gruse after all that time.

"Yeah. There was a party here that night, people watching an awards show on the tv, they were doing this thing where people put ten dollars in a hat, and whoever picks the most winners gets the pot."

"The Oscars?"

"No, the other ones."

"The music awards?"

"No, those are the Grammys. I watch those."

Winter couldn't think of any other award shows. "Okay, thanks."

Back in the car, Winter mused over the timeline. It was certainly possible that Kathy's friend had known Gruse, and Kathy was just covering for him. But if that were the case, why mention that she knew Gruse at all? Maybe there was a security camera, and Kathy had to fess up about the fight because she knew there would be evidence, or at least other witnesses. Still, months had passed. Usually bar fights were spontaneous explosions set loose by alcohol, not festered over for months.

Winter almost went back in to ask the father about a camera, but first dialed the station and got connected to Cindy. "Can you look up if any awards shows were on tv, two, three months ago?"

"Don't have to look it up. The Tony's."

Something clicked at the back of Winter's mind, where had he heard a reference to the Tony's before? "What are they for?"

"Plays, stage stuff."

"You know that how?"

"What, you don't think I'm cultured, go to the theater?" Cindy pronounced *theater* in a fake French accent.

"Do you know the date?"

Winter heard tapping. "June twelfth. Why?"

"Are you sure?"

"You think the Tony's website might be wrong?"

"No, just thinking." June twelfth was the night Melanie Upton had been assaulted. The same night Lenny was getting his nose bloodied on the other side of the city.

CHAPTER 35

Winter skipped the bypass, heading back into the central part of the city through the neighborhoods. The rain had intensified, as had the humidity, he had to run the air conditioner.

If Gruse had got his nose bloodied in a bar fight, and had been involved in any way with Upton—sexually or not—would he have gone to her place after getting beaten up in a bar? Either to clean up or . . . take his frustrations out on Upton. The timeline might fit; Gruse in the bar earlier in the evening, plenty of time to drive across town to Upton's.

Winter hadn't mastered driving and dialing numbers on his cell phone, so he pulled into a Dunkin Donuts parking lot. Winter gave the Dunkin Donuts a long look, a chocolate covered would be good right now, he'd have to remember to get lots of napkins, the topping would melt before he made it back to the car. It would make a mess . . .

A messy car. Gruse's Cadillac, filled with trash. Gruse must have driven to the bar where he got his nose bleed.

He called Andie, the crime tech.

"I hope you aren't hounding me for the SAFE kit DNA match," Andie said the minute she picked up. "You think this is television, we get results back in a day?"

"I wasn't," Winter protested. "Really. I have a different question. When you were doing collection in Melanie Upton's apartment, did you find any blood?"

"A little. Not surprising, there's usually blood where people live."

"What's a little?"

"A few drops on the floor of the bathroom. It could have been there a while. It wasn't the cleanest place."

"Could it be from a nose bleed?"

"Sure."

"Did you bag the trash at Upton's?"

"Both inside and from a garbage can out back. Nothing in the trash with blood. Not a lot anyway, there might be a trace on a tissue, we didn't go that deep. Detective Ryder wasn't so certain there had even been a crime."

"Okay. Is there any way you can find out if the bathroom blood was Upton's?"

"We can check the type easily enough, they would have collected that as part of the SAFE kit. I'll pull it up . . . Upton is O positive, and so was the blood we found. It's probably hers, but without a DNA match, we can't be certain. You want me to send that one out too?"

"Go ahead. The Gruse homicide. What was the type of the blood in the Cadillac?"

"I'll check. I thought these were different cases?"

"Probably. Maybe."

"Gruse's blood is A positive."

Winter thanked Andie and hung up, idling in the parking lot. So no Gruse blood at Upton's. Unless it had ended up in the dumpster across the street; he doubted Ryder had searched it. Ryder had been assuming that Upton was drunk or high and hadn't given the assault claim much credence.

So it wasn't going to be easy. There was still the SAFE kit though; Gruse's DNA could be a match.

Winter pulled out of the lot. He'd have lunch at The Café, healthier than a donut.

JAKE WASN'T AT THE RESTAURANT, but Tiffany the hostess was, and that's who Winter had come to see anyway. She led Winter to a booth and sat down across from him as he ordered a burger and fries.

"Jake told me you'd be by," she said. "About some guy?"

Tiffany's eyes were an improbably bright shade of green, Winter wondering if she was wearing tinted contacts. Winter showed her the Gruse photo.

"Lenny something," she said right away. "Creep."

"You know him?"

"Not really. He's been in a few times. You want to talk to Melanie, they seemed close."

"Melanie? Not Melanie Upton, by any chance?"

"The one and only."

"Close? As in . . .?"

Tiffany started to say something, stopped, then said, "I can't say for sure. But there was at least one time he was here, in fact in this very booth, and they kind of got into it, you know what I mean? Intense. Not the sort of conversation you'd have with someone you didn't have—feelings for."

The dotted line between Gruse and Upton got a little darker in Winter's mind. Upton had told him she didn't even know Gruse. "Could he have just been coming on to her, and she was upset?"

Tiffany shrugged. "Look, I don't want to say anything bad about anyone . . ."

Winter had heard that a million times, a neon flashing sign screaming just the opposite. "But?"

Tiffany dropped her voice. "Melanie wasn't the nicest person."

"To customers?"

"I don't think she thought about the customers one way or another, except for getting tips. It was all about her. She was always stiffing the busboys their cut, hiding her cash tips, stuff like that."

Winter remembered what the other hostess had said. "Lying to Jake about going off for an audition?"

"I'm sure she did, we weren't that close."

"So she's not working here anymore?"

"She quit a while back, a few months maybe? After the whole press conference publicity stunt." When Winter looked blank, Tiffany said, "For the *Shock and Awe* show. Melanie came out of nowhere and kissed Jason Ayers in front of a million people."

"And this was a publicity stunt?"

"Sure. Another woman had been cast on the show, Melanie

dressed up like her, popped up on stage, and kissed Jason to make it look like the show was going to make a cast change."

"Melanie is going to get a role on *Shock and Awe*?"

"If she is, it hasn't happened yet. She might have just got paid to do it to create a little controversy, get some eyes on the show. They probably used her because she had a thing with Jason."

"You knew about that?"

"Who didn't? Melanie broadcast it all over the place."

Winter caught an undercurrent of jealousy in Tiffany's voice; he wasn't sure if it was over Upton's acting career or over Ayers. "Seems like a lot of actresses work here, you too?"

"I get some jobs. I'm more interested in directing some day."

Winter's lunch showed up, and he swung the fries around toward Tiffany. "Help yourself."

Tiffany took a fry and carefully took a bite, then used her finger to make sure she didn't leave any grease on her lip. "They do make good fries here."

Winter didn't want to eat while he was interviewing Tiffany, but he was hungry, and rationalized that she was eating too, munching on his fries. He took a bite, swallowed, and said, "Melanie not very friendly to you either?"

Tiffany gave a diffident shrug. "I didn't care one way or another."

"You think she had a role promised to her on the show? Or would she have done that thing at the press conference just for money?"

"Melanie Upton would do anything for Melanie Upton."

"Even hang out with a guy like Gruse?"

Tiffany eyed the fries, picked up a big one, broke it in two, and plopped it in her mouth. "If he had something she wanted."

WINTER LINGERED IN THE BOOTH after he had finished his lunch. The waitress had come by a few times to refill his Coke. The Café could make a burger and fries, but their coffee left a lot to be desired.

Tiffany was back at her hostess station. He'd learned a lot from her. For one thing, Upton had definitely known Gruse. Why had Upton lied about that? All she had to tell Winter was she had seen the guy a few times. The bartender at the Marquee, Kathy at the Irish pub, and now Tiffany had all admitted recognizing Gruse. Why hadn't Melanie Upton?

Winter watched as Tiffany led a group of four businessmen to a table, walking tall, looking downright elegant. Once she had them seated, the next customers in the restaurant were two younger guys in denim shirts and work pants. With them she smiled and laughed, a different woman.

She's an actress, thought Winter. She shifted her entire demeanor depending on the customer. It made him again wonder about Upton, getting into it with Gruse at the restaurant. Had that been an act? Was she playing Gruse the same way she had tried to play Winter, and probably played Ryder?

Of course, Tiffany might not be the best reference for Upton, there was definitely no love lost there. He needed to find out if Gruse had just come on to Upton like he had with other women, and she was blowing him off, or whether there was something else going on.

He left a big tip because the waitress had let him take up the table for so long.

WINTER PULLED UP in front of the house Gruse had lived in. He hadn't called ahead. Gruse's mother came to the door, her cheeks a little flushed, her eyes droopy, Winter remembering she liked her wine.

"Is it about Lenny?" she asked.

"I just wanted to fill you in on where we are," Winter said, which was half of why he was there. She held the door open for him and he caught a whiff of alcohol as he brushed by.

Winter declined her offer of a drink as she sat on the couch and picked up a wine glass. "I want you to know we are still working on getting you closure." He hated that term, but it was better than saying *your son's case*, like it was some book report. And he'd been told that people did, in fact, like to know the how and why, or thought they did. It wouldn't bring her son back either way. If Winter was in her shoes he'd be hunting down whoever harmed his kid and take care of it himself, but that was him. If some guy had touched Audrey, it would have been Winter cutting up his groin.

"I miss my Lenny so much," sniffled Gruse. "Why would someone do this to him?"

Another box popped into Winter's head: *revenge*. Lenny committing the assault on Upton, and someone making him pay the price. Ayers, perhaps. Or another boyfriend of Upton's, one Winter didn't know about yet. Or Upton's father, was he around?

Winter said, "We're trying to find that out." He wanted to ease into the question about Gruse's relationships with women. "Mrs. Gruse, you said you didn't know any friends Lenny might have made—"

"We hadn't been here that long, he was just getting settled."

"Sure. But I was wondering, did he mention a woman? Maybe a girlfriend, or a woman he was interested in?"

"My Lenny was a good looking boy, I'm sure he was going to have lots of woman friends."

"Did he mention a name?"

Gruse took a healthy swallow of her red. "Not that I recall. You know boys, it's not something they talk to their mother about." She gave Winter a full on look, a little sultry. "You have children?"

Winter shuddered, he was in her boyfriend's house talking about her dead son and she was trying to find out if he was married. "We have a daughter." No need to add that he was long since divorced.

"Maybe it's different with girls," said Gruse, back at her wine. "But Lenny didn't tell me anything."

WINTER DIDN'T BOTHER CALLING Ryder to fill him in. Ryder wouldn't think much of the possible tenuous connection between Gruse and Upton. Winter did want to ask Upton about why she had denied knowing Gruse; if Ryder wasn't willing to, Winter would do it himself.

He didn't want to fall into the trap of looking for connections between the two cases that didn't exist. Years ago he had solved two seemingly unconnected assaults by finding a hidden linkage, and soon thereafter, cleared two other unrelated cases that shared a surprising overlap. After that he had made the mistake of looking for possible connections in his next dozen cases, all for naught. He'd learned that everything wasn't connected, that there could be two murders on the same day in the same neighborhood with the same type of gun, but have nothing to do with each other. That didn't mean such crimes were random, it just meant they weren't connected. There was a big difference.

Upton was Ryder's case, but Winter had been drawn into it. So he'd continue to poke around, though. Gruse's mother didn't know anything about her son's friends, but someone had to. Two bartenders had remembered Gruse, why not a third?

Winter drove to the Hilton.

THE HILTON BAR was being used for some type of corporate function, a buffet table set up in the corner, a woman in a stark suit standing in front of a screen pointing at a chart. No one was behind the bar, so Winter stuck his head into the back room.

Two women in waitress uniforms, whose faces looked enough alike to be sisters, if sisters could be about the same age and almost a foot different in height, were talking to a gangly red headed guy. The guy said, "Help you?"

"I'm looking for the bartender."

"That would be me," said the red head.

"My name is Winter, Marburg police. Can we talk?" The two waitresses looked like they wanted to stay and listen in, and Winter didn't see why not, so he added, "Actually, you could all help me." He showed them the photo of Gruse. "Ever see him in here?"

"We mostly do setups for special events," said the taller waitress. "I don't remember him, but we aren't in the room much until everyone leaves."

"How about at the bar?" Winter asked.

The redhead shrugged. "I dunno. It gets pretty crowded."

"You get any regulars?"

"A few. Not him."

"You know Jason Ayers?"

"Sure," said both of the waitresses at the same time.

"Me too," said the bartender. "Most of the cast, they've been in."

"They mingle with the locals?"

"Jason does," said the bartender. "He grew up around here. Not Stevens or the others as much."

Winter flicked through to the photo of Upton. "Recognize her?"

"She's been around a lot," said the shorter waitress.

"At corporate events?"

"No, just, you know, around. I see her coming in the back entrance all the time, we have to park back there. I used to think she worked here."

"I've seen her too," said the taller woman. "I thought the same thing. I heard she's friends with Jason." She used her fingers to make air quotes when she said *friends*.

"You saw them together?"

"No, not really. Just heard some talk."

Winter turned to the bartender. "You?"

The red head's eyes flicked away. "Maybe. We get lots of women customers."

Winter could understand the bartender not remembering Gruse, but Upton would be hard to miss, especially if she had been around a lot.

"Okay, thanks." He turned to go, then said, "Hey, on the way in I noticed that the sternos were out in the hot tray."

"Damn," said the short waitress. "Thanks. Come on, we'd better get that, they'll be bitching about cold chicken."

Winter waited until they had left before he asked the bartender, "What's your name?"

"Glen."

"Glen, maybe something you didn't want to say about that woman in front of your co-workers?"

Glen glanced at the door. "I might have seen her."

"With Ayers?"

"No. I don't think they are together, that's just talk."

"How do you know?"

Glen's face flushed, making his freckles glow like a lying beacon.

"She's been at the bar a few times, I would have seen them together."

"She talk to you?"

"Sure. She's friendly."

That wasn't what Winter had been hearing, but he'd also seen how Upton could turn on the charm. What was it Tiffany had said? *When Melanie wanted something.* Winter wondered if Glen was slipping Upton free drinks. He knew the bars tracked the liquor, but there were ways around that. "She's nice to everyone?"

"Melanie's nice to me."

"Anyone she's not especially nice to?"

"Guys can get a little pushy with a good looking woman, you know what I mean? I see it all the time at the bar. Women have to deal with that."

"Anyone in particular hassling Melanie?"

Glen nodded toward the tablet. "The guy you showed us the picture of. He was here one night, bothering her."

"Trying to pick her up?"

"Not really. He was babbling about how she owed him something."

"Like money?"

"Or a favor. He wasn't making sense. I offered to throw him out, but Melanie was cool, she knew how to deal with him. He left pretty angry though. He was so pissed he threw a dish of peanuts, smashed it to bits."

"Huh." What could Gruse think that Upton might owe him? Money for a smoking gun photo of Jason Ayers, maybe? Or was it something personal, enough to get him all worked up? "You think this guy might have had some interest in Melanie?"

Glen stared at Upton's photo on the tablet. "Who wouldn't?"

CHAPTER 36

WINTER POKED HIS HEAD over Ryder's cubicle wall, betting himself that Ryder would be writing up his notes. He won. "You planning on writing a book?"

"You never know," said Ryder. "Or a screenplay. This Upton case has movie written all over it."

"Then you're going to love this." Winter gave Ryder an update on what he had discovered about both Gruse and Upton the night before at the Hilton. "She seems to have known him."

"You still on that? You're running around finding facts to support your theory. Have you asked your witnesses how many other guys were hounding Upton?"

"That's a good point," Winter conceded. "But I'm more interested in why she told me she didn't recognize Gruse."

"You think she remembers all the guys who hit on her?"

"Probably not. But I have two stories about her in a heated conversation with Gruse. Does that sound like just a guy hitting on her?"

"These witnesses any good?"

Winter shrugged. "Hit or miss. One might have been a little jealous, the other a little into her."

"See?"

"Look, we got a dead guy, and so far haven't found anyone who admits to really knowing him. Melanie Upton is the one person we know who talked to him, and not just to say hi. It's the best we got right now."

"You still think Gruse might have been the one who assaulted Upton?"

"It's still possible. We'll know more when we get the DNA test back. In the meantime, maybe we can press Upton, find out what she and Gruse were fighting about. Even if it's nothing, she might know some of his friends."

"Doesn't look like he had many."

"Which makes it all the more important to talk to Upton." Ryder gave him a look suggesting he was unconvinced, so Winter pressed, "Maybe Gruse was asking Upton about drugs. And if it was Gruse who did the assault, you'd have one hell of a screenplay."

"Now you're playing dirty," said Ryder, but he got up. "Let's go see Upton."

"Before we do that, maybe we talk to the sister again, Gigi? See if she knows anything about Gruse."

"Not a bad idea. She did tell me about Melanie and Jason. But she won't talk to us at work, she's skittish about cops being around. She's worried about losing her job."

"Let's go to her place after work."

"Don't you ever sleep?"

"It's overrated," said Winter. "Don't worry, I'll get Logan to okay your OT."

IF RYDER HADN'T DESCRIBED Gigi Doyle to Winter, he might not have recognized her as Melanie's sister. The features were similar, but the package had a different wrapper. Ryder had called her *mousy*, which certainly fit. She was wearing a white blouse, buttoned to the neck, with a long gray skirt.

Her eyes grew so wide they threatened to fill the frames of her small glasses. "Oh, hi."

Ryder said, "Miss Doyle, we—this is Detective Winter—have a few follow up questions for you, if you don't mind."

"I've already told you everything I know."

"This will only take a few minutes," said Winter. "Maybe you'd prefer to do this inside?"

Doyle looked over her shoulder, then at Winter, then back over her shoulder again before opening the door all the way. Winter was careful stepping past her, but Doyle shied away anyway.

Melanie Upton was half lying on the sofa in the living room, reading a magazine. She was barefoot, wearing a scooped tank top and jeans. If she was apprehensive about seeing Winter and Ryder she hid it well. "Are you two following me?"

"We're here to ask your sister a few questions," said Ryder.

"That sounds so ominous. You aren't asking me to leave, are you? After all, it's about me, isn't it?"

"Maybe it would be better—" said Ryder.

Winter cut Ryder off before he went full bore into formal cop mode. "We're actually following up on a case that might be related." He would have preferred to talk to Gigi separately as well, but the two sisters together might actually be an opportunity. Winter headed off any objection from Melanie by waving his tablet like a magician redirecting the audience. He pulled up the photo of Gruse and showed it to Gigi, angling the tablet so that Upton couldn't see.

"Do you know this man?" asked Winter.

Gigi's eyes darted from her sister to Winter to the tablet. Winter nudged the tablet a few inches closer. Gigi squinted at the photo, took off her glasses, squinted some more.

"Who is that?" asked Melanie. "Jason?"

"No," said Gigi.

"No, you don't know him?" prodded Winter.

"I don't think so," said Gigi. "Mel, it's not Jason."

Winter had the sense that Gigi wasn't as good an actress as her sister, but he couldn't be sure. If Melanie hadn't been in the room he would have asked Gigi if she'd seen Gruse with her sister, but that wouldn't work now. He turned to Melanie. "It's the same guy I showed you a photo of, the photographer."

Upton's eyes swung to her sister. "Why are you asking Gigi about him?"

"Maybe you should take another look," said Winter. "Both of you, actually."

Upton tossed her magazine aside and stood up. "Sure."

Winter picked up a subtle interplay between the sisters; Melanie confident and at ease, Gigi reticent and anxious, looking to her sister for guidance. As Melanie looked at the tablet Gigi shrunk back, just as she had when Winter had passed her at the door. These sisters were unalike in more than just looks.

Melanie gave the Gruse photo a quick glance. "That's the same photo you showed me when you were at my place, isn't it? By the way, thanks for installing my air conditioner, it works great."

Winter felt Ryder's testosterone rising, and marveled at how Melanie had offhandedly left the impression that Winter being at her apartment was inappropriate. *She's trying to play us off one another,* he thought. *Two can play that game . . .*

"Since you said you didn't pay attention to photographers, we thought Gigi might have remembered seeing him. Maybe when the two of you were at some event?"

"We don't go to many events together," said Melanie. "Do you have another shot of the guy? Sometimes it's hard to tell from one photo."

Winter had photos of a very deceased Gruse, but this wasn't the time to shoot that bullet. "Maybe this will help. I've talked to a few people who said you had an argument with him."

Melanie pursed her lip. "Argument?" She pointed at Winter. "Why are you talking to people about me? I'm the *victim*, remember?"

"You said you couldn't remember much about that night," said Ryder.

Melanie spun on him. "Not you, too. So what if I can't remember it all? Why are you asking around about me?"

"We weren't," said Winter. "We were asking about him." He pointed to the photo, then stuck the tablet in his cargo pocket. "Some people saw you two together."

"I can tell you, he's not someone I was *with*," said Melanie. She crossed the living room, picking up a bottle of wine off the coffee table and dangling an offer. "Can I pour you some wine?"

"We're on duty," said Ryder.

Gigi, half pressed against the wall, came alive. "Water? Tea? I can make coffee."

"No, thanks," said Winter. He took Gigi's offer as an invitation to amble into the living room. Melanie had settled back into the couch, giving of an air of extreme indifference, which Winter thought odd. Wouldn't a victim's first question for two policemen who showed up be about her assailant?

"So you don't remember any photographer you had a— disagreement with?"

"If I did, it would be about some photos, and I don't remember any disagreements with my photographers."

"So this guy didn't photograph you?" asked Ryder.

"Not that I know of," said Melanie. "Of course, I've been at parties, events, there are always photographers there. I don't really pay attention to them."

Winter strolled around the room, doing a casual recon. The place was spotless, about as different from Melanie's apartment as could be. No clothes strewn about, no dirty dishes, framed prints of flowers. A glass table along one wall was filled with photographs, a younger Melanie and Gigi with who Winter assumed was their mother. Even as preteens the different personalities of the two sisters came through in the photos, Melanie out front, comfortable, Gigi in her mother's shadow. No man in the photos.

"Maybe some other kind of disagreement?" Winter said, not turning. "Personal?"

"I still don't know why you are asking us these questions," said Melanie.

"The man is a victim—also a victim," said Ryder. "We're talking to anyone who might have known him."

"Might have? Did something happen to him?"

Winter winced. He missed Brooker, they were always more in sync during interviews. He and Ryder should have prepared. "Yes," he said, but didn't elaborate. He turned and hoped Ryder picked up on it. "So if you have any information, it would really help us."

"Does this mean you're not working on my case?" asked Melanie. "Is this guy more important?"

"We didn't say that," said Ryder. "I am the lead detective on both these investigations. Detective Winter is helping out."

"While Detective Ryder is bringing you up to date on your case, maybe I could use your bathroom?" asked Winter.

"Of course," said Gigi. "It's just down the hall."

"Great, thanks. If it's not too much trouble, can I take you up on that offer of coffee? I've got an insulated cup in the car, I could take it to go. It might be a long night and I hate the stuff at the station."

"Sounds like you don't want decaf. How do you take it?"

"Black is fine," said Winter, over his shoulder.

The last thing Winter needed was more coffee, but he wanted to get Gigi busy in the kitchen area, where she wouldn't be able to see down the hallway. Melanie was not telling the truth about Gruse, he just couldn't figure out why. All she had to do was say he was a photographer she had met, nothing suspicious there. It made him curious.

In the bathroom he did his usual rifling of the medicine cabinet and vanity. He always thought that you could learn as much about a person from their bathroom as you could reading their diary.

There were two toothbrushes on the vanity, one in a stand up holder, the other lying on the edge of the sink. The holder was squeaky clean, which took dedication. A fold down makeup kit hung over the back of the door. Winter didn't need to even unzip the pockets, they were all open. Perfume, lots of makeup, three different hairbrushes with gobs of hair caught in the bristles, five condoms, two different brands. On the vanity, one hairbrush that he doubted held a single hair, a pump dispenser of chemical free moisturizer, and a jar of makeup remover.

The drawers on the left side of the vanity were organized with military precision, a small array of makeup in one, a hairdryer in another, cotton balls and the usual assortment of bathroom items in the third. The top two drawers on the right side were the same. The bottom drawer was a nightmare, a drugstore mishmash, perfume, nail clippers, more matted hairbrushes, a jumble of makeup, a few brands the same as what was in the zippered kit.

Winter sat on the edge of the tub. The bathroom reflected the two sisters, one concerned about her appearance, but a bit sloppy, and the other pragmatic, organized. The makeup kit and the one messy drawer were undoubtedly Melanie's, suggesting she often stayed at Gigi's. That was odd, given she lived just on the other side of town. Of course, Gigi's place was nicer, and Melanie hadn't had air conditioning. Maybe she had hung out here on hot days.

Winter took advantage of the toilet, took one last look around as he washed his hands, and slipped out the door. He could hear Ryder droning on in the living room, no doubt trying to impress the sisters with his investigative prowess. Winter didn't mind at all, he'd have a few more minutes to look around.

Two more doors led off the hallway. Directly across from the bathroom the door was ajar enough for Winter to see a queen sized bed with a lavender spread, a closed door to what was probably a closet, and a short rack of neatly lined up dress shoes, mostly low heels. Winter stuck his head in another foot. On the dresser another family photo, this time just Gigi and Melanie. Gigi's bedroom.

The door at the end of the hall was closed. Winter risked a quick look. A small bedroom, a single bed along the wall, made up, a row of shelves filled with see through storage bins, each carefully labeled. A maple table against the wall held a laptop docking station. A home office and a guest room, probably where Melanie slept when she was there.

Winter was keeping track of time in his head, in another minute someone would no doubt wonder where he'd disappeared to. He looked back down the hall, thought *Fuck it*, stepped into the room. The storage bins were likely Gigi's and didn't interest him. Next to the bed was a small nightstand, and Winter eased the drawer open. Inside was a neat stack of travel brochures for Toronto and the Caribbean islands. A yellow sticky note said, *Need passport for some islands*. In a brown envelope Winter found an unused passport belonging to Gigi.

He straightened up the pile, eased the door shut, and walked back into the living room. Ryder had shut up, or maybe he was catching his breath. Melanie gave Winter a glance, but it was more of a *thank god you're back* as opposed to *what were you doing in there* look, so Winter ignored her and went over to the counter. Gigi had laid out a full coffee service, mugs, Styrofoam to go cups, matching creamer and sugar bowl, polished silverware. Another difference between the sisters, Gigi as hostess.

"Thanks," said Winter. "Smells great. I'll just take some to go, if that's okay." Bustling over the coffee, Gigi looked comfortable for the first time since they had arrived. Winter turned back to Melanie. "Where were we? The arguments you had with Mr. Gruse?"

Melanie wagged her finger at Winter. "You've been talking to Tiffany."

"We've been talking to a lot of people."

Melanie curled her legs up under her on the cushion. "Now I remember. A guy in the restaurant was hitting on me—they do it all the time. Tiffany was always bitching that no one asked *her* out, though, so I pointed him at her. That must have been the guy, what did you say his name was? Gruse? I don't remember him mentioning being a photographer, I tune all that out. Tiffany was pissed, so she made it sound like I was having a fight with him."

"Why was she pissed?"

"Because the guy was a loser. I figured they were made for each other."

WINTER HATED TO WASTE the coffee, but if he drank it he'd be up all night, and not just from the caffeine. He took a sip in penance then poured the rest out on the street, down below the level of the car, in case Gigi was looking out the window.

Ryder, who'd come in his own car, paused with his door open. "Melanie sounded pretty convincing. Gruse was just hitting on her, like a lot of other guys. A woman that good looking, they probably don't even register. Your witness was just jealous."

"Tiffany isn't the only one who saw her with Gruse. There's the bartender at the Hilton."

"So she goes to the Hilton bar. Big deal. And if Gruse was the one who assaulted her, she'd want to tell us about it. Hell, if she was hazy about the particulars, just showing her Gruse's picture should have rang an alarm in her head. I'm telling you, there's nothing there."

Winter wasn't so sure.

CHAPTER 37

WINTER WAS IN COURT all the next morning, the lawyers taking turns asking for short delays that turned into hours. Before he even got called to the stand a plea bargain had been worked out.

Back at the station Gracie handed him a stack of phone messages. "Andie left something on your desk."

Winter flipped through the messages, nothing that couldn't wait. He said hello to Cindy in her cubicle, nodded to O'Dowd and Ryder, and got some coffee from the break room. He never drank coffee before court, and he needed a hit. As he poured the station swill he regretted dumping out the coffee Gigi Doyle had made, he could have saved it for iced.

The blue folder report from the lab was on his desk. A sticky note cautioned *Preliminary* with three underlines. Winter read through the technical jargon for an entire two minutes, a record for him, then punched Andie up on speed dial.

"Don't tell me," she said, "you finished reading, and have a question on what locations they are going to do the tagging on for the PCR run."

"You could have another career as a stand up comic, as long as your audiences are filled only with geeky lab technicians."

"Hey, be glad I know some lab technicians, otherwise we wouldn't have even got that prelim. It hasn't gone through review, so you can't really use it for anything."

"But you gave it to me anyway."

"Right. The full DNA match is not done, but there are useful findings. First, as you know, your Upton victim definitely had recent sex. There is foreign—meaning not belonging to her—DNA from her swabs. Second, there was lubricant from a condom. There was no semen on the internal swab, but there was some on the external swabs."

Winter processed it. "So she had sex the night before, probably within twelve hours, give or take?"

"See? You don't even need me. I'll just have the lab send you the final report."

"Is this where I'm supposed to say something about how indispensable you are?"

"At the least. A raise would be nice."

"Not my department. So what we are waiting for now is—"

"The DNA typing. That's what they'll compare to the Gruse sample, which they are already tagging."

"Can you get me the preliminary results of that before it goes through all the review process?"

"I guess you do need me, after all. I'll have to put my stand up career on hold." Andie sighed and hung up.

Winter put his feet up on the desk. So Melanie Upton had been with a man during the night, or prior evening, of her reported assault. That didn't exactly prove she was assaulted, but it certainly led some credibility to her story. It could have been Jason Ayers who'd she been with prior to the assault, or Ayers could have been the man who assaulted her. But without her specifically naming Ayers as her attacker, Winter had no way to compel Ayers to give up his DNA.

Winter stuck his head in Ryder's cubicle. "Preliminary report from the lab confirms Melanie Upton had sex the night before she called 911. Too early for a specific match to Gruse or anyone else."

"I'm betting it's in the *anyone else* category. As in anyone else but Gruse."

"Could be. I'll go back at the witnesses, see if Upton's story holds up. Tiffany didn't mention anything about Gruse getting sent to her by Upton. If Tiffany thought Upton played a trick on her, she might be mad enough to say Upton and Gruse fought."

"It still could be Ayers," said Ryder. "I called the bed and breakfast where Ayers and Mance supposedly hooked up that night. They are very protective of the identity of their guests. We'll need a subpoena, and right now I don't see how we'd get one. I'm going to go back at Ayers, see who booked the room. Won't tell us much, though, unless a witness will put Ayers there all night."

"You not buying his Suzanne Mance alibi?"

"The test said Melanie slept with someone, right? Who says Ayers couldn't have been with her before heading out to see Mance? He'd want to keep that one quiet, so it makes sense they'd meet up late, someplace out of the way."

"Busy guy."

"Lucky guy. I should have been an actor."

"You can still start," said Winter. "Listen, you just gave me an idea. What if Ayers found out that someone had seen him with Mance? That might screw up his career. I bet Michael Stevens could make Ayers's life miserable on the set. Not to mention ruining Ayers's image with Ashley Hanna."

"A witness at the bed and breakfast?"

"Maybe. Or—what if Gruse had a photo of Ayers with Mance? We know he took celebrity shots. He could have been following Ayers around and got it by accident. Or he found out about Mance being on the east coast, and was taking photos of her, and he caught a shot of Ayers."

Ryder said, "I didn't see any photos of Suzanne Mance in Gruse's stash."

"If they were special, he might have hid them. Gruse was into the whole celebrity scene. He'd know he had something good. He could have been blackmailing Ayers."

"You thought Gruse had a photo of Ayers assaulting Melanie. Now you think he might have a photo of Ayers with Mance. Which is it?"

"It doesn't matter. I'm not trying to prove a theory, I'm trying to find a motive. Blackmail is a good motive."

"It's another stretch," said Ryder, dismissively.

"It won't be if we can find some connection between Ayers and Gruse. And find out exactly what Ayers was doing at the time Gruse was killed."

Ryder picked up a stack of papers. "Gruse's call logs."

Winter, looking over Ryder's shoulder as he ran down the list, jabbed a finger at the page. "That's the main number of the Hilton."

"You think if Gruse was blackmailing Ayers he'd call the main number?" Ryder sounded skeptical.

"He probably wouldn't have Ayers's cell phone." Winter had another thought. "Unless Melanie Upton gave it to him. Maybe she and Gruse were in on it together. Upton fakes an assault by Ayers, Gruse takes an incriminating photo to use as blackmail. That's what they could have been arguing about. The Hilton bartender said Gruse was claiming she owed him something. Maybe his share of the payoff."

"First you think Gruse assaulted Upton, and now you think they are partners?"

"I don't think anything. Just looking for connections."

"Ayers didn't sound like a guy being blackmailed."

"Although he *was* nervous about his relationship with Mance being outed." Winter slapped Ryder on the back. "This is your big chance, you can follow up with Mance, dig into that alibi, and also see if she lets slip that Ayers was worried about anything. Some pillow talk."

"You think Logan will spring for a trip to California?" said Ryder, a hint of hopefulness.

"Won't hurt to ask," said Winter, turning quickly to hide his laughter. Ryder had as much chance of Logan approving a trip to California as Winter did of winning the lottery. Which was zero, since he never played.

RYDER HADN'T SEEN Logan all day, so he stopped at Gracie's desk. "You expecting the Captain today?"

"No. He's in Boston at a conference on new crime technology, something about databases."

"Yeah?" Ryder wondered why Logan hadn't mentioned it to him, since he was the only detective who knew anything about modern crime solving techniques. The conference was probably a boondoggle, a bunch of old school brass drinking on the public dime.

"He'll be back Monday," said Gracie.

Ryder wondered if he should call Logan, try to get approval for a trip. He could still catch a late flight if he hurried. He could interview Mance and have a weekend in California.

Of course, he'd have to find out if Mance was even going to be there, which meant calling her, and then Logan would wonder why he didn't just conduct the follow up interview on the phone.

Ryder's eyes drifted to a framed photo on Gracie's desk. Gracie, a man he assumed was her husband, two teenage daughters. "Your kids?"

"Trish and Janet. It's a few years old, they are both in college now."

"You've been here a while, haven't you?"

"Sometimes it seems like forever. Why?"

"Nothing, I just don't know that many people yet. I see them in the station, but not much away from the job. I'm guessing a lot of the detectives have families."

"Captain Logan has four kids, all grown and married. O'Dowd has three. Leary and Owens are single—Owens is divorced. Winter is too, he has a daughter, but you must know that."

"I met her. She's—different from him."

Gracie laughed. "Detective Winter is one of a kind."

"So everyone keeps telling me. I meant that his daughter—I wouldn't have guessed they were related."

Gracie shrugged. "I've met her a few times, she seems pretty nice to me."

Nice, and smart, and elegant, and modern, thought Ryder. Everything that Winter wasn't.

WINTER FOLLOWED THE SIGNS for the Lakeview Apartments office. He'd been bothered by the discovery that Melanie had probably spent enough time at her sister's apartment to have her own drawer in the bathroom. He'd read in Ryder's notes that Gigi traveled often, and wondered if Upton used the Lakeview apartment when her sister was away. The two sisters were so different in personality that Winter couldn't see them hanging out, although he couldn't be sure. His sister

Beth didn't hang out with him growing up, but it might be different with women.

The entire complex was professionally landscaped, upscale. Winter wasn't one to obsess about where he lived, but given a choice, the Lakeview was certainly preferable to Upton's walk up, especially before she had air conditioning.

If Winter thought that way, so would Jason Ayers. *More of a Four Seasons* guy, he'd been told. Ayers on the Executive Floor of the Hilton, meeting Mance at a what was likely an expensive B&B. If Upton wanted to hook up with Ayers, he might not want to go to her dingy apartment, or even take the chance of her being seen in his room at the Hilton.

But Winter bet Ayers would go to the Lakeview.

Inside the office, a pretty woman greeted him warmly, her smile not fading even when she found out that Winter wasn't there to rent an apartment. She was wearing a tailored suit that looked expensive, with small diamond stud earrings and a slim set of pearls. Her blond hair, showing just a trace of darker roots, was pulled back, not severely, a perfect representative for a high end building.

"No trouble, I hope?" she said. "I'm Alison Little, the complex manager. I haven't heard about a call to the police."

"No, not recently. Probably nothing to do with the complex. Just tracking down if a certain person might have been around here."

"We don't have much trouble with crime."

"Still, would you mind if I showed you a few photos?" Winter pulled out the tablet, decided to start with Gruse.

"I don't think I've seen him. I hope you don't have to go door to door."

"That shouldn't be necessary. Although maybe you have some employees who are outside a lot? I doubt anyone I'm looking for would have come in the office."

"You could ask the groundskeepers."

"Have you had any reports of thefts? People noticing their gardens trampled? Strangers?"

Little pulled a clipboard out of the desk drawer. "Here's every report we get. I log it and transfer everything to a database once a week for the insurance company. Just in case." She offered the clipboard to Winter. "You're free to look. We haven't had anything serious in four months, a car stolen from the lot. That was reported to the police, they never found the car. We set up additional security cameras on the lots, and since then nothing. Other than that, some kids left a few beer bottles in the service alley back in June."

Winter flipped through the pages. "What's this? 'Note to super about prowler.'" The notation was dated a few weeks ago.

"The superintendent found a note in the overnight box about a prowler being spotted one night. It was typed and unsigned, without any specifics. Wait, I have it." Little pulled a folder out of the desk drawer and handed Winter a single sheet of paper.

It read: 'I saw a man peeking in windows on the back side of the building and thought you should know in case he tries to break in.'

"Anything come of this?" asked Winter.

"The note is so vague. We have over two hundred units here, and without more to go on . . ."

Winter filled in the rest. They didn't want to upset the residents. "Could I see your security video if I needed to?"

"Of course. We just have coverage of the public areas though. The main entrance, the parking areas."

Winter swiped to Ayers's photo. "How about this man?"

"That's Jason Ayers, right? He's been here."

"What? Are you sure?"

"I saw him myself. I was showing a unit and he was standing in the parking lot talking on his cell phone. I was frankly hoping he was here to rent a unit. I read they are shooting his show locally and I thought he might want a place to stay. But he never came into the office. After I finished with the showing he was gone, so I just figured he was here to meet someone."

"Which part of the lot?"

Little pointed. "Back on that side, near the corner."

Which was near Doyle's apartment. "Was this recently?"

"No, not at all." Little stared into space. "A few months, at least. Back when all the news about Jason Ayers and his show was flying around. I'm not sure I would have recognized Ayers, except that his picture was all over the papers. So sometime around then."

Winter thanked her, got directions to where he might find the groundskeepers, and stepped back outside. So Jason Ayers was at the Lakeview, maybe hooking up with Melanie Upton. Ayers had probably lied about seeing her because he was afraid it would give credence to her story that they were still together, and even to her insinuation that he had assaulted her.

Winter found two groundskeepers trimming bushes behind the office. Though it was warm, both wore long sleeved shirts and work pants. A portable radio was tuned to a Spanish broadcast.

"Miss Little said you might be able to help me," said Winter. Seeing a look of wariness in their eyes, so he added, "it's not about you. Just wondering if you've seen this man." He showed them the Ayers photo.

Both men shook their heads. "I don't think he lives here," said one, in English.

"No, he doesn't. Maybe a visitor?" That only got Winter more head shakes. Winter pulled up Upton's photo. "How about her?"

"I've seen her quite a few times."

"Do you know who she was visiting?"

"Miss Gigi, the nice one, in the corner apartment. She hires us on weekends in the spring to help with her garden."

"And you never saw the guy I showed you with her?"

The two men exchanged a look. "No—but with other guys, sometimes. One of them had a bike, a motorcycle."

"You sure?"

"Yes. He went into Miss Gigi's in the middle of the day, and we talked about that since—since Miss Gigi never has men over. So when we saw the biker guy at her door, we kind of kept an eye out, you know? Making sure she was okay. But it was that woman," the groundskeeper pointed at the Upton photo on the tablet, "who came to the door. She let him in, so we figured everything was good."

"Did you see him leave? Or notice anything about him?"

"Not really. He had on a leather jacket. No colors. White guy, long hair. We just saw him from the back."

The other groundskeeper said something in Spanish, and Winter waited while they hashed it out. Then the guy who had done all the talking in English, said, "Rafael says he noticed the guy's bike had a yellow flag on the back." More Spanish. "Not a sticker flag, an actual flag."

THE MARBURG RALLY CLUB was housed in the back of Harry's Custom Wheels. Winter hadn't been there, but he'd seen bikes around the city with different colored flags and had asked a uniform who was a bike nut what they meant. The uniform told Winter there was a local bike club that did rallies, a follow directions contest, and the bikers competing often used flags to identify their teams. That led Winter to the rally club, and Harry's.

The parking lot was jammed with cars, but many of them looked like they'd been there for a while; stickers on the windows, missing fenders. A half dozen stacks of rusty used rims were balanced precariously along the side wall. The lot continued toward the back, enclosed with a high chain link fence, the whine of a spinning air wrench splitting through the air.

The front room was filled with enough chrome to blind him; it reminded Winter of those vintage cars with the big flashy bumpers, big Cadillacs . . . Gruse drove a Caddy, Winter had forgot to ask the groundskeepers about Gruse. Maybe he'd met Upton at the Lakeview. Weird, he'd asked everyone else, how had he forgotten that? That was a couple of times now something had slipped his mind, maybe Ryder was right, he did need more sleep. He didn't *feel* old, but maybe he was *getting* old . . .

Two guys were sitting on mismatched sofas in the corner, looking at car magazines. They glanced at Winter, then went back to their reading. At the counter, a clerk was talking to a customer about a detailing job, but the clerk's eyes kept drifting to Winter. The clerk had longish dark blond hair and wore a leather vest over a plain white tee shirt. Winter half listened to the discussion, he didn't have all day, but he didn't want to hustle a paying customer out either.

The shop was stuffy, uncomfortable enough to drive off customers. Hell of a way to run a business, thought Winter. He'd worn his hoodie to cover his gun, as usual. He slipped out of it, folding it haphazardly over his arm, more or less over his gun.

Winter was shaking his head over the price of a set of Asanti's when he heard the clerk say, "I'll have to check with the boss about that." Winter turned just in time to see the back of the leather vest as it disappeared through a door behind the counter. The customer, a little guy with tortoise shelled glasses, looked confused.

"You scare him off?" asked Winter.

"He said he had to go check on something, but I didn't even ask him a question."

"Let me see if I can find out what's up," said Winter. The two magazine readers were looking at him. "You two work here?"

"Just waiting for our wheels to be installed."

Winter half nodded, slipping behind the counter. He pushed on the door, it was not only closed but double locked, a thick steel job that seemed overkill for the shop. Winter fast walked back outside, tossed his hoodie on his car roof, and followed the lot around toward the back. The air wrench whined again, the compressor kicking in. Winter kept close to the building, warily eyeing the columns of used rims.

The wrench cut off suddenly, but the compressor ran on. Winter waited a few seconds, not happy with the noise. It droned on far longer than it should have, another sound barely audible, a bike starting up . . .

A sudden roar as the bike came around the corner from the back of the building, swerving to avoid Winter, a booted foot scraping the oily pavement for balance, and then blowing past. Winter caught a sight of a bearded face and dark hair as he jumped out of the way. Winter was reaching for his gun as he turned, half expecting another bike, and sure enough one revved. Winter flatted himself against the fence, but no bike. He took three quick steps so he could see around the building.

The back lot was a junkyard of cars and more rims, piled ten feet high. A large bay door was closed, the compressor banging away inside. Winter caught movement in the corner of the lot, a flash of brown, a large mixed breed dog on a chain, the dog focused on Winter, barking. Winter angled toward the garage door, one eye on the dog. The growl of the bike grew louder, coming from inside. The door started to move up, a chrome wheel poking out of the darkness.

A rapid fire series of shots, immediately followed by loud pings behind Winter. He ducked instinctively, trying to look forward at the garage and behind him at the same time, just as he felt a searing pain along the side of his left calf. His gun was out, but there was no one to shoot at behind him, just the crush of cars and rims. Someone in a car?

He didn't have time to wonder, the door was all the way open, another series of shots, wild, the bike flying out, the rider flailing with a short rifle, spraying shots, glass breaking behind Winter, relentless pings off metal. Winter dove behind a pile of rims, the bullets ricocheting like angry bees.

The compressor cut off with a gurgle as the bike screamed out the garage. Winter got off two quick shots, aiming low toward the tires, he couldn't risk standing up, he'd be cut to shreds. The bike spun out, Winter's face almost on the ground, seeing the rider fight to keep the bike up, the biker winning the battle, lining it up to run the gauntlet between Winter and the fence. Winter didn't have another shot even if he dared stand up, a hundred rims between him and the biker, still firing in Winter's direction.

Winter shimmied up, squeezed between the wall and the rims, another shot whistling by his head. Winter could hear, but not see, the bike start its run to freedom. He leaned back into the wall, braced his feet against the tall pile of rims, and pushed.

The heavy wheels tottered, and like a slow motion building collapse in an earthquake, crashed down onto the pavement. Winter slid to the next tower and pushed again, then the next, as fast as he could move.

The shooting stopped, the bike stalled out, buried under an avalanche of wheels. An arm grew out of the pile like a zombie, the hand twisted grotesquely. An ancient Tec 9 lay in the well of a rim a few feet away.

Winter gingerly picked his way toward the body, which hadn't moved. With his gun in one hand, he picked up the Tec 9, which wouldn't be doing any more firing, its shroud crushed into the barrel so hard it was bent.

Winter had to move three wheels to find the biker's head, which was twisted even more awkwardly than his hand. Winter felt for a pulse, couldn't be sure, he was never good at that. Maybe a weak one. The guy's eyes were closed.

Winter stepped back, called it in, then began heaving the rims off the biker.

CHAPTER 38

THE BIKER'S INJURIES turned out to look much worse than they were, which was fortunate for the biker, whose name turned out to be Gus Woodson. Fortunate for Winter too; there would be enough paperwork as it was.

They both ended up in the Midregions Hospital ER at the same time, Winter getting his leg treated by a single nurse, who had cleaned and wrapped where his calf had been grazed. Woodson, with a concussion, a broken pelvis, arm, and wrist, had enough doctors to outfit a small clinic.

James O'Dowd, who everyone called Jimmy because he looked to be about eighteen and had for the last twenty years, was dodging the nurse who was checking Winter's bandage. O'Dowd, who had a pasty complexion that blended into the cream wall paint, couldn't stand still.

"Man, I owe you," said O'Dowd. "I mean, I just got put on this chop shop case, and I've read a thousand pages of Ryder's notes—where does he get the time? Anyway, we've basically got nothing, I'm pissed when Logan puts me on it. We've known the Geary brothers have been moving the parts, but since we've been on to them they're not doing it at their shop, but cars are still getting chopped up. I mean, we've got *nothing*. We can't find where they are breaking down the cars. And then, boom, just like that, you find it." O'Dowd shook his head at his own luck. "I'm going to look like a fucking genius, just because I found that hidden below ground garage." He stopped suddenly, the nurse running into him again. "Ryder is going to be pissed."

Winter, who knew all this, and would have far preferred to be chatting with the pretty nurse, who reminded him of one of his high school girlfriends, or at least what he imagined she would have looked like twenty years later, didn't begrudge O'Dowd his enthusiasm. And yes, Ryder was going to be pissed.

"I wasn't there for the chop shop," said Winter. The nurse was taking an uncommonly long time to check his bandage, Winter hoping it was because she was more interested in him than some cop story. "Moron, shooting at a cop over auto theft."

"Sometimes you just get lucky," said O'Dowd. "I mean, I got lucky, you got shot."

"Thank god he couldn't shoot worth a damn. Not that you can hit anything with a Tec 9. Where'd he get it, at a flea market? Although a few more minutes and I would have been ricocheted to death." Winter smiled at the nurse, but she'd turned to O'Dowd.

"How did you find this secret garage?" she asked, clearly more interested in his story than in Winter.

O'Dowd warmed back to his tale faster than a relief pitcher. "There was this air compressor, see? And they had these extra hoses going down through a pipe. I thought, who runs a compressor line into the floor? So I looked around and found a way down, it was actually under the compressor, which was on wheels. They had a ramp leading outside that came out inside a trailer."

"Pretty impressive," said the nurse.

"That's not the half of it. There was a guy down there working on a car. Know what he says to me? 'Officer, we have receipts for everything in the showroom.' While he's pulling the engine from a Lexus."

"He's the guy who told you about Woodson?" asked Winter.

"Yeah. He gave it up pretty quick once he found out that Woodson had shot at you. He told me that Woodson worked on some of the rally bikes on the side."

Winter translated that as *off the books*. He doubted the entire IRS could track down all the off the books work that was being done just within Marburg.

Winter stood up, testing the leg, it wasn't bad, he'd had worse. Although it would itch like hell for a week. "I need to find out if Woodson ever took those rally bikes out himself. The bike he was running on didn't have a flag."

Winter gave the nurse one last look, but she had turned her adoring brown eyes on O'Dowd.

WINTER MET UP with Ryder in the hospital cafeteria, Winter with a coffee, Ryder a diet Pepsi.

"He give you anything?" asked Winter. Woodson fit the description of the man the groundskeepers had seen at the Lakeview, but so did a hundred other bikers.

"Only if you count mumbling, pissing and moaning about the pain, and constantly asking if his lawyer had arrived."

"Cheer up, you'll still get credit for clearing up the chop shop."

"What's it going to look like? I'm working on it for months, it gets thrown to O'Dowd, and he busts it open in a week."

"Just luck, that's all."

"How did you end up there, anyway?"

Winter filled Ryder in on his trip to the Lakeview. "So now we know for sure Upton was having men over at Gigi's. What if Melanie got assaulted by this Woodson guy? That would explain why he was desperate enough to shoot at me. He might have been thinking I was coming for him over a rape."

"I'll buy it that Melanie stayed at the Lakeview, but it's her sister's apartment, nothing odd about it. It's also a much better place to entertain her boyfriends."

Winter asked, "Did you find out if Goodson had a record?"

"Theft, robbery, a few drug possessions, but no assault or rape. Not even charges."

"So maybe he's seeing Upton, she invites him to the Lakeview, he spots some easy pickings, comes back one night . . ."

"And assaults a woman who is already giving it to him?"

"Maybe she broke up with him."

"She seems to have a lot of men," said Ryder. "Still could have been Ayers. Or anyone else chasing her around."

Who else did they know had been with Upton? Another piece of the puzzle fell into place in Winter's head. "Lenny Gruse was in a bar fight that night. He could have easily made it to the Lakeview to assault her. Or if he was in on some blackmail scheme, Upton might even have let him in."

"I still don't buy that."

"I'm not sure I do, either," admitted Winter. "But if Upton was seeing men at the Lakeview, that's where she could have met up with Ayers too. You said it yourself, she'd be more likely to hook up there. So she might have been assaulted at her sister's, instead of at her own place."

Ryder scratched his head. "Why wouldn't she just say that?"

Ryder's scratching was infectious, Winter reaching for his calf, getting no relief with the bandage in the way. "That's a good question. Don't you find it odd that when she talks to us she claims she can't remember much about that night, but she has no problem implying on television that it might have been Ayers? I mean, does she think it's Ayers or not?"

"Maybe it was him, and like she said, she doesn't want to get him in trouble."

"Seems she's dragging him through the mud anyway. Either way, someone isn't telling the truth here. Ayers told us he wasn't with Melanie any more. Then why was he at the Lakeview? That witness seemed pretty credible."

Ryder sucked on the remnants of his ice cubes. "If it's Ayers, or Woodson, that would ruin your theory of this having anything to do with Gruse."

"It's not a theory, just a possibility. Gruse could have assaulted Upton, and she killed him." Winter was still mad at himself for forgetting to ask the groundskeepers if they'd seen Gruse at the Lakeview. He'd have to go back.

"Just because you can make up a story doesn't mean that's the way it went down."

"You're right," said Winter, getting up. "So let's figure out what happened to Upton once and for all."

"You want to go back at Melanie?"

"Later. She's an actress, she could be lying through her teeth and doing a better job than everyone else who lies to us. I think we're more likely to get something out of her sister if we can get her alone."

"I have a few ideas about the drug angle. I talked to a guy I met a few years ago, he was on a New England drug task force. He said that the whole celebrity crowd in California is into a different class of drugs than we see here. More opioids, not just oxy, but fentenyl. Gruse might have thought he could move it here, get it from his contacts in Los Angeles."

Winter didn't think that had much merit, but it was as good a theory as any, and it could certainly get Gruse killed. Plus, he wanted to have a crack at Gigi Doyle alone. "Okay, you want to run that down? I'll go see the sister. Then we can tackle Ayers together."

Ryder crunched his last ice cube. "Works for me."

WINTER KNEW GIGI DOYLE was nervous about having cops show up at her job, so that's why he was standing outside her office building; nothing like a nervous witness to loosen the lips.

The office building, a ten story gleaming rehab in Marburg's city center, even had a Starbucks in the lobby, part of a three outlet food court. Winter didn't know enough about business to figure out whether that meant he should buy Starbucks stock or sell it. That is, if he owned any stocks. Or maybe he did, Audrey managed his savings. He didn't really follow closely, nodding when she tried to explain what she was doing with the thousand dollars he sent her every month. His house was paid for, he didn't have any expensive hobbies, and as he'd been told many times, his wardrobe hadn't changed in years, allowing him to put a small chunk of his salary away.

Gigi Doyle worked for a company called Axionics, which meant nothing to Winter. The reception area on the eighth floor was high tech steel and glass. A receptionist as cold as the furnishings frowned at Winter's cargo pants.

"I'm here to see Gigi Doyle," he said.

The receptionist peered out of impossibly small glasses. "Do you have an appointment?"

"No, but if you tell her that Robert Winter is here, I'm sure she'll see me." Winter gave the receptionist his warmest smile, but she wasn't buying it.

"I'll see if she's in."

Winter had purposely not identified himself as the police. That was a card he wanted to hold over Doyle's head.

The receptionist murmured into her headset, and Winter drifted over toward the double glass doors which led into the offices. Directly across the corridor was a conference room, empty. He could see twenty feet or so down the hall. An exit sign over a doorway suggested an internal staircase. Doyle could avoid him by taking the stairs if her office wasn't on this floor.

"Miss Doyle will be out in a moment." The receptionist didn't sound happy, which might have been her normal state of mind.

It was more than a moment, Winter again wondering if Doyle had skipped. When she finally appeared she looked even more nervous than when Winter had seen her at her apartment. She stood on the other side of the glass door, one hand over her chest, the other on the door handle, as if deciding whether to come out.

She finally opened the door a few inches. "I'm very busy," she whispered, her eyes jumping between Winter and the receptionist. "What do you want?"

Winter kept his voice low. "We can have this conversation here, or in private. Your choice."

For a second Winter thought she was going to pull the door shut and run inside. He stepped even closer, nudging her with his presence. "I haven't told anyone I'm with the police. Yet."

That did the trick. Doyle stepped out into the reception area, shrinking past Winter. "Can we go downstairs?"

"Sure."

They rode the elevator in silence, Doyle clutching at her jacket. In the lobby Winter sat her down in a corner table in the food court.

"Why did you have to come to my office?"

"Because you haven't been honest with me, and I need answers fast."

"But people will be talking. The receptionist is a gossip."

"Tell her I'm your boyfriend. After all, you've been having all sorts of men at your apartment, everyone knows that."

"I have not!"

Winter leaned over her. "See? You're lying again. I've got witnesses who say you have."

Doyle's head was shaking so hard it looked like a shiver. "I never have men at my place, who said that?"

"Look, Gigi—do you mind if I call you Gigi?—it would normally not be any of my business who you sleep with. But when one of your boyfriends turns out to be a felon . . ."

Now Doyle looked like she was going to cry. "It's not true, I don't know any—felons. I haven't had anyone at my place, I swear."

Winter felt a moment of remorse, fought it off. If Doyle was going to crack, now would be the time. "And not only a felon who's been in prison—he shot me."

"What?"

"Yep." Winter put his foot up on the chair and pulled up his pant leg. "Fortunately for me he just got me in the leg. We have him in custody. If you had anything do to with this . . ."

Doyle's shock turned into an explosion of tears. "Why are you doing this to me?"

Winter dropped his leg off the chair, using the opportunity to scratch at his bandage. He softened his tone. "I'm trying to help you, give you a chance to explain yourself in private. Detective Ryder wanted to drag you out of your office in handcuffs, bring you down to the station."

Doyle grabbed at the napkin holder, the napkins jammed in so tight she tore a handful before pulling one out, pressing it into her eyes. "I don't know what you're talking about. Any of it."

"Not even about Jason Ayers being at your apartment? We have a witness for that too."

"I haven't seen Jason in years! He's Melanie's friend."

If Doyle was an actress she was even better than her sister. "Gigi, I'm giving you one last chance, then we'll do it Detective Ryder's way. I know of at least two men who were at your apartment. The guy who shot me—he's a biker, his name is Gus Woodson. And Jason Ayers." Winter hovered over her. If he got any closer someone in the food court was going to call the cops.

"Melanie," she whispered. "I think Mel sees men there when I'm traveling."

Which is exactly what Winter suspected, but he needed to hear her say it. He sat down, giving her some space. "See? That wasn't so hard."

Doyle pulled another napkin, not drying her tears, just tearing it into little pieces, avoiding Winter's eyes. "Why are you asking me instead of Melanie?"

"I will, but she hasn't exactly been truthful, either. See, what I think is that Melanie didn't get assaulted at her apartment at all."

Doyle's head snapped up, her lip quivering. "You don't?"

That was interesting, thought Winter. Why didn't she say *'Of course she did'*? He changed his line of questioning. "No. I think she got assaulted at your place, by this guy Woodson, and she blamed it all on Jason Ayers to get some publicity."

Doyle's hesitated a few heartbeats too long before she said, "No, no, that's not true."

"Which part?"

Doyle's eyes turned down, her voice barely audible. "I swear to you, Melanie did not get assaulted at my place. I was there that night and she wasn't."

Winter waited her out, but she didn't elaborate. He couldn't think of a reason why she would lie, but he also couldn't figure out why Upton would be lying either. Something was off about all this. "And Jason? Did Melanie make that assault story up about him?"

"She never said he did or didn't. I already told you they had a thing. She said she was confused. Why can't you leave it at that?"

Because Lenny Gruse is dead, thought Winter. "How about other men? Did your sister have anyone else over?"

"I don't know. I really don't. She has a key, I know she stayed there sometimes when I was away, she didn't have air conditioning. Who Melanie dates is none of my business."

"Can you prove you were there the night Melanie says she was assaulted?"

"I'm not sure. Why should I have to?"

If she could, thought Winter, then maybe Melanie got assaulted at her own apartment, just like she said she did. By Jason Ayers. Or not assaulted at all. If either of those were true, then why was Gigi Doyle so nervous? He'd have to go back at Ayers.

"It might come to that," said Winter, trying to sound ominous. It didn't take much, Doyle had torn up the last napkin, a rat's nest of paper on the table. "If there's something else you want to tell me, now's the time. Our next conversation will probably take place in a police station."

Doyle stared at her hands for a long time. When she looked up her lip was set in a hard line. "You're a very mean man, did you know that?"

CHAPTER 39

Now that her apartment was blessedly cool, Melanie noticed its other shortcomings even more. Time to get out. Out of her apartment, out of Marburg. Her agent, Stanlish, kept dangling possibilities, yet nothing worthwhile had materialized, just amateur work. She had turned down two commercials and even an audition for a locally produced documentary, that just wasn't the image she was trying to create.

Maybe Stanlish was expecting her to put out, although he hadn't given her that vibe. Still, he was a guy, and Melanie was sure it wouldn't have been the first time he'd charged that fee. She had hoped she was past that.

Her money was running out; soon she wouldn't be able to buy the better wine she'd been drinking, the last bottle she had sitting empty on the floor. If only it was as easy to get men to send her entire bottles as it was getting them to send her drinks at a bar. She'd been avoiding the bars, maybe it was time to go back. She could drive to Boston.

First, Stanlish. While his line was ringing a call came in, Gigi. Melanie let it go to voicemail. Stanlish picked up. A good sign, he wasn't avoiding her.

"How's my favorite other woman?"

Melanie wondered if that was a hint. "Bored."

Stanlish got the message. "I'm working it. I still think you should do the commercials. It's all about perceived demand. If the world thinks you aren't busy, they won't think anyone wants you, and *they* won't want you."

"I'm tired of commercials."

"Got to pay your dues."

"You sound like my last agent. Don't go there."

"Sorry. I have stuff I could send your way, but they are worse than the commercials, so I've be screening them out."

"Like what? No, don't tell me." If they were worse than ads for local car dealers and a furniture store, Melanie didn't want to know. Her phone beeped again, another call from Gigi. Her voicemail icon was also lit.

Stanlish said, "Look, I didn't want to say anything yet, but I put in a few calls to those vacation island clubs, see if I can get you in one of their ads. Not just a commercial, a whole package. You'd get a trip out of it too."

"You mean a Club Med?"

"Similar. Places with lots of action."

"Wait, wait, you want me to be some sleaze? Men picturing me as the woman who they could pick up there?"

Stanlish's hesitation implied she'd hit the answer, but he said, "A beautiful woman at a resort. And you have to admit, it fits your image."

"Fuck you, Marv."

"Melanie, you made the bed. You don't have to sleep in it forever, but you might want to go with it. You think people were going to have sympathy for you? I can get you work along those lines."

"I'm an *actress*."

"And probably a good one. Now let's get you some roles. You know how many famous actresses started as extras?"

Another call from Gigi. "Marv, I got to go. Get me something good. Fast." Melanie switched to the waiting call. "Gigi?"

"Mel, that cop was here, at my office, he's asking all sorts of questions about men at my apartment, he got shot—"

"Wait, what? Who got shot? Slow down."

"Detective Winter. He thinks I know something about it, and unless I tell him he's going to come back here and arrest me!"

"You aren't making sense. Get hold of yourself. Are you at work? I'll come over there."

"No! I can't—Mel, I'm scared."

Melanie waited until Gigi's sobs subsided. "Tell me everything."

She listened as Gigi told her about Winter's visit, prodding her along whenever Gigi broke down. "He asked about Jason? Why?"

"He thinks I was sleeping with him!"

"What did you say?"

"That you were! Or had been."

That wasn't so bad, thought Melanie. "Okay, okay. But he already knew that. Why was he talking to you instead of me?"

"Because he thinks that you got—assaulted—at my apartment, and you're making up the story about Jason—I swear I didn't tell him that, he said it—and that it wasn't Jason who assaulted you, it was some guy named Gus, and he's the one who shot Winter."

"Wait, *Gus* shot Winter?"

"You *know* him? He's been in prison!"

"Jesus, Gigi, the cops are just trying to scare you, don't believe anything they say." What the fuck did Gus have to do with all of this? She hadn't seen Gus since . . . "Gigi, *listen* to me. This has got nothing to do with you."

"I can't keep lying to them. I just can't."

Melanie recognized that tone, Gigi's mind set. "Let's talk about that later. I think I know what's going on here. That cop Winter got shot, he's trying to blame it on Gus."

"But why are they asking *me*? I don't *know* Gus," Gigi wailed.

"Gigi, I was staying over at your place, you had AC."

"You had a felon in my apartment!"

"He's just a guy. I didn't know he'd been in prison. That might be bullshit the cops are making up. Someone probably saw Gus around the Lakeview, and Winter knew you lived there, so he's asking you. That's all this is."

"But why? That would mean Gus *did* shoot him!"

"Who knows? Don't worry, I'll take care of everything. Trust me, I'll handle it, like I always have. But this is very important. What exactly did you tell the cops about—that night?"

"I—I told them you weren't assaulted here," whispered Gigi. "Because I was here that night."

"Good, good, that will work. I'm proud of you."

"I don't want you to be proud of me for lying."

"You weren't lying, you told the truth. You didn't know Gus, you weren't sleeping with Jason, you were at your apartment that night. All of that is the truth, right?"

A long silence. "I guess so."

"This must all be Jason's doing. He's got some pull now that he's made it big. He's trying to get me to back off on my story, even though I never charged him with anything. I'll take care of Jason."

"You don't think it was *Jason* who—who—"

"Get that out of your head. It wasn't him, I'm sure."

Another long silence. "Mel, I think I should just tell the rest of the truth."

Melanie forced herself to keep her voice calm. "No, no, don't do that. Don't you see? Then they'll be really suspicious of why you waited so long. Not only will everyone find out, but they'll hear about Gus, he isn't the kind of guy you'd want people thinking you were with."

"Did he—is he the one who—broke in—did he—"

The guy who did it is dead. Those were the words that would have made Gigi sleep better at night, at least about her assailant. But Melanie couldn't trust even Gigi with that knowledge. "Gigi, I swear, if Gus did anything, he'll get what's coming to him. But he didn't, believe me. The cops are after him for some other reason. Just go back to work."

"What if the cops come back?"

"They'll come to me before they come to you." Melanie knew Gigi was going to have a hard time handling this. "You have to trust me. I won't let anything happen to you, I promise." Melanie looked around at her crappy apartment, the empty wine bottle, her mismatched furniture. She couldn't remember the last time Gigi had visited. And why would she? "I know—I know I'm not the sister you might have wanted. I'm doing my best, I am."

"I didn't mean—don't ever say that. I love you, Mel, I do, and I'll never forget how you've protected me. I think of it more than you know. But I just can't live like this."

"Just hold it together there, please," said Melanie. "Please." She didn't hang up until she finally talked Gigi down from the edge.

After the call Melanie rifled through her drawers looking for some weed, found a bag, but halfway through rolling a joint decided she needed a clear head.

She'd been right to worry about that cop Winter. All that nice guy stuff, putting in her air conditioner, he was just pumping her for information. He knew she was hiding something, not just about Jason, but about Lenny. How he knew, Melanie couldn't figure out. Sure, people must have seen her and Lenny together, but so what? He came into the restaurant, she'd seen him at the club, at the Hilton. She talked to a hundred other guys at those places.

Gus was a smokescreen, thrown up by Winter to get Gigi nervous. Gus had been a fun fling, Melanie didn't really know shit about him. Maybe he *was* a felon. If Winter really did think Gus assaulted her, that was fine.

And if not, maybe she could come up with another candidate to keep Winter away from Gigi. If Jason was putting pressure on the cops to prove his innocence, she could point them at someone else. Jason had to know that his reputation was taking a hit whether people believed the assault story or not. She could go to him and promise to make it all go away, *if* he helped get her a role. She'd probably squeezed as much as she could out of the Jason story anyway.

WINTER HAD NEVER been to the set of a filming. It looked kind of interesting, big trucks, bundles of wires snaking across the street, a flurry of activity. Ryder, who sounded like an expert, explained what was going on.

"They're getting set up for a night shot, even though it's daytime. If they shoot at night it's too dark, so they use these filters on the lenses, and make adjustments in editing." Ryder pointed to a camera on a gurney. "That camera is remote controlled. They can get what they call establishing shots, tell you where the action is taking place."

The action was taking place at an old railroad car siding. Two rusty boxcars sat on a track, looking like they'd been there forever. Winter knew they had been, he'd played in them as a kid. "How do you know all this shit?"

"I like movies. Who knows, maybe I'll write that screenplay."

"Let's find Ayers."

"There'll be a cast trailer."

Winter had called Ryder after his interview with Gigi. Ryder hadn't got very far on the drug angle yet, so they'd met at the *Shock and Awe* location shoot. Ryder wasn't overly impressed by the Gigi Doyle interview information, but wanted to see the set and talk to Ayers. Winter wasn't sure which one held more interest for Ryder.

They threaded their way through a small group of onlookers, mostly teenagers, the trucks, and a host of equipment. A bright light popped on, then off. Three trailers were lined up on a side street, just past a crumbling platform.

A security guard sat in a director's chair, as stiff as his polyester uniform. He looked about eighteen, and jumped up as Winter and Ryder approached. "This area is off limits."

"Not for us, junior," said Ryder, flashing his badge. "Where is Jason Ayers?"

The rent a cop looked enviously at the badge, but still tried to keep it together. "Mr. Ayers is—." His eyes flicked to the first trailer.

"Thanks," said Winter. He knocked, the aluminum rattling hollow. Ayers opened the door. "Now what?"

"Just a few questions," said Winter, glancing pointedly at the security guard.

"Come on in," said Ayers. "But I don't have much time, I've got to finish makeup."

The trailer was plush. Two swiveling lounge chairs, a sofa, a table filled with bottled water, fruit trays, small sandwiches. A big television on the wall.

Winter didn't waste any time. "You lied to us about Melanie Upton. You said nothing was going on, but we have witnesses who say you were together right around the time she was assaulted. We're working on the timeline now. If the dates match up . . . " Winter let it hang. He only had the one witness, the office manager at the Lakeview, and she wasn't sure of the date, but Ayers wouldn't know that.

"This again? I told you where I was. *You*," he pointed to Ryder, "talked to Suzanne."

"Were you with Melanie or not?"

"Just at that party, you know that. It's on video. I ran into her at a club once, but I was with my producer and Michael Stevens. I barely spoke to her, she was flirting with Stevens."

Winter crowded Ayers in the small space. "So you weren't at her place? We're checking security videos now. If you were there, better we find out about it from you."

Ayers's eyes flew back and forth between Winter and Ryder. "It's not what you think. I went to Melanie's apartment, I wanted to talk some sense into her after she pulled that stunt at the press conference. She's playing with fire, she has no idea how studios work. She thinks she does, but she hasn't a clue. This business is cutthroat, but everyone, and I mean everyone, knows everyone else. It's a club. They'll cut each other's hearts out for a half a percentage on a deal, but they'll also circle the wagons when they need to. Melanie is going to be on their shit list if she isn't already."

"Why should you care if you aren't involved?"

"Because she's pulling me down into her crap."

Ryder was about to say something, but Winter cut him off. "You told Melanie this at her place?"

"On the phone. I went to her apartment, but I wasn't sure what unit she was in, so I called. She said she was someplace else. I was just standing in the parking lot."

"You had a thing with her and didn't know where she lived?" asked Ryder.

"She moved. She had a dump over on Third, she told me she's living at this place called the Lakeview."

"Maybe you went back there," said Ryder. "At night? Looking for a little action? She wasn't interested, you pushed it?"

"That's bullshit. That's the only time I was there. If you have security video, check it out. I was driving my Range Rover, black. And I'm telling you, Melanie is making all this up."

"We're going to talk to Suzanne Mance again," said Ryder.

"Shit. Do what you have to do. But keep it quiet, okay? I'm ending that. I don't want any trouble with Stevens. I see what's happening to Melanie. She's totally screwed herself big time."

*   *   *

BACK OUTSIDE, away from the trailer, Winter asked, "What do you think?"

"You believe he really thinks Melanie lives at the Lakeview?"

"It would explain why he was there. But he certainly knew about her place on Third. He could have assaulted her in either apartment."

Ryder said, "Not if he was with Suzanne Mance."

"Did you ask Logan to approve a trip to California?"

"I didn't get a chance to. You think he'll go for it?"

Winter watched Ayers come out of the trailer, glance in their direction, and then head for the set. "Your chances just got better."

CHAPTER 40

Ryder didn't get the opportunity to ask for his trip to California. Back at the station, he had called Mance to make sure where she was before asking Logan for the approval. Winter listened from the swivel chair next to Ryder's desk.

"Are you sure that was the date you were with Mr. Ayers?" said Ryder, holding his phone away from his ear. Mance was so worked up there was no need for a speakerphone.

"I'm sure! Jason told me all about this Upton woman. She's evil! She's jealous of me and Jason."

"We are going to need a statement," said Ryder. "I could be in Los Angeles by—"

"I'll do better than that. I'm coming there. We'll get all this sorted out for my poor Jason. I'll take you to the little inn we were at, they'll recognize me, of course."

Ryder tried one more time. "I'm sure you are very busy, Miss Mance—"

"Nothing is more important than this. Jason has to get this behind him, his career is just taking off. I'm going to help him. I've been talking to him about going public about our relationship. He hasn't wanted to, that fairy tale about Ashley Hanna. Everyone knows Ashley Hanna is still a virgin."

"You'd do that? Go public with Jason?"

"Yes, it's time. We love each other."

"What about Michael Stevens?"

"I'm going to tell him as soon as he gets back, he's in London.

He'll understand. He will. It's been fun with him, but as soon as he hears I'm in love he won't have a problem, you'll see."

"SHE SOUNDED PRETTY CONVINCING," said Ryder. "You catch all that?"

"Who knows with these people? She's another actress."

"Yeah, but you think she'd offer to fly out here and go public if it wasn't true she was with Ayers that night?"

Winter said, "She might not be so willing once she finds out that Ayers is going to dump her."

"Maybe she already knows, and all this is to get Ayers to want her. Offering up to lie for him, get him off the hook for the Upton assault."

Winter got up. "Could be. We know one thing for sure. Somebody's lying. Or all of them are. I'm going to work it from Upton's angle, pin down where she was that night. If she was at the Lakeview, then the assault happened there."

"And it could have been Ayers or Woodson."

"Or Gruse. I'm going back to the Lakeview to see if anyone saw him around."

"You didn't ask that when you were there?"

"Wondering about that myself," said Winter.

BEFORE LEAVING THE STATION, Winter got the DA on the phone. Unfortunately, the DA he'd worked with for years, Jackson, had retired, and this new guy, Villeson, was by the book, which meant skeptical.

"Let me get this straight," said Villeson. "You want a subpoena for the phone records of a woman who is a victim in a sexual assault?"

Winter sensed he wasn't going to get anywhere, but he pleaded his case. "Her story is all over the place. I think she might be covering for the guy who shot me. I have a witness who puts them together."

"Then it's his cell phone records you want, not hers. I can work with you on that, provided of course you have a proper witness statement. That meeting between the alleged shooter and the sexual assault victim took place when?"

Winter wondered if he had dialed the wrong number and got the public defender's office. "Nothing *alleged* about the shooter, I can show you the gash in my leg. I'm not sure about the date of their meeting." That was true enough.

"If her phone number shows up on the shooter's call log, then you might have the beginnings of probable cause," said Villeson. "Provided, of course, that the call took place near the time of the shooting."

Winter gave up, Villeson wasn't buying it. "Thanks for your time." He hung up. "Asshole." He should have had Ryder call, two peas in a pod.

IN THE CAR WINTER REALIZED he wouldn't make it to the Lakeview in time to catch the groundskeepers, it was well after five. Maybe the business office would still be open. He called, but it dropped him into voicemail.

If Upton had been assaulted at Lakeview, Winter already had two possible suspects: Jason Ayers and Gus Woodson. If Lenny Gruse had been seen there, that would make three. Maybe more, who knows how many men Upton had entertained at her sister's. And if the assault had taken place at Upton's own apartment—Winter hated to even think of how many more suspects that would mean.

Gigi Doyle had denied that her sister had been assaulted at the Lakeview apartment that night. Yet Doyle had been so nervous. Something was missing from the story, a bothersome tickle in Winter's mind, a gnawing.

Woodson was lawyered up over the shooting. There might be a deal to be made, although Winter would be pissed if he had to let Woodson plea down on shooting at a cop only to find out Woodson had nothing to do with either the assault or the Gruse murder. It wasn't just because he had been the one shot, he'd have felt the same way about any other cop.

Still, Woodson could be involved. Gruse assaults Upton, she gets Goodson to kill him. Goodson had some drug priors. He could have used that to lure Gruse to a meet.

Or the blackmail idea, a Gruse photo of Ayers, either with Mance or with Upton the night of the assault. Both good reasons for Ayers and Gruse to meet. The two fought, or maybe Ayers had only meant to scare Gruse into giving up the photo, but things got out of hand.

Every time Winter talked to someone more possibilities arose.

He'd drive by the Lakeview anyway. He checked to make sure he had the tablet and it was charged. When he turned it on, the first photo that popped up was Melanie Upton's, a picture that Cindy had found on the web.

Winter knew there was some way he could access the internet from the tablet, but he hadn't learned how. He felt like a dinosaur, all this new technology, threatening his very existence if he didn't get on board.

He punched Cindy up on his cell, hoping to catch her. "You in the office?"

"Just leaving you a note and packing up. That list I sent to Los Angeles of the women Gruse had photographed? None of them reported a stalker, as far as we can tell. Logan's contact was helpful—he's going to pass the list on to other jurisdictions, easier and faster than us doing it."

"Great. What I was calling you about—the photo of Upton you put on my tablet. Any way to tell who took it?"

"It might be credited, wait, let me pull up the website. Sure, here it is. Tim Tazik. He has a website. He's local, it lists an address on Congress. Two sixty one."

TWO SIXTY ONE CONGRESS turned out to be in the older part of Marburg's downtown area, a stretch of stately mid nineteenth century homes leading into what were once early industrial age storefronts and businesses. The area had run down, then been extensively renovated and gentrified.

The display windows in Tim Tazik's studio displayed a tasteful and varied array of photos, ranging from commercial work to weddings. As Winter was about to enter, a late fortyish man was coming out, a camera bag over his shoulder. He had slicked back hair, brilliant white teeth, a little gray on the temples, and was wearing a heathered polo shirt and chinos.

"Would you be Tim Tazik?" asked Winter.

"I am. I'm sorry, I'm just closing, I have to go to a shoot. I can take your name, or you can walk with me to my car."

Winter introduced himself and said, "Did you take some photos of Melanie Upton?"

Tazik's hand hesitated with his key in the lock. "Melanie? Sure, a few."

"I know about the ones on her website. Any others?"

Tazik finished locking up. "Some. Why?"

"How do you know her?"

Tazik pointed to his display window. "I'm the best known photographer in Marburg. I'm not bragging, I've just been around the longest, and I do good work. Just about anyone who needs a photograph has probably at least talked to me. I do a lot of work for actresses and actors, I'm even the official photographer for the summer theater. Melanie is a local actress. She found me."

Winter sensed an undercurrent of affected disinterest when Tazik spoke about Upton. Tazik was wearing a wedding ring, so Winter took a shot. "You and Upton, do you two get together outside of the studio?"

Tazik opened his mouth, closed it, looked over Winter's shoulder at two ladies strolling along the street, and said, "Maybe we'd better go inside." He unlocked the door, led Winter in. "Is it okay if I just make a quick call, tell them I'll be late?"

"Sure."

Tazik set down his camera bag, pulled out his cell, hit a speed dial, and said, "Hey Joanna. I'm running a few minutes late. Can you get them started? Thanks." He clicked off. "My assistant."

"Tell me about Melanie Upton."

"What do you want to know?"

"She's made some accusations about Jason Ayers. I'm investigating that."

Tazik shrugged. "I heard. She didn't say anything to me about it, if that's what you are after."

"So you two—spend time together?"

Tazik's eyes narrowed. "She didn't claim I did anything, did she?"

"No. Might she?"

Tazik appeared to be deciding what to say. "Shit, I don't know. I can't imagine why she would, I've done nothing but help her out."

"How?"

"Taking pictures, most of them without charge. I did that shoot at the press conference, the one that went viral? As a favor. I even brought her to a party so she could make some contacts. She's a good actress, or will be, once she gets her chance."

"You do this for a lot of clients? Work for free? What do you get out of it?" Tazik's pained expression told Winter what he needed to know. "Look, I'm not the morality police. You two have a thing, that's your business. But before I ask you anything else, I would like to know if you are still in a relationship."

"So you'll know whether to believe me?"

Winter didn't see any reason not to admit it. "Pretty much."

"Does this need to get out?"

"You brought her to a party, people must know about you two."

"No, not really. That kind of thing happens all the time, agents and producers showing up with actresses, models. Think of it as a business meet and greet. To answer your other question, we don't have what you might think of as a relationship. It's more an on and off hookup. Mostly when Melanie needs something."

"Like?"

"Usually just a photo."

"Did Melanie ever ask you to take a photo of Jason Ayers?"

"Just the one at the press conference."

"How about anyone else? I mean, take photos of anyone else?"

Tazik laughed. "You must not know Melanie very well. Melanie would only want photos of herself."

That sounded right to Winter. "You know Suzanne Mance?"

"The actress? Of her. Never met."

"So Melanie never asked you to take a photo of her?"

Tazik frowned. "No, why?"

"It's complicated," said Winter.

"Why would Melanie want photos of Jason Ayers and Mance?" Tazik's puzzled expression slowly slid into a grin. "I get it. Melanie thinks—or you think she thinks—that Ayers and Mance are having an affair."

Winter was pretty good at poker, but he must have waited a second too long to deflect Tazik's thought process, because Tazik said, "Now *that* would be a photo. But I'm not the guy for that kind of stuff. I didn't even want to do the press conference, Melanie twisted my arm, and I thought she had some publicity stunt worked out with the show."

"Who would be the guy to take that kind of photo?"

"Anybody with a camera who wanted to make a quick buck. But if you're asking about professionals, check some of the paparazzi types. We don't have many in Marburg, because there aren't that many celebrities to follow around. Boston has some."

"How about this guy?" asked Winter, pulling up Gruse's photo on the tablet.

"He looks familiar. Sure. I met him at a camera shop. I think he was trying to sell some equipment. I forget his name. Said he was from LA, took celebrity photos. I told him there wasn't much of that around here. He said he had something big cooking, I don't know if he was bullshitting or not."

Something big? thought Winter. Maybe blackmail? "What do you remember about him?"

"Just a guy. Twenties—he gave me the impression he was trying to show off. Maybe a little for me, a little for Jenny, she works at the camera store. I didn't think much of it, I might have sounded the same way at his age."

"Anything else?"

"He asked about my work, I even showed him some photos of a book I'm putting together. He seemed interested."

"What kind of photos?" Winter was wondering if it was about celebrities after all.

"Artistic shots of tattoos, different people, different bodies, I morph them together to create a new person and new ink." Tazik pulled out his phone, turned it to Winter. "Here are some shots.

This is probably exactly what I showed to your guy."

Winter flipped through the photos, nothing interesting to him. Few of the photos even showed faces, just parts of bodies with tattoos.

What *did* interest him was the date on a photo of a woman's thigh, the tattoo an interlocking series of whorled rings surrounded by a row of triangular patterns.

June 12th.

"Who is this?" Winter asked.

Tazik gave Winter a sheepish grin. "That's Melanie. She has nice ink."

"You took this on June 12th?"

"That's the date stamp. Just before midnight."

"You were with her that night?"

Tazik put up his hands. "Guilty."

"I told you, I don't care about that. How long were you with her?"

"Who am I getting into trouble?"

"Maybe you, if I have to have this conversation again with you in front of your wife."

"Hey, I though you said you weren't the morality police?"

"I'm not. But this is important. Come on, how long?"

Tazik gave in. "All night. We got a room at a hotel up in Marlborough. Actually it was the first time we hooked up."

"You're sure she was there all night?"

"Yeah. We watched the Tony's, had some champagne, I got her to let me take the photos, one thing led to another . . . she slipped out pretty early in the morning. It was light out, maybe seven thirty?"

Pieces falling into place in Winter's head, the timeline. Melanie Upton had called 911 that very morning, claiming she'd been assaulted the night before. Not by Tazik, but by Jason Ayers. So either Tazik had assaulted her, and she'd pretended it was Ayers, or Melanie had made it all up. "Melanie never hinted around to you about— about you not being appropriate with her?"

"We were pretty inappropriate together. I can't imagine why she'd claim otherwise."

"Did you watch her on *The Other Woman*?"

"I caught a YouTube, why?"

"You remember it?"

"It was vintage Melanie. Hot vibe, doing her thing."

"You remember the part about Jason Ayers?"

"She mentioned the party—that's the party I brought her to, the one where she ran into Jason and Ashley Hanna. Christ, what a soap opera."

"If you watch that tape again, you might want to focus on what she said she was doing the night Ayers might have assaulted her."

"What?"

"Watching the Tony Awards on tv."

Tazik's head snapped up. "You got to be shitting me."

"I'm not. So if there's something you want to tell me about that night, maybe things getting a little out of hand, now's the time."

"You mean that I assaulted her, and she blamed it on Ayers?"

Winter shrugged. "Something like that." He hesitated, letting it all sink in. "If there is DNA . . ."

"Aww, shit," said Tazik. He grabbed his hair, bunching it in his fingers. "I swear to God, it was all consensual. She drove her own car to the hotel. I know that doesn't prove anything, but I'm telling you— we hooked up after that night again, more than once. She wouldn't have come back for more if I'd assaulted her."

"This is your business," said Winter. "But if I were you, I'd get some proof of those other times. Just in case."

WINTER LEFT TAZIK in his studio, the guy too stunned to even remember his photography session. Winter didn't believe Tazik had assaulted Melanie Upton. Sure, he could have—it would likely be Tazik's DNA in Upton's SAFE kit. Winter would keep it as a possibility, another line in his mental map of connections.

What Winter did know for sure was that Tazik was a perfect cover for Upton's story; a married guy who'd be highly unlikely to announce that Melanie's insinuation about Ayers was fake. To do so, Tazik would have to tell the world he was the one who had been with her that night.

Winter was beginning to realize that Melanie Upton was more than just a good actress. She was very, very, smart.

CHAPTER 41

W INTER SAT IN THE PARKING LOT of the Marriott in Marlborough. Nine p.m., the lot surprisingly full for a Thursday. Winter wasn't here to check Tazik's claim that he was with Melanie Upton; he'd probably need a subpoena for that, and Marlborough was out of his jurisdiction. It could be done, but he would need more evidence that Upton had committed a crime. At this point, all she'd done was vaguely insinuate an assault.

Winter had solved cases by putting himself in the shoes of the criminals, but he was having a hard time doing that with any of the players in these possibly connected cases. Upton, most of all. She was a chameleon, able to switch at will from a carefree, slightly ditsy self centered careerist to a charming vixen to a wounded victim. Winter had dealt with plenty of proficient liars, but never one with acting skills. He'd even started calling her *Melanie* in his head; he couldn't remember the last time he had used a first name to mentally refer to either a victim or a suspect.

So he'd driven to Marlborough, thirty minutes from the northern boundary of Marburg. If he couldn't put himself in Upton's head, he could at least put himself where she'd been. According to Tazik she'd left in the early morning. Winter was too wired to wait until morning light tomorrow; he felt on the verge of a breakthrough and wanted to push. He needed to determine once and for all if these two cases might be connected, and possibly hone in on how. At the least, eliminate some of the strands in his ever growing complexity of linkages.

He headed back to Marburg, taking the most likely route Upton would use to go home. Not much real highway here, the main connecting road often interrupted by traffic lights. Just over a half hour later Winter pulled to the curb across from Upton's apartment.

The Indian restaurant was busy. The night was warm enough that the outdoor tables were full. The door which led to the stairway was closed, Upton's apartment dark. If anyone had gone up to Upton's they would have needed a key, unless the stairway door had been propped open as it had been when Winter had first been there. Either way, Upton's visitor would have had to walk right by the restaurant if he had come when it was open. Far down the street, a neon red bar sign was the only other indication of life.

It was improbable anyone had broken in early in the evening. The middle of the night was more likely, which supported Upton's story. Yet Tazik had said she'd been with him all night. Why would he lie about that? It would only get him in deeper trouble with his wife should he have to come clean about his dalliances with Upton.

Unless Tazik was in on the fake Jason Ayers assault story and was covering for Upton. That didn't make sense; he'd practically ruled out that she could have been assaulted that night. Right now, Tazik was Ayers's best alibi, even more believable than Suzanne Mance.

Upton had made her 911 call not from here, but from her sister's. Winter rolled off, across the railroad tracks, again following what he thought would be the fastest route.

At the Lakeview, Winter parked where he had a clear view of Gigi Doyle's front door. From here, it would be easy to see anyone coming in or out. A dim glow peeked from the edges of the front window. No light was on in the bath or second bedroom. A security light on the end of the building illuminated a wide swath around Doyle's apartment at the far side. Past that, about fifty feet of lawn, then the next apartment unit began, also brightly lit.

The drapes on the unit next to Doyle's were partially open, revealing figures moving across the window. Just beyond, another security light. Anyone visiting Doyle's apartment would be visible by at least twenty apartment units.

Winter drove back out of the lot. Just before the main entrance was a second road. He eased down it. To his right was a six foot fence he couldn't see through. To his left was the back side of the apartment complex.

The roadway widened to a small paved lot, two medium sized dumpsters and an electrical panel, then continued on past to the next series of apartments. Winter got out of the car. It was much darker here than in front, no lights pointing toward the dumpsters, probably to keep them less noticeable. No large security lights mounted on the building like in the front, although some of the units had floods. A few of them turned on as Winter walked down the road, which he now suspected was a service alley to access the dumpsters.

A small fence surrounded Gigi Doyle's tidy garden. The drapes were pulled tight, no light leaking from either the living room area or the bedroom. It would be easy to pull into this alley and enter from the back door or break in. Or even park up the street, outside of the Lakeview parking area, and walk in.

Ayers would have had to drive from Boston. Easy enough at night, unless Mance gave him an alibi. Winter would check the security video for a Range Rover anyway. And a motorcycle; Woodson was probably stupid enough to drive his here, although he could have taken one of the repair cars from the garage.

Gruse could have been here in twenty minutes after leaving the bar where he'd been in the fight. It was easy to imagine Gruse, humiliated after being beaten up, driving here and taking out his frustration on Upton. Gruse had certainly stalked her; if others had seen Upton here, he easily could have. First thing in the morning, Winter would be back to talk to those two groundskeepers.

He considered checking the windows and back door for signs of forced entry, but didn't want to scare Gigi if she was at home, she was skittish enough. If Upton had been assaulted here instead of across town, she would probably have cleaned up any evidence. He'd check anyway when he came back. And call around to window repair shops and locksmiths. Upton, of course, could have let the guy in.

Winter took one last look around. The faint aroma of the garden couldn't cover the sickly sense that this might have been the location of a sexual assault.

*   *   *

WINTER WAS UP AT DAWN, anxious to get moving, a lot to do today, yet too early to see either the Lakeview groundskeepers or the security footage. He pulled on a pair of shorts, took a fast walk, twenty minutes, just to get his blood flowing. His was a working neighborhood, plenty of people already up, walking dogs, throwing out the trash.

He ate, had two cups of coffee. Almost eight. He would get going, call the Lakeview office from the car, and if it wasn't open yet would detour to the station. Just as he was leaving the phone rang, not the cell, the house number.

Andie, the crime tech. "Just saving you the need to call me about the Gruse DNA."

"I haven't called."

"You were thinking about it. Still not the final take to court ready report, but I thought you'd want to know that there's no match—no Gruse DNA shows up in the Upton SAFE kit." When Winter didn't reply, Andie said, "Is that good news or bad news?"

"Rules out one possibility, which is good. I think I know who that foreign DNA is from, but run it through CODIS anyway."

"I suspected you'd be wanting that, so I am now."

"Thanks. Let me know." The DNA would be Tazik's, but Winter wanted to rule out Woodson, whose DNA would be in the system since he had a felony conviction. But Gruse appeared to be off the hook. One link in the connection map snapped, that of Upton killing Gruse because he had assaulted her. Unless . . . Gruse could have assaulted her a *different* night. But why would Upton wait to report it? And choose a night where Tazik could place her elsewhere?

That left Woodson and Ayers.

A few minutes after eight. From the car Winter tried the Lakeview office, it was still closed. He called Ryder, got him on his cell, brought him up to speed. "Can you track down Woodson's lawyer?"

"Shouldn't we wait for the CODIS results?"

"I don't think they'll be a match for that night. But it would be good to hear what he offers up. Tell him we're running the test, if he has something to tell us about a possible rape, the usual." To make it more palatable for Ryder, Winter added, "Woodson had the drug priors, he still could have killed Gruse, maybe Upton put them together. You can also see if he has an alibi for the night Gruse was killed."

"That's the most reasonable theory you've had yet. The drugs, I mean. We got the lab work back on the capsules Gruse had in his pocket. Roofies, specifically Rohypnol and MDMA. Gruse was probably looking to score or find a source."

Winter said bye before Ryder had a chance to change his mind.

WINTER WAS IN THE MIDDLE of the city, just passing the Hilton, which made him think of Ayers. He punched up Cindy on his cell phone.

"Anything yet on Gruse's internet storage, or whatever you call it?"

"Cloud storage. We just got access, I'm pulling it up now. Looks like tons of photos. What am I looking for?"

"Photos that aren't duplicates of what you found on the memory cards. Specifically, any photos of Jason Ayers, especially with Suzanne Mance."

"Okay. Dan is working on a program to compare the file names, look for mismatches based on file properties."

Winter had no idea what she was talking about. "Sounds great."

He caught the long light at the ramp to the bypass road, giving him a few minutes to think. If Upton was with Tazik, then why did she claim she got assaulted at her apartment? And if she didn't get assaulted, where did she get the idea from? Just from being with Tazik, a hazy memory of having sex, leveraged into a story about Ayers designed to give her publicity?

Or had she heard about a *real* assault? Winter was about to dial Cindy back to see if there were any sexual assaults Upton may have heard about on the national news. There weren't any in Marburg around that time, Winter would have remembered. In his mind he replayed Upton's movements, from Marlborough back to Marburg, either to her apartment or the Lakeview.

Lakeview. Upton had been at Lakeview when she had called 911. Prompted, according to Ryder's notes, by her conversation with Gigi, convincing Melanie to report the assault.

Why would Melanie not call in the assault when it was fresh in her mind, at her own apartment? Why wait until she reached Gigi's? So far, there was no evidence to support Melanie's assertion of a break-in or an assault at her apartment. On the other hand . . .

Could it have been *Gigi* who was assaulted? That would certainly explain why Gigi was so nervous. Gigi tells Melanie, they call 911, Melanie blames it on Ayers for publicity.

Or because Ayers had actually done it.

Winter hit his siren switch, pulled a u-turn in the middle of the intersection, horns blaring, and roared back toward the Hilton.

WINTER DIDN'T KNOW this desk clerk, but one look at Winter's demeanor stopped any possible argument about giving him an elevator key card. As he stepped out onto the Executive Floor his phone rang. He was about to silence it, saw that it was Ryder, picked up.

"Your man Woodson was in overnight lockup on a DUI in Framingham the night that Gruse was killed," said Ryder. "And he didn't match on CODIS. He's off the hook for both the assault and the Gruse murder."

"Good."

"Good?"

"One less asshole to think about. I've got a better possibility." Winter gave Ryder the short version. "So I think it could be the sister who got assaulted, not Melanie. She just borrowed the story."

"If it's true, that's cold."

"Depends. You saw Gigi, she's scared shitless of even talking to the cops, afraid she'll get fired for lying. Can you imagine what a rape trial would do to her?"

"So Melanie is helping her out?"

"Maybe. Ayers still could be our guy. He breaks in to Gigi's apartment, thinking he's at Melanie's. Melanie tells Ayers she'll claim he assaulted Gigi unless he helps her career. He refuses, so she goes semi-public, putting pressure on him."

"I don't buy it. Gigi knows Ayers. Why didn't she just tell us?"

"Maybe the part about her being out of it is true, she can't remember."

"So there's no Gruse connection."

"There might be if photos of Mance and Ayers show up on Gruse's cloud storage." Winter had another thought, spurred by his visit to the alley behind Gigi's apartment and the anonymous note about a prowler. The timeline was off, but could that have been a resident spotting Gruse stalking Upton? "Gruse might even have a photo of Ayers going in—or breaking in—to the Lakeview. Got to go, I'm at the Hilton."

Winter knocked on Ayers's door, got no answer, pounded. A very sleepy Ayers pulled the door open. "Shit, what time is it?"

Winter pushed his way in. "Time for you to come clean. Last chance. When were you last in Gigi Doyle's apartment?"

Ayers looked confused. "In? As in inside? Never. I don't even know where she lives."

Winter prodded, "We're checking the security tapes now." Winter didn't tell Ayers that the tapes wouldn't show the front door of the apartment. "If we find your DNA in her apartment . . ."

Ayers was already shaking his head. "I haven't seen Gigi in years, since way back. Ask her."

Ayers looked believably blank, but he was an actor. Winter decided to hit him with it. "So you're claiming you didn't know Gigi lived at Lakeview."

"What? No, in the same complex? What's Gigi got to do with this?"

Winter didn't answer, this was the time when the guilty ones started protesting their innocence or claiming it was all consensual.

Ayers said, "It doesn't matter. You know I wasn't anywhere near the Lakeview the night Melanie says she was assaulted. I was with Suzanne Mance."

Winter wasn't going to let slip his suspicion Ayers might have assaulted Gigi, not yet. "Unless it was another night."

"What night?"

"You tell me. Did Melanie try to get you to help her career?"

"Shit, haven't you been listening? That's what Melanie *does*. Of course she tried to use me, that's the whole point of her story about me assaulting her. If you can't help Melanie, she's not interested in you."

"And you wouldn't help her?"

Ayers shook his head again, this time more in sadness than denial. "You know, if she had come to me, asked nicely, I would have done what I could. Not gone out on a limb for her, she's got this—mean streak in her. Introduce her to a few people? Sure. But instead of being a normal person—even normal in this fucked up business—she tries to manipulate me, manipulate everyone. Let me ask you this. Have you found even one close friend she has? Or anyone who has a single good thing to say about her? I'm telling you, she's just in it for herself."

"What about her sister?"

"She'd be the only one. Although if she could get something out of Gigi, Melanie wouldn't give it a second thought."

"You could give us your DNA, clear this up right away."

"I'd be willing to do that, but I've heard a lot of stories about DNA getting mixed up. I'd need to talk to my lawyer."

"Do that."

IT HAD BEEN SO LONG since the assault it would be a nightmare to match Ayers's DNA to anything in Gigi's apartment. But it was worth having Ayers worried about it, maybe he'd change his story.

Or not. Winter had just got back in his car when his phone rang; Ryder again. "Susan Mance is here, as in here at the station. She took the red eye. And she has red eyes, she's crying like a baby, swearing up and down Ayers is innocent."

"I just left Ayers, he didn't mention her being in town."

"Maybe he's not taking her calls. She says she's on her way to the Hilton, now that she's convinced me that Ayers is innocent."

"Her crying eyes do that for you?"

"She does do a good cry, but I've seen plenty of movies, these actresses can turn on the waterworks at will. What convinced me was the copy of her Amex bill, showing her room charge for the B&B that night. That, and a conversation I just had with the manager, after Mance gave her the okay to talk. The manager not only swears that Mance and Ayers were at the inn, but that Ayers didn't leave until morning, because the manager saw Ayers get into his Range Rover."

"I have a new idea," said Winter.

"Why am I not surprised?"

"Say Ayers did assault Melanie. Or Gigi. It didn't have to happen that night. Melanie could have just used the story. Ayers just told me that Melanie is just out for herself, she's a manipulator. I can believe it."

"I'll give you that. If Ayers assaulted her on a different night, her story is going to fall apart with Ayers's alibi."

"It still might be Gigi. I'm going to the Lakeview, ask around, see if Ayers or Gruse were there."

"What do you want me to do?"

Winter was surprised, that was the first time Ryder had offered to help. He didn't mention it; he sensed this was an apology of sorts from Ryder, or at least a grudging acceptance. "Can you check to see how long it will take Cindy to find out if there are any photos of Ayers in Gruse's cloud storage?"

"Sure. I can help look through images."

"Thanks. I'll call from the Lakeview."

THE LAKEVIEW WAS MUCH busier than it had been the night before, a steady line of cars exiting the lot, off to work. Winter spotted the two groundskeepers before he reached the business office. They were less wary this time, leaning on their shovels as Winter walked over.

He started by showing them a different photo of Ayers, a candid, and got only headshakes. Then Gruse. The guy who had done most of the talking last time said, "I don't think so."

The other one asked something in Spanish. Winter caught the word *carro*, which was in his limited Spanish vocabulary. "A Cadillac," Winter suggested. "Older, 1990 something, I think. I don't have a picture."

More Spanish. The guy who had identified Woodson's bike pulled out a cell phone and was typing away. Within seconds he had pulled up images of Cadillacs.

Winter pointed to one. "Like this, but cream colored. Off white."

"Yes. Here." The first words in English Winter had heard him speak. The groundskeeper pointed back toward the entrance. "There."

Another round of Spanish, then the more fluent English speaker said, "He says he saw the car a few times, not in the lot, but out on the road before the entrance. Does this help you?"

So Gruse had been at Gigi's after all.

CHAPTER 42

WINTER GOT IN HIS CAR, started the engine, but couldn't quite decide where to go. He now had proof—okay, not take to the jury proof, but he believed it—that Gruse had been at the Lakeview apartments. Gruse had been following Upton around, taking photos, no doubt he'd seen her here; Upton hadn't exactly been keeping it a secret.

It still could be possible that was the end of it, a semi celebrity photographer stalker. Or Gruse could have assaulted Melanie, not necessarily on June 12th, but some other night, and Melanie had conveniently turned that into a story about Jason.

If Gruse didn't do it, that left Ayers as the only other possibility, alibi or not. Too impatient to wait, Winter called Cindy.

"Anything?"

"Hard to tell. Every file on the camera cards is on the cloud, but not vice versa. But so far, every folder that is only on the cloud is dated months ago. We're going through them now, just in case, but none of the shots appear local."

"What's in the other photos?"

"More of the same. Women, and more women. No shots of Jason Ayers."

"Where's Ryder?"

"He's helping. You want him?"

"Not right now. Let me know if anything pops. Just focus on men, look for Ayers."

Winter hung up, not expecting them to find anything. The Jason Ayers idea was probably a dead end. Ayers had what would probably be a good alibi, and the one reason Winter could think of that would make him kill Gruse—a photo of Ayers—didn't appear to exist.

If Ayers didn't assault Gigi, then there would be no catalyst for Melanie to pretend *she* was assaulted. Winter couldn't dismiss the idea that Melanie made it all up; she certainly was a good enough actress. Even if Gigi knew of Melanie's plan, would that by itself make Gigi nervous talking about the deception?

Winter stared at Gigi's front door. No, not from here, that's not where Gruse had been parked. Winter pulled out of the lot, did a tight u-turn, and found a spot along the entrance road. Not perfect, but he could see Gigi's door from an angle.

What would Gruse have thought if he had followed Melanie here? He'd see her go into that apartment.

Gruse, who had fought with Melanie twice in public. Saying she owed him. Winter thought that meant money from a blackmail, but it could have been something else. Maybe she had promised him a date in exchange for taking photographs, just as she had with Tazik. Maybe Gruse had conned her, told her he had big connections in Hollywood.

Melanie blows him off, and Gruse is pissed. He gets drunk at a bar, gets beat up. For some reason he blames Melanie. He drives here, maybe parks in this very spot. He walks down the service road, just as Winter had done. He breaks in, expecting to find Melanie. Only it's Gigi. Gruse assaults her. Gigi stoned from the pills, like she said, she doesn't know who it is. She calls her sister, who comes over and co-opts the entire story, either to use it for her own ends or to protect her sister. Or both.

Gigi could have let Gruse in, not remembering. She's out of it on the sleeping pills, Gruse takes out his frustration on her. Stoned . . .

Roofies. They'd found roofies in Gruse's pocket. Gruse wasn't selling roofies, he was using them to spike the drinks of unsuspecting women.

Which would make him a rapist.

The drugs could also explain why Gigi had been so out of it during the assault, maybe Gruse had found a way to slip them to Gigi, or had forced her to take them. Melanie had used that part of the story as well. Later, Gigi remembers it was Gruse, or knew all along. Yet if

Gigi killed Gruse in retribution, she was an even better actress than her sister. Winter never said never, but the way Gigi had shrunk away from him didn't exactly give off a killer vibe.

If not Gigi . . .

Melanie.

Gigi confides in Melanie, or perhaps from bits and pieces she picks up from Gigi, Melanie finds out that Gruse did it, and it's Melanie, not Gigi, who kills Gruse. Winter had no doubt that Melanie could lure a warm blooded male anywhere, even an out of the way hotel in Greenhill.

The convoluted array of strings in Winter's mental map simplified into a series of straight lines. Gruse to Melanie to Gigi back to Gruse.

There was nothing random about revenge.

WINTER WAS ON THE MOVE, heading back to the station. There was nothing there he needed that couldn't be done over the phone, but he was at the worst kind of standstill, convinced he had it all figured out but no way to prove it. Confronting Upton without proof would be a waste of time, if she was guilty she'd run rings around him.

At the municipal building he went in the back way, the split level putting him on the floor where the evidence room and labs were. Andie was in front of her computer.

"Did you do DNA collection from Gruse's car?"

"Yes and no. There was too much—he hadn't vacuumed those carpets in forever. So we collected, but outside the blood the only specific tests we've run have been on the hair samples from the front seat area and floor that didn't have dust on them. There were no hits in CODIS."

"I need you to run anything you have, and I mean anything, against the Melanie Upton samples."

"Her again?"

"Yes. And Andie, whatever favor your friend in the lab needs for moving this up the priority list, I'll pay it."

*   *   *

GRACIE WAS ON THE PHONE but she waved frantically to Winter, pointing to the detective squad room, mouthing "They want you."

Ryder and Logan were crowding over Cindy's desk. "What's up?" asked Winter.

"TMZ is reporting that Suzanne Mance and Jason Ayers are an item."

On the screen, a photo—crooked, but clear enough—showed Mance with her arms around a shirtless Ayers. Ayers was in profile, but it certainly looked like him.

"She took a selfie," said Ryder. "He might not even know."

"If it's him."

"It's him," said Cindy. "That tattoo on his arm . . . TMZ checked it."

"What's the article say?" Winter couldn't read the small print.

Ryder said, "Mance claims Ayers loves her, they've had a secret relationship. She says, quote: Even the police know about us, because I was with Jason the night that other woman claimed she was assaulted, unquote." Ryder looked up at Winter. "I guess that totally takes Ayers off the hook for assaulting anyone, at least that night."

MELANIE STARED AT THE TMZ WEBSITE. "Bitch, bitch, bitch." Then, for the first time in fifteen years, since that night her father had snuck his hand under her covers after saying good night, she cried.

WINTER TOOK LOGAN and Ryder through it. "I can't prove it, not yet, but if we find Upton's DNA in Gruse's car we'll be a step closer. I'll go back to the witnesses that saw them together, we can show her photo at the Greenhill. Squeeze the sister."

Ryder still looked skeptical. "It's all conjecture, circumstantial."

"You're right," admitted Winter. "Melanie could have been arguing with Gruse about nothing. She might have been in his car another time. She could have been assaulted by a stranger, or no one. Gigi might not be involved at all. Gruse could have been dealing roofies, not using them for date rape." He thumped Cindy's desk. "But unless Melanie has an ironclad alibi, I'll bet Sox season tickets that Gruse assaulted Gigi, and Melanie killed him for it."

"I'm not taking that bet," said Logan.

Ryder looked back and forth from Cindy to Logan. Cindy shook her head. "I wouldn't either, even if I could afford Sox season tickets."

Logan shrugged. "Won't hurt to play it out. Upton or Doyle?"

"Both of them. Let's pin their stories down, see if there's any discrepancy."

"They've likely rehearsed," objected Ryder.

"Melanie, yes. She could hold a story together. Gigi, I'm not so sure."

"We still don't have any direct evidence," said Ryder.

Winter looked at Logan.

"Go get them," said Logan.

THAT FUCKING LOSER Lenny Gruse. Even from the grave he was making Melanie's life miserable. Yet no matter how this turned out, there was no way Lenny was going to take her down.

Her tears had long since dried. She should have known better, too much improvisation for something so important as her career. Next time she'd get it perfect.

Now she needed some distance from all of it, from Marburg and Jason and even Gigi.

When in doubt, fall back on what you did best. For Melanie, that was acting.

It took her only a few minutes to book a reservation on a flight to Toronto out of Boston. That accomplished, she reached past all her shoes in the closet and pulled out her wheeled luggage, the plain black one Gigi had given her for her birthday, the same exact bag Gigi owned. *It's so practical*, said Gigi. *You can use it for your audition trips.*

Melanie stuffed in her underwear, leggings, shorts, makeup, toiletry kit, sneakers and sandals. She needed to leave room for what would come later. At the very end, she held up her favorite leather jacket and a pair of Jimmy Choo heels. She'd only have room for one.

Fucking Lenny Gruse.

"WHERE TO FIRST?" asked Ryder, in the parking lot.

"Let's split up. I'll get Upton, you get the sister."

"Don't trust me with Melanie?"

"I don't trust any of us with her," said Winter.

WINTER WAS AT UPTON'S in fifteen minutes. He parked illegally in front of a hydrant, stuck a police identification sign on the dash, and banged on the downstairs door. No answer. The door was locked, so he went in the Indian restaurant.

There was no hostess station, only a few people eating, no wait staff visible. Winter stuck his head in the kitchen. Two waitresses and a middle aged man, all Indian, looked up at him.

"I'm with the police. Anyone know how I can get in touch with the building owner?"

"My brother owns the building," said the guy.

"I need to get in the upstairs apartment, Miss Upton. She—she's not answering, and she might be—in danger." *From me*, he didn't add.

The Indian guy barely hesitated. "I have a key."

MELANIE TOOK A LONG LOOK around Gigi's bedroom. It was far better than her place, yet not the style she herself preferred. Still, she had felt comfortable here. Gigi, as different as they were, had always made her feel welcome.

Well, except for that one time when she'd yelled about the cigarette smoke. Melanie hadn't smoked in here since.

In the bathroom, Melanie used her critical eye to review her outfit. Gigi's skirt fit just fine, although the blouse was a little tight. She'd done the best she could with her hair, cutting off a few inches, rushing a dye job that at least hid her highlights. Using Gigi's own makeup, Melanie had washed out her tan, darkened her brows—Gigi never plucked enough—and thickened her lips.

She wasn't trying to match how Gigi looked exactly, but was working from the flat, brightly lit passport photo, which Melanie had propped up on the vanity. In the photo, Gigi was looking slightly downward, probably told by the photographer to reduce the glare from her glasses.

Melanie didn't have the same glasses, but she had a few pairs of no prescription frames, standard props for an actress. She'd sometimes worn them as a joke, see if she could still pick up men. She slipped on a pair, ovoid shaped dull brown frames. This would be more of a challenge, getting guys to *not* look at her.

The outfit would help, the longish gray skirt, flats, a jacket. She'd taken a sweater from Gigi's bottom dresser drawer and a blouse from the far back side of the closet, out of a cleaner bag with a year old ticket.

Melanie realized this was the first time she'd ever borrowed clothes from Gigi. That was a depressing thought; isn't that what sisters were supposed to be doing for each other? Instead of lying. Beating up men. Killing.

In consolation for the clothes, Melanie carefully placed two new tubes of Lancome mascara on the vanity, the same type she had used up that fateful night.

WINTER'S PHONE RANG as the helpful Indian guy, whose name was Arjun, unlocked the downstairs stairway door. Cindy. "Need to be quick," said Winter, pausing on the steps.

"Two women Gruse had photographed in West Hollywood filed police reports for sexual assault. One had been drugged—positive test for MDMA, positive SAFE test. The other one had inconclusive tests on both the drugs and the SAFE. Both thought they'd been assaulted by a photographer, although there were no suspects."

"Start the paperwork to get them the Gruse DNA. Send his photo out there, see if the women can identify him." Winter hung up, took the apartment key from Arjun, headed up the stairs. So Gruse had possibly date raped women in California. It could be a different photographer stalker, but . . .

He listened at Upton's apartment, nothing. Knocked, still nothing. Arjun watched from the bottom of the stairs. Winter put the key in the lock, turning and entering at the same time. "Police!"

The apartment was empty. As it was the last time Winter had been there, it appeared to have been hit by a clothing and footwear tornado. It was oddly quiet.

Because the air conditioning was off.

Of course, Upton might be frugal, keeping her energy bills down. Winter stuck his head back out the door and looked down at Arjun. "Who pays the electric bill?"

"It's included in the rent. I keep telling my brother he's too generous. That woman's bill is almost as much as the restaurant."

Winter was pulling out his phone as he rushed down the steps.

GIGI DOYLE DIDN'T WANT to be late for the sales meeting, so she gathered up her laptop, her phone, and her notes. She could finish her preparation in the conference room.

From the hallway she could see into the reception area. A man in a suit was talking to the receptionist. Nothing unusual, except he felt familiar. Gigi slowed. The man turned, and Gigi recognized the policeman, Detective Ryder.

She ducked into the ladies room, looked around wildly, scared. The other policeman, the mean one, Winter, had said that if they came back, they'd arrest her. Detective Ryder would take her away in *handcuffs*.

Her phone rang, so jarring in the small tiled room she dropped her laptop. She fumbled for it, her file folder spewing papers, the phone yelling at her. She collapsed onto the floor, crying.

Melanie's image stared up at her from the phone, the only thing left in her hand. "Mel?"

"Gigi? What's wrong?"

A tiny ray of warmth held Gigi's tears at bay for a single moment, the realization that her sister could tell she was in distress with one syllable. It was the closest she had ever felt to Melanie in her entire life.

That was all the control Gigi could muster. "Mel, the police are here, please, help me, you'll help me, won't you? Like you always do?"

"Of course I will. Who is there? Winter?"

"No, the other one."

"Right with you? Can you talk?"

Gigi crawled into a stall, dragging her notes and smashed laptop along like a train. "I'm in the bathroom. They're going to arrest me, aren't they?" She was crying now, her tears dripping on her blouse.

"No, they aren't. They'd better not. Listen, just—it's me they want, not you. Do you understand? This has *nothing* to do with you. I'm so sorry, Gigi, I—this is all my fault. I'm going to take care of everything."

"What are you going to do?"

"That's why I was calling you. For starters, I'm going to go away for a while. I'm not going to tell you where, so when they ask you, you can tell them the truth. You don't know. You can even tell them you talked to me, you just don't know where I am."

"Are you in trouble too?"

"Not *too*. You're not in trouble. And I can take care of myself, I don't want you worrying about me. You're my little sister, I'm the one who protects you, it's not the other way around."

"Mel—"

"Shh. Gigi, please, don't fight me on this, okay? You have to trust me. They just want me, it's about that Jason story. He must have used his connections to get the cops to hound me. I'll back off from him, it will all die down without me around."

Gigi clutched her crumbled notes, her blurry eyes registering a run in her pantyhose. So foolish, she was about to lose her job, get arrested, and all she could think about was how unprofessional she'd look.

"Mel, what about the—assault? I don't want to lie any more, they'll catch me."

"I know. I should never have asked you to do that. You were trying to help me, and I love you for it. Tell them everything you feel you need to tell them. Tell them the truth, if that's what you have to do. That I talked you into it."

The truth. Finally. It would be good for her to finally be free of this lie. Melanie understood what she needed. "You were only doing it for me."

"Not only for you, but thank you. Now pull yourself together. Think of it as a business meeting. A negotiation. They want something, so do you. You want them to not make a scene, not drag you out in public. They want the truth about me. Make a trade."

"Mel, I—I can't, I won't. You're my sister."

"And I'm glad I am. Now go, do what I can't do, be a tough businesswoman."

WINTER HAD ORDERED the BOLO for Melanie Upton by the time he was back in his car. The next call was to Ryder. "Upton's not at her apartment. I have the sense she's gone for a while. She could be at her sister's, I'm heading over there."

"I'm at Gigi's office. They are trying to locate her. Says she's here, just can't track her down."

"You think they are giving you the runaround?"

"No, they seem surprised. Wait, here she comes."

"Convince her to let us into her apartment, meet me there."

MELANIE HADN'T REALLY planned for this day, so she was improvising. That hadn't worked out so well the first time, so she sat in her car and took a minute to think.

She just needed to get away for a while. She'd call Jason, make nice, promise never to bother him again. The story would fade, especially since Jason would be hip deep in the Mance story. Maybe she could help him out with that, a trade of her own.

She might be able to get on a plane with Gigi's passport, but didn't want to take the chance. International travel would also look suspicious, in case the cops were still trying to connect her to Lenny. She couldn't see how, they were probably still fishing. Still . . . Would the cops threaten to arrest Gigi just because of the Jason story?

Get away, think it through.

Driving was out, at least with her car. She could rent, but she hated driving long distances. No fucking way she'd take a bus.

That left the train.

One decision out of the way, she got on the bypass road. Boston would have more train options, but she didn't want to be on the road that long. She'd have to risk the Marburg station.

Fucking Lenny Gruse.

WINTER WAS WAITING at Gigi's front door when Ryder pulled up. Ryder had put Gigi in the back seat, and came around to open the locked door. Not a bad move; sitting in a locked police car would put pressure on Gigi. Ryder went up half a notch in Winter's book.

Ryder guided her by the elbow up the walkway. Gruffly he said, "She *claims* to not know where Melanie is."

"I don't," said Gigi.

"But she admits she talked to Melanie just before I picked her up."

"Am I under arrest?" Gigi's plaintive eyes almost were Winter's undoing.

He turned away as he said, "Not yet."

"She's not here," insisted Gigi, unlocking the door. "You'll see."

The apartment was spotless and quiet. Winter watched Gigi closely as Ryder checked the rooms. She seemed relieved when Ryder came up empty.

"See?" Gigi followed Winter as he walked down the hall. He'd look for signs of a break-in, see if that got Gigi talking. As he turned he noticed Gigi staring into the bathroom.

Winter stepped back as Gigi entered the bath. He found her holding two small bottles of makeup, a sad smile on her lips.

He was about to try to find out what had crossed her mind when his phone rang. Cindy.

"We just got a hit on a plane reservation for Gigi Doyle to Toronto."

Toronto. Where had Winter seen . . .

He ran into the spare bedroom. The travel brochures were still there, the Caribbean, Toronto.

The passport was gone.

MELANIE LEFT HER CAR in a parking garage three blocks from the train station, thankful for Gigi's practical rolling bag. Inside, she found an Amtrak brochure rack. She'd hoped to see a country wide route map, but the brochures were organized by region, Northeast, West. If she couldn't make it as an actress, she'd make a bundle as a consultant fixing the confusing mix of train travel options.

That was something Gigi would be so good at.

She had faith her sister would come through now that she could tell the truth. The lying, that wasn't Gigi, that was Melanie. She was the actress, not Gigi. She could dress in Gigi's clothes, look like her, walk like her if need be, but Gigi could never play Melanie. Sure, she could put on the clothes, could get the makeup. But she could never tell a lie, not for long.

Gigi could never have stuck the knife in Lenny Gruse.

Melanie settled on New Orleans, via New York. She was sure she could disappear there for a little while, and, if she finally understood the convoluted brochures, could catch another train for Texas. It would be an easy drive to Mexico, she'd been there twice.

She pulled a deck of prepaid debit cards from her purse, held together with a rubber band. All of them gifts from various men through the years. Most were run down to almost nothing, those Jimmy Choo shoes weren't cheap.

She used her highest balance card to buy the ticket from a very anonymous machine kiosk.

"SHE'S RUNNING," said Winter.

Ryder had sat Gigi on the sofa and was hovering over her. "Where is she?"

Gigi looked up with surprising defiance. "I wouldn't tell you even if I knew."

Winter stood next to Ryder, adding his presence. "Your sister may have killed someone."

Gigi's mouth opened and moved, but no words came out. She bit down, locking her lips. A small head shake. "You're not only mean, you're a liar. Melanie warned me about you. About both of you."

"You think you're in trouble now—if you are helping her get away, you'll be an accessory," said Ryder.

"We know what Melanie did," said Winter, softening his voice. "And why."

Gigi's eyes jumped to Winter. Just before they hardened with anger, Winter caught a glimpse of something else. Satisfaction? Approval? "You don't know anything," said Gigi. She sat up straight, uncowed.

That simple look, even more than the growing circumstantial evidence, convinced Winter he was right; that it was Gigi who had been assaulted. Not by Jason Ayers, or Gus Woodson, or some stranger, but by Lenny Gruse. Even in her defiance, Winter suspected he could pry the truth from Gigi right now. It was one thing to protect her sister, it was another to deny she had been raped.

But Winter couldn't do it. Rape was the most heinous act in all the heinous acts, a violation as evil as murder. Winter knew exactly what he would have done if Gruse had raped his sister or his daughter, Winter would have killed him without hesitation.

This wasn't the way to talk to a victim about being raped, throwing it in her face to get her to give up the sister who had protected her.

Winter pulled Ryder aside, his voice low. "We can't waste any more time on her. Are you convinced?"

"Enough for now."

"Melanie has Gigi's passport, but the Toronto flight reservation might be a smokescreen."

"You think she's going to fly someplace else?"

"Or make us believe she is. She could drive, but might not want to take the risk we'd spot her car. That leaves the bus and the train."

"I'll get uniforms to the stations."

"You should get to the airport, just in case. I'll take the train station. Get O'Dowd to the bus station. Get dispatch on the uniforms, Logan can handle the rigmarole with security at the airport."

Ryder jerked his head toward Gigi. "What about her?"

"Get a uniform, no, a detective in an unmarked car, to meet you at the airport and hand her over. Take her phone." Winter glanced over at Gigi, she was putting on a good front, but whatever courage she'd drawn on was leaking out her pores. "Go easy on her."

Ryder seemed about to object. Winter shook his head, adamant. Ryder said, "Okay."

Winter remembered the pasty photo of Gigi on the passport. "Melanie might not look herself. We need to get them a photo of Gigi too."

"No problem," said Ryder. He pulled out his phone and in one smooth motion snapped a photo of Gigi.

Winter was halfway out the door when Ryder said, "You got to get a smart phone."

MELANIE WANDERED OVER to the newsstand at the train station, picked up a few magazines. She gave the prepaid cell phones a glance, better not buy one here. Melanie missed her phone. She'd smashed it after leaving Gigi's, tossing it in the trashcan of a drive through McDonalds. She didn't want to go through all this trouble only to have the cops track her phone.

So no way to see if she was in the news. The cops might not have anything about Lenny; it could still be all about the Jason story, or even about Gus Woodson. Still better to get away. She could explain everything, the trip, even the passport—she'd say she picked up the wrong luggage at Gigi's.

Gigi would back her up. The worst that could happen was that the cops would find out the truth about the assault. But as far as Melanie knew, she was the only person who knew that Lenny had assaulted Gigi. Loser as he was, she couldn't see Lenny bragging about that.

So they had nothing.

*   *   *

AT TIMES LIKE THIS, Winter was doubly glad for his bolt on turbo. He hit the siren, ran five straight lights, and was on the bypass road in six minutes. He trusted Ryder would mobilize the troops, but didn't trust that a uniform, even with photos, would spot Melanie, the woman a chameleon.

Winter got it up to ninety for a minute or two, had to jam on the brakes for a jerk in the left lane going the speed limit, and pushed it again once past. Not weaving through traffic, just bearing down on anyone in the left lane, flicking his high beams.

He screeched off the bypass at Union, six blocks to the train tracks, although he was still three miles from the station, tucked away in the oldest part of the city, far from the highway.

His phone rang. He'd finally learned to answer with one hand. Without looking at the screen he yelled, "What?"

"It's Cindy. Ryder said you are on the way to the train station. The next train is in four minutes."

"Where to?"

"A local to Springfield."

Melanie wouldn't take a train to Springfield, it wasn't far enough away. "What's after that?"

"Albany in ten minutes. That one goes to Canada. A local to Boston, also in ten minutes. Then an express to Chicago, the Lake Shore Limited, although it does stop along the way. That's in—twelve minutes now. Boston in fifteen minutes, an express. One more after that this hour, to New York. Eighteen minutes."

Winter tossed the phone on the seat, both hands back on the wheel, too much traffic. Not much time if Melanie was getting on one of those trains.

If she was even at the station.

THE DEPARTURE SCREEN BLINKED, updating the schedule. Melanie's train to New York would leave in less than fifteen minutes. She'd skimmed one magazine, on her way to boredom, she thought running from the cops would be more fun.

Maybe it was because she couldn't see them, they might not even be coming. Well, she could pretend. It was another role, and she was very good at roles. And if the cops *were* on the way. . .

She clumsily jogged in the skirt over to the ticket counter. Three customers were in line in front of her, an older black woman and a middle aged couple. The man was going on about how he got tickets to some baseball game, the woman fumbling in her purse.

Melanie tapped the man on the shoulder. When he turned she exuded fretfulness. "Excuse me, I don't know how to read these schedules," she said, waving her brochure. "Can you tell me the next train to Boston?"

The man looked at Melanie, at the schedule in her hand, and up at the monitor. "It leaves in less than five minutes."

"Oh, no," wailed Melanie. "I've got to get on that train, my grandmother is sick . . ."

The woman looked up, empathetic. "You can go in front of us, dear."

"Thank you *so* much," said Melanie, giving her a brief smile, but not too much. She was, after all, anxious about her sick grandmother.

The black woman was just finishing up. Melanie jittered from one foot to the next in front of the window. "One ticket to Boston."

"You'll have to run, the local is one minute out, six minutes for the express."

Melanie shoved two twenties at him. "I'm fast."

The clerk, to his credit, made her change quickly.

Melanie spun her roller bag toward the tracks. Behind her, the woman in the line said, "Good luck!"

Melanie yelled, "Thanks!" Smiling. This was more fun. She still had it.

WINTER RAN INTO THE STATION, no uniforms in sight, no Melanie. He peered up at the monitors, trying to match the schedule to what Cindy had told him. The Springfield local had departed. The Albany and Boston local trains were boarding. The Chicago train was delayed. The next two were scheduled to leave in less than ten minutes, so they must be almost to the station. The Albany train was on track one, the Boston local on six, New York on nine, the Boston express on ten.

Winter ran toward the archway leading to the tracks. Track one was to the left, track ten to the right. He'd never be able to cover both ends. He was less worried about Melanie still being in the station, he could circle back. But if she got on the train, he'd have to call Springfield, Albany, god knows how many other stations, explain the situation, convince them to send cops to cover the stations to look for—a person of interest. Not an escaped prisoner, or a felon. Person of interest wasn't even a legal term.

Melanie could get off the train anywhere and be gone. With her acting skills, Winter doubted she'd be very easy to find. And even she was, then what? He might not even have probable cause for an arrest.

He changed direction, his soft shoes squeaking on the old tile. There was a long line at the ticket counter. Winter cut in front, flashing his badge. "I need to know if a woman," he fumbled with the tablet, pulled up Melanie's photo, "recently bought a ticket."

The clerk looked at the tablet through the scratched plexiglass. "I don't think so."

Winter suspected Ryder or Cindy might have sent him the Gigi photo, but he didn't know how to access it. "She might have looked different. A little—conservative. Mousy."

"A young woman just bought a ticket to Boston. Big hurry. Track six."

MELANIE SETTLED BACK in the seat, it was more comfortable than she had expected. Maybe she needed to travel by train more often. She'd taken off the uncomfortable jacket, and in deference to Gigi, had laid it out carefully on top of her luggage, which she'd hoisted onto the overhead rack.

The car was about half full already, passengers working their way down the aisle. The first time Melanie had been to New York, for an audition years ago, she'd played a game, trying to use nothing but her eyes and her body language to pick the passenger who would sit in the empty seat next to her. Not that one, not that one, he's good looking, him. She'd been successful in both directions, to and from New York.

She was much better actress now. She'd want a seatmate, in case the cops were looking for a single woman. She wanted to be in such deep conversation with some man any conductor would think they were lovers.

WINTER WAS WRONG, she was going to Boston. If the ticket buyer had been Melanie. He took the stairs to the train level two at a time.

The conductor was leaning out of the door of the end car on track six. "You have to hurry."

"I'm a cop," said Winter, holding up his badge. "Can you hold the train?"

"Trouble?"

"Just need to see if someone is on board."

"I can give you a minute, two tops, otherwise you'd better have paperwork, or something."

"I'll run through the cars," said Winter.

"Anything I can do?"

"Just keep an eye out for a young woman getting off."

Winter sprinted to the front car, worked his way back quickly. On the next track the Albany train pulled out, Winter praying Melanie wasn't on it. The Boston train was almost full, but definitely no Melanie.

He got off, waved to the conductor, and stood there on the platform as the force of flushed air from the train blew musty dirt in his face. The next two tracks were empty. Beyond that a gleaming seven car train, New York, if he remembered right. Winter couldn't see past it, but the Boston express train would be beyond that, which would be leaving next.

Passengers were hurrying onto the New York train, Winter trying to sort them out. A few women alone, none looked like Melanie. Or Melanie pretending she was Gigi.

He started up the steps so he could get to the other tracks just as he heard "All aboard! Boston express!" That would be track ten. The announcement jerked Winter's head around. There wasn't time to go back upstairs.

He jumped down onto the track area, gingerly stepped over the rails, not sure what was electrified, and pulled himself up the other side. Did the same at the next track, his shoes squelching in the grease and muck.

To reach track ten Winter had to get through the New York train or go up and over. A slight rumble in the platform told Winter he wasn't going to make it in time. Winter caught a glimpse of the passengers in the New York cars looking out at him, their attention drawn by the hubbub, surprised.

Except for one woman, who didn't seem surprised at all.

WINTER PLOPPED DOWN in the seat next to Melanie just as the train started to move. "Buying the Boston ticket, that was pretty slick," he said.

Melanie took in his greasy pants and dirty hands. "Christ, you're a mess." She reached down for her bag, Winter tensing, ready, but all Melanie came out with was a plastic bottle of sanitizer. "I have some makeup remover up top, it will take out the grease, an old trick I learned as a waitress. This will help a little."

Winter cleaned up his hands as best he could, catching his breath, the train rolling along now. "Thanks."

"I always thought you'd be trouble. All that bullshit while putting in my air conditioner. The other one, Ryder? He never would have found me." Melanie looked out the window. Quietly, she asked, "Is Gigi all right?"

"She's fine. We had to take her in, so she wouldn't call you. But no handcuffs. We didn't make a scene, she was in an unmarked car. She's not under arrest."

Melanie took off her glasses, Winter glimpsing the real Melanie. "Thanks for that," she said, sounding sincere. "She—she didn't do anything."

For some reason Winter believed her. Not because of her words, but because of what he had seen in Gigi. "I know. She should have come to us."

Melanie's eyes flared. "And what would *you* have done? This isn't the first time with her. Even with the 911 call, nothing was going to be taken care of."

"You didn't help matters, making us look at Jason Ayers."

"Do you have a sister?"

"I do."

"What would you have done?"

"That's not the point."

Melanie's anger didn't seem to be an act. "Fuck you. You're telling me you would have handled it. So it's okay for you to do it, but not me. Fucking men."

"You don't know me," said Winter, knowing how lame that sounded. She'd seen right through him. "So it was all for Gigi? Just for her?" It was a cheap shot, but she'd hit him harder than she could possibly know.

Melanie leaned back in the seat, her eyes closed. The train swayed rhythmically. "I don't know. I really don't, and that's the truth. I wish I could say it was, but I'm not Gigi, I'm not that good of a person."

Neither am I, thought Winter. He looked past her out the window, the train picking up speed, the landscape a blur, it could be anything out there. He needed clarity. "I have to know one thing. Are you sure it was Gruse?"

Melanie opened her eyes, looked at Winter, calculating. "One hundred percent."

Winter nodded, doing his own calculations.

"What now?" asked Melanie.

"Ryder builds a case," said Winter. "Look for your DNA in Gruse's car. Get witnesses who saw you arguing. Find Gruse's DNA at Gigi's."

"Ryder. Not you."

Winter couldn't hold her eye. "The police."

"Sounds pretty weak. I could have been in Lenny's car anytime. Or rubbed up against him in the club."

"Unless you confess," said Winter.

"Why?"

"Because—." There was only one reason why she might. "We could make it ugly for Gigi. Does she have an alibi for the night Gruse was killed?"

"You wouldn't." Melanie's voice turned as hard as the rails. "You can't."

Winter wasn't sure he could either. Ryder wouldn't hesitate for a second. "I told you, it's not about what I'd do."

"Lenny Gruse was a slimy excuse for a human being," hissed Melanie, her voice filled with venom. "He attacked my sister, one of the nicest people in the world. If it comes to that, I'll make sure any jury knows what he did, and how he and you cops ruined her life. How you spent more time going after the victim than the man who assaulted her. I'll tell them he came after me too, that I was just protecting myself, it was self defense."

"That's not the truth," said Winter.

Melanie's features shifted, a magic transformation. Gone was any vestigial hint of the vixen, the sultry seductress. Her shoulders stooped, her lip trembled, the seat seemed to be swallowing her up. Winter had to resist the urge to put his arm around her, this wounded little girl.

As quickly as the change had come about it was gone. Still the flattened hair, the pasty skin, the boxy clothes. But the Melanie gleam flashed a confident challenge. "Who do you think the jury is going to believe?"

CHAPTER 43

B ROOKER HAD LISTENED without interrupting, the story had taken longer than Winter expected. It was because they were no longer working together every day; all the details had to be filled in, even the wrong turns he had taken, the dead ends.

"You let her go," said Brooker. It wasn't a question.

"Ah, you know why. What was I going to do?" Winter paused. "Once I heard about the roofies and the stalker attack in California—Gruse must have done this before. And Melanie, she *knew* it was Gruse. You know what I would have done if I'd been in her shoes."

Brooker stared at Winter, nodded once. "Is Ryder going to squeeze the sister?"

"I don't think so. He's still pissed I was right, that there was a connection between the assault and Gruse. He'll just be rubbing it in on himself. And he knows we really have no proof of anything, even if Gigi admits she was the one who was assaulted. If she doesn't, we don't even have a reason to look for Gruse's DNA in her apartment."

"It doesn't sound like Melanie's the type to go into hiding. Easy to find her if you need to."

"Yeah," said Winter. "She'll probably be on a television show in a month."

Brooker's nurse, the attractive ebony skinned woman, glided into the room, a mug of coffee for both of them. Winter picked his up, took a taste to be polite. The coffee was black, no sugar. She'd remembered.

He'd forgot her name again. Embarrassed, he said, "Thanks."

She gave him a little smile, puffed up Brooker's pillows, and slipped out, leaving a subtle hint of jasmine in her wake.

"Still have your nurse," said Winter, his voice flat.

Brooker was staring at the door, then he turned back to Winter. "Maybe more than that."

"As long as she gets you better."

Brooker leaned forward, lowered his voice. "No matter what happens, I won't tell her."

Winter thought about Gigi, having to keep secrets. "Not a good way to live."

"You got to do what you got to do. Just like we did." Brooker's eyes softened, and he took a sip of his coffee. "Fucking decaf."

Winter grinned, raising his mug in salute. "Fucking decaf."

Coming soon:

The next book in the Detective Robert Winter Series

Random Melody

Sign up for our mailing list for updates on new releases at

www.varzarahouse.weebly.com

About the Authors

William Michaels is the pseudonym of W. R. Pursche and Michael Gabriele. They also co-wrote *The Eternal Messiah* and *Immanence*. Pursche is also the author of *Lessons To Live By: The Canine Commandments* and the fantasy series *Chronicles of the Third Reckoning*.

CPSIA information can be obtained
at www.ICGtesting.com
Printed in the USA
BVHW04s0812190418
513820BV00026B/56/P